The Ideal Wife

The Ideal Wife

Geraldine McCaughrean

RICHARD COHEN BOOKS · London

British Library Cataloguing in Publication Data:
A catalogue record for this book is available from the British Library

ISBN 1 86066 107 6 (tpb)

First published in Great Britain in 1997 by
Richard Cohen Books
7 Manchester Square
London W1M 5RE

Typeset in Bembo by Palimpsest Book Production Limited,
Polmont, Stirlingshire

Printed in Great Britain by
T.J. International Ltd, Padstow, Cornwall

For Emma

Contents

PART ONE

The Age of Simplicity

CHAPTER ONE

Two Girls

'*Two* girls, your letter said.'

'Two, yes.'

'It speaks highly of your charity, sir, that you should think in terms of two.' But the look on the warden's face was not quite one of admiration.

His visitor laughed genially. 'How can you say so, when your own charity extends to a hundred poor souls?'

There was a strong smell of carbolic soap mixed with cabbage water and cheap tallow. The through-draught brought in the sweetness of horse dung off Lambeth's busy street. The sun was out and it was the recreation hour, so that girls were walking about the open courtyard. In their white bib-aprons and double caps, on the swept bright squares of flagstone, they had the look of chess pieces moving about a board. Their leather-soled pattens made no sound.

'What is the youngest you have?'

The warden paused at the distant sight of knitted hose flapping on a washline above the herbs and vegetables of the kitchen garden. His lips moved in silent calculation. 'Nine,' he said. 'The girls in my charge are all between nine and twelve . . . On which subject, might I venture to mention, sir, that you seem very young yourself to be contemplating this particular act of benevolence.'

The young man wore no wig; his own, brown, unkempt hair was tied in an unusually long queue. He hastened to reassure the warden. 'I have come into my estate, I do assure you, Mr Argent. My lawyer is waiting in the hackney; he can vouch for my means. . . . Though, to be honest with you, I consider them of no importance whatsoever myself. A yoke I would gladly share with my fellow men.'

'Yoke, Mr Wootton?' said the warden, thinking he had missed some turning in the sentence.

'Wealth, sir,' said Wootton with another brilliant smile. 'Wealth is a yoke, don't you think?'

Mr Argent, warden of the Lambeth Female Asylum, was hard put to see wealth as a yoke. He had just spent the morning struggling to make lists of voluntary donations into columns long enough to haul the asylum through another thrifty month. It did not make him like any better this young man with the rural accent and round hat, that he thought wealth was a yoke. He answered briskly, 'It's simply that our founder, Mr Fielding, made it a binding rule: girls should be released only into households carefully scrutinised by the asylum guardians. It has to be said, Mr Wootton, that our founder envisaged placing these girls in domestic service. Or failing that, a trade.' He again took time to look the gentleman over with narrow, sceptical eyes. 'Nothing of this kind.'

Wootton was undaunted. 'How much better, then, to adopt them. Raise them. Educate them in the *true* sense.'

Mr Argent was a small man with large responsibilities. He knew, from the letters on his desk, that Robin Wootton had already secured the approval of the guardians; perhaps one was a friend of his. Argent knew he should probably speed the matter through and return to his administrative duties. And yet he was uneasy that this . . . youth – he could not be above twenty – should be choosing adoptive daughters like a man choosing apples from a barrow. Still, it was probably not his concern. He would be businesslike.

Just then, two girls presented themselves to the warden, curtseying briefly while watching, with huge-eyed intensity, the stranger.

'In anticipation of your visit,' said Argent, 'I took the liberty of selecting out two personable girls of excellent character: Miss Marianne and Miss Alba Padock. Girls, this is Mr Wootton of Winding Hatch, in the county of Berkshire. Bid him good day and show him your shirts.' He applied unnecessarily to the ledger he was carrying. 'Their father was a hairdresser, but is now at sea in a man-of-war, and their mother . . . well, a worthless, low woman.'

The two girls did not flinch at the mention of their mother. Both were as fair, the younger as blonde, as any Scandinavian, with features symmetrically and geometrically perfect. They curtseyed deeply to Robin Wootton, blushing and smiling, their mouths a little tight with terror. Each held out a shirt, unfurling it like the sail of a galleon. The littler girl's shirt was held together only with pins.

Mr Wootton was nonplussed, so Argent explained. 'We ask of our girls

4

that, before leaving here, they should be able to cut and sew a shirt, make their own linen, clean kitchen and household furniture, undertake simple cooking, and read a chapter of the Bible.' They were words he was obliged to say or write almost every working day. He was also carrying a Bible, with the express purpose of demonstrating Marianne Padock's accomplished reading. 'You will see from their bearing that both have been stayed: the guardians consider carriage and personal appearance a vital factor in placing the girls.' He added rather bitterly, 'Even though the outlay is well over a pound apiece – even for leather.' The littler girl scratched along a crease in her dress which marked the base of her leather stays.

'Ah. Well, now.' Robin Wootton's irrepressible good humour bubbled up even through his misgiving. 'The *reading* might be a detraction.'

Argent's face coloured. 'Why, sir? Do you have some objection to the teachings of the Bible?' His lips were rigid with indignation.

'Not at all! Not at all! It's simply the reading itself, Mr Argent. You see, I have certain theories of my own concerning education. Little Alba here will do very nicely,' – and he crouched down so as to address her face-to-face – 'so long as she cannot read.'

'I can't do seams yet eever,' she said, jutting her head a little forwards and swallowing. With obvious trepidation she glanced sideways at Argent's Bible.

'That's of no consequence,' said the young Mr Wootton. 'None in the world.' Finding he had nothing else to say to the child, he straightened up again. 'In any event, I thought a *brown* girl would make a pleasing comparison, if you have one unlettered like Alba here.'

Argent looked around him. His arrangements had been upset. He bridled at the thought of anyone selecting girls according to the colour of their hair and the level of their illiteracy. 'Girls are not book-ends, sir.' Robin Wootton only laughed again, good-naturedly.

The elder girl did not move away, but neither did she follow, as the visitor took Alba by the hand and sauntered farther into the kitchen garden. Alba looked back over her shoulder until the pea canes hid from sight her sister and the bright courtyard with its chessboard flagstones.

'What I mean to say, Mr Wootton,' said Argent without ever having started to speak, 'is that you are not of a . . . how shall I put it . . . of a natural age to have daughters of nine or ten. I wonder you do not address yourself to Mr Coram at the Foundling Hospital. For children newborn, I mean.'

'Ah, yes! It's true, of course it is,' agreed Mr Wootton enthusiastically. 'The younger the child, the freer she is from society's persuasions. But I fear I'm not patient enough. Passionate men do not make patient men, I'm afraid. I crave results! And the age difference, you see. The age difference would be just too . . . No, for the purpose of my experiments, I needs must settle on older girls.'

Experiments? The warden did not hear the word. His attention had been drawn away by the washline and its row of grey knitted hose. After a morning spent working on figures, he could not stop himself counting and re-counting them. There were fifteen.

Experiment. Alba heard it, though: a word she only dimly understood but which turned her blood to salt. Like Lot's wife, she stood powerless to move, observing her casual purchase by a young country gentleman for the purpose of an 'experiment'.

'Tell me,' said Argent sharply to a girl passing by with pegs. 'Why are there fifteen hose?'

'Don't know, sir,' said the girl. In case she was being accused of something, she added, 'Not me, God's honour.' She was as dark as Alba was fair, with eyes too large for her face, and hair too excitable for her cap, so that it gave the impression of a split pillow stuffed with black wool.

'Why are there *fifteen* hose?' Argent repeated irritably.

Panic-stricken, the child looked from face to face, saw fear written on Alba's, saw a visitor, a stranger. Often, she knew, the visit of a stranger to the asylum required the girls to recite in answer to questions: 'What is your name? Who made you?' Was this one of those questions? 'Why are there fifteen hose?'

'Don't know my catechism yet, sir!'

The stranger laughed out loud, and twirled his round-hat between his hands. 'This one will make up my pair, Mr Argent,' he said. 'What's her name? Does she have a name?'

Alarmed, the dark girl drew closer to Alba who, despite her fright, drew away.

Argent dropped his voice a little – not so much as to prevent the girl hearing but to keep his words from passing beyond the perimeter wall of the asylum. 'This one's not an orphan, sir.'

'Oh! Is she your own? I'm so . . .'

'No, no, no! Of bastard stock, sir. A foundling,' said Argent hastily. 'Tin merchants passing through, in all likelihood. Abandoned at the gates of the St Giles Poorhouse.'

'I was cottaged out,' the child volunteered.

'Cottaged out, yes. But only, of course, to the age of seven. The practice becomes uneconomic at seven. So she was returned to St Giles. Being over-stretched at the time, they asked we find room for her here. We have several dozen bastards.'

Argent spoke with nice precision when he said it. 'Her name is . . . something Cornish . . .'

'Z —' said the child.

'Zena?'

'Zennor, sir,' said the child. 'Gawd knows the reason.'

Argent hit her sharply on the upper arm with his open hand, but she did not seem to know the reason for that, either.

'Here is my choice. I have chosen!' exclaimed Robin Wootton, jubilant with triumph, 'I shall take them both home!'

Zennor dropped her little basket of pegs and clashed heads with Alba as they both stooped for it. Overcoming her repugnance towards the tinkers' bastard, Alba brought her face close to the lawn cap bulging with fleecy black hair. 'He wants us for experiments,' she said, and Zennor dropped the pegs a second time.

Argent saw his authority being circumvented by the sheer speed of events. He tried to slow them down. 'I wonder, sir, that you do not bring your *wife* with you, too, sooner than your lawyer. To make such an important choice. Such a very major undertaking, after all, and so much more her labour than yours, surely?'

'Oh, I'm not married,' said Wootton delightedly, helping Zennor gather up the pegs. 'That's entirely the point.' He seemed to have been waiting the opportunity to say it, like a man who savours a good joke.

Argent opened his Bible, not looking for inspiration or guidance — his eyes could not focus on the page — but he needed time to govern his anger. Let this libidinous youth damn himself however he cared to, out in the muddy shires; what enraged Argent was being made party to the sin. Without looking up from the Bible, he said, between clenched teeth, 'What do you take me for, sir? A pander to your *country* vices?'

Unfortunately, Wootton had moved too far off to hear him. He had taken each girl by the hand and was leading them through the asylum portico and down the steps towards the street. They hung back from him, trailing at the ends of his long arms, jarred and rattled when he unexpectedly and energetically broke into a skip. He skipped them down the driveway. He whirled them into the hackney carriage, from which, in turn, a man in black got down.

Hearing the warden's running feet clattering down the steps behind him, Wootton turned and came back, still smiling, pink-cheeked now from the skipping. He introduced his lawyer, then continued the conversation as if

7

nothing had interrupted it. 'No, to my mind, of course, a man shouldn't marry till he's fully thirty. That allows me seven or eight years to bring them up after my own precepts. Then, when I see where nature and my own meagre efforts bear best fruit – I shall make my choice.' He was not disappointed when Argent continued to boggle at him, not understanding. It gave Wootton a chance to spread his slender hands expressively and say, 'These are not prospective *daughters*, Mr Argent. They are prospective *wives*. One or other I mean to marry!'

Sitting opposite each other in the hackney, Alba Padock and Zennor known-as-Giles looked at one another like sheep in a butcher's yard.

'Experiments, he said,' said the pale one.

'Black arts, is that?' said the dark.

They contemplated jumping down from the other side of the coach, running full tilt down Lambeth Walk and out along the Thames mud-flats into the distant city. But life at Lambeth's Female Asylum, though it had not yet taught them needlecraft or reading, had instilled absolute obedience. They were obedient to their fate. The devil himself could have come requiring their company and they would have been powerless to say no.

Alba had seen seven brothers and sisters die since her father went to sea, and her mother to the gin. She stood cornered now, on a narrow promontory of which all but the tip had crumbled into oceanic death. The world would do as it liked with her.

A month before, the guardians had given leave for all the girls to attend a public hanging at Millbank. (They had said it would instruct the girls to cherish one another and to fear God.) It had instructed Zennor that waking nightmares lurked everywhere in the world – pent up in the poorhouse, or loose and swinging in the streets. She looked down, and realised she was still holding the pegs.

They did not run, but they held hands – girls who had never spoken before – across the well of the coach.

Presently, Wootton's lawyer returned and climbed in. Zennor eyed his black clothing. 'Is this a hearse?' she asked.

He peered at her, suspecting insolence.

'Where will he take us?' said Alba.

'To Berkshire, child. To Winding Hatch in the parish of Wootton. You are fortunate children, past question. The Lord has provided most comfortably for you today. As has Mr Wootton. I hope you do justice to his kindness.'

'Why, *is* he kind?' said Alba.

The lawyer took a fob-watch from his waistcoat pocket and examined it closely. 'I travelled here with Mr Wootton from Wantage,' he said, in a voice which stretched out the distance still farther. 'I seem to remember the word occurring a great many times.' At this he sighed, and settled himself into a corner, averting his eyes so as to forbid further talk.

Zennor felt her life at stake. 'Are we to be scullery or out in the fields, or what?' she hissed at Alba, supposing the other girl knew more, since she at least had been sent for on purpose, not stopped on her way to the washline.

'I don't know. If he doesn't want sewing or reading, it must be simple. Will we sleep with the cows, do you think?' Alba was town-bred.

The lawyer stirred and, to steel himself against the long journey home, took snuff from a small pewter box. The coach was deathly quiet; he could hear the blonde girl's teeth chattering with fright. 'What gooses you are,' he muttered, still looking out of the window. 'Do you suppose servants can't be got well enough in Berkshire? Mr Wootton don't require *maids*. Does a man *adopt maids*? I think not.'

'What are we for, then?' asked Zennor, appealing to him, her white neck stretched out so long above the coarse blue cloth of her dress that she did indeed look like a goose.

'Experiments,' said Alba, again shivering uncontrollably.

The lawyer's dull, pebbly eyes watered as he looked at them, but it was only an effect of the snuff. 'I'm sure it's not my business to speak of it. Mr Wootton will tell you himself in good time.' The only message they could read for certain in his face was disapproval of Mr Wootton and of the enterprise which had brought them both to London.

Then Robin Wootton came, the papers of adoption all signed and sealed. Boisterous and grinning, the skirts of his frock coat swinging, his buckles glinting in the sunshine, he set the hackney swaying as he leapt aboard it. Alba crossed the well of the coach to huddle against Zennor, but Wootton wriggled his hips in between them, an arm round each, patting their bony shoulders. 'Let's go home,' he declared, 'and begin the great adventure of living!'

As the hackney moved off, a window opened high up in the street wall of the Lambeth Female Asylum and Argent put out his head. 'Their baggage, Mr Wootton!'

'What do we need with baggage?' Wootton asked the girls, beaming and flicking his hands out of the window. 'Baggage only ties clogs to a person.'

'Then, if you could return their clothes, sir. The outlay was nigh fourteen shillings!'

'Wave goodbye to incarceration,' Wootton instructed the girls, 'and open your hearts and minds to liberation.'

Mr Finch, the lawyer, took another pinch of snuff.

Argent's voice, trailing after the hackney, faded with distance. '*Their leather stays, at least!*'

CHAPTER TWO

A Contract

The Reverend Samuel Baydon stood at the window, facing the light, his thumbs locked together behind his back. He seemed unwilling to turn round and address his visitor face-to-face.

'As you may be aware,' he said, his voice emerging in a high bray which he coughed to rectify. 'As you may be aware – well, naturally you are – I lately lost in childbed a wife who saw fit to leave me with three young children. . . . There are pheasant in the garden again!' he rapped loudly on the window. The pheasants ignored him.

'They do so weed up the small plants,' said the lady by the door. 'I grieve for you in your loss. The loss of your wife, I mean.'

The Reverend Baydon nodded. 'As you can imagine, this parish makes a multitude of demands on my time and energies. I am Surveyor of Highways in these parts – also, Justice of the Peace – as you know, naturally. It requires an ordered life, an orderly household to fulfil these . . . these various duties. Presently they tend to . . . overwhelm us. Besides that, the children require the tenderness – the, ah, tenderness and instruction of a gentlewoman.'

'Naturally.'

'Also –' he nodded his head as he went on – 'also, I feel the need of a . . . second pair of hands. This house. The servants. I fear I came to rely heavily on my late wife. It has left me somewhat . . .' His movements were small, constrained, like a fly caught in a web. Somewhere in the house a child was crying noisily.

The woman by the door was dressed in widow's black – a collarless cape and a black calash ribbed with hoops of cane. Her angular, bony face was as pale as cuttleshell, her hands hung loose by her sides. 'That is surely the place and pride of a wife,' she said quietly. 'To be relied upon.'

'Quite. Quite.'

A hiatus hung between them, filled only by the distant crying. 'That's George,' said the Reverend Baydon wincing. 'A little big for crying, I know, but he has the earache.'

'Have you tried oil of cloves?' murmured the widow.

'No. I don't know. Is it efficacious?'

'Warm from a teaspoon. Sometimes, yes.'

'I'm obliged to you, Mrs Inchpen.'

The silence washed back, tidal between them, deep enough to drown in. He invited her to sit down, but she declined, as if to sit down would have been to call business to a close before it had even begun.

'My inclination was to wait, of course,' he said. 'To let things run on: certainly I would not wish to be rash in such a . . . critical matter. But then, when I heard of your . . . great misfortune, there did seem to me – perhaps I'm wrong – a remedy at hand. More than one, indeed! The hand of Providence at work – if that's not too presumptuous a thought.'

Outside on the lawn, the white willow swayed its crinolined skirts in a whispering breeze full of the cooing of wood-pigeons. His horse was rolling, for the sheer pleasure of it, in dew-wet clover, sending up a glittering spray of water drops.

'I was very sorry that you and your children – where are they today? Are they well?'

'With a neighbour, sir. Yes, quite well, thank you, praise God.'

'Ah. Yes. Very good.'

He lapsed once more into contemplation of the garden. Pied wagtails were jumping and chasing one another in and out of the camellias. The radically pruned stubs of rose bushes each sat on a dark knoll of fresh manure. It was a well ordered garden; it gave him more satisfaction than the house.

His visitor cleared her throat. 'It's their long-term welfare I fear for,' she said. 'With no father and no roof over their heads, and no food in their mouths but what charity and kindness put there. But I shall keep them out of the poorhouse. While there's breath in my body, sir, I will.'

He seized the opening, almost turning to look at her in his eagerness. 'So you don't feel the need to observe a period of mourning before . . . changing your domestic circumstances?'

'Far from it. Surely, the best way I can honour the memory of my husband is to put bread in the mouths of his daughters. Surely,' she added uncertainly, pushing the cane ribbing of her calash back from her face. It was a tired face, undernourished and overburdened with worry, but there was a stillness, a calmness about it, as though Sophronia Inchpen had reached an armistice with grief such as Samuel Baydon had never done.

'In that event,' said the parson, moving sharply across to a bureau and taking out a roll of paper, 'I have ninety pounds a year, to which you may add occasional fees – weddings, christenings, funerals and so forth. I've listed all the details here, I think. For you to read at your leisure. But to summarise; the living furnishes me with this house and three acres, one of clover for my horse; I keep my own chaise, one cook and two maids. I like to see to the garden myself – not out of scrimpen closeness, you understand: it's a passion with me. Well, you know it, like as not. I do believe it causes some merriment in the parish. As well as being parson of this parish (by the grace of Lord Wootton) I am a prebend of Winchester Cathedral – not without hope, I may say, of some degree of furtherment one day – a canonry, perhaps. Would it discompose you, would you say, if we ever had to shift ground to the cathedral precincts?'

'Shift ground,' said Sophronia Inchpen. 'In the capacity of your . . . ?'

'Wife. Wife, yes. Wife.' Having refrained from saying it for so long, the Reverend Baydon repeated himself, his fist in front of his mouth, as if he were coughing. 'Wife, yes. As my wife.'

Sophronia Inchpen rested her hip against the arm of the settle and unrolled the sheet of paper he had given her. The clover was mentioned, that much she took in.

Their only acquaintance previously had been to shake hands at the church door after divine service. They had not so much as sat down at table together.

No mention passed between them of Baydon conducting the funeral rites for her dead husband, of him waiving the burial fee. There was no mention, either, of the addiction to laudanum which had robbed John Inchpen of his livelihood, his sanity and at last his life. It would have overstepped the bounds of intimacy to refer to such things.

Presently, she stood clear of the settle. 'And there would be room for both my children?'

'Sarah and Suzannah, isn't it? Ideal company for Grace – my own,' he said brightly. 'There's much to commend it, you see? I've given it many hours of prayerful consideration. It does seem an eminently suitable arrangement, given our similar . . . predicaments. The only plain demerit is, of course, myself. My person, I mean. An unalterable factor, I'm afraid. . . . Shall we take chocolate in the garden? It will deter the pheasants, and I can show you my asparagus. Seven years it takes to establish a crown, and I have ten will crop this year!' Real enthusiasm lit his pale brown eyes. He rang the handbell for the cook, but she might have been picking herbs for dinner or trying to stop George's crying, because she did not come. While they waited, they discussed the portrait hanging over Baydon's fireplace. It was like a third person in the room, to whom they could look for neutral conversation. The portrait was of the parson's patron, Lord Wootton.

'Have you seen very much of his lordship's nephew?' asked Sophronia Inchpen. 'I've seen him in church. He looks a very personable young man.'

'We dine, you know. We dine,' said the parson, his hand spread on the high white stock which hid the entire length of his neck. Above the stock, his jawline was soft, weary, imperfectly shaven. 'Naturally, gentry and clergy – we're thrown into society with each other, in simple search of conversation, if not out of perfect . . . sympathy. He's a very *modern* young man. Some of his ideas are very modern. But then he is very young. I suppose the young cannot very well help being modern. Youth excuses a little . . . outlandishness.' Good manners forbad any more adverse comment about his patron's nephew, though secretly he felt a hearty contempt for these fashionable young men who professed to prefer anything Italian to home-grown good taste.

So he was startled when she observed, in a low speedy murmur, 'I suspect there's a little macaroni in that particular recipe.'

It caught him off guard. He gave a loud bark which might have been a laugh if he had not taken out his handkerchief and blown his nose. Fearing they were poised on the brink of parochial gossip, he tightened his lips, smoothed the curls of his physical wig – the kind worn by doctors and academicians – and rang the handbell again.

'Perhaps you would care to glance over my late wife's wardrobe while you are here. She was much your size, and it's a shameful waste of good clothes, to go empty . . . Whatever your decision, I mean. Whatever you decide.'

Sophronia Inchpen did not point out that she was a hand taller than the dead Mrs Baydon, and broader in the beam by far. The parson of Wootton parish was more puritan than cavalier and unlikely, she thought, to take in such details when he looked at a woman. On ninety pounds a year, he could have married women of better background, younger, prettier and a lot less encumbered than the apothecary's widow. She was not about to carp at his charity.

The cook set up the card-table in the garden, and on it the jugs of chocolate and cream. On their way there, after visiting the asparagus beds, they paused to examine the espaliered pear tree spreadeagled against the warm southern garden wall. There was a sundial there, too, which they checked to see whether the sun was keeping time with Mr Baydon's pocket watch. But an obelisk of shadow cast by the church tower obliterated the little triangle cast by the dial.

'As for the other aspect . . .' he suddenly said, 'I am not yet past fifty.'

'Your paper said as much,' said the widow. 'I am thirty-five myself.'

'I know,' he said, by which she guessed he had looked up her birth in the church records. 'I would expect – or hope . . . I would like to think, in time.' There was no end to the sentence. He had never intended one. But she could supply his meaning.

'Naturally,' she said. 'It would not be a marriage, else.'

The pheasant, which had a nest within the parsonage garden, gave its shrill, craking cackle and Samuel Baydon went after it, in full cry, clapping and running and shouting. He crashed into the board fence that separated the garden from the churchyard, and came back examining the palms of his hands for splinters. 'You probably want to consider my offer for a day or so,' he was saying as he came.

She looked at him across the bladed sundial, but could not engage his eyes which now moved uneasily between his pocket watch and the church tower. She thought he must have a sermon to write before evensong. So she smiled when he said, 'I should feed the pig.'

'No,' she said. 'No.'

'But she commonly breaks out if I don't feed her on time. Pigs can be a most unruly . . .'

'No, Mr Baydon, I mean you may have my answer now,' said Sophronia Inchpen, and the pig was entirely forgotten. 'I shall most gladly make a marriage with you. I am indebted to you for thinking of me. But if you'll excuse me, I'll go now and find oil of cloves for George's ear.'

So it was arranged. On the card-table (though Reverend Baydon abhorred waste as a rule), the drinking chocolate went cold in the morning sunshine.

CHAPTER THREE

Winding Hatch

He did not mention Rousseau to the man at the Lambeth Female Asylum. The ignorant, if they had heard of him at all, knew Rousseau only as a religious dissenter, a subversive. There was no point in making the path to adoption any harder than need be.

But all Robin Wootton's plans and schemes had their being in Jean-Jacques Rousseau. He had not met the man, not quite *met* him, yet he had stood where Rousseau had stood, and felt the presence of the man like the warmth left behind on a nest the moment after flight. In a little riverside cottage on the Harcourt Estate at Nuneham Park, he had lain down on a bed where the divine philosopher had slept, exiled from his native land.

The cottage had reverberated with words. The fringes of the river had turned back on themselves as if still harkening to hear the great man's voice. Robin had smelled flowers descended from the selfsame ones Jean-Jacques had smelled. He had walked in a garden shaped by Rousseau's precepts, meditated on landscapes which had inspired Rousseau. He had even met the second earl, asking, 'What did he say? What was it like to be with him?' like some first-century Christian interrogating Saint Peter.

Every book of Rousseau's which had ever been published now lay on the round table in the centre of Wootton's library, their margins marked with a constellation of asterisks. It made him smile to remember how his uncle, the third viscount and a grand example of the grandiose breed, had walked around the table as he might have done a dung heap, lips rolled back in disgust. He had read nothing more modern than Seneca and never understood that. Had Robin been his son, there would have been a conflict worth seeing: bigotry beating its bewigged and ponderous head against the rock of pure conviction. There would have been threats of disinheritance, bombast and blackmail! But Robin was only his dead brother's boy. The viscount had fumed and cursed, but he had not taken reprisals. Indeed, he had fulfilled his avuncular obligations and given Robin his recreational country villa at Winding Hatch, and bought another to develop, near Marlborough.

A small plot in which to re-establish Eden; but Robin had made a start. His first act after moving in had been to call together tenants, estate hands and staff, and declare his dislike of privilege, his wish for a simple, unflamboyant life free of pomp and ostentation. The least of them, he said, was, to him, equal to the highest-born in the land. And he had given them extracts from Rousseau, specially printed in tiny, scarlet bindings, declaring them his 'manifesto for Winding Hatch'.

They had shown precious little interest – asked no questions as they turned the ribbons over and over in their horny, labourers' hands. They had thanked him and reverently tugged at their hair or curtseyed. It had left him with a terrible feeling of fatigue, as if he had had to pull them all uphill in a cart. But such was the stomach and disposition God had given him, such was the energy and glee he drew from nature and philosophy, that Robin had not let it dampen him, not one jot.

At first his intention had been to marry the daughter of a tenant or farm-hand. But somehow when he applied his mind to it he could only picture that room full of worried faces, silent and glumly suspicious, between them and him a gulf of misunderstanding. There was so little *joy* left in them, and he such a *joyous* man. As he had told the lawyer on the long ride from Wantage to London, 'joy cannot fly with misery in its claws'.

So the scheme to adopt and nurture himself a wife had struck him like the lightning of divine inspiration. Rousseau had only written *about* educating an Emile, a Sophie. Robin would find a real girl – flesh and blood – grasp her, mould her, recreate her in the image her Creator intended. In the image, at least, that Rousseau favoured for his new Arcadia.

The man who gave money – tin charity – to the hungry could always be accused of condescension, of salving his privileged conscience. But to share his very life with someone! To share with them the discovery of truth and beauty – that would be real *caritas*, true largesse of spirit. He was a convert to happiness, and with a convert's zeal meant to preach the virtue of joy.

'Forgive the building,' he said, reining in the hired chaise outside Hatch House. 'I have plans to make it more picturesque.'

The girls stared at his apology of a house, a small Palladian mansion, precisely square, with slender pillared porticos to both the east and west elevations. It stood like a box of chalks placed there to keep flat a map, a map of perfect geometic precision: straight avenues, hexagonal parterres, low pilastered walls, square shallow pools full of fish. The asylum had been a vast, imposing building – London had no shortage of grand piles – but this was airy white, isolated by acres of green ground, acres of blue sky. Even the sky was producing columnar cumulus clouds in imitation of Hatch House. Alba began to count windows, using the latest skill taught her – that of counting the threads in sewing canvas. The house was as white as canvas.

'Alba, Zennor, welcome to your new home!' said Wootton. 'We shall make it a home, shan't we? All our thoughts and cares and feelings we must pool, you and I. Don't be afraid. Don't let the house cast its shadows over you. Myself, I'd rather live in a tree house or a pavilion of red silk on the lawns – or some little thatched cottage down by the river yonder. But we shall muddle along, shan't we? It's the souls inside a house who give the house its soul. Isn't that right, my little disciples?'

Alba laughed out loud at the thought of Mr Wootton living in a tree house, but it was a shrill, unnerved laugh. She and Zennor held hands.

'Come,' said Wootton. 'There is someone I wish you to meet.' He led them up shallow Portland steps, to a terrace, to where a fine new statue stood on an older plinth. The man depicted was slight in build, with a prominent hooked nose and tidy wig; his small, intense face looked out over the classical garden with an expression of aggravation – a man turned to stone by the prospect of tending fifty acres. It was very lifelike. 'Did you do it?' said Zennor, already feeling her flesh stiffen into stone, her blood congeal into stonedust at this petrifaction.

'No, no, no! I fear I'm no mason!' He laughed, wrinkling up his long, exquisitely narrow nose. Robin Wootton's features were as regular and per-fectly placed as the elements of his garden. 'Ladies, I give you Jean-Jacques Rousseau, your benefactor, author of your redemption! Bring him flowers in the summer and in due course you shall give him your hearts!'

'Jesu Judas,' said Zennor under her breath. What kind of idol-worshipper was this, with his graven image which required flowers and the hearts of young virgins? Did he mean it literally? She shivered under the gaze of the beak-nosed statue with the knitted brows. There was a grim smile about the grey lips which made it seem all too likely this was truly the prime mover of the day's events.

But Alba was entranced by the statue, by the gardens, by the house, by the perfectly ordered prospect of lawns and paths and trees. They all said, 'Here is money. Here is plenty. Here is a world within a world, where nothing unpleasant has ever been suffered to happen.' She had passed inside a breakwater, and all the storms and sickness and danger of sinking were left outside.

'We lead a simple life here,' Robin Wootton was saying. 'The comforts of the rich are the discomforts of the poor. So you'll find us plain and ordinary, plain and ordinary. Still, at least we are all friends here. That's our merit. All friends. And that's the only thing a man needs, don't you agree?' He threw wide his arms. There was that grin again, that bright, excitable starriness of the eyes that they had never seen before in adults, except maybe in tavern doorways. There was no smell of drink on Mr Robin Wootton. That in itself endeared him to Alba.

Inside the house were more statues, more pillars and shallow marble stairs, though no sign of servants. None at all. Round, polished tables stood about, with no apparent purpose but to reflect the stucco ceilings and cornices. A painter was at work behind a door, creating a *trompe-l'oeil* of Pan-pipes and a lyre. Alba put out a finger to touch. She saw in the painter's face a desire to smack her hand away, yet he did not. Wootton laughed as she smudged the work. 'Ah! You see? All possessions are illusory!' The painter passed her a rag; the desire to smack her was still there. But he could not: being with Wootton protected her. It was a strange and marvellous feeling.

'You'll want to wash and rest after your journey,' said their protector. 'Let me show you the way.'

And Zennor thought, 'Now. Is it down or up?' For this was her Judgement Day. Either she would be elevated to some realm beyond the elegant curving sweep of the stairs, somewhere unimaginable, beyond all deserving. Or else she would be thrust down a back stair to the scullery. The abyss she could imagine; it held no fears for her. It would make sense of this uprooting and transportation out of London. But if the lawyer were right, and they had not been brought here as servants, then something else awaited them, so unimaginable that it filled her with terror. 'Seven years from now I shall be dead, or I shall understand,' she told herself. It was her banner, her nostrum, her way of surviving the moment.

The room he showed them was bare and uncarpeted, with a single white bed, a chair and a narrow darkwood cupboard. Windows reaching almost to the floor gave a view of the terraced rose gardens and beyond them a rising farmland with stands of ancient trees, like atolls on a green ocean. Both girls assumed the bed was for the two of them – top and tail, or sharing the soft white pillow. But Wootton opened a door into an adjoining room, and there stood identical furniture, scrupulously imitating the first room.

'Tomorrow we must furnish you with clothes,' he said, and Zennor (who thought he meant her to sew them) contemplated running away in the night. 'For now, pray wash and refresh yourselves, then come and find me. I shall be in the library.'

Halfway down the stairs, he called to mind the leather stays and went back. When he opened the door, Zennor was unlacing Alba and stood behind her like a charioteer with hands full of reins. They started several inches into the air, and froze, eyes round with terror.

'Away with those!' he said rhetorically, and took possession of the stays. It gave him some hardship, as he was not acquainted with how they fastened, and the strings kept tangling in Zennor's long hair. But at last he left, triumphant, and was just bounding down the stairs when the maid opened the front door to a visitor.

Baydon had called to inform his neighbour and patron of his decision to marry, and was not quite sure how to tackle it. He had been part expecting Sophronia Inchpen to take a cautious line and several weeks to consider his proposal. It occurred to him that the neighbourhood would think him hasty, observing too short a period of mourning. He thought so himself. 'But the plight of the children . . .' he said, as he spilled his news, with anxious haste, over Wootton's threshold.

'Baydon! Samuel! My dear man!' Wootton greeted the news. 'That's excellent. Truly excellent. I hope you bring joy and comfort to each other. Come in. Come in! We must toast your good news. And you can meet *my own* . . .'

'Really, I hadn't meant to intrude. I understand you're just home from London. You must be weary.' But he only said it to be civil. Wootton was never weary; he was the kind of man who gave Baydon eyestrain simply by never standing still in one place for more than a second.

As he followed Wootton into the library he noticed the stays clasped in one hand. At first he could not believe what he was seeing; then he could not take his eyes off the tangle of leather and laces: like stable tack. Whatever could it mean? Had he arrived at some completely inopportune moment? Alarums sounded in Baydon's head. He wanted to go. He feared to stay. If nothing else, he was confirmed in his fear that young Wootton was guilty of . . . *peculiarity*. 'Wootton, look here, I –'

Then the door re-opened behind them, and two children – one blonde, one swarthy and black-haired – came into the room. Their hair was unbrushed and, despite wet splashes down their smock fronts, they still looked grubby and hot.

'Come in, girls, and meet a friend. Reverend Samuel Baydon of this parish. Congratulate him! He's about to be married.'

Neither of the girls spoke – only bobbed down where they stood, as if someone had taken a shy at them. The dark one looked around her at the books lining all four walls of the room, the huge, smoke-stained portraits of viscounts and viscountesses, dogs, horses and landscapes.

'Samuel, permit me to present Miss Alba and Miss Zennor Wootton – or so they shall be when my man-at-law has scribbled his scribbles and dripped his wax. My new wards. My protégées!'

'Oh! Wards!' exclaimed Baydon with relief. He tried to place the faces – whether he had seen them in his church, whether they were local to Winding Hatch. They were definitely not blood kin, not distant nieces or godchildren. There was no breeding in them. But he had never seen either of them before. 'Miss Alba. Miss er . . . your servant.' One looked distinctly foreign. They were surely not sisters. Even so, he prepared to be reassured. There was charity afoot here. Wootton was renowned for odd outbursts of charity. Reputedly, as a boy, he had given away his horse to a vagrant, so that his father had been put to the expense of buying him another.

Robin Wootton drew the girls over to the pedestal table in the centre of the room. Open on it was a dilapidated book, thumbed and dog-eared; in most houses it would have been the Bible. He poured wine into four crystal goblets standing ready alongside: four glasses, so that Baydon looked around him for other adult visitors.

When Robin put the wine-glasses into their hands, Alba and Zennor held them as though they contained hemlock, in two hands, well away from their bodies.

'Let's drink to marriage! To joy and love and comradeship!' he said.

That same silence which had greeted Wootton's declaration of liberty and equality at Winding Hatch settled again over the library. The parson wanted to explain: it was not a desire for joy which had decided him to marry. But he did not want to go into it in front of the girls. They all sank their mouths in the wine.

Suddenly the girl Zennor spoke – so unexpectedly that, beside her, Alba spilled wine down her smock. 'Shall we learn reading?'

Wootton laughed and hastened to reassure her. An arm round her shoulder, he rested his other hand on the book on the table. 'This is the only book that concerns you, Zennor. The pattern of your days.' Zennor supped her wine, ducking her face awkwardly over the crystal.

Baydon turned his head on one side to identify the book. 'Emile? Who, pray, is Emile, Mr Wootton?'

'Rousseau, Samuel! The divine Rousseau! The inspired educator! I mean to educate these girls according to the philosophies of Jean-Jacques

Rousseau. Fashion and shape their natures . . . that's to say, allow their natures to grow untrammeled by the false presuppositions of society. To free their spirits! To let their souls grow as God intended!' (Baydon's eyes rose in surprise that his neighbour should be privy to the Almighty's intentions.) 'To let their spirits draw breath unconfined!' To add emphasis, Wootton pitched into the fireplace the stays he had been brandishing.

The girls both uttered inarticulate cries of horror. A pound apiece! A log fell out of the grate, and Baydon kicked it back in, trying not to look too closely at the items of female underclothing spread like racks of lamb on the embers.

'Yes, but you mean to take a governess,' he said, laughing uneasily.

'Why? That would defeat everything! I shall be teacher, friend and parent to them! And in due course, when they're grown, when their personalities have . . . *ripened*, so to say, I shall make one or other my wife!'

'Oh now, really . . .' The room began to fill with a strange smell which, to the parson's mind, might have been the whiff of scandal. He furtively pulled the bell-rope beside the hearth and set his wine-glass down on the mantle. 'I mean, Wootton – look – can we . . .' He looked between man and girls, wanting to remonstrate in private, but the master of the house was preoccupied in watching the effect of his remark – beaming at the girls, who boggled back at him dumbfounded.

Baydon felt bound to take charge. He opened the doors of the library (which had begun to fill with acrid smoke) and ushered Alba and Zennor out into the hall. 'Your indulgence, girls. A few moments,' he blustered, and shut the doors on them. 'Wootton, have you seriously thought this through? Have you given a mind to how this will look? Taking in young girls not kin to you – are they kin to you? – without a female to chaperone them? Reputation, man! Think what the talk will make of it!'

'*Honi soit qui mal y pense*,' said Robin serenely. 'Of all the things I prize on God's earth, Baydon, reputation isn't one of them.'

'I didn't mean *your* reputation, man! I meant theirs!' With difficulty, he lowered his voice to a whisper. 'You can't seriously mean to hold them both to your chest like a pair of cards? Play one and discard the other?'

Robin ducked his curly head like a carriage horse and snorted. He did not trouble to moderate his voice. He had not thought as far ahead as the actual making of his choice, but it was hardly the potential for a tragedy. 'These are girls your chattering "society" would cheerfully suffer to starve or run depraved, for the sin of their poverty. Do you really suppose they stand to fare worse for coming here?' He signalled round him at the sheer opulence of Winding Hatch, though he did not mean the gilt chairs, the linenfold panelling, the ceiling-high shelves of leather-bound books. He meant his republic. He intended the girls no harm, therefore they would come to no harm. Baydon's misgivings fell on waterproof feathers. 'Of course I shall see to it that the one I don't . . . I mean, the one –'

'Left surplus,' Baydon interjected.

'The one whose temperament proves less well suited to mine, I shall naturally provide for. Naturally. What do you take me for, man? I shall see her married and provided for just as any father provides for his daughter. I promise you, she'll want for nothing!'

'Yes, but she's not your daughter, is she? She's your prospective . . .' Baydon broke off. He could not thoroughly express the welter of unformed misgivings that rose up at the thought of a man adopting two daughters with a view to training up one wife. He was not a good impromptu speaker. He hadn't the gift of debate. He wrote all his sermons down, and felt the need coming on now, like a head-cold, to get away and write something down so as to muster and order his thoughts. Besides, he was arguing from a weak position. Wootton could always retaliate, throwing in his face the unseemly haste of his own planned marriage, the dubious morality of forcing his attentions on a woman lately bereaved and made defenceless by poverty. He had to content himself with saying, 'I can't see any good will come of this, Wootton. Do think again, there's my bully man.'

A servant, as unobtrusive and silent as a stick insect, all his joints bent in carrying himself low, opened the door a crack and crept inside. Keeping to the wall, he circled the library to reach the grate, then retreated the way he had come, the blackened remains of the stays held in the firetongs, like the ribcages of two dead deer. Robin Wootton might seem to get by without servants, but in truth they just came and went with the utmost discretion.

Out in the hallway, the girls stood on a single marble paver, their hands on each other's wrists. They watched the servant go into the library, letting a little puff of leather-smoke escape as he did so, saw him come out again and creep soft-soled down a passageway towards the kitchens. He did not cast a single look in their direction; it was as if they were invisible.

'Marry us. Is that what he said?' Alba's little red mouth was pursed tight to keep in the wonder of it.

'All those books,' said Zennor. 'Why *can't* we read them?' It increased their mysterious allure. The sight of them had been more marvellous to her than any mention of marriage, since marriage was far, far off, and the books were substantial, there.

'Does it mean we can live here always? Be grand ladies? Dresses like this!' Alba spread her arms wide. 'Rich! Like princesses!'

'One of us can,' said Zennor.

'Oh, I'll share, if you'll share,' said Alba. She had a dim, confused notion of marriage. Her father had walked with several women on his arm – fat, thin, elderly, young. While her mother had been ill, her little hairdresser husband had sometimes walked about the alleys with a woman on each arm.

'I *want* to read them,' said Zennor, harping back to the books.

'But you can't read,' said Alba, and did not understand why Zennor glared at her with those dark, scowling eyes. To escape an argument, Alba ran up the staircase, to the top of the straight flight and proceeded to come down, step by wobbling step, pausing too long on each foot to make a steady descent. She cocked out one elbow and rested her hand over an imaginary arm as she and an imaginary husband descended to the sound of imaginary trumpets. Zennor, shelving the thought of books, ran to take the place of the invisible bridegroom, and they came down together, arm in arm. 'Make way for Mr and Mrs Robin Wootton of Winding Hatch in the county of . . . where are we?'

'Paradise,' said Zennor.

'. . . in the county of Paradise,' said Alba. 'Oh, Zennor! Really, will we? He means it! He does! He said so. He means to marry us!'

'One of us,' Zennor corrected her.

CHAPTER FOUR

Freedom

The pig had never known such days. All of a sudden, it was regularly fed on time, thanks to Sophronia Baydon's organised domestic routine; and almost every evening the parson could be found standing beside its sty scratching its back with a stick.

His son often came and balanced on the fence beside him; they declined *porcus* together – *porcus porcus porcum* – or Baydon told him Bible stories: Gideon and Daniel and Samson. Once he started on the story of the Gadarene swine, but George stopped him saying it would upset the pig.

'You know it already, then?' said Baydon.

'Mrs Baydon told me,' said the nine-year-old.

Mrs Baydon. It was not quite what Samuel Baydon had intended, and he could not help but suspect he was partly responsible for the present state of . . . confusion at the parsonage. Sophronia's children kept asking when they would be going home; little Grace kept packing their bags for them, generously loading in fruit and cushions and books, the quicker to see them gone. Perhaps he should have allowed them all to attend the wedding, after all. Perhaps he should.

Still, Grace's nightmares had stopped. For a little while, after her mother's death, Grace had searched the gardens during the day, calling out, and barricaded her door at night against ghosts, crying herself to sleep. All that seemed to have stopped since the arrival of 'Mrs Baydon'. And the baby, of course, was too young for prejudice.

'Do you like your new . . . Mrs Baydon?' he asked George, watching the boy throw rotten apples to the pig.

'*Optimissimus,*' said George categorically. 'Why? Don't you?'

Most confused of all, perhaps, was Baydon himself. He could not get out of his head the matter of Robin Wootton's adopted girls, and the more he thought the less he liked the business. Perhaps he should have taken a stronger line, stated his opposition more cogently. The fact that he had said so little he put down to his weakened moral position. He had himself undertaken a marriage for reasons of domestic convenience, and although no one could deny the order it had restored, the increase in his output of work, he could not totally square his conscience. Hence his long hours communing with the pig and with George.

Fortunately, the woman apparently lacked curiosity; she did not pepper him with questions as to why he had given her a bedroom on the far side of the nursery and made no further mention of that 'other aspect' of marriage.

Robin Wootton thought that because he *had* no improper intentions, it was not improper to introduce two young girls, unprotected, into a bachelor household. Intention had *nothing to do with the case*. One had always to bear in mind what misunderstanding and malice could achieve behind a man's back.

'*Optimissima*,' said Baydon, correcting his son's Latin. 'And do try to avoid exaggeration.' But George had long since got down and gone to play inside the box-hedge. Time often escaped Samuel Baydon as he stood scratching the pig's back. There was a great deal on his mind, what with the forthcoming Quarter Sessions, the monthly removal of vagrants, the Highways Maintenance Committee and the Parish Council. Luckily Mrs Baydon had taken over the running of his Penny-Savings Scheme. He could not quite recall asking her to do it, but the callers at the door seemed just as content to hand in their pennies to the parson's wife as to the parson, and so far Sophronia had not shown any difficulty in keeping the ledger up to date.

Then there was his brother to worry about. Always his infernal brother . . .

There was the army encampment, growing like a tumour on the edge of the parish, and the problem of overcrowding at the poorhouse where he was a governor – that request from the warden for a sermon on the abuse of poor relief. It was just as well that Mrs Baydon, on top of everything, gave no cause for concern – only that slight nagging uncertainly that he had done an improper thing.

Time and again Baydon's thoughts returned to those two little girls, imported like blackamoors, and withheld from the civilising influence of the dame school or a governess.

'Great Henny!' he burst out at the tea table that evening. 'Does he really mean to pit them against each other like cocks in a cockpit?' (Though he believed that oaths broke the third Commandment, he was the kind of man who needed an escape valve for his feelings, so that all his expletives came from the household gazetteer. Sophronia was just becoming accustomed to the geography of Baydon's wrath.) Discreetly wiping the baby's vomit from her bonnet strings, she transferred her daughter's uneaten crusts to George's plate, picking eggshell from the tablecloth as she did so, and signalling to Grace to gather up the plates.

'What if I were to befriend the girls a little?' she suggested quietly, pouring him another cup of coffee. 'Give them to know they are always welcome here. If they need advice. Or feel the want of female company.'

He scowled at her, but she did not take it amiss. She had seen him scowl at many a congregation in the same way without having anyone in particularly marked down for a sinner. 'Hmm. Yes. That might ease their minds a little, yes,' he said. 'Yes, it might,' forgetting to mention that it had eased his own.

Alba and Zennor sat down on a log and prepared for a long day.

'I'm sure it was dung,' said Alba a fourth time. 'I trod in dung.'

They were wearing scarlet muslin chemise gowns fastened down the front with ribbon bows, embroidered with lilies-of-the-valley and adorned with coppery sashes of silk. Each sash matched the ribbon band round their wide, bergère hats. Their collars, too, were vandyked with exquisite bronze lace. But their feet were bare.

Zennor fingered the row of tiny buttons close-fastening her muslin sleeves; she thought hers was the most beautiful dress ever made. And here she was, in a wood, put to the labour of keeping it clean. Already the leading strings – the beautiful, corded, ornamental, golden leading strings – had caught round a twig and almost been tugged off. 'We're supposed to climb a tree,' she said, looking up at the elm boughs, the white-candled chestnuts and the mare's-tail clouds beyond. She could not put out of her mind the possibility of rain. 'Climb trees, he said.'

'Yes, but he won't know if we don't,' Alba pleaded. 'I've never climbed a tree.'

'That's why we have to do it, I suppose. To learn.'

'But why? Why does he need a wife who can climb trees?'

It was not a proper wood – only one of the stands of trees surrounded by the grazing and harvest land which made up the Wootton estate. They had already come through a bed of cabbages, a field of cows and over two stiles to reach the spinney. At least now they were out of sight of the house. He could not be watching them – unless he were standing on the roof with a spyglass.

The thought brought Zennor sharply to her feet. Robin Wootton might do anything. The heads of slimy white fungi broke off under her bare toes.

'I did. I stood in dung!' said Alba examining the sole of one foot. 'At least at Lambeth we had shoes!'

On the day the dresses had arrived, tailor-made, from Wantage – the dresses and nightgowns, the petticoats and capes and half-capes and bloomers, the straw hats and morning wraps, with four other gowns to follow – Zennor and Alba had looked everywhere for the shoes. Clothes lay across every piece of furniture, like swooning ladies, bonnets capping the bedposts. But though they scrabbled under the beds and lifted up whole armfuls of cotton and toile, shoes were nowhere to be found. Nor hose. They could not mention it; perhaps Mr Wootton had overlooked them, and it would have been carping to mention shoes and stockings in the face of such generosity. 'He'll soon notice, when he sees us,' Zennor had reasoned.

But it turned out that Robin Wootton did not intend them to wear shoes. 'Let Emile run barefoot all year round – upstairs, downstairs and in the garden!' he had declaimed delightedly. 'Now go out and play! The child's work is to play! Go anywhere you please. Do anything you care to. Make as much noise as you want. This is your Age of Nature, when reason sleeps!' So saying, he had thrown open the great windows of the breakfast room and lifted them out into the garden.

'Who's Emily? You or me?' said Zennor, two hours later, in the spinney.

'I am,' said Alba swiftly. She knew how fond Wootton was of using the name.

Overhead, the wood-pigeons crooned monotonously. A lime-white dropping splattered down on to the log where Zennor had been sitting a moment before. 'Emily is a boy,' she pointed out.

'No!'

'He is. He's French. They call boys Emily in France. They call boys Mary, too. I've heard that.'

'Well, then, I'm Sophie. I'm not going to be a boy,' said Alba. 'Nor I'm not going to climb trees. Are we?'

They were unwilling to refuse Robin Wootton anything. In fact, they were eager to please him, in any way they could. Nothing was too good for a man who would deck them out like a church pulpit in flower-embroidered collars and dormeuse caps. But they were accustomed to doing what they were told, from first light to after dark, and now, to be left to their own devices in a wood was hard indeed. 'Climb trees! Pick flowers! Leap into haystacks!' he had enjoined them as he urged them out of doors. 'Play in yonder woods! Smell the summer! Listen to the earth's heartbeat! Let her beauty ravish your senses!'

Zennor sniffed. 'Do you smell summer?' she asked the other girl nervously.

'I can smell dung,' said Alba. 'I trod in dung in my bare feet.'

They had picked poppies out of the edge of the barley field – blood-red fragments of tissue such as must have been left on the tailor's floor after their dresses were made. But the poppies had wilted within minutes, shrivelled to pellets the size of flies. Rose-bay willow-herb was the only flower they had seen in London, and that had been growing, hardy and reckless, out of chimney-pots and guttering. Perhaps it had removed itself from the danger of little girls sent out to pick flowers.

'There's no helping it,' said Zennor with sudden ferocity. 'We'll have to take off all and lay it by. We can climb in our linen.'

So they took off their fabulous gowns, those elaborate assemblages of bodice, petticoat and skirt, and wandered unhappily about, looking for trees that might just be climbed. There were twigs and brambles, and tree roots which stuck through the ground like the backbones of hibernating dragons. Zennor was glad, finally, to pull herself up into the fork of an elm tree. Boots would have made climbing a lot easier. But she wormed her way around and up, up and along, until she began to see beyond the spinney and back the way they had come.

The house looked more beautiful than ever amid its tailor-made prospect of immaculate grounds. She could see one ugly yellow scar, like a smallpox blemish, where something – a maze? – had been uprooted. 'This one does well enough!' she called to Alba. 'Come up. You can see all of Winding Hatch.'

But Alba, after circling the tree a few times, resting a hand against the trunk, lifting one bare foot hesitantly in the air, declared it was impossible and sat herself down like a broody chicken on the ground. 'I'll just sit here until it's time to go back,' she said.

Moving round to the other side of the trunk, Zennor could see the church and graveyard and, beyond them, another house. It must be the parsonage. Its garden, too, had an ordered, multi-coloured beauty, but had largely been given over to vegetable beds. There were straight lines of carrot tops, netted berry bushes, a chicken coop and a pig pen. Washing hung from a line between two apple trees – brightly white in the sunshine, every shape and size of garment from baby pilches to a man's big nightshirt, all jostling close; they looked like ghosts trouping single-file out of the graveyard next door. In just one corner, between the raspberry canes and chicken coop, one bed of flowers had been allowed to persist (despite the terrible increase in food prices which had lately turned every gardener into a smallholder). Canterbury bells and campanula, peonies, honesty and Michaelmas daisies and the rest were so tightly compressed that, from the top of the tree, the flower-bed looked like a bright Turkey rug.

'He told us to pick flowers,' said Zennor, reminded.

'We did. They died,' said Alba, pulling the dead poppies out of her hair. 'It's not a place for flowers, this.'

'There are some down there.' It was only an observation.

Alba thought immediately that they should go and pick them, but Zennor said they would get into trouble for it.

'No, we won't. Robin can take anything, hereabouts. He's gentry,' was how Alba saw it. Zennor might have quibbled – with the idea or with Alba using the gentleman's Christian name. But she had just discovered that she was stuck in the tree. Flowers went entirely out of her head.

'The branches have gone I came up by,' she said.

'Don't be simple.'

Zennor eased herself on to another branch, looking for a way down. The ground below rippled. A sudden sweat came to her hands and feet. Shutting her eyes, she bent one leg and felt with the other for the branch below. The branch melted out of existence. Long threads of blown gossamer drifted towards her like spittle.

'You're being simple!' Alba insisted. 'You got up!'

Zennor's legs, which just now had been strong enough to raise her, were spongy and treacherous. She sat down, and the tilt of the branch overbalanced her, sent her sliding, so that she collided with the trunk, yelping. 'I'm strait-wedged!' she called down. 'Get someone! Get help! Down there! That house! Quick!'

But Alba did not go quickly. First she allowed time for Zennor to change her mind, for Zennor to be fooling, for Zennor to be mistaken. Then, slowly, she backed away from the elm tree, every moment expecting to be called back because Zennor was all right; but Zennor only whimpered in her strait place.

When Alba reached the edge of the spinney, she told herself Zennor must be getting down by now – would get down better for not being watched. Anyway, she did not want to run; did not know what her bare feet would step on. So she picked her way carefully through the barley, spiking her ankles on broken stems, fearing snakes. The English countryside was exotically dangerous after the stoney sterility of London.

She could see the parsonage now, its domino-tile vegetable beds, its corner patch of flowers. Flowers! She need not disobey Robin after all. Here were flowers. No one would deny their local gentry flowers. He could surely take whatever from wherever he pleased. So, too, could his wards. Zennor would be down by now. Zennor would surely be down.

Being in her underwear, she could hardly present herself at the parsonage door and ask for the flowers. Besides, she had only to reach between the slats of the fence to help herself.

A boy about her own age was playing in the garden, trying to toss and catch a ball on the blade of a garden trowel. A baby with a cloth pudding bound to the top of her head sat swatting the dapple of an apple tree with a leafy twig. Alba reached through and began tugging irises out of the ground. Soil and roots and leaves rattled against the palings, and drew the attention of the boy, who sauntered over.

'What are you doing?' enquired George.

'Picking flowers. I was told,' said Alba. She grunted with the exertion of heaving a big cluster of iris corms through the narrow slit. The corms broke off in a shower, like pebbles.

'Who told you?' said George.

'My husband–as–will–be,' said Alba. 'Give me some of those blue ones, boy, will you?'

Fascinated, George climbed up on the chicken coop to look over the fence. Yes, he had been right; his perforated view through the fence had not misled him. 'They give out shoes and dresses at the poorhouse. You should go there.'

'Don't need shoes,' retorted Alba, demeaned to be pitied by a fellow child. 'Emily doesn't wear shoes summer or winter, upstairs or down.'

'Who's Emily?'

George climbed down from the chicken coop and began picking the blue flowers, as he had been told. He pushed some through the slits, but they got broken, so he threw them over the fence instead, one by one.

It was this blue parabola of Michaelmas daisies, flying one by one over his fence, which drew the attention of Samuel Baydon as he sat in his study writing a letter. He took off out of the house at such a run that he collided with the washline prop and dislodged it. A nightshirt fell over the baby. '*Mrs Baydon!*' shouted the parson.

George was so startled into guilt that he ran backwards into the fence with a bang, saying, 'There's a poor girl! A poor girl!'

Baydon set one foot on the chicken coop and loomed up over the thief, for all the world as if he would vault the fence. Alba dropped all the flowers in her arms.

'You!'

When he saw who it was, Baydon was so shocked that he momentarily forgot the plunder of his flower-bed. 'What are you doing, girl? Great Snoring! What are you thinking of? Where are your clothes? Where are your shoes?' He dropped the questions on her like clods of earth.

'She doesn't have shoes,' George offered in a diplomatic whisper.

'Robin said to,' the girl said, her note of defiance belied by the fright on her face.

'*That macaroni told you to pick my flowers?* . . . Where's your sister?'

'Lambeth, sir!'

'He sent her back?'

'He never brought her!' They were shouting at each other now, he in his booming pulpit roar, she in a high, desperate wail.

Behind Samuel, Mrs Baydon unearthed the crying baby and picked her up. She let the fallen washing lie, sensing a more important crisis. Bouncing the baby on her hip, she walked through the picket gate to the churchyard, and round the perimeter of the garden to where Alba danced agitatedly on a strewing of flowers. George, seeing her through the slats, called out like a prisoner through his bars: 'Her husband told her, Mrs Baydon! He told her to!'

'*George, be quiet!*' thundered his father, and the chickens burst themselves like feather cushions against the far end of the run, trying to get away from the noise.

Alba turned an appealing face towards the parson's wife. 'Zennor's stuck in a tree up yonder!' she said, and burst into torrential tears.

They went up the hill like a hue-and-cry, Baydon hauling his miscreant son behind him, Mrs Baydon carrying the baby, Alba picking her way through the vipers and porcupines of Hatch Hill. The first Zennor heard of them was George's, 'She's called Emily!' and Alba's 'waspish, 'I am not!'

By the time Baydon reached the spinney, he was so hot that he appeared puce with rage. George too was puce, but only because his cheeks had run the gauntlet of the wiry barley whiskers. Alba hung back, knowing she had spent over-long fetching help. 'It's an outrage!' said the parson, apparently to the occupant of the tree.

'I can't get down,' said Zennor, the tears making a slurry of the dirt on her face.

Mrs Baydon took charge of her husband's camlet waistcoat and his stock, and he climbed the tree, encouraged from hesitating by his son's scorched, admiring face.

'Have you neither of you one shred of decency?' puffed the face emerging through the leaves on a level with Zennor's. 'Is this how you behaved at the asylum?'

Zennor shook her head, but she was beyond explaining the dilemma of the tree and the clothing. Instead she flung herself in his direction, closing her arms round his head and neck so that they both almost tumbled out of the tree. Mrs Baydon covered her eyes.

'Ogbourne-Maizey,' said Baydon, climbing gingerly down. 'Wootton had best have some answers ready why he blesses us with two thieving, trolloping, ragamuffin, shameless . . .'

'I'd best get back down to the house, Reverend,' said Mrs Baydon, brushing the leaves off his back, and out of Zennor's hair. 'The children are alone. I could maybe take the girls back with me and find them something of Sarah's for them to wear.'

'Oh, we have *dresses*,' said Alba in surprise, going to fetch them. 'It's only shoes we ain't.'

'But we couldn't climb trees in dresses,' Zennor explained, 'and he said we must climb trees.'

'I couldn't,' observed Alba dismally. '– But don't tell Mr Wootton, sir, please!'

The parson told them they were ungrateful, trolloping besoms and led the way down the hill to Hatch House, still holding his son by the wrist. A stem of Michaelmas daisy still hung broken from George's other hand. The girls followed behind, their scarlet dresses lifted high above their knees, white liberated feet picking a path between cowpats.

But Robin Wootton, when they found him in the rose-garden, was not abashed in the slightest. 'This is their Age of Nature,' he declared, looking with evident satisfaction at their dishevelled hair. He wore a straw round-hat which gave him the ingenuous look of a goat-herd in Arcadia. 'Let them find out! Let them touch and smell and try and fail and see and wonder!' There was no trace of anger in his soothing, contented voice. It fell like a balm on Alba. It barricaded out the parson's fretting and fuming, soaking up his angry indignation as a pillow soaks up tears. Nothing he said could batter down the serene cheerfulness of her Mr Wootton.

Baydon, too, had collected himself. 'I think you will find, sir, that discipline adds greatly to the charm of children.' He said it as politely as he was able. 'If you could tell them not to pick my flowers in future, for instance, I'd be obliged to you.'

'I fear I can't even be of that much help, Samuel. You see, the words "obey" and "command" don't enter into our vocabulary presently. No curbs. Just the freedom to discover the world in their own time and their own way.'

Baydon was thunderstruck. 'You mean you shan't tell them what they must and must not do?'

'All the first impulses of nature are good and right,' came the reply, too pat to be an original thought, and so self-evidently untrue that Baydon stood open-mouthed, images of Eden tumbling through his head, waiting for his neighbour to modify this preposterous claim. Instead, Wootton waved a pacifying hand. 'Trust nature, Samuel. Trust nature, and trust God. You of all people should trust the Almighty God who made these girls. You'll see. Right-thinking will spring from them as naturally as grapes from the vine. Trust me.'

Baydon cleared his throat, dipped his head and moved closer, almost brushing cheeks with the swain in his linen smock. 'And what if the stock's bad?' he said in a mumbling bass, not wanting the girls to hear.

Every muscle of Wootton's mobile face was engaged in the smile which followed. Taking advantage of the parson's closeness, he took hold of his arm and stretched it out to the side. 'You may train stock to grow along the ground, my friend; the new will always shoot upright. Rousseau himself said that, and *he*, sir, was a gardener.' He could not have been more pleased with his unanswerable horticulture.

'I'll venture he didn't suffer little children to pull up his flowers, sir,' said the parson, shaking an irritable arm free of Wootton's grip. 'And how shall you keep them from hurting themselves, might I ask? Eh? I found this child here forty feet up in a tree and incapable of climbing down. What if she had fallen?'

'Then next time she would know her limitations – or climb better!' replied Wootton joyously. 'That's exactly our principle of education. Learn by doing! Learn by *feeling*! . . . And a child never died yet of *playing*. You must read *Emile*; you truly must, Samuel. As a parent it would open a window – a window, truly. Heart and mind. It's a revelation, I swear to you.'

'In my experience, Mr Wootton,' said the vicar testily, '*Revelations* is full of monsters and demons. We can see the end of the world in *Revelations*.'

34

A tide of darkest ennui rose up in him. He had work to do, letters to write. Also, he had just realised that, in his haste and anger, he had come out bare-headed, without his wig. He did not want to stand debating the education of children, under a hot sun and in front of the girls in question. He had come for an apology and to redeliver the man's charges, and had got neither his apology nor thanks. His energy was already depleted by climbing a tree. He also knew that Wootton's mind would not change if they debated all afternoon.

Still, the man was advocating anarchy! And with the souls of two little girls at stake he felt obliged to make one more bid on their behalf. 'Children need guidance,' he pointed out with (he thought) admirable restraint. '*Educare*: to lead out.' A painful hand wrung his guts as he saw what pleasure his comment apparently gave Wootton.

'Ah, Latin! And we all see how well the Roman Empire fared on a diet of Latin,' said the young man, with lapidary irony, poking his tongue into the side of his mouth to restrain a grin.

The girls concerned wore the vacant, inexpressive faces of children weathering adult conversation. Wootton saw it. He abhorred it. To startle them back into vivacity – to involve them actively in the democratic process of their upbringing – he flung an arm round Alba and drew her head close to his chest. Zennor he included, with a theatrical tilt of his head. 'We three are not bound by the past, you see, Samuel. We disciples of Rousseau, we're older and at the same time we're moderner than any of your classical *magisters*. We have re-invented childhood the way God intended it. We have given ourselves back the freedom of natural man. Children of this age don't need guidance, man. They need freedom!' To lend his point graphic potency, he reached out and caught hold of the leading strings of Zennor's dress.

Vestiges of babyhood, wizened down by fashion into nothing more than pretty decorations, the strings had no real purpose. But they were symbols of a guiding parental hand – of restraint and reining in. So with a swift sure nick of his bill hook, he cut them off short, and flung the golden cords far out on to the ornamental pond. 'We have found a better way, Mr Baydon,' said Robin without the slightest reproach. 'We have broken free.'

A small, shuddering cry escaped Zennor, and her eyes followed the golden strings, and her fingers flew to the stubs of unwinding cord left sticking out of her bodice like a whippet's dugs. George, who was the only one to notice, proffered her the broken stalk of a Michaelmas daisy, his eyes filling with sympathetic tears.

★

35

'What fiddle-faddle the man talks,' said Mrs Baydon, as her husband raged through the parsonage, slamming all the doors, repeating aloud Wootton's philosophies in a shrill, baleful, disbelieving rant. 'Children not hurt themselves playing? Must be three children a year drowned in the Kennet, never mention those that step out under a mail coach.'

Up the box stairs and down the main, she followed him, showing her solidarity, taking care not to be hit by the doors but never dropping quite out of earshot.

'It's their *moral* welfare, Mrs Baydon,' he said, turning at last towards her with outspread hands. 'That's what I fear for most.'

She picked a last leaf out of his short-shaved, greying hair. 'Myself, I think it's their feet,' she said. 'I'll maybe knit them some socks before the cold weather comes.' And hitching his baby higher on her hip, she went in search of her knitting bag. He watched her go.

'Very good, Mrs Baydon,' said the parson, in a small, defeated voice.

CHAPTER FIVE

Removals

It was the first time in Alba's life that she had outdone her sister. The older girl had always overshadowed her – more competent, more clever, better able to cope. More loving.

'How that Marianne girl do tend after that sister of her'n,' the voices at the asylum had said. 'Ain' she just the perfick little mother?' But Alba had not felt compensated for the loss of her mother, had bitterly resented her sister's attempts to stand in for the real thing. Marianne was nothing like her, after all: sober, hard-working Marianne – nothing like their slatternly, drunken, flabby, incomprehensible mother.

Marianne had owned more, too: a pair of their mother's drawers, and a scar on her back where their mother had hit her once with a broken gin bottle. And memories. Marianne had remembered times in their father's barber's shop, playing among the snipped hair and beard shavings on the floor. Alba's head was as bare of such recollections as a robbed tomb.

So Alba gloried, now, in the fact that her sister had been passed over, that she, Alba Padock, had been chosen despite her lesser skill with needle and thread. She triumphed in her isolation. When Zennor asked curiously, 'Are you missing your sister fearful?' Alba burst out laughing and said, 'Never!'

It was only after a time – passing one of the mirrors and mistaking her own blonde hair for that of her sister – that Alba discovered an unaccountable sense of loss.

'She will write, uh? Your sister?' said Zennor, hearing the tears at night, going as far as the door of the adjoining bedroom.

'No!'

It was said in panic, for any such letter would certainly instruct Alba to blow her nose, wipe herself well after using the closet, not to grind her teeth or walk her heels over to the side. That was Marianne's way of trying to be a mother. With Alba unable to read, someone would have to read the letters out to her, so that she would be, like a prisoner in the pillory, pelted with her shortcomings.

Besides, alongside Zennor, dark and fiendish, she felt she could hold her own. Against her sister, she never had, and probably never would. Life had always been a struggle: that much she did remember. So like a piglet latching on to a maternal teat, Alba Padock pursed shut her mouth and determined to hang on grimly. Here was succour, if she only had the tenacity to hold fast. If it meant shouldering aside the memory of a sister left behind at Lambeth – well, that was no more than their mother had done when she left her parcel of children at the gates of the asylum.

Robin hoped they liked him. He was trying very hard to make them happy, and not just because his experiment demanded happy subjects. He found it very hard to measure his success, even so. They would *look* at him so, expressionless and silent – suspicious, he might almost have said, if it were possible for the woodworm suspicion to have infested timber so green. He was aware, after being with them, that the muscles of his face were tired from smiling – from trying to imbue them with his own joy. They were not quite sullen. No, they were more like small animals cowering at the back of a dark cage, needing coaxing before they would show themselves.

It was no good applying to his own childhood for guidance; he did not remember anything of relevance there. His mother had been a wholly unsmiling woman. She had not even smiled when she said, 'One would think the boy a changeling for all the resemblance he bears to his stock.' Fortunately, he had known it must be a joke: changeling babies are known by the fact that they never smile, whereas Robin had smiled and smiled as though his small life depended on it. Only his mother had remained implacably straight-faced. As for his father, he had believed in the simplest possible regime for child-rearing: mothers should supply affection and nourishment, fathers punishment.

Robin found himself buying Zennor and Alba a great many pretty clothes, even though Rousseau would not strictly have approved. He had always tended to give presents, even as a child – horses, jackets, gold coins to the servants. It at least provoked a response. He would have to stop that, of course, with the girls. Materialism was banned from his curriculum; he had to teach Alba and Zennor to be enriched by a sunset, by a rose unfolding, by a frosty morning. As he was.

It was true he did not greatly care for their childish company at the moment – found it never quite accorded with his mood – like a neck-band which clashes with whatever outfit is put on. But all that would change, in time. He did not even find them very appealing, now that he had got them home. . . . But then he often felt like that with girls and women. They were a little like the butterflies he had hunted as a boy: when he picked them out of the bottom of the net, they had never retained quite the magic of free flight. The ladies he gallantly invited to Hatch House after a dance or a soirée elsewhere never smiled quite as much as they had on first acquaintance. And without a smile, how was one supposed to take soundings, to judge one's depth?

Alba opened the rear door to go out, and screamed. She slammed the door shut, and ran through the house shouting, 'Mr Wootton, Mr Wootton! There's a redman at the kitchen stoop!'

Stiff Abney was shown into the octagonal room, with its gilded French furniture and its mythological paintings. He was a bright, sunset-orange colour, with short-cropped hair and a jacket made from a hessian flour sack. If he had ever worn an expression, it had long since dissolved in the red steam of the Wantage tannery.

'Was asking myself if you had work, y'honour,' he said. 'Summat. Anything.'

Wootton did not answer at once; he was fetching a chair into the middle of the room for Stiff to sit on. 'Tell me about yourself, sir,' he insisted. 'Alba, bring some tea.'

Stiff eyed the chair dubiously; it did not look strong enough to take his weight, and was upholstered in cream silk.

'Up to yesterday, I was a reddleman at tannery, y'honour,' he said without sitting down. 'But I'm turned off. So I'm seeking work, yes? And I thought . . .' His appeal tailed off. He had not expected it to get so much of a hearing, and had, after all, said everything which needed saying. As far as Stiff was concerned, the world was divided into men with jobs and men without; no one could fail to know the difference. But the young gentleman of Hatch House continued to look at him eagerly, encouragingly, urging him to sit down. Stiff lowered his heavy thighs on to the rim of the chair: it racked dangerously. 'Thing is. Iwuzzen born in these parts. Wife was, but she's gone on.'

'Gone on?'

'Into the ground, y'honour.' It felt like a long time that they spent waiting for tea.

39

When at last it came, and he was handed a cup by Alba, his cracked, mahogany hands entrusted with some tiny china ornament half full of tinged, strange-smelling hot water, he saw the look the girl cast over his orange features. 'Mine's not the visage for working-in, see – serving, or such, or coach driving. But I'm good in a garden. Could ever me things come up. 'N you got almighty gardens.' The longer a hearing the gentleman gave him, the higher Stiff's hopes rose.

'Well, look here, Mr Abney,' said Wootton. 'I never insult my fellow men with charity, but you're welcome to stay to dinner. The Dunches are coming over for piquet. Do you play piquet, Mr Abney?'

Stiff stood up. He suspected he was the butt of a joke too subtle for a man of his simplicity to grasp. The idea tasted as bitter as the tea. 'I must find work, me. If you've nought, maybe you'd speak to the Dunches of me. Ken do gardens. Wuz only a reddleman since I come in Wantage. Before that, gardens an' me . . .'

'Oh, then I must show you what I'm doing! It will interest you.' And Wootton jumped up and went out of the room leaving Stiff uncertain whether to follow or wait where he was.

A picture of the third viscount looked down disapprovingly, while a legendary Horatio manfully held the bridge between the candlesticks and the end of the mantel: held it against just such men as Stiff, to judge by the sneer on his classical face.

Stiff had already got wind there was work afoot within the grounds of Hatch House. All the way up the drive, grubbed up plants lay about, their roots like matted hair. An avenue of limes had been felled and dragged away by horse-and-chain, and green grass had been flayed off the hillside behind the house. He did not greatly care why Robin Wootton should be marring the work of his ancestors; he only cared that it meant work; for a man with a strong back, it surely meant work. Once, he might have taken exception to the scarifying of an ancient rose-bed, the dissolution of box hedging, but all curiosity and opinion had drained out of him like earth from a broken flowerpot. He had to find work. He was not local, and his name was already on the constable's list.

Alba, once she had overcome the alarming strangeness of his colour, found nothing strange about Stiff Abney being there. The room had entertained many such passers-by. Almost anyone who called at the kitchen door was shown into this exquisite octagonal room with its swags of stucco laurel and its octagonal laurel-pattern carpet. Robin Wootton's hospitality astounded her, though it stirred in her very slight feelings of jealousy to think that she was not the sole recipient of his goodness. Clearly she and

Zennor had not been strange enough to satisfy his taste for the outlandish. All these others had followed: gypsies, tinkers, drovers, icemen, lost recruits looking for the encampment on the downs. . . . Fortunately, he never gave them money – said that charity demeaned both getter and giver – so they never stayed long. But she marvelled in the interest he showed in his fellow men, the generosity of sympathy he showed for their chaotic, desperate little lives.

She personally had no interest in them. She had met every kind of want and ruin in the other girls at Lambeth Asylum. Even left alone in a room with Stiff Abney, she felt no need to speak to him.

But the servants did.

They came in, in a body, all three of the house footmen: paunchy Job, tall Curragh, and William, spare and pallid as a wire-worm. Failing to see Alba by the bright window, they dispensed with their usual creeping, silent unobstrusiveness. They took the teacup out of the visitor's hand, and Curragh tipped him off his chair with a twist of one hand on the chairback. 'You're leaving,' they told him.

'Don't want no house job,' he insisted, getting up as quickly as he could off the octagonal carpet for fear of their buckled shoes. 'Only gardening.'

But they did not choose to argue. Curragh twisted the man's arm behind his back. Job gathered up his hat and satchel, and they put Stiff out through the window, throwing his things after him, promising to pass on his regrets to the master.

They were housemen, saw their place as in the house. But more and more, Wootton talked of liberation, took trays out of their hands, apologised to them for his crime of making a slave out of other living souls. To Job and William and Curragh it smacked of dismissal. They did not see how he could run Hatch House without staff, but it was not worth the risk. They had to keep employment. Times were such that hands were two-a-penny, and the destitute went past the gate in cartfuls, twice a day.

Together, they had plunged into panic, like sheep into a dip: Job, Curragh and William. But Job's wife (who was cook at Hatch House and less in danger of being noticed, down in her subterranean kitchen) had given them her advice. Wootton plainly had grand plans for the reshaping of the gardens. All his current interests were out of doors. His need, therefore, was of gardening men. That is why Job and William and Curragh, at times when they would formerly have been napping in the boot room, were volunteering to dig out the foundations of an orangery wall, or burning out the roots of ancient trees. Wootton had some landscape in mind, of which he often spoke to them, spreading his arms, nodding his head towards some unplanted prospect. They would nod, too, and grunt with enthusiasm, and pretend to see it in their minds' eye. Then they would strip to their shirt-sleeves, leap to their barrows, and get to work. But what they were building with this unaccustomed, disagreeable toil, was a bulwark against disaster. Out there, unemployment and destitution were loose and rampant in the countryside, and Job and Curragh and William had no intention of tasting them, no intention of losing place to any of the strays Wootton so liked to ask into his house. That is why they put Stiff Abney out of doors.

The lesson was not wasted on Alba. Standing in the window, her slight shape obliterated by the light behind her, she learned that Wootton was someone to cling to. Like drowning men round a wet and slippery rock, men were prepared to fight for a hand-hold, cling on and let no one and nothing dislodge them back into the swallowing cold. How much more should she, with prospects such as hers, cling on tight to the shining smoothness of Robin Wootton?

The text for his sermon was 'A man of sorrows, acquainted with grief.' But Samuel Baydon could think of nothing to say on the subject.

Tiny black harvest flies settled in scores on the blank paper, like living punctuation marks looking for the sermon which ought to be there. Though his quill hovered over the page, and his other hand was spread on the open Bible, his mind refused to grapple with the topic. A letter from his brother, which lay screwed up in the grate, held a far tighter grip on his concentration.

Oliver was threatening to visit.

'Does he visit often?' asked Mrs Baydon, who was pinning up the hems of new curtains. She did not generally intrude on his privacy, but for some infernal reason, had decided this morning to pin up the curtains. Ever since she had fetched that letter up from the village, she had been to and fro with pins and lemonade and chatter, wanting to discuss it. 'What manner of gentleman is he, your brother?' she asked.

'A man of shallows, acquainted with sloth,' he answered tartly, but she only laughed, spraying pins from between her lips. 'What does he do?'

Baydon could see no easy escape; he laid down his pen. 'As little as he can, for as long as he's suffered to,' he said. 'My brother, Mrs Baydon, came late into the world, and ever since then, he has contrived to outstay his welcome.'

He could recall his youngest brother's arrival – an unprecedented racket of pain and shouting and fright, smashing the peace of his father's cavernous, silent rectory. As a boy of fourteen, he had been instructed to kneel on the carpet beside his father and pray for his mother's safe deliverance. Deliverance from what? They seemed to think that, at fourteen, he must know. But always before his mother had travelled away to female relations for her confinements, returning childless after a succession of stillbirths which were scrupulously never mentioned in front of the boy. No such unseemly words as 'pregnancy' or 'childbirth' had ever been let inside the house. There had never, in his lifetime, been such a clamour as this – nothing to prepare for that endless vigil on aching kneecaps, no explanations of exactly what peril his mother was in. Somehow he had taken it into his adolescent head that she was possessed by demons, and that they were praying for those demons to be cast out. Nothing since that first atrocious night had given Samuel much cause to change his mind.

'Yes, but do you *like* him?' asked his wife, with maddening impertinence.

'He's very well made,' said Baydon down his nose. 'Ladies find no difficulty in liking him.'

'Yes, but do—'

Before she could bend his patience to breaking point, a figure passed the window in front of Baydon's desk, making for the front steps. At the same moment, his daughter Grace came in and said there was a reddleman at the kitchen door.

As if Samuel's day were not blighted enough already, the constable had brought the weekly list for signature. He was a big man with a child's face and a drayman's body, rounded off by regular beer-drinking. The only thing thin about Constable Gervase was his hand-writing – an etiolated menagerie of letters so tall and thin that he could compress twenty words on to a line. He took immense pride in his 'list', laying it down in front of Baydon (in the parson's capacity as magistrate) with a childlike eagerness for praise. Men who wrote more, had less reverence for the beauty of the written word.

Baydon looked it over. The only white space was the one left for his signature. 'It gets longer every week, Gervase,' he said, picking up his pen.

'None of 'em born Berkshire,' said Gervase, which was his standard reaction.

There was so little gap left between words that the actual names were hard to decipher. Still, the parson felt it his duty to try.

Edward Allen
Louis Stepney & three small ones
Mary Isham
Ann Shad & boy
Stiff Abney an 2
Thomas Ethell & wife . . .

They were vagrants. At least they were unemployed, destitute and liable to cause a drain on the county exchequer. If they had been born within the county, then the county would have accepted responsibility for them, paid them poor relief. But they were not 'born Berkshire'. Consequently, they could be seized on by the constable, clanged into the lock-up, then put into a cart and transported east into Oxfordshire. Half of them had probably arrived in Berkshire off the Wiltshire wagons. It was an expensive solution, costly to police and flawed in concept. Where, Baydon wondered, did their futile journeys end? At some east-coast beach, dumped like rubble on the foreshore?

Foolishly, he allowed the spindly, overcrowded letters of Gervase's handwriting to take on human shape. Crammed together in a jostling convoy, they leaned all towards the east, Edward Allen and Ann Shad, the three Stepney children taking up no more room than the emaciated e's and o's of their family name. If he added his signature, it might be trampled by the relentless feet of all these migrating words.

'For half the money it costs to move 'em,' said the parson, 'we could feed and clothe 'em.'

'Long as they's out of Berkshire, the beggars,' said Gervase with relish. 'There be no bread by Christmas, without they mouths eating it up.' He was a man invested with huge powers for one of his age, and with no prospect of unemployment. There would never be a shortage of beggars to crate up and ship out of his native county. So he had no difficulty in thinking of them as verminous, vicious, superfluous. They were a plague on his Egypt, the rats in his Hamelin. When, in a rash moment of pride, Samuel had shown him the pig, Gervase had looked over the pink expanse of Porcus-Porcus and said, 'But she be'nt Berkshire, be she?'

Needing to escape his duty, Baydon seized on the excuse of having another visitor, and hurried through to the kitchen, only to be confronted by a man the same size as Constable Gervase but as orange as Seville. His wife had given the reddleman a glass of applejuice. 'Mr Abney here is looking for work,' she said. 'I told him you do all your own gardening but you might know of something.'

Stiff Abney stood up and mangled his cap between cracked, orange hands.

44

There was a small cut over his left eye, and one sleeve of his flour-sack jacket had come adrift at the shoulder. 'The tanneries are all renting in, now, and laying men off. Anything. Anything, sir!' Even his eyes seemed orange.

Samuel Baydon turned straight round and went back to his study without a word. Running his eye down the list, he found the name crushed into its tumbril of loops and serifs. Stiff Abney ought, even now, to be awaiting his fate in the town lock-up. 'This man here. The name's familiar. Does he not work at the tannery?'

'Yea. But now they're renting in,' said Gervase, colouring up a little at the mention of Abney.

'What is this 'renting-in?' demanded Baydon, exasperated by a phrase that had crept into everyone's comprehension but his.

Gervase loooked at him, puzzled. 'You know. Like a farm do's. Rents hands out of the poorhouse. Money goes to the house. Best thing is, it empties out the poorhouse, come daylight; makes the beggars work. An' it do save using offcomers not born Berkshire.' The concept was as plain as day to him, and sweet in its simplicity. He would have put it into practice years since, if policy-making were his. It was Gervase's crusade to purify Berkshire.

Baydon was glad the constable did not admit to having let Abney escape custody; it meant that Baydon did not feel obliged to mention that the man was in the kitchen now, seeking salvation. 'I shall be with you again presently,' he said, and went out of the room to think.

Grace met him in the passageway. Her eyes rolled up into the top of her sockets as she endeavoured to remember the message she had memorised. 'Mrs Baydon says to say the Dunches were complaining after church on Sunday about the dust on the turnpikes. How it needs laying. And please to remember what the constable said about the pig last time.' Her eyes rolled down again, and she gave him one of her sweet, vague smiles.

Baydon gave an exasperated honk. He could make no sense of messages like this, and persevered as far as the kitchen to tell Stiff Abney there was nothing he could do to help him. Best if he surrendered himself, of his own free will, back into the custody of the constable.

When he opened the door, he found . . . no one — only his wife, studiously beating a batter. She looked beyond him, for signs of the constable. 'We thought it best,' she whispered. 'Gervase generally comes looking for a bite of refreshment after he's brought his list.' She saw his eyes come to rest on a beaker circled with orange fingerprints, and hid it away in the stone sink.

Sure enough, the constable had drifted out of the study and wandered through the house, poking his head into each room he passed, out of habitual nosiness. Now he arrived in the kitchen doorway, a hopeful, hungry expression on his face.

Little by little, the meaning of his wife's message was filtering down through the unhappy preoccupation and misgivings of the Winding Hatch magistrate. He was also a presiding official on the Borough Turnpike Committee responsible for fixing tolls, erecting milestones and waterpumps, and ensuring those pumps were used to damp down the dusty turnpikes during the hottest summer months.

'I need a pump man for the turnpike at Letcombe,' he said, turning a strange and unhealthy colour, avoiding his wife's eye. 'Stiff Abney can do that, for the duration.'

Constable Gervase's mouth opened once to protest, once to mention the unfortunate absence of Stiff Abney from the lock-up. Then it occurred to him: if Abney were not found, he could not be told of his new post; if he were not told, the pump would not be manned, and if the damping down were not done, Abney would get the blame. The end result would be the same, without anyone ever knowing that the constable had . . . mislaid a detainee. 'I'll tell him, right off,' he said. Then Mrs Baydon offered him a pickled onion, and the onion stopped up his mouth, as surely as a kiss.

All three went back to the study, where Magistrate Baydon crossed through the immaculately written name of Stiff Abney before signing his own name underneath.

'Poor souls,' said Sophronia Baydon quietly. 'It's a wonder their tears don't damp down all the whole summer's dust.'

The harvest flies had spread from the document into every recess and plain of Baydon's desk. They crawled across his wife's collar bones; he could feel them in the creases of his face. 'It may be a bad bread harvest, but I've never seen a better one for these creatures,' he observed.

Constable Gervase knew better where the tic-ish flies were from. ''Tis not harvest. 'Tis Mr Wootton improving his garden, will be,' he said sagely, lifting his full-bottomed wig and rubbing a white, shaved scalp vigorously with the flat of his fat hand.

Baydon had purposely kept from crossing the hill for several weeks, so he knew nothing of any improvements. 'What part of his garden?'

'Well, now, every bit and twig, if you believe people. 'Tis all to go, says Jack at the Post Inn. Make way for ruins and deer and suchlike. '*Romantic*', is the word for it.'

'Romantic' was not the word which sprang to the Reverend Baydon's lips.

The view from the top of the hill had changed, as though, at his feet, one map had been rolled up and another unrolled in its place. On the first had been tightly packed flowers-beds, parterres, concentric pathways, a grid-pattern of avenues and rides, with fountains, dew-ponds and walled orchards. The new map was a battle plan, with scars and ditches and trenches, weals of brick-dumps, welts of felled timber. Everywhere, prospects of sublime order had given way to scenes of devastation.

Even as Baydon watched, fetched to the hilltop spinney by alarming, repeated thuds which shook the windows of the parsonage and sent the cook running out of doors, a chain of explosions gouged open the green face of the great lawn, making a ring of pockmarks which gradually settled and collapsed into one large crater. Out in the surrounding fields, shockwaves of rabbits were propelled outwards, dark amid the dry grass.

Smoke was left hanging in smuts, trapped by the bowl-like natural basin in which the house stood. Sappers emerged from shelter like ants unearthed by digging, and shouted over-loudly at one another, deafened by the explosions. Several of the windows of Hatch House had been broken.

But Robin Wootton, a buccolic and incongruous figure in his white, shepherd's smock, standing on the roof among the chimneys of the main block, showed no sign of displeasure. His dreams for Hatch House were as rash and uncontainable as gunpowder, and he had long since accepted that some damage was unavoidable. It was of no consequence. Everything that got broken belonged to the past, and the past was done with. He had a romantic vision, and could see prospects already, in his mind's eye, which his ancestors had been quite incapable of imagining. On either side of him, his wards, in their scarlet dresses and bare feet, sat on the chimney plinths with their hands over their ears: two more gardens ripe for cultivation in the romantic style.

The sappers were packing up their cart. There would be no more explosions. Baydon turned back towards the house. The cook was being comforted in the garden by Mrs Baydon. The children were starting up a game of cricket. Constable Gervase would be in Wantage by now, loading the latest carts with 'sturdy beggars' not Berkshire-born. Stiff Abney would be gone from his hiding place in the cellar. With no more interruptions to keep him from working, the parson could safely return to the matter of his sermon: 'A man of sorrows, acquainted with grief.'

But inspiration did not come, even now. What could he find to say, he asked himself, on the subject of Christ's suffering, which would have any genuine relevance to the Sunday congregation of Winding Hatch?

CHAPTER SIX

Incentives

The fire moved restlessly in the grate then, settling like a thing disappointed, caved in on its incandescent heart. In the firelight, the picture-frames looked empty, as if the portraits had walked out of their frames to wander disconsolately about their much-altered house.

Zennor tried to move the table, but it was too heavy for her. So she dragged a chair as far as the edge of the carpet, then walked it on its back legs, so as not to make a scraping noise on the planks. There ought to have been a ladder, but Robin had removed it. He neither wanted the books himself nor for the girls to reach them. As long as his great project lasted, the words of Rousseau were all in all to him. Like a Puritan fundamentalist, believing all books other than the Bible are frivolous, Wootton found Rousseau had said all which needed saying on any and every subject. As for reference books, Wootton saw no purpose in them, saying, with gleaming eyes and a gesture of rapture, that 'living was the great and best encyclopaedia'.

There was one exception to his ban on books. After dinner each night, he read to the girls from *Robinson Crusoe*, confiding in them that it was Rousseau's favourite. They presumed its story was true, since there was no one to explain to them the concept of fiction. They half-expected the man with the goatskin clothes and parasol to arrive for tea one day in the octagonal room, with his savage in tow.

He would teach them how to eat frogs or light a fire using their hair as kindling, Zennor just knew it.

She stood the footstool on the seat of the wicker chair, knotted her nightgown on one hip, and climbed up on top of both. The curved leather spines of the books ranged along every shelf smelled sweet and rich. Here and there, the firelight fell on gold blocking. It was like climbing up the flank of a sleeping dragon, and the knowledge that she should not be there lent a similar terror. Somewhere in the room, mice were devouring a book, with scholarly enthusiasm.

One foot of the stool pierced the wickerwork of the chair below it with a sharp bang. Zennor gasped and, to keep from doing more damage, stepped across on to the face of the bookshelves. There was only room for her fingers and toes, and the weight of her body seemed to double, pulling her away from the leathery cliff face.

But Zennor had set her heart on reaching the topmost shelf. Like a bird-nester scaling a cliff, she looked only upwards at her goal, her incentive not to fall. Here was the purpose in climbing trees – so that other, far more important heights could be scaled. The bookcases gave the illusion of keeling out from the wall towards her. In places, books filled the shelves to the very edge, so that there was nowhere to get a handhold, and she had to traverse into the next bay. Her fingers and toes screamed with cramp.

But at last she reached it – her face hard up against it. It was resting flat on top of the topmost books. Zennor tried to nudge it loose with her nose, but only pushed it farther in. In fact it almost slipped off the back, down behind the other volumes. A spider hung in the angle of the shelves, blackly horrible; her cheek broke its web.

Zennor looked down. Just below her, an unlit lamp with a glass chimney stood on a narrow reading-table. If she fell, or if the book fell, they would smash the lamp in a tinkling din that would rouse the whole house.

Holding her breath, galvanising her body, she swung to one side for long enough to snatch her right hand off the shelf and sweep the treasure free, before snatching hold again. Her prize flew out in a wild parabola, over the lamp, over the soft rug, to fall flat on the dark floor with a noise like a single clap of cupped hands.

Surely someone would hear it? Zennor started down. That was far more difficult, and the fright of the noise had brought a clammy sweat to her fingers and feet. It was as if the wood of the shelves were ice, melting in a thaw of panic; she could not keep her grip a moment longer.

She did not fall far, but her tailbone hit the side of the reading-table, and she saw the lamp rock eagerly forwards. It fell right on top of her, and she caught it on her chest, cradling her arms around it, feeling the glass, still warm, feeling the spilled oil run round her stomach. The pain in her tailbone made her gorge rise, but she continued to lie there, on her back, cradling the lamp and listening to the silence of the house. It seemed to her that the explosive bang must still be echoing round the room, but it was not. Even the mice were silent now.

Carefully she set the lamp to rights then, wiping her oily hands on her nightdress, picked up her precious acquisition. She would not let herself stay and look at it; there was barely light enough even to find it on the plank floor. So she took it back to her bedroom. Going to light her candle, she smelled the reek of oil on her hands and chemise and dared not strike a spark, for fear of setting herself alight. So all night long she lay awake, waiting for the blackness in the window to weaken and pale into daylight.

Then she drew it out: a small book bound in green leather, with red marbling on the page edges and gold blocking on spine and cover. The pages were tissuey thin – a little furry at the edges, where the knife had slit them. The endpapers were marbled, too. Zennor looked at the title page through a single translucent fly-leaf as gauzy as rice-paper, then, brushing it aside, saw the filigree of ornamental print come into sharp focus before her eyes. She was so tired that the words jumped about on the page.

She had caught sight of this book on that first day in the library – the very first day she arrived at Hatch House. Ever since then, each time she had found the library unlocked, she had gone and stared up at that little green volume resting sideways on top of the others, at the very summit of the bookshelves. She did not know why it should appeal to her more than the others, but its green cover, the sandwiched red swirl of marbling between, the tiny gilt letters had come to represent a treasure casket on which her heart was set.

The ornate type of the title page was completely incomprehensible to her, but as abstractly beautiful as the Arabic patterns on the domes of the Alhambra. She knew the names of the letters, but not what they said. Her fingers traced the loops and angles, the wrought-ironwork of this bridge which ought to carry her over from the old life to the new. That was, after all, what distinguished the thriving from the poor, those of consequence from the invisible, herding, vacant poor. At Lambeth they had begun teaching her to read: she considered it their greatest kindness to her. But Robin Wootton had come along too soon for her to grasp even the rudiments. She would not let him withhold reading from her, no matter what Rousseau said.

Three or four times she had asked Wootton if he intended them to read, thinking he had mistaken her the first time, thought her lazy or unwilling. But he had just smiled his godlike smile and told her, 'No book but the world' or 'The child who reads ceases to think.' They were words he had read in a book: words he did not mean her to read, like God forbidding Adam and Eve to eat of the tree of the knowledge of good and evil. God was at fault, Zennor thought, to tempt Adam and Eve like that. She supposed them quite content before He mentioned it, quite eaten up with curiosity once their attention had been drawn to the apple. Like her. Here, amid an orchard of knowledge, she had been forbidden so much as to taste one word. It kindled in Zennor a desire she could barely keep hidden. She was Tantalus ringed with water but fasting in fire. If Robinson Crusoe lived in just one of those books in the library, who lived in the others? What heroes, what marvels, what spells for the working of magic, what secret notes passed by God to man?

Was it stealing? How could it be, if this was her home as Wootton insisted it was; if one day she might be mistress of the house, mistress of that library?

The day before, the parson's family had resumed a routine (broken for several weeks) of coming over the hill to supper on the last Friday of each month. The atmosphere had been cold at first, but after a glass or two of wine Reverend Baydon had begun to talk about the son sitting beside him, saying what a clever boy he was, wanting him to show how well he could con Latin, wanting him to stand up and recite. Poor George had not wanted to, his ears red as beetroot slices, his fingers working the buttons off his jacket in embarrassment. Mrs Baydon had laughed and said to let the boy alone. But Zennor had wanted him so much to do it, to recite that poem, that she had found herself on her feet, fork in fist, saying, 'Go on, boy. Do it.'

She had wanted to know the kind of thing *she* would one day be able to do; what manner of skill was able to make a father's jaw tighten with pride, and his eyes consume the pink boy with such devouring admiration.

'How happy is he born and taught
That serveth not another's . . .'

George had begun. But Robin Wootton had cut in, tinkling the little silver bell on the table, summoning the next course of food. 'Poetry, I regret, is quite barred from this house just now,' he had said, smiling with rueful chagrin. 'Poetry, eloquence, rhetoric, they are all strictly outlawed.'

Zennor did not know what eloquence or rhetoric were, but that prohibition made her want them with a passion. That cutting off of George had seemed far more of an unkindness than making him speak. That was when Zennor had decided. She would do everything Wootton asked of her – climb trees, cut her bare feet on stones, uproot wild flowers, look at sunsets, eat berries off the cotoneaster and squeeze wet clay through her fingers. But she would do more. She would read. Somehow, despite Rousseau, she would read every book in the Hatch House library.

Clutching the little stolen copy of Andrew Marvell, she had just fallen into a vivid, pleasant dream coloured scarlet by the sunlight through her lids when a loud banging woke her again. It was her professor, her tutor, her redeemer.

'Tight sleeves, comrades,' Wootton shouted through each bedroom door in turn. 'I've set your saw-horses on the terrace. Carpentry today!'

Wootton himself was not a carpenter. He would have liked to be, but the confounded classical education he had now come to despise had left him with no practical skills in the world. His protégées would be better served, he vowed it. 'I shall tell the carpenter to teach you everything he knows!' he assured them. 'Where is the man?'

Just for a moment, he blenched from the sight of Zennor and Alba in their thick canvas smocks, standing on either side of a saw-horse and at either end of a rip-saw. But after he had told them they were helping to build the Bower of Troth (a feature of his new romantic garden) they went at it with such a will that all his worries were dispelled. He felt quite happy to leave them and go back to designing his ruin for the end of the eastern vista. Even from indoors he could hear the satisfying growl and rip of the blade chewing through the branches of his felled elms. Carpentry could not be too difficult, then, if two little girls could do it.

The two little girls in question looked at one another across the saw-horse. Zennor saw the desperation well up in Alba's eyes, the certainty that she could not do it. Alba's pale, lily-like prettiness came of physical frailty, an undernourished, febrile delicacy which might one day pass very well for breeding. Zennor was far more robust. Alba did not want to fail her adored Robin, but (Zennor could see) was about to despair and burst into tears. She was about to fail this test Wootton was setting for them. It was a test: it had to be. What other purpose could it serve? There were plenty of strong, capable men on the estate who could saw his wood for him.

Zennor did not want Alba to fail, even if it meant that she, Zennor, might thereby stand to lose. Winding Hatch was far too strange and frightening a place to face alone. The ground here was fluid and unstable beneath her feet; she needed a sister beside her, to reach out and take by the hand for balance – even if it were a sister foisted upon her by random selection. Alba's weakness made Zennor feel strong; if Alba were to fall short of Wootton's demands and be sent away, the only feeble, confused and isolated girl left behind would be Zennor. Out of her depth, she needed Alba, to keep afloat.

So snatching hold of the saw's truncheon-shaped handle, she said, 'Up there's where he'll do it.'

'Do what? Where?' said Alba, letting go the saw.

'The Bower of Troth. That's where he'll ask me to marry him.'

Alba stared at her with a trembling lip. The whole of her pointy chin – even her shoulders – trembled. 'Won't.'

'Oh yes, he will. He's mine!' And she dragged the saw towards her as if it were Robin Wootton.

Alba snatched the handle at her end and dragged it back towards her. 'Mine!'

'Mine!'

'Mine!' Her bare feet took several involuntary steps forwards and back with each jolt of the saw. The saw-horse, too, rocked on its four feet.

'Mine!'

'Mine!'

Chewing and sticking, the big rip-saw flexed and warbled. Sawdust fell like blood from the unclean wound they were making. But Robin Wootton, poring over his design for the East Ruin, could hear the rip of the blade, and purred with gratification. Tearful and angry and startled, Alba finally guessed from the grin on Zennor's face, her taunting tone of voice, that she had been tricked into sawing. She gave a sobbing snicker and a cough, as her arms were once again pulled half out of their sockets, and the log bounced up and down on the saw-horse. 'You beast!' she said, but she did not stop pulling, pushing, pulling, dragging the rip-saw through Robin's ancestral elms.

Ten minutes later, their soft, fleshless hands were ripe with blisters. With a terrible splintering noise, the first branch snapped, leaving spiteful jags sticking out of each half. The carpenter, wheeling an empty barrow down from the Bower of Troth, swore loudly and broke into a run. He snatched up his saw and gave a roar of misery. 'I'll needs set every bloody tooth! Just wait till I tell you master 'bout you meddling!'

'Robin told us,' said Alba adenoidally, tossing back her head. 'He'd have us learn woodwork.'

And once again, the magic worked: the magic of that name, white as a cabbalistic circle, keeping out the demons. The carpenter swallowed his anger, like a mouthful of nails. He looked to these apprentices foisted on him, and his apprentices looked away, sniggering. So he hurled aside the two halves of their sawn branch and turned back towards the scoured site of the Bower of Troth. 'Is him teaching you 'mself?' he called over his shoulder.

'No,' said Alba. 'You are.'

Later, accordingly, the carpenter tapped a row of copper nails into the rustic arch of the bower, gave them each a hammer and told them to practise. The beam would have been too high up for them to reach, but for the delivery that morning of two new statues for the arbour. Cupid and Psyche, carved in pinkish Portland marble but still thickly wrapped in sacking and rope, lay like pupating larvae along the ground.

Zennor wrapped her smock round her blistered hand, bit her lips and closed one eye. Alba looked sideways at her, courage once more failing.

'That's Jean,' said Zennor, putting a small forefinger on a nail-head. Then she reached across and pointed to one in front of Alba. 'That Jacques.' She pointed to another. 'And that's Rousseau.' Then taking a wild but ferocious aim, she brought the hammer down on Rousseau's tack-head.

So Alba stood on Cupid, and Zennor on Psyche, and they hammered two dozen nails into a buckled entanglement of copper curlicues. The carpenter, too intimidated by their raucous giggling, left them alone, praying they would not fracture each other's skulls in the frenzy of the game.

By the end of that day they had sworn to be friends for ever. Both girls climbed into the same bed and described to each other the things they would own when this obstacle race of a childhood was over and they were great ladies together.

'. . . And I shall have a fan made all of peacock feathers,' said Alba, 'and a powder-puffer full of gold dust for my wigs.'

'And I shall go about in a sedan chair carried by four black men,' said Zennor.

'And I shall wear a butterfly cap with jewels – like that countess that came to Lambeth and paid for us to wear frieze.'

'And I shall eat nothing but strawberries.'

They spoke in whispers, already knowing that Wootton would not approve, that he had other things than jewels and strawberries in mind for them. That was part of the joy of it: to be joint conspirators with a swag of secrets carried between them. It was the stuff of true sisterhood.

Even so, when Alba laid her head down on Zennor's pillow, and sank into an instant sleep, Zennor crabbed her little blistered hand in under the pillow and retrieved her green-and-red book. She slipped the precious object into a pocket, in case Alba's fingers fumbled upon it in her sleep. Some secrets did not need to be shared.

There were two pockets, muslin ones, sewn to a muslin belt which was worn under the topmost overskirt. Next week, on the way to the forge,

Zennor could feel the small hardness of the book bang against her hip, a familiar comfort.

She had felt it banging there on the day she walked over the hill to the parsonage as a respite from woodwork. (There was one thing to be said for Wootton's curriculum: it permitted them, quite soon after beginning a task, to express boredom and weariness, and to wander off, without being reproached for it. Perseverance and application did not seem to be important.) Climbing and descending still pained her after her fall in the library, but she was becoming inured to pain, thanks to Wootton's programme of practical activities.

Mrs Baydon had been busy preparing a bedroom for some visitor due to arrive, but she had not made Zennor feel unwelcome. In fact she had presented her with a gift: a pair of woollen socks, the soles knitted double for extra cushioning thickness. There was a pair for Alba, as well.

'I don't know,' Zennor had said, doubtfully. 'We'll be not allowed, maybe.' But she was already ruching up her skirt as she said it, to put the socks in her empty muslin pocket.

She stood there for a moment, her skirt gathered up under her armpits, looking like a ruffled black swan. Then she drew out the book.

She did not say anything, only turned it over and over in her hands, until Mrs Baydon noticed, and took it from her.

'Marvell?' she said. 'A pretty poet.'

'Poet?' said Zennor. 'Is he?'

They had sat down together at the kitchen table, Mrs Baydon's sleeves rolled back, hands red from washing-soda holding the little book. She read out loud, as if that were the way it suited her to read, but she turned the book a little towards Zennor as she did so, her wrinkled fingertip sliding below the words. Nothing was said, not in so many words, but she offered Zennor reading lessons just as plainly as Zennor had asked for them. It was as if she had had the key lying there, on her scrubbed kitchen table – the key to Zennor's stolen casket.

Sophronia Baydon was a broad-shouldered, broad-hipped woman, in a Watteau gown. In her small round-cap with long, lace-edged laps hanging down over her ears, she looked rather like a beagle, amiable and soft-mouthed. The lids over her brown eyes were starting to hood. She did not smile inordinately – not as much as Robin – yet all the lines on her face came from smiling. When Zennor slipped the stolen book back into her pocket, it seemed to have found its perfect counterpoise in the rolled up socks: both secrets burdened her equally with happiness.

★

'Can't have all they skirts a-puffin out, like,' said the blacksmith, when confronted with Alba and Zennor. 'They kindle them fendangels, they go up like beaconfires.'

He could not refuse Wootton's request to teach the girls metalwork – his forge was on estate land – but he could glare at them, like Vulcan at the gods who maimed him – and object to their clothing. Although they were wearing their canvas smocks (as hot as horse-blankets in the stifling forge), the skirts of their overdresses still bulged out to either side.

Wootton instructed them to slip off their skirts and 'just fling them anywhere'. He sensed the smith's hostility to his plan, but was unwilling to deprive the girls of their promised treat. He breathed deep the rich mixture of smells: soot, fresh dung, leather and incandescent metal. If he shut his eyes, he said, he could 'almost commune with Wayland himself who had shaped these Berkshire hills and made the sparks of nature's magic fly up . . .'

The smith, who kept a gobbet of solidified iron in his mouth, turned it over with his tongue, rattling it against his teeth before pouching it in his cheek. His foot worked the bellows which gave a long flatulent belch with every kick.

Alba and Zennor brushed shoulders as they hung their neatly folded skirts over the saddle-stand by the door. The glance they gave each other said, 'How much more?' But with each other's confederacy, even metalwork could be endured. Besides, Wootton did not persist long on any one tack: carpentry had given way to horticulture, horticulture to beekeeping, beekeeping to ironwork. He was galloping pell-mell through his curriculum, impatient for novelty, more than to see his girls perfect any one skill. When they did not show an inordinate thrill over one handicraft, he hurried them on to the next, hopeful of them discovering their true métier. Woodwork, metalwork, gardening. Agriculture, weaving, wickerwork.

The landscaping of his gardens made such demands on his time: otherwise he would gladly have shared in their lessons. He only wished he *could* spend more time doing these things himself. His soul yearned towards them passionately. But it would be self-indulgent. And so he allowed himself only the vicarious enjoyment of his girls learning such simple, noble occupations as winnowing, thatching and milking goats. Regretfully, he left them at the forge for their first lesson in metalwork.

There was undoubtedly a kind of beauty in the plume and fall of golden sparks as the smith brought down his hammer on to a white-hot bar. Alba did not like the noise, and edged as far as possible back from the anvil –

almost to the door. But Zennor was mesmerised by the sheer power – the gleaming plait of the man's bare shoulder-muscles, the terrifying force of metal striking metal, the secondary clang as the hammerhead bounced off the incandescent rod, the ear-splitting hiss and white exclamation of steam as he plunged ingot and tongs into the tempering water-trough.

When he told her to pick up the hammer, she could not even lift it. He had to stand behind her, his two arms under hers, before she could manage to swing it up high and drop it down on to the anvil. In doing so, he pinched her narrow body tight between his elbows, almost squeezing the breath out of her. Perhaps her hair got by accident into his mouth, but at one point, he held her black plait between his teeth and she could hear his teeth cut into the hair. When the gobbet of iron came dislodged from his cheek, and fell down the length of her back, she thought he had spat on her.

'Know what he's keeping you for?' she thought he said. 'Be'nt smithying.'

Just then, Alba, ducking down behind the saddle-stand to escape the noise of cold water tempering molten iron, caught sight of Zennor's muslin pockets. She saw the angular bulge of something small and rectangular and, curious, pulled out the little green-and-red volume of Andrew Marvell.

'What's this?' she said, rising into view once more.

Zennor broke free of the metalwork lesson and ran and tried to snatch back the book. 'Please, Alba. Give that back. It's mine.'

'You can't read!' said Alba scornfully. 'Anyway. Not allowed.' She was resentful of finding a secret existed between them.

'Shall soon,' retorted Zennor in a petulant whisper the smith would not hear. 'Parson's wife's teaching me.'

Alba was startled, but not so startled that she gave back the book. Instead, she went outside with it, into the sunshine, to think. She was hurt and taken aback, and yet the inkling of something good was beginning to dawn somewhere in her head. She needed somewhere quieter to take proper hold of it. Once round the forge she carried her discovery: Zennor was trying to learn to read: Zennor was disobeying Robin's express command!

When she re-entered the little inferno of a building, her 'sister' was standing right beside the door, pink-faced from her exertions with the hammer.

'I'm going to tell Robin,' Alba said. 'I'll tell him you're reading books. He'll never marry you, after I tell him. Said we mustn't. I never.'

The smith had a strange look on his face, different from before. He had come halfway round the anvil and held his hand flat, extended towards Zennor, as if she had taken something he badly wanted back. Alba was too absorbed in her marvellous discovery to pay any heed. She held up the little green book and wagged it in Zennor's face. 'He'll send you away. I'll show him it. Where did you get it? Steal it? Never going to marry a thief. Not Robin.'

A half-circle of light seemed to fly up and around Zennor's body. It came from behind her, and struck the book clean out of Alba's hand, leaving behind it a dark vapour trail of ashy smoke. The book flew towards the water-trough, but fell short, and Zennor ducked down and tossed it farther on, into the furnace of the forge. As she did so, she prevented Alba from interfering by holding out the red-hot poker she had pulled from the bottom of the grate. Now she lunged with the poker at Alba who, driven backwards out of the door, promptly fell over her petticoats and sat down in the dirt.

The tip of the poker, though cooled to black, was still so hot that Alba felt it through three layers of clothing, as Zennor held it poised over her stomach. 'You won't tell him. Where's your proof now? Won't. I'll end you, if you tell him.' The heavy poker hovered and trembled; Zennor's fingers were splayed by the great weight of it in her fist. Alba sucked in her stomach, her fingers scrabbling the folds out of the front of her canvas smock. Still it charred, strand by open-weave strand. She dared not draw breath. She could not speak for want of drawing breath.

So she shook her head – spread her hands open, palm up, on the gritty ground, to indicate her submission. The tip relented an inch or two. 'I won't tell. I won't,' Alba said, dragging herself out from under the poker at last.

The smith stood in the door of the barn – could see that the danger was passed, and chose not to intervene. When Wootton returned to collect his pupils at lunchtime, he asked, 'And do they show an aptitude for the science of Hephaestus? My protégées?'

The smith blinked at him with inexpressive, impertinent, bloodshot eyes. 'They's fiery enough,' was all he said.

Robin Wootton could not have been more pleased.

CHAPTER SEVEN

A Proposal

The rain fell on Wantage in such quantities that it set the sewage afloat at the bottom of Mill Lane. On the upland, by the Ridgway and along the Vale of the White Horse, all the crops lay flattened. A hole in the roof of the shoemaker's shop made Maurice Blackfield's entire stock of leather slimy and sodden. John House the currier could not deliver his load of hides to the tannery because a pile of planks in Jig Alley had floated hugger-mugger into the passageway. No one could remember why the timber had been piled there in the first place: there had been no building done thereabouts for months. Outside the chandler's a dozen rats sat, in plain daylight, drinking from the puddles. The rattle of traffic in and out of the market place did not disturb them; they knew they had precedence. Their station in life was higher than any of the souls who eked out an existence in the streets behind the tanneries.

'That's what I'm saying!' exclaimed the doctor, banging his fist on the dining-room table. 'A canal would be like a main artery pumping blood into the very heart of the town!'

'Hawkers and didicoys, that's all it'd pump in,' declared Constable Gervase. 'Outsiders. Don't need more'n we got hitherto.'

But the mood of the meeting was against him. Canal mania was rife that autumn, and those around the table were interested parties – men with money to invest, if they could just find a few more like-minded individuals to share the risk.

Samuel Baydon had no money to invest; he saw the profit in terms of reduced social evils. He knew of three young women, for certain, who had fallen pregnant for the sake of the poor relief. The system of renting-in from the poorhouse meant that, although the tanneries were thriving, no money was going into the economy of the town. Those wraiths with 'P' embroidered on the breast of their smocks haunted the square on market days and were pelted with rotten vegetables for their lack of buying power. The mooted canal, linking the Thames to the Somerset Coal Canal, would engender more trade than one tannery could handle, jobs for the builders, the boatmen, the suppliers of the builders and boatmen, the suppliers of the investors profiting from a new canal. It gleamed in his imagination like a vein of silver in an otherwise grey rock.

Everyone there, in the Lamb Inn, knew someone who had met someone who lived in a canalside town. And though Constable Gervase sat back in his chair with his thumbs in his belt and said, 'Itinerants, gypsies,' most talked of the canal funding infirmaries and penny schools and missions. Even the parson's visiting brother, Oliver Baydon, had stories to recount of prosperity, renewal, entrepreneurial fortunes being made, slums transformed into thriving mercantile communities. He had travelled considerably, had Oliver Baydon. He was a tall, handsome man bearing little resemblance to his brother, and younger, much younger. The members of the committee were impressed with this unexpected addition to their number. His nankeen breeches and double-collared redingote were fashionable and, along with the big Kevenhuller hat, made him appear abnormally tall; even though he did not often speak, the swish of the coat's long, split skirts made the other men continually aware of his presence in the room. He held himself like someone in a painting by Gainsborough. Strange: they had not even realised the parson *owned* a brother before this evening.

'In the words of Isaac Watts, the children of the poor are abandoned to the wildness of their own nature, like brutes of the earth – without knowledge of God or Christ!' declaimed Service Gibbins, the surveyor, who was also a lay preacher. 'It's been so for sixty year, and the state of things is only worse for the wait!'

Baydon looked at Wootton. 'Abandoned to the wildness of their own nature,' eh? It was galling to have to refrain from comment, but he needed Wootton's support if the canal project was to gain momentum, and the project was sufficiently dear for him to hold his tongue. The tanneries might be the most up-to-date of their kind in the entire country, but if the projected canal were built somewhere else Wantage could become a backwater – worse, an ox-bow, cut off from the mainstream development of the country. Newbury or Lambourn would take the plate from under Wantage's nose.

Baydon wondered why his brother cared, why Oliver had invited himself along to the meeting. Did it signify an intention to stay in the area? He certainly had no money to invest. To Samuel's certain knowledge, his brother hadn't a sovereign to his name. Regularly, once a week, he would touch Baydon for 'a shilling or two' to save his face down at the Post Inn. With a room of his own at the parsonage, and regular meals (which he consumed like a harpy) there seemed no reason in the world for him to move on.

But why should Samuel care? At long last there was a canonry vacant at Winchester. His heart thudded at the mere recollection. Rumours were rife about candidates, but his hopes had to be as good as any. His uncle's friend, he knew, had spoken well of him to the bishop. Last time, it was said, he had missed out only by reason of being newly widowed: the bishop favoured married men. This time, Samuel was married, had fulfilled every requirement it was within his power to fulfil.

Winchester! In Winchester canals, built or unbuilt, would not so much as feature on his life's map . . .

Still, this was Wantage, and while he lived near Wantage he felt required to care about canals. And in this (he guessed) he was probably in one mind with the macaroni Wootton for the first time in his life.

He heard the swish swish of his brother's coat as he stalked about the room. Like a card-sharp's assistant spying out the hands of the other players, thought Baydon uncharitably. But the truth was, he was touched by Oliver exerting himself on behalf of the canal. Just possibly he was doing it as a favour to his older brother. Just possibly.

Samuel could see that the Dunches liked Oliver, were pleasantly surprised by Oliver, had not expected the staid Reverend Baydon to possess a brother as debonair and fashionable as Oliver. Secretly, it gave him a degree of pride, to see Oliver so well received. Even if the man were a charlatan and a sponge. Mrs Baydon liked him. Every day she said something which suggested she found his visit an unforeseen blessing. But then, thought Baydon dismally, women had always liked Oliver.

The Dunch brothers had said nothing so far. They were waiting to see which way Robin Wootton's vote would go. Truth to tell, they were severely aggravated by young Wootton at present. The wreck of his ancestral lands at Hatch House had been hard to swallow, but then Wootton had spoken of creating a deer park. Deer would have gone a long way towards excusing his vandalism. *Then* it proved that the deer were not intended to provide Wootton and his neighbours with venison and good sport; they were merely for *prettiness!* To satisfy the aesthetic demands of some romantic vision!

No, several esteemed households were deeply disenchanted with Robin Wootton just now. But that did not alter the fact that Wootton's land lay directly in the path of the projected canal. They needed him to be in favour of the scheme, or it could not go ahead.

'Well, Wootton, what do you say?' asked Service Gibbins. 'You're a modern man,' he added with a degree of distaste. 'Full of new ideas. Are you game for this new river of ours? This Wiltshire-cum-Berkshire Canal?'

Robin rocked back in his chair, one knee against the table. His striped Italian waistcoat was unbuttoned, and its flaps brushed the floor. He wore the ruffled cuffs of his shirt pushed back from his wrists, and there were grass-stains on his lapels. (How does one get grass stains on one's lapels? Baydon wondered.)

'You see . . .' said Wootton, and put the tips of his fingers together. 'Nature abhors the unnatural. A river flowing down from a mountain summit flows with the curves of the earth.' He put his palms together and snaked his hands through the air. 'It shrinks, it floods. It does not *dissect* the countryside like a scalpel!' Around the table, there was a tightening of lips. 'If we surround ourselves with constructs – tools . . . conveyances . . . intending, in our arrogance, to *tame creation*, we fail to *bend* to the forces of nature, just as the canal fails to *bend* to the contours of the land.' He leaned precariously sideways out of his chair.

George Gadby sighed a whimpering sigh. It was not for this that he had come seven miles, in a chaise, on a wet September evening.

'Your plans do you credit,' Wootton went on. 'Your ambitions are all well meant, I don't doubt it. But I'm sorry. I'm truly sorry. We have to be realistic.' This was new. No one had quite expected the macaroni to call for realism. A dozen brows puckered, as the committee racked its brains for some obstacle they had overlooked. 'Society is in flux!' said Wootton, barely leaning on his vocal cords for emphasis. 'There are revolutions even now tearing apart the old fabric of the world. A crisis in every monarchy between here and Russia. God alone knows what the future holds for you and me, gentlemen. Personally, I run towards it with open arms; it will be a huge adventure! But I fear the profits we see won't be counted in coin of the realm. Kings are about to fall! I don't believe this is a time to be planning ahead – except – except, mind you, to put ourselves in accord with nature.'

The snorts of disgust running round the table grew to a roar of protest. Accusations of blasphemy and treason tumbled on his head, but Robin Wootton was wearing his implacable, invulnerable smile.

'Planning ahead is for the restless man. I thank God I am a contented soul

63

leading a contented life – mindful of my blessings. I ask you: what manner of man would contemplate scarring the face of his beloved mistress?' He looked around him triumphantly at faces blank with incomprehension. '*Nature* is my mistress, gentleman! We have to live in harmony with nature! Once we've learned to do that, there will be no need remaining for this restless going and coming, this hastening along straight lines.'

The surveyor, who was rolling up his charts by this time, banged the roll loudly and unnecessarily into shape on the table. The Knollys were lighting pipes. Constable Gervase was emptying the porter jug. The corn merchant, Seaton, was buttoning his jacket.

'Permit me if I mistake,' said Baydon, as if sipping the words off an overhot spoon, 'but are you not a member of the Society of the Dilettanti? And do we hear you carping against restless to-ing and fro-ing?'

Robin gave a sheepish chuckle, resting his elbows now on the table and spreading his hands wide like arum lilies. 'It's true! I travelled. I took pleasure in travelling. I am inconsistent. I know it. I learn, I understand, I alter. It's the great flaw in a reasoning man,' and he dipped his eyes, accepting their reproof for being a reasoning man receptive to new wisdoms.

There was no purpose to be served in arguing with him after that. Once Wootton's mind was made up to be inconsistent, he would hold to an opinion all night. Everyone there knew it. The canal stopped flowing through their corporate imaginations, the sluice-gates wound down on it by Robin Wootton and his mistress Mother Nature. Baydon confined himself to muttering dyspeptically, 'Burbage, Burbage, Burbage.'

'Is it true, what the surveyor told me?' said Oliver Baydon, following his brother out of The Lamb. 'That Wootton's on brood over a pair of chicks?'

Baydon declined to understand.

'Truly? Is he breeding up two girls to find out which suits him best?'

Baydon walked faster, his hands made into fists behind his back. 'It's true he's undertaken some unadvised social experiment.'

'Breeding them up for marriage! The man's a genius.' Oliver laughed as he said it, rattling the words in his long, aquiline nose. 'How will he choose? *When* will he choose? Have you seen this Mary and Martha? I'd wager a pound one of them's dark and the other's fair. One for weekdays and t'other for the Sabbath, to keep it wholly . . .'

'You would think the man might prefer to keep such a shameful notion out of the ears of his neighbours,' Baydon interrupted hurriedly, to prevent Oliver saying something lewd.

'No, but tell me! When he's made a pair, what will he do with the card he discards?' Oliver's voice was rich with mirth. There was no avoiding the subject.

Unwillingly, the parson described the outline of Wootton's unsavoury plan. He never liked to talk of women to his brother: it felt very like lending the man a clean handkerchief and getting it back fouled. True to form, Oliver found the idea both hilarious and bawdy.

'What, marry one and marry off the other? The man's a genius! Hedging his bets with an each-way!'

'I have expressed to him my doubts that such a thing can be accomplished quite as cleanly as he imagines.' Samuel could feel his sentences growing, like convolvulus, into long, strangling toils. His brother always made him pedantic.

'Yes, lor', but what a meal of crumbs for some lucky dog under the table, eh? Licking up what Wootton lets fall from his plate.'

Fortunately the thinking behind this graceless and disgraceful remark was too silly to give Samuel a moment's unease. '*You*, sir, haven't the patience to sit that long under any man's table. The girls in question are only eleven or twelve apiece. I fancy your appetites are too large to keep hidden for five or seven years . . . Besides, both girls have been promised a *favourable* match, come what might. You, brother, do not constitute a "favourable match".' And for once he allowed himself the luxury of a smile.

Oliver shrugged and moved off ahead of his brother, striding out on his long legs, so that Samuel was hard put to keep up without breaking into a run. On the unlit street, the puddles waited like invisible mantraps, but only Samuel seemed to tread in them.

With the coming of the rain, there was no more need for Stiff Abney to man the turnpike pump at Letcombe. Baydon might have delayed longer in telling him so, but he knew that the constable would not. Unless Abney secured another job, he would find himself aboard one of Gervase's carts and shipped out of the county, at the worst time of year.

'Go to the Weyhill, man! Get yourself hired. You're young and fit: you can thank God for that!' Baydon made a fist and punched Abney's shoulder encouragingly.

Stiff Abney was a paler orange now, as if rinsed down by the rains that had put him out of work. The dye left in his skin only made him look swarthy and weatherbeaten, and disguised the toxic damage five years of tanning had done to his lungs. He tottered slightly under Baydon's fist. He had been so sure the parson would keep the constable off his back, as he had done before. 'I kept my road wetted. I did,' he said defensively.

Baydon knew he had. So assiduously had Abney gone at his road-wetting on the turnpike that come-heat, come-cold, there had always been a large patch of mud for the post coach to splash through on the Letcombe Hill. When the pump had broken, Abney had had his little children carry buckets of water from a distant ditch, to maintain the swamp while he dismantled the equipment. It was a wonder the little mites had not been ridden down by the traffic. Baydon had no wish to be the cause of that. So he hardened his heart against Abney, did not wrestle with the problem of ending his employment.

Stiff Abney's great desire to work only cast into relief the enormity of Oliver Baydon's idleness. To Samuel, it seemed as if there were no bottom to his brother's indolence. He was in the parlour now, tinkling on the spinet, while Mrs Baydon tried to concentrate on the household accounts. Laziness incensed the parson, whose chief prayer was for time and energy to overtop his mountain of weekly duties. And his irritation made him the wrong man for Abney to be asking for help. 'The mop fair. That's your best move,' he said, declining to meet the man's orange-pip eyes.

Besides, there was so much to be done. The bishop might be arriving at any moment. This week, next week. His letter had been extraordinarily vague on a matter which might change Baydon's whole life everlastingly. 'Weyhill Fair, yes,' he said again. 'That's your best bet. Now you really must excuse me. I've got a great deal . . .'

'How say I maybe mend your fence, parson? There's couple a boards . . .'

'I thank you, but there's nothing needs mending that I can't mend myself. A sedentary man should keep up the practice of manual skills, I've always thought.' An unfortunate remark to a manual worker with no work to keep him out of the poorhouse; it fell between them like a hurdle separating sheep from goat, rich from poor. Baydon felt in his watch pocket for a shilling and held it out to Abney. 'You get yourself down to Weyhill, that's my advice. Skip out of the way of the constable. He's a zealous man, I fear.'

Abney twisted his head on his neck, like an orange withered on the tree. 'I be a tanner, me. Not a farming man.' But he took the shilling, even so, and went.

To ease the disagreeable feeling he was left with, Baydon turned his mind to Winchester once more. The irritating tinkling from the spinet had fallen mercifully silent. His imagination carried him to the silent cloisters of Winchester. George might enter the cathedral school there

– even sing tenor in the choir when his voice broke. (The boy would have a good voice if he could just learn to hold a tune.) The baby could go there, too. And Grace and Sarah and Suzannah would have a choice of dame schools: not just the one in the village. The household might even run to a dog-cart for the children and a better cook than Marion Coppler – though no-one in the world was likely to rival Mrs Baydon in the matter of honey slab cake – yea, even unto a simple roast, as the psalmist would have said if he had ever eaten at Mrs Baydon's table on the cook's day off. Rightly, a man should not look forward most to the days when his cook is absent, thought Baydon.

In fact, his first fear, when he saw his wife's face appear white round the study door, was for the dinner. Something had burned. Something had proved rank.

Sophronia started to speak, but could not find the words. She came in and shut the door behind her. She looked panic-stricken.

'The children?' said Baydon jumping to his feet.

'The Penny Savings.'

And at once he knew it was gone: the tin box and inside it the slub satin bag containing the worn-smooth coppers of three dozen villagers.

'From where "gone"? How? How "gone"?'

'I was reckoning up. Checking the ledger,' said Mrs Baydon, her eyes brimming. 'I stepped out to see to the baby . . .'

They went back to the parlour, and he began to search – as if the several pounds' weight of copper might have become mislaid or slipped behind the furniture. He looked under the table, behind the spinet; he twitched at the curtains and poked behind the door. The tin box and the ledger still stood open on the table, but the satin bag was gone. The parson leaned his knuckles on the table, his face colouring through several shades of rage.

'That pewsey luggershall ingrate. That baulking shirkoak! That purse caundle. How much was there?'

'Six pounds. A little more,' said Sophronia.

'*Six pounds?*'

It suddenly occurred to Baydon that a man carrying six pounds' worth of pennies would be bowed down by the sheer weight; he would certainly not be able to hurry from the scene. It was not too late to run after Abney and treat him to the thrashing he deserved.

But though Samuel ran as far as the main road, there was no catching up with the tanner; he seemed to have disappeared out of the landscape. Walking back, Samuel wrenched at his bands; the blood vessels in his throat flickered and swelled, and the sweat poured from his brow.

At the door, he met up with his brother, redingote on, preparing to go out. 'Good man. Are you going for the constable? Did you see which way the wretch went?'

'Who? The reddler? He certainly left at a run,' said Oliver, scrupulously checking his appearance in the mirror. 'Why? What's afoot?'

'The fiend has filched the Penny Savings, that's what! I'll have him transported, the culshabbin weem, so help me!'

But Sophronia Baydon, though still trembling with shock at the enormity of the disaster, showed precious little hunger for vengeance against Stiff Abney.

'It was my fault,' she said repeatedly. 'I should never have put temptation in . . . anyone's path. It was my fault for leaving the box open.'

Baydon could not contradict her there. He agreed wholeheartedly that it was her fault, but saw as far more pressing the arrest of Abney and the return of the money. 'If it's not returned I shall have to furnish it myself, you know? Things will have to go! I shall have to sell the spinet!' He seized on the example maliciously, knowing that of all the things in the house the spinet gave her the most pleasure.

'That would be hard on Grace,' Sophronia said. 'Her playing is coming along so well.' But the soft answer, as usual, did not turn away wrath; it only fuelled Baydon's hotter. Her failure to condemn Abney made her seem somehow confederate with him.

Could she possibly have encouraged him? Offered him the chance of a new life, at the expense of all those thrifty, God-fearing parishioners who had entrusted her with their weekly pennies? He could not believe it of her . . . and yet she had hidden Abney in the cellar to keep him out of Gervase's hands. And she did not seem eager for him to be caught – not one jot eager.

In his disgust and perplexity, Baydon arrived at more and more unkind ways of replacing the stolen money by means of domestic economy. 'We couldn't afford to keep on the cook, of course,' he announced at supper. 'You realise that. If the money's not recovered, you'll have to make do without Marion.'

'That would be hard on Marion,' she said softly, but her husband, having reprieved the spinet, had positively no compassion left to squander on the cook's feelings. 'To Helvellyn with Marion!' he yelped at her, thumping his fist on the table. 'Six pounds is six pounds! – And to think I gave the snishival horse-tick a shilling in charity!'

Oliver Baydon did not come home to supper that night. He took it at the

Fox and Grapes, and slept it off in the post stable (though he did remember to report Abney's thieving to the constable). His route back to Winding Hatch next morning was a roundabout one, by way of Hatch House.

Alba and Zennor, out rowing on the new lake, saw him coming a long way off, in his highwayman's coat and the tricorn with the silver braid. From such a distance, it was impossible to see the slight imperfections of his dress: the beer stains, the frayed hems, the scuffed heels.

'Who is it?' said Alba to Zennor.

'The parson's brother. Remember? We met him at Sunday service.' They watched him loping up the long drive, white breeches flashing as he let the coat fall open and billow behind him. He was evidently in cheerful mood, and they wondered what business he had up at the house.

But he did not turn up towards the house. Instead, he came to the shore of the lake. He had had them in his eye all the way up the drive, watching them stationary on the lake. 'My compliments to you, ladies,' he said, circling the water until he reached the stretch of bank closest to them. 'Are you quite warm enough?'

The girls were pretty much inured to the cold, having spent large parts of each day enjoying nature. But they would have gone ashore some time before if they could have done. 'The lake is not rightly finished yet,' Zennor called back, though Alba sat primly, hands on her knees and her face averted from the stranger. 'Somewhere, the water drains out,' by which she meant that the level of the pretty, irregular lake had fallen yet again, leaving insufficient depth for the draw of the rowing boat.

'Are you wedged?' Oliver called. 'Do you require assistance?'

'We shall float in somehow,' Zennor returned. 'I suppose.'

'I have a present for you each,' called Oliver. 'A small token of my admiration for two beautiful girls. You so much add to my pleasure, these days, of taking my sins to church.' From the depths of his pockets he pulled two packages, untying the shop ribbon, letting the tissue blow out on to the lake and float and grow sodden and sink. With a flourish, he flicked out two embroidered shawls, fringed with rose-coloured silk, and knotted them, each by a corner, to a newly planted sapling by the waterside. The shawls billowed out like banners.

Alba leaned forward and snatched up the oars, although she was facing the wrong way to row. Splashing ineffectually, she only succeeded in putting the boat hard aground on the mud shallows, ten yards from the bank. Zennor told her, in choice Lambeth English, the colour of her bloodstock. The boat rocked alarmingly.

The man on the bank gave a theatrical sigh. 'There now, I see I must indeed rescue you.' And before they could answer, he had dropped his coat off his shoulders and walked straight out into the lake.

A half-ton of topsoil had been dumped into the water in an effort to plug any fissures in the clay, and to give a footing to waterlilies. The resultant brown quagmire reached over his boot-tops and high up his white breeches. The girls stared at him, at his unwavering smile despite the squelching treachery of the lake bed. Uprooted lilies gathered round his thighs, clustered in front of his fall. Reaching the boat, he took hold of the prow and pulled it in to the bank. Then, handing them out, he offered each a low bow and swung his coat round his shoulders once more. It jingled with money.

As if as an afterthought, he reached down deep again into the huge pockets and brought out a pair of penny pieces, pressing one into each girl's palm, before laying his fingers to his lips, for secrecy.

In all their lives, it was the first time anyone had ever given them money. And if the embroidered shawls flapping in the tree were not enough, those pennies fixed sharp in their memories, the image of Oliver Baydon striding away down the path, his boots squelching only a little, his swagger the positive epitome of panache.

CHAPTER EIGHT

Republicans

Wootton came home from The Lamb in contemplative mood. Everything he had said was true, and he took pride in having said it. Baydon had drawn attention to his inconsistency, and Wootton gloried in inconsistency. 'A man of soul cannot be consistent in his beliefs, but he can be true to the truth!'

Still, the fact that a coachman had been waiting outside in the rain for him that night, and had driven him home, while another servant warmed his bedclothes, and a third cooked his supper – that troubled him. It did, it troubled him, as it had troubled him many times in the past. More and more it troubled him that he was setting a poor example of egalitarianism. Many, many times he had turned the matter over in his mind. But this one evening, an idea had hatched during the comfortable tossing of the carriage, and it kept him awake all night, in a fervour of excitement.

Next day he summoned all his staff, and his wards, too, instructing them to assemble at the newly completed ruin at noon, in two days' time, for 'a declaration intended to change the substance of their lives'.

William's wife, Alice, said that it was a shame he could not out and say it in the hall, sooner than put knees and backs to the labour of toiling up a poxy hill. But she only said it to William. She, like the men, was in terror that the moment had arrived, the dreaded, desolate moment which had overshadowed them ever since the young barbarian had inherited Hatch House. Him with his radical ideas and his ungodly practices. He intended to be the ruin of them all. He surely intended to turn them off.

Even as they leaned into the steep-sided slope of Hatch Hill, Alice relying heavily on her husband's arm, they were not free to mutter and compare their dreadful premonitions. Those girls (those unbred ragamuffin bastard waifs the barbarian had fetched in) were tagging alongside, their unseemly bare feet lipping out from under skirts far too good for their kind. The Zennor girl was *brown*; positively *brown*. Even Alice prided herself that her skin was paler than that sunburned hoyden.

The ruin, which was built of best Portland stone, looked (just for the present) brand new, with half a sparkling arch, an array of pristine broken pillars and a dome balanced on columns, like an upturned porcelain bowl. Newly planted ivy stood in mounds of gingery mulch, too young and unambitious yet to clamber over the tidy stonework. In a year or two, the gardeners said, it would have swallowed up the ruin from pediment to architrave, 'so 'im might's well of used brickles'.

They all sat down, each on a column base which was the convenient height of tree stumps. In fact the undergardener and gardener were of the opinion that if they had simply cut off the trees on the summit of Hatch Hill (instead of grubbing them out to make way for the ruin) Wootton would have been left with much the same effect. Especially after the ivy grew.

Alba and Zennor did not grieve for the loss of the trees. There were too many left, as far as they were concerned. They still associated Hatch Hill with that first unhappy time they had been sent to climb the horrible trees. Through the pierced stonework of a ruined balustrade, they could just see the parsonage where Alba had run for help.

They could also see, in the other direction, the raw wound of the Bower of Troth, the Muses' Walk planted with tamarisks, and the sadly diminished lake.

'Yon's bleeding out round cemetery way,' said William darkly. 'Set the coffins floating, shouldn't wonder.'

It did not surprise them either that Wootton was late. He moved much faster than they did, but never in a straight line. They could see him now, crossing the garden below like a bee moving from flower to flower, accomplishing this, attending to that, ever purposeful, never weary. Never on time, either.

Today they could muster limitless reserves of patience. They did not want him to arrive. This surely was the day when he would fulfil his frequent hints at 'liberation'. The servants and hands firmly believed that Wootton was about to turn them off.

Curragh was more panic stricken than any. His wife Marion, through no fault of her own, had just lost her place at the parsonage, and starvation was staring him in the face.

When Wootton did finally come running up the hill he was carrying under one arm a lidded cane basket. There was a kind of stele or altar-post within the ruin, where libations must have been offered up in the unremembered days when the British had worshipped Greek gods. On top of this, Wootton set down the basket and took off the lid, pulling out a succession of parchments. 'My dear brethren,' he said, trying to capture their eyes with his. They glanced away from him, sullen. 'This little community of souls is as dear to me as Alexander's empire was to him. You are, I consider, more like family to me than my own kin. As Rousseau sees it, some things cannot be altered; some changes, in this imperfect world where we find ourselves, we cannot sanely contemplate. A man is born to his station, and his station is the place given him, to make of what he can. But that is not to say that one man is worth more than another.'

'Just some has 'nother seven hundred a year,' muttered Job, and had to suffer the glare of that yellow-haired Alba chit who thought of herself as prospective lady of the house.

'It is for this reason that I have settled on a new order – a republic, here at Hatch House. A community of souls all equal under God: a communal example to the world of commonalty.'

'Him sharing out his portion?' breathed William, gripping the sides of the pillar under him.

'Not a chance,' Job's wife whispered back.

'No more talk, then, of "master" or "your honour"! No more doffing of caps, or dropping of curtseys! If we begin with domestic democracy, shall we not infect the world at large with democracy? A seedbed to plant out the world: that's what we shall have here at Hatch. As Rousseau tell us . . .'

'That bugger again,' murmured Alice.

'The will of all is the law, the supreme rule!' And he began to unpack the documents.

They said little, either because they did not know if he had reached his main point, or because they were still toying with the marvellous possibility of sharing out the Wootton Estate between them.

'So shall we each have a piece?' said William, almost without realising it.

'A peace?' said Wootton.

'A piece of land,' said William.

The idea seemed to take Robin unawares, but he quickly rallied. 'A piece of land? A garden of your own, you mean? Why not? And why not indeed. I shall set by a corner of the linseed meadow for allotments.'

'Ah,' said Williams, subsiding. Just for a moment he had entertained a wild and foolish error, but now everything was plain.

Robin began to call out their names, one by one, summoning them forward to present them with a scroll and to pin a red ribbon on to their chests. To each in turn he said, 'I deem you as you deem yourself, from this day forth, a member of the Republic of Hatch House.' When he kissed Curragh on both cheeks, the man all but turned and fled.

The axe had not fallen, and yet the servants and hands were not reassured. 'T'aint 'gainst the King, is it? I am't 'gainst the King,' said the ostler. 'Not even this one.'

They tossed their heads about, muttering, foreseeing armed struggle and them on the side of rebellious treachery. Robin laughed and explained that no, he was not advocating riots and revolution, only the peaceful democratisation of one Berkshire estate.

Last of all, he summoned the girls forward. 'You too shall be members of my republic,' he said, his head fondly on one side. As the ribbons were pinned on, every eye was drawn to those immature breasts. Already Zennor was starting to fill out. The rumness of the situation was once again brought home to the staff, who had opinions of their own about the master's unseemly domestic arrangements.

He looked for his republicans' eyes to shine, but they remained blank, puzzled, bewildered, suspicious. They were pleased about the allotments, loudly grateful for the allotments, and yet those had not even been a part of his plan. They did not stand more erect, did not throw back their heads and delight in having parity of esteem with their master. Their tortoise-like slowness exasperated him. They held their hands over the ribbons as they picked their way out of the ruin, and wagged their heads, talking about other things: beans, peas, potatoes, carrots. They were unsettled and uneasy. He had expected them to stride down the hill, wearing their lives at a jauntier angle. But they did not seem to understand; did not seem to value the dignity of the republican man or woman, the nobility of being on a par with the King and all his court.

Alba had already begged Zennor's twist of ribbon to pin to her left breast and prettily balance the one on her right. Only Zennor was reading and re-reading her scroll, eyes bright, cheeks flushed, her hand holding the hair on top of her head, to keep it from obscuring her view. She looked so intent on the words, so excited by their meaning, that he was almost compensated for the damp and unlit dullness of the others . . . until he remembered that she could not read.

Urgent to break the hold of dull-eyed ennui, he was moved to shout after his workers, 'In celebration whereof, I declare today a holiday, this year and ever after!'

At this, his staff turned about and started to descend the other side of the hill, heading for the village, to enjoy half a day at the inn.

They did not seem to expect him to follow.

'Is that the sum and parcel of it, then?' said William, edging down the hill on the sides of his feet. 'A free afernoon and a piece of ribbon?'

He and Job and Curragh and Alice moved lop-sidedly down the slippery slope.

'Leastways we're not turned off,' said Alice.

'Will of all is the law, is that what he said?' Curragh was in one of his sour, black moods. 'If that's the case of it, I'll take that Baydon to court.'

'Who? The Reverend? Oh, for turning out your wife.'

'Well, it weren't my will, that's certain,' said Curragh. 'No word of why. Nothing to say her's unsatisfactory. 'Conomies, they said, somesuch. 'Conomies! What's 'conomies to a man like him? More money for his claret, likely. Don't trouble that it's winter fuel and meat to us. Kindling and crackling t'us.' He liked this. He repeated it several times, the gall tasting sweeter every time. 'Kindling and crackling t'us.'

'If the will of all be the law,' said William (who had been wrestling with the idea all the way down from the ruin), 'then we could just walk 'bout a-helping usselves, couldn't us? S'long as we all wanted.'

'Like to kindling,' said Curragh. (There was not such a fearful shortage of firewood in Berkshire that autumn, but the rain had made the log piles wet, and Curragh had spent a frustrating morning trying to light fires in the many grates of Hatch House.)

'I mean to say, who'd choose to be a pauper, if you asked him?'

'Be Sodom and Gomorrah,' was Alice's way of thinking.

'Not *all*. Got to be *all* to count,' said Job, drawn in to the novelty of the idea. 'Some'd want the poor kept poor, to be rich 'longsider them, some would.'

'Like the parson,' said Curragh, unable to rise above the personal.

'Be Sodom and Gomorrah, everyone helping thesselves.'

'No levy. No pressing. No prison.' William was engrossed. His face fell into a doggy grin. 'Not my will to go to Bridewell, y'honour, nor missus don't will it neither!' It was breathtaking, the folly so-called educated gentlemen could spew out when the spirit moved them: "the will of all is the law'."'

They had reached the bottom of the hill by now, and the footpath which skirted both churchyard and parsonage. Some nails had rusted through in the parsonage fence, so that a couple of shingle boards sagged loose. There were specks of cold in the air, and the leaves were trembling; it was about to rain torrentially on their half-holiday.

Curragh's wife would be home now, always at home now, rehearsing her grievances, wanting to take them out on him. He pulled at one of the planks, but instead of twanging back against the rest with a hollow bang it came right away in his hand. The others looked at him, shocked, thinking he had done it wilfully. He made a joke of it. 'Fuel 'gainst the winter,' he said, letting his jaw sag in a grin.

William sized up the fence. The hot summer had made the wood dry and brittle. 'It's the will of all,' he said, tearing off another slat.

'And mine,' said Job, and pulled the finial off the fence post.

They expected Alice to tell them to stop.

'See what I said?' she complained. 'Sodom and Gomorrah, it would be,' and she moved her ample body between the men and the fence, to protect the parson's property.

'You heard the master,' said her husband. 'The will of all is the law. Well? Don't you will it?'

'How would you feel if you was my Marion? Turned out of your post.'

Alice thought. It was a holiday, and holidays were supposed to bring a change from the normal. She was sorry for Marion Coppler – mostly for having Curragh as a husband, but a little also because she had been turned out of her post without a word of an explanation. She pressed her rump against the fence and, with a cry of surprise, achieved a triumphant splintering of timber, falling backwards in among the parson's lupins. The pig in the sty set up a noisy commotion, but the house remained quiet; there could be no one at home. For a moment, the little group of holidaymakers stood half inside the immaculate parsonage garden, with its tidy rows of beetroot tops and marigolds and short-sheared grass and sickly green kale. It was peculiarly different from the wild wet hill behind them.

Then the men helped Alice to her feet, and gathered up the smashed pieces of split plank – for tidiness rather than firewood. It was no one's will to steal the parson's prizedand cosseted vegetables; he had not offended them to that extent. But the great daring of their republican stand made them snigger and snuffle and swear and joke – 'All know where *you*'d put your will, if you had your way, Curragh Coppler.' – all the way into Winding Hatch and the Post Inn, running ahead of the rain which might wash out their holiday mood.

'Could it be, do you think? One day?' said Zennor, furling up her scroll and the one Alba had left on her pillar. 'Everyone sharing? Every-one equal?'

'Did you see? Did you?' said Alba, who was not listening, indifferent to such things. 'Did you?'

Below them Robin's newly imported, free-roaming fallow deer were wandering, with patrician rectitude, through Muses' Walk, cropping the newly planted tamarisks, pausing now and then to listen, as if for distant gunfire, the fall of kings. Their individual beauty merged, as they grouped and regrouped, into an amorphous dapple, a cloud-shadow wandering over the gardens of Hatch House, as improbably scenic as any rustic bower or Portland arcadia.

'If people can think to write it down, it must be possible,' said Zennor. 'I'll ask Mrs Baydon.'

'He kissed me. God's truth, he truly kissed me!' Alba was standing by the shining white stele, gazing down at Hatch House. Wood-pigeons were making a dull, monotonous drone in the few remaining trees.

'When Adam delved and Eve span . . .' Zennor tried to break out of the cocoon of thoughts and imaginings which seemed to hold her in a trance – tried to interest herself in Alba's excitement. 'He kissed everyone. He kissed William.'

'Not like *that*,' sighed Alba, her hands clasped prayerfully against her chest. 'You didn't see. He was so . . . that waistcoat likes him so well.'

'The waistcoat does?' Zennor was confused. Alba was trembling – shuddering. Over a waistcoat? She looked most odd, her facial muscles gripped by a kind of rigor, and her lips pushed forward poutingly. 'Are you ill?' Zennor asked.

'Very, *very* well,' said Alba – hardly a whisper, her pale face even paler. 'God knows . . . the gods knows . . . the gods . . .' She faltered, her mouth full of strange plurals. Wootton's garden and house were full of Olympians, and she had found it hard all along to grasp whether he was a Christian or not. Once or twice, speaking to Zennor, she had been quite priggish about it, but today she stood in a ruined temple struggling with a deckful of gods and goddesses as doggedly as Zennor struggled with the notion of democracy.

All of a sudden, Alba dropped down on her knees, and put her arms round the marble base of the stele. The spreading sacrificial dish surmounting it forced her head backwards awkwardly, but she did not ease her grip. Her eyes were tight shut. 'I make this solemn vow . . .'

'Whoa! Wait,' said Zennor, suddenly wide awake. 'What are you doing?'

'. . . before all the gods in heaven as on earth.' Her face was screwed up like a ball of paper.

'Alba, give over. Stop.'

'. . . to love and serve Robin Wootton for ever and ever and ever, and give him my heart and soul, so help me Jesus Christ and all the angels and gods and everyone looking down. And *to be a good wife*.'

'Alba!' Zennor stamped her foot.

'Hear my oath,' said Alba very loudly, to drown out Zennor's presence. 'And may I die if I break it. In the name of the father and the son and the Apollo and Diana and Zeus and Hermes and Horatio and the Holy Ghost. Amen.'

Opening her eyes again, she glared at Zennor defiantly. 'You're my witness,' she said. It was partly confiding, partly a warning. Alba considered herself in love with Robin Wootton, and though there was no one else but Zennor to share the happy news, Zennor also needed to understand: her own hopes of marriage to Wootton were at an end.

CHAPTER NINE

That Same Day

The Bishop of Winchester, on the previous occasions when Baydon had seen him, had seemed more brightly coloured than the man who got down from the London stage. Though his looks were just as saintly and ethereal, haloed in white hair, his black frock coat had a less rounding effect on his cadaverous frailty than purple or heavy embroidered ceremonial robes. His stained-glass saintliness was more transparent viewed in the daylight than from inside the cathedral. Baydon did not grip hard the hand extended to him, for fear it break into powdered glass.

The bishop had brought with him one of the incumbent canons – for bodily support, by all appearances. Canon Pyle was a dark, square, muscular man, with a wig which coiled around his ears like rams' horns, and he wore a broad lambswool collar. The bishop leaned so heavily on him, in fact, that Canon Pyle resembled the ram being plucked from the thicket in place of Isaac.

'Have you been waiting long?' asked the bishop.

'No time at all, Your Grace,' said Baydon, who had been waiting all afternoon, watching the skies darken over Wantage like the Day of Judgement, until the rain had swept down the Vale of the White Horse soaking him to the skin. He just hoped the roof was sound over the guest bedroom.

It was indeed the Day of Judgement for Baydon. On this visit hung the future of his clerical life. For this had he grown; for this was he ripe. Such a venerable bishop surely did not put himself to the discomfort of a fifty-mile coach journey unless he inclined strongly towards one particular applicant.

'You wrote to me,' said the bishop, without preamble. 'A pleasant letter to receive on a pleasant day. I thank you for your consideration towards all my relations.'

They squeezed into the chaise: the bishop, the canon, the parson and the parson's wife. He was sorry he had brought Sophronia now, as it was rather a crush. Even if the bishop did favour married candidates, he might not necessarily want to ride in a carriage with all the wet volume of their skirts and furbelows. It was good of her to reach across and place a hand in his, within his lap; he could not have primed her better to display wifely affection. But she really ought to have stayed at home, where she could have put the children to bed at a civilised hour. Now they would come flooding out of the house and be forward and make inappropriate remarks. That Padler girl did no more, in minding children, than prevent them killing each other till their parents reappeared. And where was the unexpected canon to sleep? There would be no bedroom aired for him. And what manner of disaster would dinner be without a cook or his wife in the house to prepare it?

'Mr Gilbert writes glowingly of your pastoral abilities,' said the bishop, fragile as a pane of glass propped on the leather upholstery opposite. 'Does he pass often through your parish?'

So soon to business! He had expected the journey at least would be spent on pleasantries. He had been going to tell the bishop about his asparagus. 'Mr –?'

'A friend of your uncle's, isn't he, my dear?' said Sophronia.

'Oh yes! Mr Gilbert. I don't see him as often as I would wish, Your Grace. He is a very educated gentleman. Mrs Baydon and I prize his visits greatly for the conversation they bring.' He made a mental note to write and thank Mr Gilbert for his kind offices as soon as the bishop had gone; also to remind himself of the fellow's Christian name, which had utterly deserted him. A country parson is hard put to make the kind of influential friends who can help him at such a time as this. Baydon wondered if his brother would stay good to his word and pass the night at the Fox and Grapes. Was there anyone less calculated to impress than Oliver in one of his facetious and blaspheming moods?

'I might have expected you to enlist your *patron*, in seeking after the canonry,' said the bishop, his vitreous blue eyes still bright amid the shadows of a chaise closed up against driving rain. 'You are on good terms, are you, with your patron Mr Wootton?'

'I hope, Your Grace, that I am on good terms with every Christian fellow, but Mr Wootton . . .' He *would* have gone on to say that he ranked Robin Wootton among the unbelievers, an ordeal to be endured with Christian forebearance.

But his wife's hand, concealed by the hat which rested on his lap, had snatched hold of such a part of his anatomy as robbed him of speech.

'Mr Wootton is so completely busy with the restoration of his garden,' he heard her say brightly, as he gasped with shock and pain. 'Though we dine there regularly on Fridays. Your cousin's son is a marvel of hospitality! The Reverend is loth to trespass on his time too greatly. Especially for such a personal favour as a commendation. We are so deeply indebted to him already for our well-being.'

The ram bucked and wriggled bad-temperedly in his corner of the chaise; it was plain Canon Pyle did not approve of women participating in a conversation between professionals.

Baydon removed his wife's hand from his fall and patted it to acknowledge the service it had done him. 'My patron is a very *modern* young gentleman, too. Well, I'm sure you know better than I, being his godfather. I suspect he may not place such importance on the great continuity of the English Church as, say, Canon Pyle here. Or I.'

The bishop sighed. 'Yes. Young Robin drove his uncle to desperation as a child,' he said unnostalgically. 'Giving things away which were not his to give. Liberating horses from between traces and songbirds out of cages.' His pale blue eyes had hardly moved from Baydon's face, as he searched it for tell-tale indications of character. But his journey had tired him; he was an old man, and his lids began to drop now. 'Nevertheless,' he said, suppressing a yawn, 'Saint Francis was a similar trial to his father, we are told. And I hold it a rule never to disparage a man merely for being young. That would smack of jealousy.'

Baydon smiled. He felt the muscles of his face relax from pretending to smile, into smiling. He liked the bishop. He would like to work for him, learn from him. He carried with him an aura of the cathedral, just as a pig man carries with him the aura of pigs. His hands were as old as its flagstones, his bearing as ancient as its vaults, his stillness contracted from a cloistered lifetime. Baydon was tempted to breath him in, like the odour of an old book.

Hatch Hill came into sight, and the little Grecian temple which generally made his lip pucker with irritation. Today it had no effect. The rain had passed, and the sinking sun was retrieving a beautiful evening from a dirty day, lighting up the hilltop like the hairs on a baby's head. He was glad the children would still be up: the bishop could meet George. No one could fail to like George. And there would be the chance of a turn in the garden, to see the asparagus mounds – scene of recent triumphs – and the espaliers, too.

At the sound of the coach, the children came out of the house, Sarah and Suzannah, Grace and George, with Annie Padler holding the baby. She had got the little ones into their night clothes and armed each child with an umbrella, in case any were needed by the visitors. ('Annie Padler never thought of that herself,' he whispered to his wife, as he helped her down from the carriage.)

The girls curtseyed. George made a creditable bow – and the vicar of Winding Hatch thought he could hear the clamour of cathedral bells all the way from Winchester.

'Dinner will be ready the sooner you excuse me, Your Grace,' said Sophronia curtseying. 'A pot roast I prepared this morning.'

Baydon gave an ill-disguised cry of relief that the problem of dinner had not been overlooked, then explained, in an outburst of emotion, 'Jacob would have sold Esau's birthright back to him for a mess of my wife's pot roast!' The evening was surely set fair. 'Come and see my asparagus mounds,' he said upon a sudden, generous impulse which encompassed both canon and bishop. No one could underrate a man who produced tender asparagus and could espalier his own plum trees.

If the bishop were too tired he concealed it well, for he smiled at the prospect of seeing Baydon's garden and inclined his great white head like God agreeing to walk in Eden in the cool of the evening. He was alert enough, too, to deduce that Mrs Baydon cooked her own dinners. 'You keep no cook, Reverend?' he said, as they passed through the house.

'We try to live frugally,' said Baydon, barely recalling the matter of the stolen Penny Savings. 'I abhor extravagance.' He knew it had been the right thing to say, the moment it was said. The big white head was nodding again above the narrow, ascetic frame.

'If we might just *wash* ourselves . . .' said Canon Pyle peevish, halting obdurately at the foot of the stairs. The bishop smiled apologetically at Samuel, and said he would come into the garden directly, as soon as he had 'washed off the dust of the turnpikes'. Then he delivered himself into the care of the canon, whose assistance he needed to climb the stairs.

Evening sun lapped yellow even through the drawn curtains of the garden room. Full of optimism, Baydon opened the door to survey his pride and joy . . . and found the god Cerne looking back at him, mirrored two score times in the delicate features of his followers. A spread of antlers, a pair of liquid brown eyes, hooves among the marigolds, a scut-tail lifting . . .

Then the entire herd of deer bolted – lifted free of the ground, and sprang for the gap in the fence. The stag's rump was ponderous, by contrast with the does; he made an audible thud–thud–thud as he climbed Hatch Hill, his females spilling past him or channelling off along level ground to either side of the hill.

Baydon went after them fifty yards or more, slashing with his best frock coat, using it for a flail. But the deer melted away like insubstantial things, into the evening light, dapple into dapple, antlers among branches, leaps dissolved by the acid brightness of the last blinding rays of the sun. Returning to the gap in his broken fence, he rested a hand on the post to recover his breath. The nail which had once held on the finial pierced his palm.

His garden had been eaten bare, the roses plucked from the thorn, the flower and green tops cropped level with the ground. Here and there, the delicate bark of the espalier had been peeled off like skin from a flayed man, and the whole tree hung forwards from the wall as if contorted in agony. The bay, the new wood of the vine, the carrot tops, the strawberry runners – they had all been systematically stripped by the deer. Even the wisteria against the house wall had been cleared of greenery along a geometrically straight line the height of nibbling mouths. Baydon went from canes to herbs to ridge to shrub, touching his plants, as a camp follower might close the eyes of the dead on a battlefield. And all the while, there trickled out of him, like water from a fractured pipe, a stream of seething, scalding, involuntary invective.

'Volester! Wootton, you pitten weem! You hucking copdock! You pode hole!' His voice broke, and the anger burst out of him, the leak turning to great welling sobs. 'Sladdery eyke!' He turned and began bawling up the hill, towards the temple where a large stag stood at bay against the altered skyline. 'Are you content now, Wootton, you prickwillow? You gort? You and your visigoths? What did I ever do to you, you pigdon wannock?'

When he turned round, he could see that all the little windows under the vicarage eaves had opened. His daughter and step-daughters were at one, the lace of their nightcaps flickering pale below their faces. George was at the next, intrigued more than aghast. Canon Pyle was at the next, bringing his ecumenical hat down in short swatting movements, as if trying to catch a moth under it. But at the end window loomed the pale, Lindisfarne face of the Bishop of Winchester, washing-water glistening in his white hair, his eyes on the madman below violently defending the breach in his garden fence apparently against an invisible army of demons. The ancient face, having long since gained mastery over mere human emotion, was wholly inexpressive.

Proud as she was of her declaration in the ruined temple, Alba knew she must now keep a careful watch on her step-sister. She had a keen intuition that Zennor was more clever than she, what with her reading and her thinking and her large, high forehead full of irregular curls. Above all, there was her hair.

Alba was under the impression that the brain extended, like tree sap, into a person's hair, so that the extreme curliness of Zennor's surely afforded her miles more labyrinthine storage for wit and cunning. Hers must be an infinitely complex, coiling cunning, the like of which Alba could never house inside her own straight, fair intellect. She would have to take care of Zennor, now that she had confessed her love for Robin. In fact, it would be best if she could somehow lessen the threat Zennor represented.

That hair. Its wild, glossy magnificence combined with Alba's own rather wild theories of anatomy made her brood over the problem of Zennor's hair.

Despite the declaration of a republic there was no afternoon off for the Wootton girls. Robin had declared the rest of the day a holiday only on the spur of the moment, whereas their lesson in withying and basket-making had already been arranged for that afternoon. So, as the hands and servants trooped off to the inn, Zennor and Alba trailed over the fields, all the way from Hatch Hill to the river, knowing it was going to rain, knowing all along it was going to rain and put a stop to the lesson. Robin never noticed such things as the weather.

Watching the basket-maker pollarding a willow for canes, Alba reached a drastic decision. The ugliness of the tree was frightening. The grotesque stump, like the maimed limb of some war veteran, leaned towards them, begging without any fingers to beg with. Not a flank of the trunk was free of tumorous, bulging scars. One cluster of lumps resembled a human face; the weaver even drew their attention to it. 'Got a smicker eye on you, this 'un, see?' he said, as he hacked spindly withies off the white, lumpen brow.

On the far side of the river, unpollarded willows, too inaccessible to crop, swayed in lime-green dresses, trembling at the promise of rain. They were beautiful, feminine, ethereally pleasant, dancing on the water's edge. Yet cut off their tresses of slender leaves and they too would be like this: hideous, obscene, gurning faces fit only for mundane household use. The resolve formed in Alba's head like a headache and, in the course of the day, sank down through her body to lodge in her narrow hips.

Once or twice she wandered away from the basketry lesson, to where the grasses were high, and crouched there, her skirt round her ears, and tried to void the solid piece of pain inside her. But she decided it came simply from knowing what she was going to do that night: hack off Zennor's bouncing abundance of hair while she slept.

Rain came down the river like a tidal bore, eliminating the countryside behind it with a wet, grey mist and setting the skirted willows tossing like mourners. The girls had to walk all the way back to Hatch House in the downpour; the basket-maker gave them big withy baskets half as big as coracles, to carry over their heads for shelter. Alba, walking behind Zennor, could still see black hair swishing below the osier dome. There was so *much* of it, that hair.

Tomorrow, Zennor would tell Robin what her sister had done, but Alba would deny it – say it was a lie – that Zennor had done it herself, wanting to be more boyish, hankering after boyishness. Robin would not like the thought of her lying, no more than he would like the sight of her pollarded, shorn. The ache grew in Alba's belly. Was it guilt? She had thought guilt came after the event.

She knew Zennor was plotting to win Robin for herself. The girl had said nothing about Alba's vow, only, 'Wait and see. Let's wait and see.' She thought she would be able to make Robin love her, with that hair, all that hair. But Alba had vowed, in the face of all the gods, and Zennor would have to make do with a farmer or a blacksmith or a soldier. Alba had been first to cry 'Snap!' and by all the laws of fair play that entitled her to the crimson jack on the table.

If only her guts did not ache so much!

Sophronia Baydon closed the bedroom door softly behind her. Her husband sat on the edge of the bed in his breeches and shirt, his wig rolled up between his hands. It seemed to him that dinner had lasted at least fifteen years – a fifteen years passed in almost total silence, as he descended, like Dante, lower and lower through the several storeys of hell.

The bishop himself had said nothing about the scene in the garden. When invited to say grace, he may, of course, have always favoured Alaric of York:

> '. . . And you that eat, give thanks for it to Christ
> And let the words you utter be only peace,
> For Christ loved peace.'

Baydon did not think so. The bishop might also have intended to visit Winding Hatch purely for the pleasure of eating Mrs Baydon's pot roast, never a thought in his mind of the vacancy for a cathedral canon; certainly, the matter was not mentioned again during dinner. But Baydon had gone up to bed that night with the sure and certain conviction that he had ruined his chances of advancement for ever. He would remain a country parson as long as Canon Pyle or the bishop drew breath, as long as the implacable God of deer and catastrophe held sway over the Church of England.

'I think we can discount any change of address in the near future,' he told Sophronia, as frostily as he was able. He hoped to deter her from any reproaches. He had, after all, as good as promised her a change of station, at the time of proposing marriage, and no doubt her sights had been set on Winchester when she accepted him.

'I am very fond of this place,' she said. 'So are the children. Children like things to stay the same round about them.' She began to undress, laying her clothes in an orderly row along the lid of the press, for want of her own wardrobe. When she saw his surprise, she simply said, 'We lacked an aired room for Canon Pyle. The loose canon. I had to give him mine.'

'Ah. Yes. I see.' She came and helped him off with his boots. 'At least we were spared the company of my dear brother tonight. Where has he taken himself? He didn't ask me for money.'

'He still has a few pennies, I believe,' she said, without inflection. 'Maybe even the King's shilling by now. He's considering joining the army, you know?'

It was a moment or two before he could assimilate this piece of news. Oliver had never mentioned any such thing. 'Oliver? A soldier? The fool! Doesn't he know there's a war coming?' A new anxiety stabbed him in the guts: a fear for his brother's safety. 'The fool. He fancies himself a beau in a uniform. Never reads a broadsheet. Vanity of vanities. Anything for a new set of clothes. He likes the scarlet, that's at the bottom of it. The fool. I must –' He stirred himself, struggling up through the dark earth tumulus which had buried his hopes and his career, to the greater worry of Oliver's safety. But Sophronia laid a hand on his sleeve and sat down beside him on the bed.

'We all have our battles to fight, my dear,' she said. 'We could not hope to enjoy his company endlessly.'

He shot her a look, suspecting irony, but could not catch her eyes. She was busy unknotting his bands for him. As the knot round his throat relaxed, the madness of wrath and panic, horror and shame which had thumped inside his skull all evening subsided through him, making all the pulses of his body flicker as they passed. Then Sophronia climbed into his big double bed, as if she had always been sleeping there. She did not ask his permission. She simply climbed in, her plaited hair making peculiar distortions within her cap.

Resentment stirred in Baydon. To crown a vile day, was he really supposed to give up his bed as well?

It seemed not. 'Come to bed, Samuel. There will be better days.'

It was the first time she had ever used his Christian name. Perhaps it was this novelty which made him forget his prayers – something he had not done for twenty years. Perhaps it was the thought of a new and unexpected consolation for all the rat-brown regrets gnawing on his guts which made him undress at speed.

As for Sophronia Baydon: she deliberately laid aside, once and for all, the knowledge of Oliver's theft, her guilt at forcing his hand in the matter of enlisting, her guilt at deliberately leaving the money within Oliver's reach. A woman has a limited armoury in the face of a lewd and pestering bully; she must use what means she can to protect herself and her daughters. She would never again mention the Penny Savings, only pray that the war kept Oliver away a long while, and expiate her crime by doing the extra work it had brought on her.

Consolation is rarely given without some being returned.

'After such patience with the asparagus, I wonder you could bear to think of moving away from Winding Hatch,' she said, placing her hand once more in his lap. 'I'm sure there's nowhere to equal this.'

'I fear my crowns are all cast down,' he said. It made him sound like a saint in the celestial city.

'They will come again, Samuel. You'll see,' said his wife. 'It may be slow to come, but asparagus is wonderfully resilient.'

Alba could eat nothing at dinner-time, and pleaded the need to go to bed early. Indeed, once she had stolen the scissors from the kitchen, she could think of nothing but going to bed. But she must on no account fall asleep. Not until the thing was done. With her hair gone, Zennor would not have the wits to think up a clever retribution.

Unfortunately, Zennor was solitious and kind – said Alba did look fearfully ill, and offered to fetch her beef-tea and a warmed stone for the foot of her bed. Alba sent her away, surprising herself with the rudeness she could muster to achieve it: she had only to open her mouth and nastiness spilled out, snide and venomous.

Staying awake proved to be no problem at all. The pain was going through her now like wind through a field of grass, in pulsing waves that made her whimper and curl up in a ball. Would it stop when the thing was done?

She waited until she heard Zennor come to bed in the room next door. She waited till the room fell silent. She reached under her pillow and pulled out the scissors – huge, iron-bladed shears capable of cutting through meat bones. Then she moved over to the door and listened for proof that Zennor was asleep.

It was while she waited that she realised her nightdress was wet. In the dark, she could not tell why, only that she smelled peculiarly vile. Was it the smell of wickedness?

As she opened the door, to her consternation, light spilled out to meet her. Zennor was not sleep at all, but sitting up in bed reading a book. She looked up, her face like the moon within that wealth of black hair, and drew such a gasp of horror that Alba dropped the scissors.

'What have you done? Have you stabbed yourself?' gasped Zennor, seeing the scissors fall.

Alba looked down at the huge, glistening patch of blood soaking her nightgown, and shook her head. 'I think I'm having a baby!' she wailed.

Nothing else made sense of the pain, the blood, the despair. Babies came of loving a man: that much had permeated the cloistered ignorance of Lambeth Asylum. She had fallen in love with Robin Wootton, and this was her reward: to be in labour at midnight in the nursery of Hatch House, at the age of twelve. 'Tell Robin! Tell Robin!' She wanted to tell the gods: she had not loved him *that* much, thank you very kindly mum, sir.

Zennor ran, as if from brandished scissors, along the corridor and downstairs to the floor below, where Robin Wootton slept. 'Robin! Robin! Robin! Alba's having a baby! Alba's dying! Come quick!' A few minutes later, she stood in the doorway, clutching his hand, trying to draw him farther into the room.

Robin Wootton remained behind her, his head slightly averted from the sight of Alba's dripping blood. Alba clutched the door handle, while Zennor clutched Robin's hand, but the inequity gave no rise to jealousy. Jealousy was too puny an emotion to survive the feelings at large in that bedroom.

Zennor was baffled as to why Wootton did not act – do – take charge. He seemed quite helpless even to speak, other than to repeat, in strangely swallowed tones, 'She is not giving birth. She is not giving birth. Children do not give –'

'Shan't I fetch a doctor?' Zennor implored. But Wootton did not believe in doctors. They were against his philosophy.

It was Alice the cook who explained, both to Alba and to her employer, the female menarche: the Blight, as she called it. Wootton tried several times to curtail the explanation – said that he was well versed in simple biology, and had just been confused by the child's foolish panic. Why such an immoderate reaction to a natural phase of development?

''Cos no one never told her?' suggested Alice pointedly. 'Girls weren't born knowing.'

'Neither were boys,' said Wootton unguardedly, but it was as close as he ever came to admitting ignorance. (Yet another shortfall of his classical education, he thought darkly, though he could cheerfully have continued on not knowing.)

He asked Alice to instruct Alba and Zennor in 'future modes of discretion' and went back to bed. Alice, put to the trouble of explaining menstruation at two in the morning, took it hard that the favour was not returned: no one would tell her what her jointing scissors were doing on the nursery floor.

PART TWO

The Age of Reason

CHAPTER TEN

Herschel's Telescope

Alba's devotion to Robin Wootton did not diminish with time. Indeed, it grew, in adolescence, to the kind of passionate obsession so all-consuming that it becomes an end in itself, a self-fuelling combustion. She obeyed his injunctions not to read. She suppressed her loathing of the open air and the countryside, and learned to milk a cow and curd a cheese and carry buckets on a yoke. Wootton had them both painted carrying milk-pail yokes, but the picture was not good. Increasingly, he believed that portrait-painting was a vanity of the rich, and that it should be undertaken only by the poor. The artist chosen, consequently, was accustomed to painting inn signs, and to concealing the crudities of his brushstrokes with several layers of amber varnish. (The finished effort was given to Curragh to prettify his cottage, and he turned it to the wall, put hooks into the stretchers and hung his fishing rods across it. He would have sold it to a pub for cash, but could not find one with a name which suited the subject.)

Zennor's passion, on the other hand, was still for books. With the help of the vicar's wife, she became fluent and widely read long before Wootton adjudged the Age of Nature past and the Age of Reason due to dawn in his two wards. They were fifteen when he decided the Age of Reason had come.

Suddenly he was impatient to convey ideas, disciplines, an assortment of knowledge which would explain the world in rational terms before, in the Age of Morality, the girls began actively to participate in changing it. It was a frustration to him, therefore, to find that Alba could not learn to read overnight.

She had looked forward with some pleasure to the moment when Robin discovered that Zennor had betrayed his trust, had gone behind his back, disobeyed his wishes and slunk guiltily over to the vicarage for lessons, expressly contrary to the theories of Rousseau. 'And now! To reading!' he had said one morning when they were twelve. Alba drew breath to inform on her companion.

'I read already,' Zennor had said quietly and quickly, before Alba could make the revelation.

'You read?'

'I read,' she said. 'It came to me.' Just like that.

And Robin, saved the arduous task of teaching her, had been pleased – not annoyed, not disappointed – *pleased!*

And Alba had found herself wading through a mire of consonants and vowels which threatened to drag her down in Robin's esteem. Reading did not 'come to her', did not settle on her head like some dove denoting divine approval. She had not the facility she might have had at six. She felt old and slow-witted, intimidated by the wire entanglements of the printed word. Wootton could remember nothing of the process of learning to read, and therefore believed that it must have 'come to him', as Zennor said, spontaneously. So he named the letters to Alba, and Alba named them back to him, but continued unable to read whole words. Later, Robin shouted at her, to implant the seed of reading deeper in her head.

'Mrs Baydon taught *her*! *She* went to Mrs Baydon!' protested Alba, in self-defence, tears of bitterness rolling down her cheeks. But Wootton only concluded that Zennor, who had mastered reading at an earlier age, with no apparent difficulty, must be cleverer than Alba. And no amount of reasoned argument dislodges such impressions once they have taken root.

Zennor grew into a young woman of unusual proportions for the time. Alba took heart at that. Thanks to long hours spent out of doors, doing strenuous manual activities and none of the small, pernickety pastimes which generally occupied young girls, she developed a broad pair of shoulders and a strong, high bust. Her movements were large and energetic, which made attractive clothes look an encumbrance on her; and her wild black hair brooked no restraint. Alba, on the other hand, had participated sacrificially but as little as possible in Emile's rustic timetable, perservering only as long as anyone was watching, giving up breathless and afraid of the great unwellness which threatened to engulf her whenever she taxed her small, narrow frame. She grew into a slight, delicate woman, pale despite the fearsome outdoors, with collar-bones like the pediments of a Greek column and a cloud of ethereally pale hair. She took heart from the great mirrors which lined the sumptuous quilted treasure-box of a house in which she felt so immensely safe and valued.

Zennor kept other treasures in mind. Perhaps through having fixed her own heart on the top shelf of Wootton's library, or having lighted accidentally there on Marvell, she could make better sense of Rousseau's admiration for the gardens and woods and sky. She coveted the diamante night, as Alba coveted the gilded plate floating in smeary glass cabinets, the gems painted with such scrupulous precision on the despised portraits on the stairs.

Though she no longer needed Mrs Baydon's help with the mechanics of reading, Zennor was being conducted along as many pretty corridors of knowledge as the travelling library afforded. Mrs Baydon also turned a blind eye to Zennor pilfering books from the library at Hatch House, tending to agree with the child that the books were better used than left to moulder. She too gained delight from the books, and was glad of the continued excuse to read with her at the kitchen table. Only Goldsmith sent her irresistibly to sleep.

Once Zennor could read, the Reverend Baydon was doubtful as to the purpose of his wife spending more time with the girl, especially as he had found out it was a secret kept from Wootton. He justified it grudgingly to himself by slipping books of a religious and uplifting nature across the breakfast-table, or seeming to leave one accidentally under the napkin beside his plate, where his wife could find it as she cleared the table: *Aesop* and *Pilgrim's Progress* and the *Life of Saint Francis*. Foxe's *Book of Martyrs* was such a gigantic edition, complete with woodcuts, and a commentary by the Archbishop of York, that it had to be left by chance on the hall table with no more than a passing comment to draw Sophronia's attention to it. He just wished his son George would show as eager an interest in books as the Wootton girl.

George, as he grew up, was aware of some covert education of Zennor progressing parallel to his own. He looked forward to the days when she came, but not with any prospect of play or companionship. Her greater height intimidated him, and the aura of anxious disapproval which emanated from his father every time she or her household were mentioned made George think of her as something dangerous: forbidden ground. He would drift past the kitchen door each Thursday morning, while she and Mrs Baydon sat at the table reading, but he would never have dreamt of going in. In fact, he sat at his bedroom window, watching for her to arrive, watching her walk back over the hill, but he never pictured himself ever speaking to her or walking alongside her. She put him in mind of Pallas Athene who, in standing head-and-shoulders taller than mortal men, struck the kind of reverent fear in them which made death and battle pale by comparison.

So it was an event in the young man's life very like a visitation of the gods the day she spoke to him. He was sixteen, Zennor seventeen. He stood loitering outside the kitchen door while Oliver Goldsmith sent his mother inexorably to sleep. On one of his casual, unpremeditated passes, he saw Sophronia's head go down on her arms, while *The Deserted Village* crumbled into picturesque and wordy decay and Zennor's voice rose and fell with a hypnotic regularity, stanza by rolling stanza.

Suddenly Zennor's face came round the door jamb very close by his. 'Herschel,' it said.

'What?'

'Herschel's telescope. I want to see it. Have you seen it? I want to go there.'

'Go, then,' said George backing away, flattening himself against the wall.

'We don't ask for things. We mustn't ask for things. Whims are not to be granted. It encourages wilfulness. But I want to go. Take me there! I want to see Herschel's telescope.'

Herschel's telescope at Slough was the wonder of the hour. Tourists by the hundred were travelling from all over the Home Counties for a glimpse of the monumental machine, window on to starry landscapes. George had heard it talked of as one of the wonders of the world and had, as a result, lodged the idea of it in the same part of his mind as the pyramids, the submarine, the laws of Hammurabi, Leonardo's flying machines and the projected Channel tunnel: it was not something he had expected to see in his lifetime. Now, this Amazon of a girl – a wonder in her own right, with her shining, bushy hair and socked, shoeless feet, her peasant-style dresses of fabulously impractical material hemmed in mud, this reader aloud of luxuriant poems, this eater of forbidden fruit – wanted him, George, to take her there. She wanted him to take her on a journey cross-country – run away with her while his mother slept at the kitchen table. She seemed to be commanding him, expecting him to fall in with her plans. And yet it was not resentment, that blazing heat around his ribcage, that liquefaction of his bowels. He was extremely loth to say he had no idea *how* to set about such a journey.

'Don't you *want* to see it?' she asked, genuinely puzzled. 'I can't go alone. I must have an escort.' She leant round the door in a way that brought her lips level with his burning ear.

'Yes. Absolutely. Of course you must,' said George, feeling through all the pockets of his jacket and breeches, as if in search of the fare. 'Now?'

'Next week. This day next week. I shan't come here.' Her hair flicked his cheek as she looked back towards the kitchen table. Mrs Baydon was lifting her head a little, blinking at the creases of her sleeve. 'We can meet at the Post.'

And George knew he would do it, was powerless to refuse. Gentility demanded it, and his father was always urging gentility on him: manners, consideration, chivalry. Besides, she had given him no chance to refuse, and though he lay awake that night thinking of ways to decline, he knew (in some part of his chest where fear properly belonged) that he could not refuse the girl from Hatch House.

'I would like to go to see the great telescope at Slough, Papa,' said George at breakfast next day.

Samuel Baydon was startled: George rarely displayed a desire to see much of life, beyond the wildlife in the area and whatever fish he could catch on a breaded hook. When he got over his surprise, however, Baydon was pleased; he nursed a secret desire to see the Herschel telescope himself, and an outing with his son would be just about as agreeable a day as he could imagine. An expedition. A joint expedition of discovery as far as the back of the universe, in a hackney chaise.

'Yes, yes. Very good,' he said, trying to convey grudging compliance, guarding against over-enthusiasm. 'Very good. I shall see what we can do. Perhaps Mrs Baydon and the girls would care to go as well, if we can all squeeze into the carriage. No. Perhaps just you and I, eh?'

George blushed scarlet. 'Well, in point . . . what I meant . . . it's a 'micus from school. Asked my company. I thought . . . the journey on our own would be half the . . .' He ducked his head, so as not to see his father's feelings hurt.

Baydon, like a crayfish that has left itself over-exposed, withdrew with awkward confusion into a protective hardness. 'Ah. I see. With an amicus. Hmmm. That needs consideration. I doubt you could be trusted.' And wiping crumbs from his mouth, he abandoned his breakfast and went to his office, by all appearances sulking.

In fact, Samuel was appalled to find how disappointed he was, how discomposed. Why could he not have instigated such a trip without waiting for George to say he was going with a schoolfriend? He was a fool. He was also ashamed by the fact that he had no idea whether George was *capable* of travelling by himself to Slough and back. If he was able to think of it, Baydon supposed, then he must be old enough to do it . . . but perhaps that did not follow. He would have to ask Mrs Baydon, and that galled him, too. Though he knew he could trust her answer, still it would have been preferable if he knew himself. He experienced a sharp stab of fear felt once or twice before – that his children, in growing, would get away from him, slip out of his hands somehow, like brook trout evading the net.

Perhaps he could redeem his grasp on the situation by arranging accommodation for the boys? Yes. He would do that. He would find out the name of a parson in Slough and arrange hospitality for them. That was his role in the outing. Even so, he allowed himself to say, in a moment of resentment, 'Snodsbury. I'd've liked to see that German's pipe.'

The German's pipe was forty feet long, with the circumference of a brewer's tun, and lenses ground to the transparence of purest water. Its brass body was wonder enough to the hundreds who crowded into the observatory of Sir William Herschel, private astronomer to King George. Leafy Slough was suddenly the fashionable place to be seen.

The tourists, ignorant of any practical astronomy, were content to admire the gigantic proportions of the precision instrument, to pace out its length, to glance bewildered at the pencil drawings hanging framed around the wall – drawings of refraction and parallax, planetary alignments, constellations, comets and nebulae. There was a model of Georgium Sidus, the planet which Herschel had discovered on the outermost bounds of the solar system. The tourists bought catalogues and woodcut-pictures of the telescope. But of the night sky they saw nothing, and most were content not to, for they would not have known what they were seeing; the point was to have *visited* it, this wonder of the modern world; to say they had been there.

Zennor was not content to look at the brass housing. She wanted to see the starlight flow down it, to milk the sky of images, to see what had never been seen by human eyes before this telescope was built. George, on the other hand, had not given it a moment's thought, eaten up as he was by worries much closer to hand.

What was he to say to the vicar of St John's, Slough, who, in answer to Baydon's letter, was expecting two schoolboys to stay overnight with him? 'Such comfort as they can win from a bed among the eaves is theirs for the asking,' he had written back. It was torment enough to tell all the lies necessary to meet Zennor at the Post, to secure tickets for Windsor.

He was sure the coachman suspected them of elopement, that the other passengers were watching him with lewd and critical eyes, noting his youth alongside her age. 'Must be a whole year younger,' they seemed to whisper. 'Not seventeen, and already a rake!' As the coach clattered through Maidenhead (praze-an-beeble, how did a town get a name like

Maidenhead?) he worked out a complex fiction by which to explain away Zennor Wootton. He would knock at the vicar's door and say that he and his 'micus had found this poor girl left destitute by cut-purses, and would rather see her provided with a bed for the night than have one themselves. Then he would sleep in a haystack. (He would just have to hope St John's vicarage did not have more than one spare bedroom.)

On getting down at Slough, George had begun to explain this plan to Zennor when she asked, 'Why should we need a room? We shall be at the observatory all night, watching the sky!'

It made a better excuse, he had to admit, but George was not at all sure the observatory would be open to visitors all night long. He was also fond of his night's rest. If they stayed awake all night, the only sleep he would get for forty-eight hours would be on the coach returning home. Already he was weary, emotionally fatigued by carrying his great burden of guilt across the county single-handed. Zennor gave him no help with it; she seemed perfectly unashamed.

She had been reading everything she could on the subject of the sky. He could make no sense of her chatter about spheres and falling angels and thunderbolts. He could recollect one passage by Livy he had had to translate at school – about omens sighted in the sky when Hannibal was coming. But he was only alarmed into silence when he mentioned this and Zennor pounced at him, asking what the omens were and if he would have believed in them if he had been alive then? He was not accustomed to taking a personal viewpoint – it was not required of a scholar – but no, he said, no of course he would not have believed them. Livy did not believe them.

'Livy was enlightened,' said Zennor. 'Enlightenment doesn't believe in anything beyond what's proven. Wouldn't you *like* to believe in apparitions in the sky? Lions with cannon on their backs? Fiery hailstones? Plagues of frogs? Ixion lashed to his wheel?'

George did not want to sound unenthusiastic, but there were reprisals enough in store for him without wanting to consider Ixion.

Still, he went to the vicar of St John's, and explained that his amicus and he would be passing the night at the observatory, so would not put him to the trouble of hospitality. He did not think the Reverend Gibforth believed him, but then he could feel the word LIAR branded hotly on his forehead, so that was hardly to be wondered. At least the Reverend Gibforth had never been to the observatory himself, and did not care for it enough to know whether or not it stayed open at night. In fact, the Reverend Gibforth seemed to think the German and his telescope were an extravagance Slough could well do without. So perhaps it was just contempt which George read in his face.

Zennor jumped out from behind the vicarage hedge with a 'boo!' and startled George half out of his wits. She put her arm through his, and he was, on the whole, more ashamed to admit he had never linked arms with a woman before than to be seen walking with Zennor Wootton.

People *did* stare. Men looked at Zennor, as George had seen gypsies look at a horse: appreciatively. Women looked at Zennor because her clothes were beautiful, though pretentiously Arcadian. (She looked as though she were dressed in character, to sit for a portrait: a Dresden shepherdess, perhaps. Her hems were too short. But at least she was wearing shoes. Wootton had finally come round to shoes.) No one stared at George, though he felt as if he were standing in the beam of the eye of God.

George was wearing knee-breeches himself, and a cutaway frock-coat, all in fawn corduroy which his sister Grace had said made him look like a retriever. His hair still curled long over his ears, brushing his collar. No one would mistake him for anything other than a schoolboy (or a retriever) and every time he glanced at Zennor he felt a peculiar resentment – not *of* her, exactly, but of not being old enough to contain her – like a bird confronted with a fish too big to swallow. It made his belly ache, somewhere low down.

Sir William Herschel did not choose to spend that night in his observatory, though the sound of an oboe, sweetly melancholy over the dankly misty gardens, testified to his being at home.

'He plays tonight,' said Caroline, his sister. She was dressed in a sleeveless coat and fingerless gloves against the cold of the comfortless observatory, and wore a large velvet beret. She was noting down the calibrations of the telescope, in a hard-bound notebook, her elaborate German handwriting like a cipher interspersed with pictograms. Her sharp Germanic voice, as spiked as her handwriting, was discouraging, but she did not, even after a day-long infestation of tourists, close the door against Zennor and George. 'If you be patient,' she said, still writing in her notebook, 'I shall the telescope turn towards constellation of Telescopus Herscheli. This constellation is named for my brother by his excellent colleague, the professor. You will ask also to see the planet Georgium Sidus, discovery of my brother. But this is not just now in the night sky easily to be seen.' She spoke with the flat intonation of a guide who has said the same thing a great many times.

'Please don't trouble,' said Zennor. 'We don't want to interrupt your work. If we could just look . . . If we might . . . whatever you yourself are looking at presently? Are you searching for comets?'

Caroline Herschel looked them both over: a dispassionate, scientific appraisal, and nodded her head curtly. 'You know of my work?'

'I know you've discovered two comets. Where are they now? Are they nearer or farther off? Which way were they travelling?'

The lady softened under the flattering interest of Zennor, whose desire to visit Slough had been as much inspired by the thought of a female astronomer as by the giant telescope. They were permitted, as a result, to sit on the little gilt chair at the lowest end of the massive brass cylinder and to bring their faces up close to the spy-hole, at the angle of a child putting its face up to be kissed. While Zennor looked, George held his hat and lowered his head, as if in prayer. He did not want to confront the acute, bird-like stare of the middle-aged Fräulein Herschel. He felt obliged to grip the back of Zennor's chair, to show that they were there together, not independently. He hoped, when it was his turn, that he would find something intelligent to say about the images contained within the telescope.

'Where do you sleep tonight?' asked Fräulein Herschel.

'In our cloaks,' said Zennor without removing her eye from the aperture. 'Small pain, to see this.'

'Your brother has no cloak.'

'Oh,' said Zennor. 'Doesn't he?'

Zennor was ravished that night. But only by the stars. What she saw, through the glass cornea of Herschel's lenses, were the terraces of heaven. Her Rousseauian education in the garden – she only discovered it now – had taught her the gestalt of beauty, the aesthetic genius at work in nature. The sky was one boundless garden, drifted with white flowers. The clarity of vision of the telescope, which excluded all peripheral distractions, reaped whole stooks of stars and tied them up in ribbons of night. While she looked she hardly breathed, she bit her lip, and tears crawled from the corners of her eyes, simply because she forgot to blink. The night beyond the telescope had no edge, because it was sky without horizons. It existed beyond the cosy, domestic hearth of the solar system's sun. It was so large, had such a dense weight of blackness, that it bore down on her like an edgeless body, the stars pricking her skin with rapture. Her hand, when it touched George's as they changed places, was icy cold.

George, by contrast, was sickened. The cacophony of silent darkness, the pelting rain of stars, the hideously large scale of space all made him want to shut his lids. Pressing his eye too hard against the aperture, his universe decayed within exploding red circles of pain. Where was man in all this dark? Where was earth? Looking up a telescope excluded the whole of planet earth from the picture. It became an irrelevance of microscopic smallness.

'Some of the stars is now gone,' said the lady astronomer, wishing to be informative. 'The light only to us arrive after many million of years. Star itself is maybe burn out and gone.'

George shuddered convulsively, locked for the night within an icy atrium of darkness in which the candles were one by one going out. He tasted dissolution, and at sixteen he did not greatly care for it.

'The wonders of the Lord are manifold,' he said politely; it was what his father or schoolmaster would have said in the same circumstances.

It is not possible to spend an entire night peering into a telescope. Fräulein Herschel, when her brother was not using the telescope, would spend perhaps two hours painstakingly progressing across the night sky, with specific discoveries in mind. But even she was ready to retire by midnight, and Zennor and George had long outstayed their welcome. They were ushered outside in a pleasant but brisk manner. 'Fräulein may sleep in kitchen. Sir may sleep in summer house,' she told them, declining any discussion by looking each directly in the forehead. 'I rise late. Please leave more early if you have the need. My pleasure is great in meeting you.' No smile accompanied this injunction to be gone by morning. Even so, such hospitality was remarkable in the wake of the hundred tourists who had already interrupted her work that week. Caroline Herschel had a sense of proportion born of studying the universe, and ten minutes after going to bed she had forgotten the pair entirely.

Mrs Baydon was not in the least surprised when Zennor did not appear for her weekly visit. The smell, which now permeated every one of the lower rooms, was, to Sophronia, so objectionable that she wondered anyone chose to call. She had tried everything to be rid of it – that mouldy, musty reek such as lingers under the cover of a bad well. The water from the pump was not always perfectly clear these days, and George had told her she must boil all the water meant for drinking or cooking. When his father told him he would have to fetch in the extra fuel to make this possible, George had said perhaps it did not matter so much, after all. But Sophronia had decided to follow his advice anyway. And so the range was continuously shrouded in clouds of steam, only adding to the damp atmosphere in the kitchen and scullery.

On the day George was due to return from Slough, Sophronia, scrubbing a patina of green mould off the pantry wall, found a host of snails behind the flour bin, encrusting the corner like barnacles on a ship's hull. As she gouged them off, plaster and powdered brick crumbled away like biscuit crumbs.

She was loth to tell her husband: he would see it as an appeal for funds, and he was, in any case, brooding about George's trip. To divert him, she had persuaded him to play cricket with the remaining children. Suppressing the girls' astonishment, with her 'mother-has-her-reasons' tilt of the eyebrows, she had sent them all out into the garden, and they were still there, despite the raw cold of the day. She could hear laughter, and that was not worth interrupting over the matter of a few snails and some crumbling plaster.

Out in the garden, the youngest Baydon, Sam, took a swing at the cricket ball and knocked it towards the pig sty. Since it was the first time he had managed a square hit, the fielders were taken unwawares. The bowler cheered and said, 'Well done, son! Well done! Fine stroke!' Susannah put a foot out to stop the ball, but it went straight between her legs. Her skirts and petticoats slowed it down enough for Sarah to get a hand to it, but she was wearing woollen mittens and it slipped straight through and struck the sty fence, where it found a gap just big enough to swallow it. The pig, granddaughter of Porcus-Porcus, and known as Hoxa, eyed it sidelong then turned, like a ship boxing its compass, and picked up the ball in her teeth.

Sarah rattled the pail at her. Grace pleaded with her, and Susannah beat her across the shoulders with a switch of dead lupins torn out of the garden bed, while her father restrained her bodily from falling into the sty. Sam meanwhile ran doggedly to and fro between the wickets, accumulating the highest score of the match.

Constable Gervase, who every Tuesday, with punctilious regularity, neatened his mother's grave, was drawn to the noise, as to any disorderliness. There was no longer any portion of fence around the vicarage garden low enough for a man to look over. High, deer-proof fencing had been put up (at horrific expense), and though it excluded the sunlight from certain of the beds, it enabled the vicar to maintain a garden. So the constable's voice came disembodied through the larchlap. 'It's happened, then,' he called lugubriously. 'Anarchy. Rabbling. Come to our parts.'

'What's happened, Gervase?' Baydon called back.

'Rioting. Pillaging. The Lord knows what. I'd hang 'em all, if I had the parish.'

'Rioting where, Gervase?' called Baydon, signalling the girls to come within reach, circling them with his arms. The pig's teeth rattled against the hard interior of the cricket ball. Little Sam ran to and fro, flapping his feet down flatly on the lawn.

'Up Wantage,' said Gervase, gratified to be first with the news. 'Drunkards and roisterers loose on the streets. That's what this talk fetches up to. Breakdown of the commonweal. Rape and plunder. An excuse is all. Fools and jades stirred up to't by incomers. That's what you get with incomers. Foreigners. French, I wouldn't wonder. We surrender us to 'em, we surely do. They drunkards surrender us into the hands of the French!' Gervase warmed to his subject, unaware that the garden beyond the fence was now empty. The vicar and his children were running for the house. The pig's grunting drowned out the noise of Baydon calling to his wife. 'Sophie! Sophie! Help me with the chaise! I have to get up to Wantage! Be quick, woman!'

Sophronia emerged from the kitchen holding a scrubbing brush, her head tied round with a cloth. 'What's the matter?'

'There's a bread riot in Wantage! The boy's coach will drive into the midst of it!' He was still holding the cricket bat and, as she helped him on with his coat, passed it absently from one hand to the other, throwing it into the chaise before they wheeled it out of the shed by its shafts. He allowed her to back the horse into the shafts; she was not so like to infect it with fright. He had taken off his pocket watch to play cricket and sent her to find out the right time from the kitchen clock.

It was only after he had left, whipping up the horse to an unprecedented canter, that she realised the kitchen clock had stopped. Another victim of the oddly damp atmosphere. It crossed Sophronia's mind, with a twinge of superstitious dread, that the house itself was sweating with anxiety, or weeping with preternatural foreboding.

CHAPTER ELEVEN

Riot

As the coach from Windsor to Oxford rolled into Wantage, it was struck by several stones, then by a pack of stick-wielding louts who took an irrational dislike to the coachwork.

The real trouble was up around the Corn Exchange and the Tatchells, where benches and handcarts were burning in the street. The bakery itself had been set alight, and there was a smell of burnt toast mingled with tar and the usual unwholesome stink of the tannery. A recruiting sergeant with a detachment of guard had found himself in the middle of the riot and, in an effort to quell it, had let his men begin a fist fight which now extended for the full length of Mill Street.

The coach driver, though slow-witted enough to drive into danger, kept his nerve sufficiently to put on speed and outrun the louts with the sticks. He did not try to pull up at the Alfred's Head, his official stopping place, but drove straight on, scattering soldiers and rioters, and plunging down Oxford Street. He might have pressed on into open countryside again, if he had not been confronted by a haywain barricading the road and on fire. With so little time to stop, the lead horses all but ran their noses into the fire, and their manes and nostrils were singed by a great flapping curtain of burning straw. They reared and staggered, and the horses behind cannoned backwards into the chains, crushing the footboard up against the coach like a fold of paper. The driver was struck across both thighs, and had to let go the reins and grab the roof-rail to keep from falling down between coach and horses. The netted luggage shifted and slid, breaking loose and threatening to crush his fingers, but his chief thoughts were for his legs and whether they were broken. The postillion, pitched off by the sudden halt, was nowhere to be seen, though his post-horn was rolling in the road, catching the red glimmer of the fire.

Zennor and George and the print-caster who was the only other passenger aboard, heard the luggage sliding overhead, the horses shrieking, the rattling of the chains, the swearing of the driver and the soughing roar of the fire. Wisps of burning straw blew past the window, some coming to rest on the paintwork, but the upholstery, which had broken free of its brackets, stood on end in the footwell, holding all three passengers in parenthesis between its cushions. The print-caster's case of die-cast font samples burst open against George's back, releasing a grapeshot of hard words. If he had not been holding Zennor to his chest, the case would have burst in her face. One of the doors would not open, but he managed to unlatch the other, and they slithered out, all three entangled, into a heap on the road. The printer got to his feet and ran off, only to be floored, at the end of the street, by a soldier using his musket for a club.

Zennor and George found themselves outside a barber's shop deserted, by all appearances. Brass bowls stood half full of soapy water, towels lay on the floor. As George pushed the door open a row of razor strops were set swinging like brown, panting tongues. The top corner panes of the window nearest the burning wain cracked in the heat: an ear-splitting noise. He crammed Zennor down between two chairs, for safety.

'Has it begun?' said Zennor. 'Is it now?'

'What?'

'The revolution! Is this the revolution? Is the King brought down?' She seemed excited, expectant, unafraid.

George had no way of knowing what was happening: an army mutiny? an uprising? a strike at the tannery? If indeed it was the beginning of Wootton's promised revolution (which he doubted), George cursed the republican who had chosen today to bring down the monarchy. 'As I see it, Wantage is not quite the hub of England,' he said.

'Perhaps this is happening all over. In every town! Everywhere!'

For a moment he was almost swept along by her eschatalogy, picturing the kingdom sinking into a sea of blood. 'Then I hope your macaroni is contented by it – to see Christian folk go up in flames!'

'What macaroni? What's a macaroni?'

'A fop who left his brains in Italy and his politics in the wardrobe!'

Outside the window, a soldier and a tanner moved slowly by, like dancers locked in some immodest Tudor dance, each with only one fist free, thumping it rhythmically into the other man's body. Even through the smeared window and the smoke George could tell that both of them were drunk.

'We should go and help,' said Zennor standing up.

He pulled her down again. 'He can hold his own, I think.' He had no illusions about his own chances in a fight: George was slight and quick on his feet, better built for flight than brawling. If any of the rioters fell into the shop he knew he would do his best to defend Zennor, but he was equally certain they would pelt and gut him and hang him up like a rabbit from the beams. He unhooked a steel razor which hung beside one of the strops, unable to put out of his mind the fact that he had never yet used one to shave, and might get his throat cut before he ever had cause. Right beside his head a dozen leeches suckered and squirmed over the glass of their jar, never-endingly thirsty for blood.

'I mean the revolution! We should go and help fight for the revolution!'

'Mistress Wootton, I'm a Whig,' he exclaimed, as if it were a species, a genus, an inherited trait.

Just then, someone with a stolen musket came down the street, smashing panes of glass with a systematic crack, crack, crash. George wrapped his legs around the shapeless muddle of Zennor's skirts to draw them out of sight of the door and, to restrain her from jumping up or calling out, wrapped one hand round her face, one arm around her body.

As the musket hit the barber's shop door, it swung open, and the looter lurched inside – a labourer wearing a leather apron and dragging a gunny sack. Looking around the shop, he picked up the barber's brass bowls one by one and dropped them into the sack, slinging the cold, soapy water out of them in wide catherine-wheels of spray which splashed the two hiding between the chairs.

Suddenly, another window-pane cracked in the heat from the burning cart, and a jolt of fright shook an enormous belch from the looter, who mistook it for a musket shot. Swinging the sack over his shoulder, he reeled off balance, up against the wall, banging his head. The sack swept a bottle of oil of wintergreen off a shelf, and it landed in the seat beside them; the ground-glass stopper slipped out, and the oil ran down cold on to Zennor's hair. Takings his bearings from the daylight, the looter made an approximate attempt on the door, bouncing off both door jambs before moving off into the burning miasma of drifting straw.

The downfall of this particular bread riot was a wagon of cider drawn up outside The Lamb. The rioters captured it and, after that, their grasp on strategy and righteous indignation and single-mindedness and all the other requisites of a successful revolt degenerated into drunken hysterics. Their hunger was no less real – indeed, it made the cider quicker to take effect – but it made them easier to quell and, subsequently, easier to discount as hooligans.

Samuel Baydon, running down the Tatchells, shouting his son's name, had no opinion just then on the fair price for bread. Forced by a military blockade to desert his carriage on Chain Hill and run the rest of the way, he thought only of getting his son safely off the Windsor stage.

He saw Curragh Coppler sitting astride the block-and-tackle of a warehouse winch, two storeys up, drinking cider, but he saw it like the image in a dream or through a coach window, unrelated to him. A tanner, maroon in hands and face, came at him with a reddling paddle, but Baydon struck him with the cricket bat he found he was still holding.

The coach had arrived an hour since – that much he had established – but what had become of it he could not glean from anyone who ran past him: man, woman or militia. It was not in the market square, nor was his son. It was not outside the Alfred's Head, which refused to open its doors to his knocking. He ran towards the church, hearing musket shots, though he could not tell how near or how far away. Turning into Mill Street, he would have gone on down the hill, but for a glare of fire to his right. He looked down Oxford Street and saw the Windsor stage burned down to its wheel rims, the charred hulk holding its shape like the ash in a grate before the poker shatters it. Burning straw had kindled a succession of fires along the street, but nothing had burned so completely as the Windsor stage.

Baydon picked up from the cobbles the bent and dented post-horn and was standing – a cricket bat in one hand, horn in the other – quite still, regarding the skeleton of the burned coach, when his son and Zennor Wootton came out of the barber's shop directly alongside him.

He looked at them for a long time without speaking. He did not speak much all the way home.

First there was a need to inform the coaching company that no one had died as a result of the incident. This, and the sudden, unexpected meeting with his father, did not give George or Zennor the opportunity to concoct a lie; it soon became obvious that they had been together for longer than a day. George was not, in any case, accustomed to lying. He was appalled at what his father must be thinking.

Wrath occupied the empty seats in the carriage, as it struggled up Chain Hill and over the Ridgeway. But his father did not speak. George fixed his eyes on the cricket bat and coach-horn rolling to and fro on the seat opposite, and could not bring himself either to excuse himself or explain. He could not presently think of any good excuse. He would sooner have died of shame than blame the excursion on Zennor, a woman.

Zennor too kept silent. Baydon's silence silenced them all, so charged was it with anger. It overhung the carriage like a corniche of snow awaiting a gunshot to bring it down in an avalanche that would swallow them all up.

He drove directly to Hatch House. The gates to the main drive were shut and he had to get down to open them. George tried to atone by leaping out and opening the gates for his father. Their hands collided over the latch.

Baydon's grip closed around his son's wrist and pulled him close so sharply that the boy's forehead struck him in the face. 'Did you sully her, boy?' The whisper was like a jet of compressed steam.

'*No!*'

'Have you before?'

'*No!*'

Robin Wootton heard the carriage on the drive, and came out smiling, unstartled at seeing them together, since Zennor had told him she was staying at the parsonage overnight. Alba, too, came to the door, disappointed that her time alone with Robin was over. They had heard nothing about the riot.

As Baydon opened the carriage door for Zennor, eyes over-wide with pent-up anger, he said, 'Did you wish, mistress, to drive your guardian quite mad with worry?'

She tipped up her chin and tossed her hair, in an attempt at devil-may-care. 'Oh, he won't give a fig. No harm came of it.'

She was right, too.

George did not need to blame the trip on Zennor: she instantly volunteered, 'I asked George to take me to see Herschel's telescope.'

After a moment's startled silence, Wootton clapped his hands in applause. 'What ingenuity! What spirit, egad! What enterprise!'

Told of the riot, the loss of the coach, the bullets flying in Wantage streets, he shared Zennor's conclusion that, since no one had been hurt, no real harm had been done. No lasting harm. Sniffing the air, he smelled wintergreen and said that she 'smelled of doctors', expressing the hope she had not resorted to medical science, knowing his views on it. Assured she had not, he repeated, 'No lasting harm, then, eh?'

Samuel Baydon clenched shut his eyes and his brows knitted so tight that his whole face changed shape. He leaned forward from the waist, and George thought he was perhaps going to vomit, then and there, on the octagonal carpet of the octagonal morning room. 'If one of my children,' he whispered, still leaning forwards at this precarious angle, the fingers of one hand tapping his chest to eject the words choking him. 'If any one of my children were in danger, I –'

His breath exhausted itself, and he never finished expressing the thoughts which had gone through his head while he stood looking at that coach, that skeleton of ash clasping a dead horse in its charcoal shafts. This was his patron, after all, and were it not for Wootton's casual unorthodoxy the children's excursion to Slough could have plunged both families into scandal.

'Ah, but that's because you look on your children as mere *possessions*, Samuel,' Wootton assured him. 'Myself, I never talk of "mine", or "my children". I never could feel a right of ownership over a fellow being.'

Baydon did not argue. He ran his hands over his bare head and took one step back. 'I am assured that no . . . flirtatiousness passed between our . . . the boy and girl,' he said, like a man picking his way over the hot ruins of a burned-out stagecoach, 'although I shall of course be at pains to impress upon my son his utterly' – it burst out of him like a sneeze – '*inappropriate* behaviour. Beyond that I can only extend my regrets at the disturbance to your household, and thank God Almighty that . . . no real harm came of it.'

He meant to, as well. He meant to flog out of George every mote of adolescent admiration for Zennor Wootton, like the dust out of a carpet – to make him vow, out of purest terror, never, never, never to see the girl alone or in secret again. He remembered from his own youth the obduracy of infatuation, and steeled himself for the strife.

He meant to show no sentimental pity when, crop in hand, he summoned George to his study next day. 'I wish to make this one thing very plain, my boy: you will see no more of Zennor Wootton.'

But the boy shook his head with such ear-flapping, neck-cracking, pink-cheeked urgency that Baydon lost his momentum. 'Saints preserve me, Father!' George said, his hazel eyes round with unfeigned strength of feeling. 'She's a mad woman, that one. Root and branch! A madwoman! I always thought so.'

The riding crop clattered to the study floor as Samuel Baydon caught hold of his boy in his arms and held him so tightly that neither of them could draw breath. 'Christ spare us! Think on it! You might have had to marry the wench!'

★

Zennor Wootton was not so much as reprimanded for her adventure. The enterprise of it twinkled brighter and brighter in Wootton's imagination, until he was prepared to recount it at dinner: proof of the daring and thirst for knowledge which he had inculcated in his two protégées.

Zennor was gratified – relieved, too – that the adventure had not blackened her in Wootton's good opinion. But she could not suppress a slight jealousy of George, a slight hankering after the kind of parental care which fretted and raged and stamped and struggled wordlessly with the possibility of loss.

When Robin asked her, in front of his dining companions, her impressions of Herschel's telescope, she baffled them by saying that she had found Caroline Herschel the most marvellous revelation. When pressed to describe what she had seen in the night sky over Slough, she found herself at a loss for words, looking from guest to guest in the hope that they would read it in her face. After a reproachful look from Robin, the subject was dropped in favour of other topics.

Later, after she had retired to bed, Zennor suddenly thought of a way of describing what she had felt. She remembered a passage in Marlowe's *Tamburlaine* which had provoked in her much the same feelings as Herschel's window on infinity. Next morning she ran over the hill to borrow the copy of the book, for she had read it with Sophronia Baydon at the kitchen table.

Sophronia went and fetched the book and gave it to Zennor, telling her she might keep it. But to Zennor's dismay Sophronia said that it was time their weekly reading sessions came to an end. Zennor postponed her sadness, still excited by the prospect of showing the passage to Robin – of sharing the words with him which had the same effect on her as the starry universe funnelling in at her eye.

She read it aloud, standing in front of him in the library, head erect, the book at arm's length in front of her.

> Now walk the angels on the walls of heaven,
> As sentinels to warn th'immortal souls
> To entertain divine Zenocrate:
> The cherubins and holy seraphins,
> That sing and play before the King of Kings,
> Use all their voices and their instruments
> To entertain divine Zenocrate:
> And in this sweet and curious harmony,
> The god that tunes this music to our souls

Holds out his hand in highest majesty
To entertain divine Zenocrate.
Then let some holy trance convey my thoughts
Up to the palace of th'empyreal heaven,
That this my life may be as short to me
As are the days of sweet Zenocrate.'

He said, 'I don't know it. I am not sure I greatly trust poetry myself. A man of honest passions can oft-times find poetry – I don't know . . . *contrived*.'

Contrived. She could see he was telling the truth; the lines did not move, did not so much as touch him. Zennor drew the book against her stomach, the covers tight closed. It was as if she had shown him her likeness in a mirror and he had breathed on it. She could not make sense of her feelings. Just at the moment, she wanted to run to Mrs Baydon now, this minute, and ask her how it could happen, how beauty could fail to be beautiful. But that was no longer possible.

'George Baydon said the universe makes us small,' she said, for no better reason than that the conversation needed to be brought to a close. 'He said he felt lost.'

'And you, what do you think?' he said, reading through a letter from a Frenchman in London whom he had set to work on a translation of Rousseau's last work.

'I think it's a reason to . . .' she began.

'*Sacré*! Maurice says he can send me the first fifty pages of *Confessions* next week. Isn't that *très excéllent*? . . . A reason?'

'To live like a signal flare,' she said, already sorry she had started the sentence.

But Wootton liked that. He liked it enough to quote at dinner parties – 'like a signal fire, as one of my wards expressed it. We must live like signal fires in the dark void of space.'

Such remarks, in the opinion of Alba Wootton, were another very good reason to snuff out Zennor, and the sooner the better.

CHAPTER TWELVE

Notes

'Some people – some people of *this parish* – some people known to me and to this congregation *were there*,' said Baydon, leaning forward over the pulpit rail to be sure of being heard. 'And let those people know that *they were seen*!'

The congregation quailed, as they were required to quail, a few (including Curragh Coppler) from personal shame. Mrs Coppler elbowed her husband sharply in the ribs but did not incriminate him by turning her head.

'I could, you know, invoke the Black Act and remove iniquity from our midst.'

Mrs Murphy gave an audible gasp, and rolled in her seat, shunting her whole weight against her husband in a paroxysm of fright. Transportation and obloquy loomed up before her.

'But I am persuaded by the merciful example of my Saviour to close my eyes – this once – to their crime. Let mercy bear the fruit of repentance! I will not blink twice.'

In fact it was Mrs Baydon who had prevailed on Samuel not to invoke the Black Act against parishioners who had taken part in the bread riot. She had taken it upon herself to educate him in the iniquitous price of bread relative to the income of a reddleman or a seamstress. He had simply asked her for one of her bread-and-butter confits, and she had served him up a pair of Sam's boots and a muffler (mercifully uncooked) in the confit bowl. When the children boggled at the dish, and Sam asked why his shoes had come to table, Sophronia told him it was to demonstrate to them (the children) what some people in the world must go without in order to eat bread. She had said it to the children, but of course it had been meant for him, and he was not in a position, at the dining-table, to enter into an argument about morality-in-the-face-of-want.

He contented himself now with preaching a sermon about the widow's last mite. Then he concluded his homily, clumsily and with gruff embarrassment, by saying, 'I should earnestly thank God for acquainting me with any one here who can rid a house of rats. The parsonage is at present overrun.'

That had been Sophronia's idea, too. She said that Curragh Coppler would feel obliged to do the job free of charge.

Once again, she was correct.

It was one of Zennor's duties, from the very first, to go down to the village for the post. Everyone knew it. In fair weather or foul, she could be seen picking her way along the footpath, over the plank bridge and home again. It was a pleasant enough walk in the late spring, when the bluebells made a knee-deep flood of blue and the hollow hedge was full of green growth and urgent bird song, and there were fish in the brook. Even Alba was tempted out of doors by such weather, and decided to walk with her. There was every likelihood that Robin's fifty pages had come from the translator, and she fancied delivering them to him herself rather than letting Zennor steal the happy moment.

The pages had come; Alba laid proprietorial hands on the packet. So, too, had a letter for Zennor, which Zennor no sooner saw then she screwed into a ball, without even opening the envelope.

'Who wrote to you?' asked Alba in astonishment.

'No one. It's nothing,' said Zennor, and turning sharply set off for home again, taking quick, long strides. Alba had to run to catch her up.

'Someone wrote to you. I saw. Show me! I'll tell Robin!' Zennor ignored her and walked on. So Alba (who was wearing gloves) picked a spray of nettles and once again ran to close the gap between them. From behind, she brushed the nettles across the back of Zennor's ungloved hand, so that she started and the screw of paper fell to the ground. Alba snatched it up. 'It's from a man! You're receiving love letters from a man!'

The discovery was so unexpected that the full implications were slow to dawn on Alba: the advantage to her, the leverage it gave her over a rival. She was simply intrigued – and a little jealous – that someone should be paying court to Zennor and not to her. She set Robin's parcel down on the rail of the footbridge and ripped open the envelope.

'If you will have it, Miss Long-Nose,' said Zennor, 'Oliver Baydon writes to me. The vicar's brother. From Canada. I don't know why. I did not ask him to. I don't encourage him. I never wrote back. But every month or thereabouts a letter comes from Canada. He is on campaign there. For me, if you care to know, I hope he stays there and never comes back. I never *asked* him to write to me.'

Alba had by now smoothed out the unread letter against the bridge rail. 'This is not from Canada.'

Zennor was sufficiently surprised to stop at the bridge's end and come back, looking from the letter to Alba for signs of mischief. It was true; the letter did not come from Canada, but from the Liverpool docks.

Alba was so excited and surprised by its existence that she was slow to pick the words off the single sheet of paper; they jumped about, incoherent. In any case, the handwritten word always gave her difficulty. Words like 'dear' and 'longing' and 'heartfelt' and 'desire' sprang out at her like wasps, stinging her with vague, shapeless, erotic fancies. 'He says he's come back,' she deciphered. 'He's posted to the Encampment. Your lover's come back here. Canada, phoo!'

Zennor made a grab at the letter, but Alba snatched it to her, clenched it to her chest with both immaculate gloved hands.

'He's not my lover. I don't even like him. He has no right to address me secretly. Did I ask him to?'

'Did you ask him not to?'

'A man can write on a wall. Is the wall defamed?'

But Alba's imagination had at last begun to work. She was holding her certificate of safe passage, her passport to marriage with Robin. The gods had delivered Robin into her arms, by this simple expedient of a love letter. It did not occur to her to believe Zennor's protestations. Who, after all, would remain indifferent to a man who wrote such things as Oliver Baydon had written? 'I shall show Robin. He can decide,' she said.

Zennor lunged again at the paper. Repeatedly she tried to snatch it, but Alba only backed away across the bridge, taunting her with it, holding it up high like a crumpled handkerchief. Then she lifted up her overskirts and made a great show of putting the letter in one of her linen pockets.

'Alba. Please. Give it up. I can tell Robin: I never gave that wretch a word or a look.' But Zennor knew, better than Alba, the kind of sickly sweet hyperbole of which Oliver Baydon's letters were concocted, the way in which they assumed an intimacy, referred to things unspoken, harkened back to promises never made. Their implicit untruths had always terrified her, ever since the first one arrived from Canada and she was only twelve. Now this latest scared her even more, for it threatened not only the return of her persecutor but the loss of home and future and reputation, for no crime she had ever committed.

Alba could not possibly imagine the kind of temper Oliver Baydon had provoked. Zennor turned, as if determined to go, and when she considered Alba off her guard, ran back across the bridge.

She did not try for the letter but went for the whole girl, colliding with her and carrying her bodily over the rail of the bridge. They fell ten feet into the water, which was at its deepest and coldest, full of meltwater and upland rain. Alba went in on her back, Zennor on top of her. No sooner did Zennor's knees and knuckles graze the chalkstone bed than she broke free and stood up, wading towards the shore. But Alba, who had been taken unawares, and thought she was drowning, remained sitting on the riverbed, screaming, the neck-deep water piling her pale hair the wrong way over her head, hands groping for a hold on the pushy, unruly water. She screamed and screamed, until she realised that no help would come of it, then scrambled towards the shore, panting and gasping with cold and indignation. The weight of her sodden clothes tripped her twice, so that she sat down again in the water. Not until she had crawled out on to the bank did she think to unearth the letter from her pocket.

The envelope came out intact, but with only a smear of blue where the address had been. When she tried to draw out the letter inside, it disintegrated into pinch-sized pieces, the words reduced to plucked grapestalks of running ink.

Zennor had gone too far now, thought Alba. She would tell Robin anyway that Zennor had pushed her in the river (which just then seemed a far worse crime than having a secret lover). She would tell him about the letter, too, even if she did not have the evidence any more. He would believe her – why would she make up such a thing? Zennor would be gone by the end of the week, married to the first chimney sweep or swineherd who would have her. The prospect warmed Alba all the way home.

She was warmed, too, to find that Robin had been watching out for her with eager anxiety – he came running down the drive. Somehow she seemed to have reached home first; perhaps Zennor was hiding herself from the wrath to come. Alba's outer dress had largely dried, and though her hair was a fist-sized knot halfway down her back, and her white gloves were stained with duckweed, it was not immediately obvious she had been swimming. Not to Robin, in any event.

'Where is it? Where? Where is it?' He was wearing his outdoor jacket and round-hat, which increased the childlike ingenuousness of his delicate face. Hermes, thought Alba: Hermes was the god he personified. He had purposely dressed with the intention of walking the estate while he read as much of Rousseau's *Confessions of a Savoyard Priest* as had been expressed in English for his sole benefit. The packet.

'Oh, Jesus Judas Christ,' said Alba. 'The packet. It's in the river.'

He did not hit her hard – not by his own reckoning – but she was reduced to such helpless stupidity by the blow that he would have struck her again if Zennor had not intervened.

'It wasn't her fault!' she said, appearing from nowhere to interpose her body between Robin and Alba. 'The bridge rail broke. It wasn't her fault, I swear it! We both fell.'

'She pushed me in,' mewed Alba, her nose bubbling with blood and tears. 'Look at me! Zennor pushed me in the river!'

'*And did you get out – and leave my book?*' yelled Robin, pushing against Zennor's restraining hands, reaching to slap Alba, round her. '*And forgot it? And come home without any thought of it? A handwritten copy? An irreplaceable manuscript?*'

'Zennor had a letter! Zennor has a lover!' squealed Alba. But Robin was roaring too loud with exasperation, deafening himself to her puny excuses. She made excuses, while his precious fifty pages lay steeping in the brook! He took off down the drive, cursing Alba for her incomprehensible callousness, her bubble-headed carelessness, her cruelty.

While Alba howled, Zennor held her close, soothed and shushed her, like a little child, stroking her dirty hair, holding her own petticoats to the girl's bleeding nose. 'I'll put it to rights, I promise. I'll make things right with him for you.' Alba tried fitfully to push her away, but Zennor held her too tightly, soothing, whispering. 'Listen! You can have him! Hoo! Do you think I want to marry a man with fists? Have him! Marry him! I'd rather live single. . . . Only don't have him turn me out. Not now. Not yet. Not your little Zennor, eh? Not until you are married. Think! When you're married, I can be your friend still. I shall make things right between you. I promise. Only don't tell him about those foolish letters.'

It was Alba's turn to honk, 'Huh!' down her swelling nose. She did not believe for one moment Zennor's indifference to her soldier beau. But to be left alone with Robin – with him hating her, and no words in her head to make him understand. How could she make him see that a secret lover was more important than a book, that love was more important than fifty pages, that *she* herself was more . . .

When Robin came back from the brook, the sodden remnants of Rousseau's *Confessions* cradled against his chest, he could not bring himself to speak to Alba. For over a week, she crept around him as though he were a phial of phosphor which at the creaking of a floorboard might crack and blind her with incandescent fire. The house, meanwhile, was festooned with a bunting of peeled-apart pages hanging over every chair-back and banister. It was Zennor who undertook to salvage the manuscript, and thanks to the nature of the French translator's ink she was able to redeem pages ten to forty in near legible form. The rest were lost. (She only wished the river could have swept away the existence of Oliver Baydon, the threat of more letters.)

When Zennor delivered the crispy sheets of brittle paper to Robin one morning at breakfast he looked at her with such tender gratitude that Alba dropped her fork. Seeing that look, she lost all faith in Zennor's promises. Robin was bound to choose for his wife this resourceful, cunning, shiny-haired minx. 'She pushed me in the river,' Alba blurted out, forgetting her mouth was full of scrambled eggs.

'*And jumped in herself, too?*' Wootton came back at her down the table. He had just come to terms, in his own mind, with Zennor's version of an accident – an unforeseen collapse of the old footbrige; had just begun to feel a twinge of guilt at hitting a young woman in the face. Now here she was trying to capitalise on the disaster by telling lies about Zennor! Always one eye on her marriage portion, that was Alba; always panting after him like a dog. Though Wootton said nothing so specific, Alba could read in his eyes that he had made up his mind against her, then and there.

'Nonsense,' Zennor told her. 'Nonsense. You read too much into him. He's distempered. He's choleric. He's out of humour.' She rested a tentative hand on Alba's back as the girl lay on her bed sobbing distractedly.

'No! No! No! He hates me! He's right to! I'm good for nothing! What am I good for? You, you're Sophie and Emile rolled in one. Me, I can't be anyone but me. I shall never please, if I live to be a hundred!'

'At a hundred, no one pleases,' said Zennor absently. At some level she was intrigued and appalled that Alba could revert so quickly to unqualified adoration of a man who had hit her in the face, who shut his ears to her, who thought such unjust ill of her. But since she, Zennor, had done everything in her power to keep the precise truth from Robin, she could hardly hold the man to blame for his ignorance, she supposed.

And if she were to keep a roof over her head Zennor needed to win Alba back to her side. If Wootton made his choice of wife now, and chose Zennor, Alba would never keep quiet about the letters. 'Perhaps what we need to do is to make you shine in his eyes,' she suggested, stroking one of Alba's small, delicate hands. 'To make you . . . yes. Shine.'

It had been suggested to Robin, over dinner one night, that the girls should play an instrument. That is to say, Constable Gervase had bluntly suggested they play something to entertain the gentlemen, and, being told they could not, puffed out his cheeks in astonishment, protesting, 'A woman's nor use nor ornament without she can knock out a tune!'

And Robin had laughed indulgently, and said he had been 'saving the project for the apt time in their spiritual development'.

One project on which Jean-Jacques Rousseau exerted himself, before turning to education, was a system of musical notation. It did not conform to any of the classical disciplines, and had met with scorn and indifference wherever he had taken it. But at Hatch House that spring Robin Wootton determined to remedy the injustice. He would teach the girls to play according to Rousseau's theories. That is to say, he would have them study the system and pick it up for themselves. He was not musical himself (though his soul, of course, responded ecstatically to music). No one had had soul enough to teach him a solfa.

That spring, Zennor in turn determined that Alba should learn to play better than she — should outshine her, and so impress both Robin and Robin's dinner guests.

The only drawback to this plan proved to be the impenetrable difficulty of Rousseau's system. She read and reread, but she could not come to grips with it. Wootton had had the text translated (as he had every work of Rousseau's, right up to the *Confessions*), but the translation was literal, crude, and had become disconnected from the examples which originally punctuated the text. Now the examples were all bundled together at the end, the original order forgotten, ignored. The two girls stared at the pages till their eyes were red, but could no more play music at the end than read Chinese.

'I'm a dunce! I'm a donkey!' wailed Alba self-pityingly. 'If Robin would only help us to understand!'

'He may not understand, himself,' said Zennor, preoccupied. 'I know Mrs Baydon plays,' she added thoughtfully.

So, soon after, Alba took Zennor's path over the hill to the vicarage, visiting Sophronia Baydon not weekly but daily, to learn the spinet. Zennor did not go along, sensing that (though she did not know why) she was no longer welcome to call there. She envied Alba, with a keen hankering envy, but more for the warmth of Sophronia's parlour than the mystery of music. She wrote a note to Sophronia, saying that it was more urgent for Alba to master a few tunes by heart than for her to wrestle with music theory; and she enclosed some of Rousseau's examples.

Sophronia Baydon took one look at the cipher, entitled *Le Rossignol*, turned it upside down, looked overleaf, said 'Humph,' then slipped it under the spinet lid for safe keeping. 'Something French, then. Let me consider,' she said to the pale creature perched like a wood-pigeon on the edge of her piano stool. '"On the Bridge at Avignon." That should serve for the soup course. . . . I only wish this spinet would hold its tune these days. It's the damp, you know.'

At the next party, Alba would be able to play – nothing very clever for a seventeen-year-old young lady in an aristocratic house, but well enough to widen Robin's blue eyes. Zennor, on the other hand, would have to admit she could not play, had not mastered the genius's brilliant system of music. Such a humiliation should be enough to incline Robin's face away from her and towards Alba for once.

But for Alba the price seemed high. To achieve this one small triumph she must traipse daily over the hill, and endure the peculiar mouldering stink of the vicarage – what was it about the place? – while Zennor stayed home inside Hatch House, alone with Robin.

'What's the matter, dear?' asked Sophronia, as Alba played a discordant jangle at the keyboard.

'She wants to be there alone with him! She did this to have me out of the way!' she said aloud, though not to anyone present. Then she looked at Sophronia, her cheeks hotly pink in front of her ears. 'Could you kindly oblige me with a sheet of paper, Mrs Baydon? I have a need to write a letter.'

CHAPTER THIRTEEN

Manoeuvres

In 1792, the 66th Berkshire Regiment of Foot were among the seven thousand men who pitched camp at Wickham Bushes, Easthampstead. That seven thousand does not include the hundreds more civilian spectators who travelled there to witness the stirring sight of so many red coats massed under an English sky. The aggression of the French was an indistinct worry for all but the politicians and generals, and the prospect of the world's first peacetime manoeuvres was greeted with the same holiday enthusiasm as a Christmas goose fair.

No one was more glad of the event than Oliver Baydon, fetched home from Canada to rattle his sabre at the French. Since learning of his regiment's return to Berkshire he had invested more time on strategic planning than any general at the War Office.

He hated the army. Without sufficient rank to turn things to his advantage, he found his existence reduced to bestial brutality, boredom and the possiblity of sudden death. Canada he liked. He had plans for Canada, preferably for making large tracts of it his own. But army service would never bring him that. He therefore applied himself to a private, long-term project, much as a convict sets about carving his indentity on a dungeon wall. Patience, though it had never been a strength of his, was forced on him by the prospect of years in foreign provinces. The only women to whom he had access were whores and officers' wives, so he was not often distracted from his plan, not tempted to let it go, even when it bored him catatonically.

The only crucial factor outside his power to bring about, was a return to England before Robin Wootton made his marriage choice. As the years bled by, as thickly black to Oliver as Canadian troop molasses, he feared that he had missed his chance: that Wootton must have chosen by now. But regular correspondence with his brother brought no news of a marriage, even though the girls must have reached – what? seventeen? eighteen? Oliver sometimes wondered if Wootton were enjoying the delights of a triple ménage too much to marry; such daring public lechery inspired more admiration than jealousy. And if it delayed Wootton's marriage choice until Oliver could get back to England, all well and good. All he needed was a chance to convince Zennor she was in love with him: Wootton was so completely self-absorbed that he would not care what became of his superfluous ward, so long as he was left in peace and quiet with his 'ideal Rousseauian wife'.

The very first time he had heard tell of this bizarre experiment in wiving Oliver had formed the intention of securing Wootton's cast-off, and thereby tapping into the vast Wootton fortune. Robin Wootton's promised dowry was not, in itself, worth such years of effort, but there were others in the Wootton family who would pay much more to suppress scandal. If he applied himself, with all his best endeavours, Oliver would be able to wedge his spigot so deep into the Wootton barrel as to keep the money flowing his way in perpetuity.

Once he had suceeded in marrying the girl in secret he would offer to remove both the girl and her socially sensational revelations to a safe distance – Canada – so long as he was furnished with the means to live in comfort there.

Whether or not Zennor *had* any sensational revelations to make about Hatch House, Oliver neither knew nor cared; he could soon enough invent some so scurrilous that the earl would pay thousands to keep them out of the papers. He had tried to elicit some scurrilous gossip from the child each time he wrote to her, but she had never actually written back. So perhaps, after all, she had acquired the tedious respectability of her tedious betters. It made no difference. What mattered was to land the fish, to make his killing.

He had fixed on Zennor not by taste – he could take pleasure in almost any breed and colour of female. But he had taken the gamble that Wootton would opt for the blonde – the one who promised to fit the Berkshire country mould: refined, effete, decorous. There was too much of the mongrel about Zennor: Wootton would surely never choose her. Even so, that, more than anything else, had given Oliver Baydon pause during the long cold of Canadian nights and the gut-churning voyage back to England. Had he targetted the right 'sister'? Had he let his own predilection for bonny, boisterous, big-bottomed women make him favour the wrong girl? Would he have had any replies to his letters if he had sent them to the blonde instead? He comforted himself that the choice had in fact been made for him. Zennor was the only one he *could* write to. It was Zennor who fetched the post up from the village. Always Zennor. Everyone in the locality knew that. It was only possible to write, undetected, to Zennor. But why had she not written back?

Once Oliver woke with a start, the thought rising like a bubble through his blood: what if Zennor were taken ill, or found out, or supplanted in her daily trips to the Post Inn? What if his letters had already fallen into the wrong hands? From that day forward he had phrased his letters in such a way that they implied the wooing had been all hers – a long-term adoration of the kind men can do nothing to deter.

It was nerve-racking, but exhilarating, posting letters into a void, never knowing whether they arrived, how they were received, what look they brought to the reader's face – even how that face looked now that it had pushed through the briars of adolescence into womanhood. But Oliver possessed the vast, egotistical self-confidence of a successful philanderer. Sexual conquest came easily to him. Young women like Zennor were all too ready to believe that a distant admirer loved them to the point of madness. All he needed was for circumstances to conspire once or twice in his favour.

Restored to Berkshire, encamped at Wickham Bushes and stretched out on an army cot among the gargling snores of stinking men, it pleased him to imagine Zennor Wootton lying in her bed, wishing wistfully for her handsome soldier-beau, one hand between her thighs . . .

So when he received a letter – an actual letter, written in a woman's badly formed hand – it was minutes before he could bring himself to open it. His hands shook. His heart thumped. He swore at this peculiarly self-inflicted ordeal.

'Belovied Oliver, Come to me at the tempel ruin, sweet hart. Come at noon on FriDay 3 October. I long for your tuch. Do not rite again. Your own Z.'

The nib oozed a blot as she wrote the letter Z; Alba thought that very fitting, since Zennor was indeed to be blotted out by the simple expedient of this one forged love letter. Alba had had to ask Mrs Baydon the spelling of 'ruin', and thanked her politely for providing it, keeping her arm tightly curved round her letter as she wrote, like a defensive wall.

'You are welcome, my dear. In these days, a girl must hope to get by without ever needing the word,' Sophronia had said, with one of her creased, sidelong smiles.

But Alba understood jokes no better than she understood Rousseau's musical notation. Jokes had not been included in her life's curriculum.

'I hear the Reverend's brother is come home,' Alba said, in order to change the subject. She had quite forgotten how she knew this.

'Fancy your knowing that,' said Sophronia non-committally.

'I expect the Reverend will be happy to see him.'

'Happier than anyone,' said Sophronia, with greater conviction. 'Now . . . To Avignon.'

Alba allowed a safe margin of time for the letter to reach Oliver Baydon, for she had no idea how long it would take to find him among seven thousand men, in an encampment of tents. Would it find him at all? Would a sergeant major open it and sneer, or a cavalry horse trample it into the mud? The posting of that letter carried Alba's heart and happiness with it, and she knew nothing would restore them to her until the plot had run its course. Now all that remained was to send Zennor to the ruin at the appointed time and bring Robin – jump – upon the damning scene: Zennor with her soldier lover. If her heart had been at home, it would have quailed from the consequences – might even have pitied Zennor. But her heart was on its way to Wickham Bushes, care of 66th Berkshire Regiment of Foot, and she went about her machinations almost empty of feelings.

Whatever Sophronia Baydon's feelings were about the return of Oliver Baydon, she concealed them well. She said nothing to her husband of what Alba had said, hoping the girl was in some way mistaken. But sure enough, a couple of days after the music lesson, Samuel received a letter from Oliver saying that he was posted to the encampment, and would be taking part in the manoeuvres.

Still Sophronia did not mention that Alba knew this already. But it puzzled her how or why word had reached Hatch House *before* the vicarage. She hoped Oliver was not trying to touch Robin Wootton for money, or to buy his discharge from the army. She liked Oliver better as a soldier; it meant that someone other than Samuel was responsible for his behaviour.

Of course, Samuel was pleased. He tried to conceal it, with talk of bad pennies and prodigals, but the thought of Oliver coming home gave him real joy. All along, the idea of his little brother being billeted in the farthest-flung British colonies had filled Samuel with horror. He had even made enquiry – casually, and with feigned disapproval of the practice – as to how much it cost to buy a man out of the army. And he had investigated the possibility of borrowing the money, with his stipend as surety. But at the back of his mind he feared he would be too late: Oliver would be killed – in a foreign place, among people he despi . . . of a different temperament; without benefit of good chirurgy or sympathetic clergy. And, for all his doubts concerning Oliver's probity, he found the idea heartbreaking.

So when Oliver's regiment bivouacked for the manoeuvres not ten miles from Winding Hatch, Samuel was hard put to hide his delight. He informed the family that he thought it 'important to witness the nation's preparedness to defend itself in the face of war'. Privately, he told Sophronia that he thought it would calm any fears in the younger children about French invaders.

'Yes, and on top of that it will be agreeable to see your brother Oliver again,' said Sophronia, smiling down at her needlework.

'You ladies. You always reduce the grand scale to the small particular,' said Samuel, carefully cutting out the newspaper item concerning the army manoeuvres, his jaws working in time with the scissor blades. 'We shall drive over on the Friday, I think. Do you suppose the children remember their uncle?'

'He is memorable,' said Sophronia, still thinking in terms of bad pennies.

When Robin Wootton read in the papers of the army manoeuvres planned at Wickham Bushes he saw it only as an occasion for generalised political comment.

'War is born of the vices of society,' he said from behind the newspaper. 'It favours private interests. Man is naturally peaceful – he only becomes fierce through habit and experience.' He certainly had no wish to go to see seven thousand men pretend to join in battle so as to perfect the dubious art of war. 'There is no war between men; only war between states,' he said, quoting as usual.

Zennor hankered after the grandeur of the spectacle – 'like a scene from *Tamburlaine*', she said – but was not so reckless as to argue with Robin once he had voiced his opposition.

'When are these manoeuvres?' asked Alba, yawning and reclining languidly, to show her indifference.

'Tomorrow and the day following,' said Zennor. 'Friday, Saturday.'

Alba yawned again, in a rictus of nerves. What a day to have chosen! Should she have made the assignation another day, another place? How would Oliver ever be able to get away? She had foreseen a difficulty in getting Zennor to the ruin at the appointed time, but not that Oliver might be prevented from getting there at all. Were intrigues always so difficult to arrange? One thing at a time. She must think of only one problem for now. The ruin. How could Zennor be made to go to the ruin?

Alba's yawn turned to a hiccup which almost ruptured her diaphragm, as she suddenly glimpsed the gaping flaw in her plan, her catastrophic oversight.

The ruin had not been built when Oliver Baydon went away. He would not know where to go.

Oliver was cock-a-hoop. Zennor had no notion of what she was asking, by suggesting a rendezvous so far from the camp: he would have to abscond for the day. But by fixing the assignation for the day of the manoeuvres – clever girl! – she had at least given him the means of obliging her.

All passes and tickets-of-leave were cancelled; there was not a man permitted to leave the Easthampstead marshalling grounds. But the truth was that the chaos and confusion of the manoeuvere would be so great that no one would miss a single trooper gone missing. What was one man out of seven thousand? He could be gone all day.

The mention of 'the ruin' had caused him no puzzlement at all. His brother (determined to 'keep dear England green' in Oliver's imagination) had written him interminable letters. He was forever describing the countryside to him, Wootton's hare-brained schemes, the propagation of common weeds in the flower-beds of Hatch House . . . And since the ruin dominated Samuel's view from his study it featured often in the letters he wrote at his desk.

'. . . The good Lord has seen fit, in His great mercy, to clothe the macaroni's monstrous ruin in ivy. It is scarce visible at the height of summer.'

Oliver could picture it. He could picture Zennor waiting within it, and the pleasurable task of persuading her towards an elopement. Even allowing for the subtlest, most cautious groundwork, he had hopes of marrying her by Christmas.

He had no friends within the regiment. The other troopers mistrusted his flamboyant, fashionable manners, and the officers despised his poverty. So he told no one of his plan to slip away during the manoeuvres. He could easily reach Hatch House by noon and be back in the encampment before the evening counting-of-heads.

He was right. It was easy. The British Army had never attempted anything of the kind before in peacetime, nor so much in the public gaze. Everyone was so eager to shine that any shortcoming was something to be concealed, covered up. And anything could be blamed on the untoward nature of the day: 'I was commanded to hold bridle for Captain Y,' he would say. 'I was sent with a message by General X.' Who would know any better? Who would challenge him? Being by nature a cynic, Oliver was a good judge of human failing.

Being by nature a cynic, he unfortunately failed to take into account such dangerous factors as brotherly affection.

'Where might I find the 66th Berkshire Regiment of Foot?' asked a clergyman with his wife on his arm and five children clustered behind.

The sergeant posted on the outermost flank of battle-lines grew more exasperated with every enquiry. Women with lap dogs, newspapermen with portable ink-stands, old women with wicker baskets full of cake strolled up to him as they might a lamplighter, looking for directions, looking for good vantage points, looking for relations, for a friendly chat. Sir Henry Englefield of Whiteknights had arrived with half a dozen servants carrying cane chairs for the ladies in his party. He had carried field glasses, and a map torn from the *London Chronicle*, as he might have done for the Christmas cross-country steeplechase, or a public execution, and asked the sergeant if the ordnance wagons could not be moved, to allow a better view.

At first, the sergeant attempted to turn back this tide of sightseers but, like Canute, realised he was unequal to the task. To the tittering ladies in military-style shakos or wigs like cumulo-nimbus, he became just another obstacle to be negotiated, like the guy-ropes and the wagon horses, and the mud. By the time Samuel Baydon asked after the 66th Berkshire Regiment of Foot, the sergeant had decided in favour of profit. 'For a shilling, Reverend, I shall have a man show you directly.'

The allocation of space to the 66th Foot was only three chains in from the left flank. The sleeping tents were being dismantled and a pair of light cannon hitched behind two pairs of gun horses. As the Baydon family picked its way through the muddle several troopers whistled at Grace, who blushed and bit her lip, wishing she had stayed at home. She remembered her Uncle Oliver; the memory brought a dark, unspecified fear with it which tied her stomach in an overhand knot.

'I'm looking for trooper Baydon,' said Samuel, raising his voice above the noise of a distant bugle. 'Please will some one of you direct me to trooper Oliver Baydon?'

★

'Job, please saddle me a pony,' said Alba, in her most imperious tone. She meant it to sound casual, but it only sounded imperious.

'I ben't the groom,' grunted Job sulkily.

'Then tell the groom,' said Alba, her blue eyes a little proud of her head, and her small white bottom teeth pushing forward of the top ones. It was as though the dam of her mischief had collapsed on top of her and she was having to chew her way out, log by log. She dared not abandon her plan; then she would have no clue, and no control over what Oliver Baydon was going to do. If she were quick, she might get another note to him explaining the first – explaining the whereabouts of the ruin. Or she might intercept him on the road and, in some nonchalant exchange – as if she knew nothing of his romance with Zennor – manage to send him on in the right direction.

So small an error, and yet it grew in contemplation into the spark which would burn down the forest, the rut which could overturn the coach. She had to put it right. In the meantime, there was Zennor to be primed. Time, which generally hung about Alba in muddy clods, seemed this morning to run through her fingers like sand. In no time at all it would be noon, and either everything or nothing would have happened.

'Zennor,' she said, but nothing came out of her tight, dry throat. She coughed. 'Zennor. I am going for a little ride.'

'Mmm? Do you want me to come?' Her head was in a book, as usual.

'No! . . . Um, Zennor. Robin wants to speak to you.'

'Mmm?' Zennor got up from the settle, her eyes still on the page of her book, finishing the paragraph.

'Not now! At noon. Did you hear? At noon.'

Zennor folded one leg under her and sat down again, her eyes still on the book. 'Very well.'

'At the ruin. You are to wait for him at the ruin.'

Her paragraph finished, Zennor looked up, aware of the strain in Alba's voice. The face looking at her was paper white. Inside her chest, Zennor's heart twitched like a sleeping cat. At the ruin? What did it mean? An appointment at the ruin? Another of Wootton's *grands gestes*? More republicanism? Or something different enough to make Alba go riding (which she hated to do) and to turn that ghastly deathly white?

'You will go, won't you?' said Alba.

'I – Yes, of course. I must, if I am sent for.'

'Good,' said Alba, and Zennor was even more baffled.

★

As she rode the little white Welsh pony down the driveway, Alba tried to wear a cunning grin. But her face would not oblige her. Instead, it twitched and flickered and grimaced, even when she used the flat of both hands to restrain it. Zennor probably thought Robin wanted to meet her at the ruin to propose to her. Vanity of vanities! Well, before the day was out, Zennor would be shamed and dishonoured. At half past noon, Alba would take Robin by the hand and lead him up the hill to the ruin. And there (where she had vowed by all the gods to love and serve him for ever) she would show him Zennor and Oliver, Oliver and Zennor *in flagrante*.

What would they be doing? What would Robin see? Kissing? Or some Old Testament crime which had a name but no illustration beside it in Alba's naive imagination. She shuddered and shivered, and the pony (which she so hated to ride) crabbed and baulked and played with the bit in the front of its mouth, until its lips dripped saliva.

When Samuel Baydon could not find his brother he became a little alarmed. Wickham Bushes was beginning to resound to cannonfire and blank shot. There was a smell of smoke, and a level of chaos which mirrored true battle conditions. He exhorted Oliver's fellow troopers to look harder, to search farther afield. He incurred towering impatience from everyone, but his concern was so great for his brother that he persisted all morning long. He even borrowed Sir Henry Englefield's field glasses, and climbed up on top of a forage wagon for a better view of the field.

At last Sophronia took him by the arm and led him away. 'Later, later, Mr Baydon,' she said soothingly. 'It will be more easy to find him *after* the manoeuvres.'

So Baydon withdrew to the sidelines, where by now the crowds of spectators were four- and five-deep. A hackney coach had been hired, and its roof was packed with drunken dandies peering at the proceedings, with massive distaste, through a shared pair of lorgnettes. A spreading plane tree was completely overrun with boys and young men waving flags which they had bought from an enterprising hawker.

'I could climb up there and look for Uncle Oliver,' suggested Sam.

'Don't be absurd,' said his stepmother tartly.

'Quite,' said his father. 'George will do it.'

So George climbed up the tree, despite the efforts of those already there to kick him down again. Wedging himself between branch and trunk, he twisted round for a view of the heath. Chains of men were moving forward or back in a complex and incompehensible game of human chess. Orders were shouted. Horses galloped about. It was war, and it was not war.

Blank cannonfire was directed at a seemingly indestructible foe, for no one fell, no one pitched to the ground screaming, no hams of dismembered horses hung in the bushes, no bloody dwarfs screamed for their legs. Regimental banners progressed, by complicated moves, from north to south and east to west, with pauses for the watering of horses and for various dignitaries to salute one another or contemplate the weather. Overhead, clouds supplanted one another in a succession of westerly routs. It was war, and it was not war.

'Do you see him?' Samuel called up into the tree.

'No,' George called down. 'But I see Alba Wootton on a pony!'

All morning Zennor tried not to wonder why she was summoned to the ruin at noon. She had to keep it in mind – it would be dreadful to forget – but a large part of her did not want to go. It was probably something utterly trivial, or else a gathering of the whole household again, for some new declaration. But Alba had been so very, very agitated by having to deliver the message. Zennor had never seen her so agitated. That surely signified something?

She went early, passing Robin in the stable yard. He did not look at her in any way oddly – paid her as little attention as he usually did. 'Until noon, then,' she said, and he looked at her and smiled. Sometimes his smile meant agreement, often that he had not heard. Part of her wanted to ask, 'What is it you want to say? Life is not conducted on the tops of hills.' But, of course, she did not.

At eleven o'clock she climbed Hatch Hill. Its summer ivy was dull-leaved and brittle. Giant spider-webs, hung with the dampness of autumn, stretched like crazed windows between the pillars, and a bird came to bath in the puddle on top of the stele. Zennor read her book.

What would she say if Robin proposed? Not today, perhaps, but at any time. Why, when *Alba* thought of nothing else, had Zennor never once pictured the scene, the words, the feelings, the triumph? It was as if she knew it would never happen. Sometimes, when she was face-to-face with Robin, it was like looking into the barrel of a gun – something hollow, something dark. But it never occurred to her that the gun would go off in her face.

That was it. The gun was not loaded. And though this thought made no sense to her, no sense at all, it enabled Zennor to put Robin Wootton completely out of mind, and concentrate on reading Fanny Burney's *Evelina*.

Shortly before noon, without warning, a pair of hands covered her eyes from behind. They were cold, hard, large hands. She knew at once that it was not . . .

'Robin?'

The hands moved down her cheeks, over her mouth, her chin, her neck, and came to rest on her shoulders. 'Zennor. Oh my dear, dear Zennor,' said Oliver Baydon.

CHAPTER FOURTEEN

Ruin

Samuel Baydon was slow to scent scandal, and his wife was unwilling to bring him downwind of it. When he caught sight of Alba Wootton riding her pony up and down behind the impenetrable crowd of spectators he assumed that, like her sister, she simply liked sightseeing. She had presumably been curious to see the manoeuvres and had, following the devices and desires of her own heart, made her way unchaperoned to Wickham Bushes.

'They are born *tourists*, I tell you,' he said under his breath to Sophronia in tones of deepest disgust. 'He has raised them up to be *tourists*.'

When Alba caught sight of her neighbours pushing towards her out of the crowd, her face froze over like a pond. The anxieties of the day, the widening cracks in her flimsy plan, the ten-mile journey on horseback had all conspired to give her indigestion, and she held her thin little hand to her stomach like a claw. 'Reverend Baydon. Oh. Mrs Baydon. Oh.'

There was no question of her riding home; the parson upbraided her soundly for travelling alone, and said she must accompany them at the end of the day, her pony tied on behind. He would hear nothing to the contrary.

Thanks to the press of the crowds and her ignorance where to look, she had not succeeded in getting anywhere near Oliver Baydon's tent. She had no idea whether or not he had received her letter, understood her letter, gone to Hatch House as a result. Even if he had, she was no longer there to spring the trap, to betray the lovers to Robin. Zennor and Oliver would meet and part – she had helped them to it – and the only person in trouble would be her. Her top lip and the plains of her pale cheeks grew longer and stiffer as the tears gathered behind her eyes and she tried to think of yet more lies, this time for Reverend Baydon's benefit.

'I beg your pardon, child?' said Samuel, frowning as he bent his head closer to hers. 'What did you say?'

'I said I should like to go home *now*,' shouted Alba above the noise of cannon and the crack of muskets and the blowing bugles and the shouted commands of sergeants and the admiring cheers of the crowd. 'The noise is fearful.'

'What did you expect?' asked George in astonishment.

'War is not a peaceful pastime,' said Sophronia, her fingertips to her aching temple.

'We shall go as soon as I have spoken with my brother,' Baydon dictated. 'He has been in Canada these five years with His Majesty's forces.'

'But no one can seem to find him,' said George. And that simple, obvious phrase sent an unaccountable shiver through Samuel Baydon, who up to that minute had assumed his brother was simply out of sight somewhere nearby.

'Softly now. We cannot be seen from the house. We are quite alone. No one shall disturb us,' said Oliver Baydon.

'I fear you mistake, Mr Baydon,' said Zennor. 'My guardian will come at any moment.' Zennor stood up, brushing the creases out of her skirts. 'Besides, should you be here? I thought every soul in scarlet was at Easthamstead today, rehearsing for the French.' Her voice shook a little. She tried to steady it, instinctively knowing any sign of weakness would somehow put her at risk.

Oliver had gone to pains with his uniform, shining his boots with spit and rag, whiting his belt and securing any loose buttons on the jacket. He had worn a cloak to make a stealthy departure from the encampment, but now he threw it on the ground by Zennor's feet and sat down on it, obliging her to sit down again or to pick her way around him. 'My heart had a greater duty to you,' he said. 'You know I would risk all for you, Zennor.'

She picked her way round him. 'I have to say, sir, that your letters were a great trouble to me.'

'I was troubled myself when I wrote them. To be kept so far from you!'

'A nuisance. I mean a nuisance,' said Zennor. 'Your letters were a great nuisance. I wish you had not sent them. I cannot think why you did, since I never wrote back.'

Oliver, at a disadvantage sitting on the ground, got up again. 'A letter is a poor way, I know, for a man to express his feelings. But you must own, I was a great way off, and living among wolves and savages. I had

to worship at the altar of love the best way I was able. If I write badly
. . .' He was put out, in truth; he prided himself on writing a good love
letter, in a fair hand. Perhaps Wootton's advanced education methods had
left Zennor incapable of reading, as well as spelling. Slow to emerge from
the role he had been expecting to play, he began to perceive things were
not going quite to plan. 'Tell me, have I not touched your heart even once
with my entreaties?'

'You should not have wasted your leisure nor your ink, sir. I tore them
all up unread.'

A thread of anger like a wire-worm crawled across Oliver's vision. 'You
could have a spared me pains if you had written of your indifference.
You and your sister liked me well enough before I went to fight for
the King.'

'Liked you? I hardly recall you. I remember a man who spent a shawl
and a penny and a smile on two young girls. I have seen old men do that
in London before, believe me.'

Oliver broke out in an unpleasant barking laugh which rattled all
his sinuses. 'Oh, what? Am I too old for your taste? Is that where I
fall down?'

Zennor straightened her spine and looked back at him over one shoulder,
her hair appearing to bristle like the mane of an Abyssinian lion. 'Oh please,
please! Pray do not hold your age to blame, Mr Baydon. I find your *brother*
a very proper man, in all respects. It is not your *age*. I am sure you were
unpleasant *all* your days.'

'Jesu!'

'Did you really suppose yourself a match to equal Robin Wootton?' said
Zennor.

'No,' he snarled back. '*Did you*, you Lambeth whore?'

'I have a better chance of it than Alba, I do assure you. You should have
set your sights on her, if you really wished to pick up the droppings behind
Robin's horse.' Her words startled her as much as him, for she had never
knowingly thought them before. She in the ascendant over Alba? She, the
probable lady of Hatch House?

'Damn,' said Oliver, kicking up a divot of dirt. 'In that case, why did
you send for me? For a jest? A spite, to have me cashiered?'

'Send for you? I did not send for you.'

'But you are here. Here you are, look.'

'I came because Alba said . . .'

She did not need to go on. There grew between them the slow
understanding that Alba had made fools of them both.

'Fond girl,' said Zennor.

'Intriguing little trollope,' said Oliver.

'She must mean us to be discovered together. Are we to oblige her, or will you go? . . . Oh, and in case you think to start paying court to Alba, I must tell you she is in love with Wootton. I mean "in love". As you and I are not.' She held him for a moment with her eye. It disturbed him, that look: so much awake to the danger and yet unflustered by it. Somewhere at heart he found it faintly shocking – at odds with his notion of how a woman should be. He wanted badly to extinguish something which had shone too bright in his eye.

'I should take some recompense before I go,' he said. 'Something for what's lost to me.' And he stopped his backward drift towards the trees and propped his musket against a pillar.

'Shall I refund your postage?'

She saw quite plainly the sexual aggression take hold on him. It colonised his face, feature by feature, his stance, the expression of his hands. He uncinched his ammunition belt, and let it fall to the ground. He unfastened a button at his waist. He advanced a step.

Within the same length of time Zennor considered flight, considered shouting out for help, her stupidity in insulting him and the novel sensation of blind panic. Then she too took a step forward, placing one hand on the ivy-clad, birdbath altar. 'I am always interested to see what I have never seen before,' she said, staring at his trouser front. 'I have been raised to have a lively curiosity.'

The surprise was only enough to halt him for a moment. Now both his hands went to his waistband, and he came on again.

Zennor put both sets of fingers under the rim of the altar and tipped it over. Several strands of ivy rose up taut from the ground like guy-ropes, but snapped as the little marble pillar fell over. Its spreading dish landed across Oliver's feet and shins. His forward momentum would have pitched him on his face, but one foot was pinned to the ground; ballasted at the base, he rolled like a lead-weighted toy clown.

Zennor did not wait to see if he were badly hurt, but picked up her skirts and ran round him to where the musket was propped against the tree.

'*Oh, my foot! My foot's broken!*'

It was probably not loaded. She ducked down and pulled the bayonet from his discarded powder belt and fastened it to the musket barrel, dislodging the ramrod, which fell into the folds of her skirt.

'For Jesus's sake, get it off me! My foot!'

She took out a piece of wad, the powder horn, a ball from his belt.

'How can you do that?'

'I had a practical education,' Zennor panted, spitting the ball down the muzzle and ramming it home.

'I mean how can you stand by, doing . . . are you going to shoot me? For Christ's sake!'

He got the stone column off his foot, as she had known he would, but by then she was pointing a loaded musket at him. 'Pick up your cloak and go,' she said.

'How can I go? My hellish foot is broke in half, bitch!'

'Even if it misfires,' said Zennor (who had never loaded an army musket before) 'the noise will bring Wootton.' She pointed it at his head. 'Go on! You must be 'waited back at the Bushes.'

The curses bubbled out of Oliver Baydon as though from a vase holed at the base, but he managed to clutch up his cloak and hop over to the brink of Hatch Hill. 'Give me my gun, at least! How can I go back without my gun?'

'You will excuse it. You have such a plausible tongue.'

She had one moment's uncertainty when Oliver, from shock and pain, suddenly vomited into the nettles. But after that she watched him, unflinching, as he slithered on his backside down the slippery hill, in the direction of the church. Only then did she throw down the musket, thinking to lose it in the deep nettlebeds below the bald summit of the hill. With a noise like a ripping sheet, it went off, loosing a spurt of flame simultaneously out of the barrel and the pan. The ball passed so close to Zennor that it kicked up the ornamental apron of her dress. Right in front of her womanhood. Though she would have liked to do it, she thought that, on the whole, this was not an apt time to faint.

Had it not been for Samuel Baydon's attempts to visit his brother, Oliver would almost certainly not have been found missing, absent without leave. Had he not been posted absent without leave, his tent would not have been searched that evening, and the letter from a young woman found. The Baydon family and Alba Wootton were all standing there, their Union flags drooping at half mast from their hands, as the unpleasant smell of army cooking engulfed the encampment, and the cheerful crowds melted away into the growing gloom. A soldier with a face like a yard of cobbles, and with two fingers missing from his left hand, scooped the letter out of its envelope and passed it to his sergeant who let the saliva gather on his lower lip as he read it. When he had finished, he held it up in front of the parson's face with a finger and thumb, saying, 'Shareshay la fame, hey? Shareshay la fame.'

Samuel had to push the man's hand away to a distance to be able to read the small, impacted handwriting. Though his face must have registered something, he did not so much as turn his head in the direction of Alba Wootton. What purpose would it serve to implicate her? – to deliver both her and his brother into the hands of the miltary? He had done enough harm for one day. Instead, he snatched the letter and pushed it, in a crumpled ball, into his pocket. The sergeant had not intended that, at all, but was too slow to stop him.

'It is time we were going, Mrs Baydon,' Baydon said, shrugging his cloak higher round his ears. 'Children. Miss Wootton. Shall we return to the carriage?'

The sergeant, who did not know how to get back the letter from a church minister, was only glad he could remember the contents. 'Might you, by any chance, know of the ruin wrote of in the billy doo?' he called after them, as the family group moved off in silent convoy.

Samuel Baydon did not reply. Only his wife turned, her hand on her husband's sleeve and the hood of her cloak pulled forward. 'Wherever there are soldiers, Sergeant, can there be any shortage of ruins?' she said.

'It appears I must apologise to you,' said Baydon, slapping the reins on the horse's rump. His voice was sharp and piping and sarcastic. 'It seems that, all unknowing, I have kept you from your rendezvous.'

He had insisted on taking the reins and driving home, and on having Alba Wootton sit up beside him on the driving seat, while the rest of the family huddled, abject, on the chilly bench-seats. None of them understood what was going on, except for Sophronia, who wrapped her long arms around as much of her family as she could reach, and talked softly about nothing very much, so as to stop them eavesdropping. George, however, sat perched perilously on the back transom, his feet on the seat, glaring out across the countryside. All he could hear of the conversation on the driving seat was Alba's voice piping up continuously, 'Zennor! It was Zennor!'

Nobody supposed it was Zennor with whom Oliver Baydon had made his tryst. Zennor had a good large hand, and immaculate spelling. Besides, Zennor had not been caught out riding unchaperoned around the perimeters of a military settlement looking for Oliver's tent.

Even Robin Wootton, when he was shown the letter, had no difficulty in recognising Alba's handwriting. There were many things he did not know about Alba, but her handwriting he knew. He and Baydon, Alba and Zennor climbed at once to the ruin on the hill, though Sophronia was sent home with the children, to protect them from any further unpleasantness.

But apart from finding the stele-post fallen over there was nothing to show of any lovers' tryst up at the ruin. Presumably Oliver, if he had come at all, had sat out the afternoon, imagined himself let down by Alba, pushed over the stele in a fit of pique and headed back to camp. They walked back down to the house in silence, the girls walking wide apart on either side of the men.

Alba, her store of protests used up, sat down at the harpsichord in the octagonal room and began to play. It was not like the spinet at the vicarage, but she played it anyway: 'On the Bridge at Avignon'. Discordantly. On and on.

Samuel Baydon, as brother of the seducer, felt it lay with him to find an avoiding route around scandal. 'My brother is newly returned from the Canadian colonies, sir. I do not believe this can have been any more than a fancied romance.'

> On the bridge at Avignon,
> All are dancing, all are dancing . . .

'There was plainly no meeting today, and I cannot see that there has been much . . . opportunity for misconduct . . .'

> On the bridge at Avignon,
> All are dancing in a ring.

'As for my brother – why he has barely seen the girls above twice or thrice, and that when they were no more than children.'

> Ladies all go this way,
> Gentlemen go that way . . .

'I do not believe the army's displeasure with my brother will in any way be felt by your household. I cannot help feeling . . . I realise you must hold me responsible for the presence of my brother in the vicinity . . . I can only say . . .'

Robin Wootton, who had been reading the household accounts from a large leather-bound ledger, looked up with an eager smile and slapped the book shut. 'Nonsense! We are all responsible for our own actions, *mon cher Samuél*! Truly, you must try not to expend energy on things of such small consequence.'

> . . . Ladies curtsey this way;
> Gentlemen bow that way.
> On the bridge at Avignon . . .

'You see, what people fail to understand is that the moral sense comes late to the unfurling soul. Pish! I have not even *begun* to instruct my wards in matters moral. One cannot awaken a person within a house – shout as one may – if that person is not there to be waked . . . Is that not the truth of the matter? But if you will excuse me, I must speak a word with Constable Gervase. When you arrived he had just called here on the matter of a broken footbridge, but I have other matters he can help me to settle. Allow me to send you some claret. – No. Please. You must not think of leaving. Some claret, yes. I shall be with you again presently.'

Even after he had left the room, Alba kept on playing.

Somewhere in the countryside, Samuel's brother was at large. Deserter? Absconder? Seducer? Was he even now returning to the encampment, delivering himself up, unwittingly or deliberately, to arrest? Samuel tried hard not to speculate on exactly what had passed between Oliver and this . . . this *child* at the harpsichord, but whatever the truth, the last place he needed to be was here, drinking claret in the midst of this unnatural family where no sin seemed too grave to be blinked at.

When he could stand no more of the jumble of twangling discords he went and gently closed the lid over the keys. 'It seems there is very little Monsieur Rousseau finds unacceptable in a young woman,' he observed. 'Youth apparently excuses all.'

Alba did not answer him. She kept her eyes fixed on the hieroglyphs of *A New Musical Notation*, which sat propped on the music holder of the harpsichord, her hands in her lap now.

'*What is, is right,*' said Zennor. Over by the window, she stood looking out across the garden. He had forgotten she was even in the room.

'Is that what he says, your Monsieur Rousseau? Echinswell! What a sinner's charter! May God have mercy on his soul!'

'Pope,' said Zennor. 'Rousseau is quite a Puritan, really. Pope said it. I have been reading Pope.'

'Then you would do much better to read your Bible, miss!' huffed Baydon. He wanted very much to get away. He found he craved the comfortable good sense of Sophronia. Even the musty rotting smell which pervaded the vicarage was preferable to the elusive, undeterminate smell of Hatch House: he could not pin it down better than to call it the smell of something *amiss*, something un-sane.

The claret came, and while he was drinking it, still wishing he were somewhere else, the door opened, and Constable Gervase looked in. 'Gervase! My excellent fellow. Good-day to you. Here, have this claret. I must leave.'

But Gervase did not even appear to hear him. He looked straight past

Samuel into the room, craning his head to one side a little to see the girl at the window, the girl at the harpsichord, the furniture and fittings. A big purple vein was throbbing in the side of his forehead. 'Gervase?' But the constable ignored Baydon. Only his big belly jutted into the room, a fob-watch lying almost flat on the top of it, jumping to the subterranean beat of his heart. Was he about his business? Looking for an army deserter or his female accomplice? Gervase's mouth opened, leaving a seal of transparent spit which no word burst. He breathed stentoriously through his nose. Then he turned and lurched back down the reflex corridor, bouncing off one wall, steadying himself, straightening a lithograph of a shepherdess, then continuing on, his head jutting forward like a charging bull.

'The man is drunk,' thought Baydon, but could not bring himself to care. He set down a full wine-glass, and left.

In the kitchen of the parsonage he found his wife serving leek soup to a soldier in dishevelled uniform. One army boot stood empty on the table. It took Samuel a moment to recognise his brother.

'Our visitor has suffered a mishap,' said Sophronia in a sharp high voice she did not customarily use. 'I found him asleep in our bed.' He saw that there was a frown clewed to her forehead as if by a staple between her brows. He saw, too, that Grace stood in the very corner of the room, trying to be invisible.

Oliver turned the soup over with his spoon, filled and emptied, filled and emptied it, as if he were looking for something among the curls of leek. 'That callet . . .' he began. Then he remembered the disservice the family had done him by being out when he got there. 'Where were you? I need to get back to camp. Can you drive me?'

'The horse is done in,' said Samuel, non-committally. 'We just got back from there ourselves. You were . . . away.'

Oliver, though taken by surprise, was quick to comprehend from their faces the predicament he was in. 'What? Am I missed? Hell! Swyving hell!' Grace flinched, hollow-eyed, backwards into her corner. Oliver did some quick and politic thinking. 'You see, how it goes is this, brother. . . . I was coming over here, to see you. Yesterday. Plenty of time to come visiting and be back before the manoeuvres. I was set on! Roadmen. Stole my gun, pox on them. Broke my foot. Look at me! What could I do? Couldn't get back to Wickham. Come here, I thought. Sam can drive me back. But no one home. You'll have to speak out for me, Sam. Give me good character. Those cheese-hoppers will take it hard I missed their war-games. Call me a deserter or some such. Try to hang irons on me without someone to give me a character, tell them the way of it. – Five years, eh man? Has it been five years? It has! I needed to see you all – see how all my nieces and nephews are grown! Five years, among wolves and savages! There were times I thought . . . Five years, eh? Five years is too long for a man to be apart from his family.'

'George,' said Samuel Baydon to his oldest boy. 'Go over the hill to Hatch House. You will find Gervase there. Tell him we have your uncle here in the house.'

Oliver looked unsure but gratified; a ride, he assumed, in a coach with a fresh horse between its traces. Of course, he needed Samuel to travel with him, if he were not to end the night in the brig.

His brother had turned his back in order to look out at the garden through the open kitchen door, assessing the weather written in purple clouds across a rising moon. 'An absconder from the encampment, tell him George,' Baydon went on. 'Request him to come at once; as a Justice of the Peace, it compromises me to be giving shelter to a fugitive.'

George looked across at Mrs Baydon, who nodded. That was all the confirmation he needed, and he dashed out of the door, scrambled over the high garden fence and pelted off up the hill.

'Sam, what is this?' Oliver half rose.

'You were always a lecher, Oliver. Always a fornicator. And a liar. But to prey on young girls for no reason better than their prospects . . . Grace!'

'Yes, Father?'

'Fetch out clean sheets, and help your mother to change our marriage bed. I do not want the smell of this man to keep me awake tonight.'

Gervase did come over from Hatch House, as asked. If he were in an odd mood it passed unnoticed amid the curses and foul language which overspilled Oliver Baydon like a blocked sewer. But as the constable bound the prisoner's wrists to the pommel of a borrowed horse and paid out a leading-rein by which to lead the beast away, he did have one neighbourly favour to ask of the Reverend Baydon.

'Would you do me a marriage, Reverend? Soonest as can be?'

'Yourself, do you mean? You're marrying again, Gervase? I had no –'

'I was approached. As being an eligible gentleman. As I be, ben't I?'

'Of course, of course, Gervase. I shall read the banns this Sunday.' The constable's face gave him somewhere to look, somewhere to direct his eyes rather than at his brother who was still cursing and spitting and threatening all manner of retribution. Samuel could not honestly say that at that moment he cared what farm-widow or grocer's daughter had agreed to marry Gervase; he only wished him gone, swallowed up by the dark. But courtesy made him ask. 'Who exactly . . . forgive me. Should I know? Who is the bride to be?'

Gervase mounted up, standing in the stirrups to pick the tight folds of cloth out of the tight folds of his fat thighs and buttocks. Slowly, carefully, he settled himself into the saddle, his face turned upwards, his thoughts drifting among the picturesque Berkshire stars. 'Mr Robin Wootton has put it to me that he would not oppose a marriage between myself and his ward. Miss Alba Wootton.' He smacked his lips around the name. He had not tasted it before – had never once thought of it before Wootton's suggestion. But it tasted good. It tasted of money. A great deal of money. 'Miss Alba Wootton. Yes.'

PART THREE

The Age of Strength

CHAPTER FIFTEEN

Appeals

'Please, Zennor. Please! He listens to *you*. He speaks to *you*. He'll not even *see* me. Please!' Alba's voice was muffled by her pillow, and sodden with the tears which welled out of her like syrup from a maple. 'Oh God, Zennor, make him listen!'

She reached out a flailing hand to seize hold of the other girl, but Zennor stepped sharply back from the bed, unwilling to be touched. 'You are past belief, Alba. Yesterday you were plotting to shame me, ruin me. You set Oliver Baydon to me like a ram to a ewe, and now you want –'

'I'm sorry, I'm sorry' howled Alba, but in truth she needed all her sorrow for herself, to mourn the tragedy which had overtaken her. 'I love Robin. I can't marry that . . . that great *beast*!'

'The constable is a respected man hereabouts. Important. In the county. When we were small . . .' Zennor wanted to say how far beyond the hopes and expectations of a Lambeth pauper such a marriage would have been when they were young. But even as she said it it rang untrue. When they had been small, Gervase had already been a fatstock boar big enough to break the back of young sows. Zennor tried hard to rejoice in Alba's fitting downfall, but an unaccountable pity gathered in her chest each time she thought of Constable Gervase. 'He has a fine big cottage. You'll be mistress of a good home.'

But Alba only groaned and sobbed, and beat the pillow with her fist. Her dress creased into little concertinas of silk. Her fur tippet, hung on the back of a chair, looked like a malevolent dwarf hunched headless on the far side of the bed.

Zennor was hotly incensed against everyone who had brought her to this: against Alba and Oliver, against Gervase and Robin. Why could the whole absurd folly not have lapsed back into the familiar regime of lessons and fantasy? She wanted to slap Alba, to pull out her hair, maybe even to throw her down the stairs. She wanted to shout in her face: cheat! forger! schemer! But she did not want to see her married to Gervase – to a virtual stranger, to a pompous, boorish widower with an eye only to her dowry and the social advantage of marrying the Wootton family name.

George Baydon's head was up and back like a carriage horse short-bridled. 'How is it anything to do with me?' he asked defensively.

Zennor shrugged. She could not rightly say why she had asked him. Perhaps if she had met Service Gibbins outside the Post Inn, she might have asked him, but she had met George instead. Though she no longer visited the parsonage, George still spoke to her amicably at church on Sundays. Indeed, he seemed to make a point of it – not, she thought, because he liked her but as a point of principle: to show that his parents could not dictate to him whom he should and should not consort with. She rather admired him for that.

Not that she had any great hopes of George successfully dissuading Robin, but someone had to try, and it was not going to be her. 'You are impartial, George,' she said. 'People talk to you. *I* talk to you. People must.'

'You talk to anybody,' he reasoned. 'And I'd have thought Miss Alba might count herself very lucky. In the circumstances.'

She kicked him in the ankle for his priggery, then apologised, remembering she had said exactly the same thing herself to Alba. George was wearing his stout walking boots, however, and had not felt the kick. They floundered for a time in a welter of misunderstanding.

Secretly, George was flattered to be thought a man of influence, a man whose opinion might deflect a member of the gentry out of his chosen path. He wanted to say, 'Do you really think he would listen?' but Zennor was busy rehearsing him in what he must say, how he should heap scorn and obloquy on Gervase, how he must prevail against a cruel work of spite.

All inspiration withered inside him as he sighted Robin Wootton in Muses' Walk. He was left thinking that, once again, Zennor had persuaded him to a mischief from which he stood to gain absolutely nothing. It was the telescope all over again.

'Mr Wootton. A word, if you please.' It came out sounding quarrelsome: he must be careful Wootton did not think he was being called out, especially since he was currently holding a scythe.

Wootton, though he appeared to be simply enjoying the view, was engaged in yet more garden planning. He was striving to establish an eyeline between Muses' Walk and the terrace of the house. At present an overgrown box-hedge and an arbutus had encroached on the vista. Nature had intruded on his plans for a natural paradise.

'Regarding this marriage,' said George.

'Good. Stand here,' said Wootton pointing to the spot where he was standing and moving off down the slope. He whetted the scythe with a stone as he went. George had to raise his voice to be heard.

'I hope your mind is not wholly made up. I mean, I believe there was no . . . affection, no acquaintance even, between Miss —'

'Ah, I see.' Wootton's head nodded exaggeratedly. The scythe fetched down a sprinkling of arbutus leaves. 'So you partook as well, did you?'

'I'm sorry?'

'My ward. She cast her net wide, did she? You were favoured with her "openness".' Showers of twigs flew outwards from Wotton like expletives, but his voice never rose above the conversational.

George started down the incline. 'No! By my life, no!'

'Why else would you speak against her marriage? Oh, pray, how can I keep my line straight if you leave your marker?'

George's outrage gave him courage, but robbed him of the power of articulate speech. 'Such a heap of a man! Against her will? He's a bully and heartless. There's no sympathy in him. His office has marred him . . . there was always a liming smell about him . . . I mean to say, Mr Wootton, *nothing* commends him as a husband to such a very —' He stopped, unable to find the right word to describe Alba. 'Spindly' had sprung to mind. A chair too spindly to survive sitting on by Gervase. 'Spindly' would not give way to the right word.

'Very well.' Robin Wootton was hewing now at the box like a collier working open-cast. The springy density of the hedge soaked up his blows like rubber and he was panting and frustrated. 'Very well. To show I am not closed to persuasion, and since you make your gallant offer — you may marry her. I won't thwart you. Have her, do and welcome. Gervase will master his disappointment in time, I dare say.'

He was prepared to stop work at last and look George over. The boy's discomfort plainly amused him. It confirmed in him his belief that Alba was beneath further consideration, beneath everyone's consideration. George's pale brown eyes were aghast that Wootton should have turned the things about so. He feared the wind might change and fix this dreadful moment, unalterable.

'No, no. I never meant —'

'No? Forgive me. I thought you were proposing yourself as a preferable bridegroom. No?' Wootton climbed back past George to Muses' Walk and checked the eyeline again to see if he had hacked away enough of the shrubbery. He looked directly through George, as though he were less of an impediment than arbutus or box.

Zennor was waiting for George on the hill. 'Well? What did he say?'

George was inclined to walk straight by; she should never have set him to it in the first place. But she ran alongside him tugging at his sleeve. 'Tell me, tell me!'

Grudgingly, gruffly, he hinted at his humiliation. 'He thought I must be in love with Alba myself that I wanted to stop the marriage.'

Zennor put her fingers to her mouth. 'Oh!'

He felt freed now to keep walking, but she still ran after him. 'Will he really do it? He won't. He won't give her to the constable!'

Exasperated, George turned on her. 'He said I could marry her instead, if I cared to,' he said. 'I'm sorry. I was not the person to send.'

The hand withdrew. For some reason he felt his failure settle on him like dust.

'Well?' she said, her voice inflected sharply upwards.

'Well what?' He had always been slow to follow her train of thought.

'Well, you would have been better than Gervase.'

George made a noise somewhere between a gasp and a laugh. He waited for her to apologise, to laugh it off as a joke, but she stood on the edge of the hill, shoulders back, belligerent fists clenched by her waist. Her dress blew between her legs, her hair stood on end. George thought he had never been more offended in his entire life. Resentment roared around his heart.

'Oh, I see Wootton's done a fine job of patterning your nature on his!' he retorted. 'Ready to dispose another's life to your liking. Ready to landscape your fellow creatures. You ask too much, madam. You ask a great deal too much!' Dropping on down the hill, he cursed Zennor as he went: Zennor and Alba and his uncle and Gervase – the whole pack of them.

'*All the same, you could have*,' she shouted after him, and only the sob in her voice said that she knew she had overstepped the bounds of fair comment.

Despite his indignation, George persisted in believing it was wrong for Alba to be made to marry Gervase. He went to his father and asked him, 'Can you do nothing to forbid it? Wootton's shedding her like a spent horse.'

Unmistakable signs of fear flickered across his father's face. 'Great Tew,

148

boy, you're not enamoured of the girl yourself, are you?' he said, and was taken aback by the uncharacteristic roar of annoyance from his habitually soft-spoken son.

And so the weeks came and went, washed away by Alba's noisy tears. The little household rode to and fro to church, to hear the banns read, stiff as three card puppets on a single rod slid back and to along a single groove. The congregation watched Alba sobbing, pink-eyed, white-faced, and speculated lewdly as to why a bride should be so unhappy, why the marriage should be so hasty. But no one intervened, saying, 'No. Look. The bride is not willing.'

Constable Gervase also sat in the church, wearing a faint, curved smile, and acknowledged their congratulations with a slight dipping of his head. He was a man of influence, a local dignitary. For years they had been watching to see which girl Robin Wootton would choose. Now it seemed Wootton had made his choice, and kept to his word in finding a prestigious match for the girl left surplus to requirements. Gervase was buying himself a large, new house in place of the modest one he had shared with his first wife. All in all, they considered it ungracious and ungrateful for Alba to show her disappointment; given her origins, she was lucky to do as well as she had.

But Alba had no picture of herself as a rescued waif. Up on her Olympian plateau, separated from the real world by romantic landscaping, she had thought of herself as Apollo's consort, his future wife, and had set about loving him as dutifully as any wife ever had. In her own way, she had herself expended a fortune on Robin Wootton.

'Please, sir. Please may I say –'

'Ah, Zennor! What would you say to bluebells? Here, and along there.' Wootton was planning a herbarium between the lawn and Muses' Walk – somewhere to be planted out solely with wild flowers collected while out taking his walks in the lanes and fields. He liked to talk of it as 'inviting nature into his garden', though it necessitated carrying a trowel with him everywhere and sometimes netting off areas against the deer.

'Pretty. Sir, I –'

'Take out the fritillaries, I thought. So colourless at a distance. Too meek. A garden should be bold, do you not think? Nature is bold.'

'Sir. Tomorrow. You surely won't force Alba to marry against her conscience?'

'Strength,' said Wootton. 'Strong, rich, primary colours lend character to a scene.'

'She is very unhappy.'

'Happiness,' said Wootton, 'is an attitude of mind. A limberness of spirit. Happiness is a rightness with God and with nature. Happiness . . . We must keep to our curriculum, however. The Age of Happiness is still some way off. For now we must confine ourselves to the Age of Strength, must we not? A time of *consolidation*, yes. Consolidation.'

'She loves you,' said Zennor, a good deal louder than she had meant. Indeed, she had not known she was going to say it at all. He looked up at her, a clump of turf in one hand and a trowel in the other, a look of such distaste on his face that she thought he must be in pain. 'I mean, she *fancies* she loves you. A long while, now. It is hard for her to think of marrying . . . someone else. Her heart is so given over to . . .' She was afraid to go on. It occurred to her that if she angered Wootton sufficiently, or persuaded him of Alba's regard, she might find herself married to Constable Gervase in Alba's place.

But she need not have worried. Wootton was dry-caulked; sealed up against Alba as sound as any ship against a breaking sea. 'Any slave to passion is greatly to be pitied,' he said, closing the subject as he might a jar of strychnine once a fox was poisoned. Zennor knew there was not another word she could safely say regarding Alba. Alba was a closed book, a room walled up, a clump of colourless fritillaries rooted out.

'I shall pretend it is him,' said Alba, on the morning of her wedding, and the tears which Zennor had begrudged her till then welled up and overflowed. 'I shall pretend it is Robin beside me all the while. All the way through. All through . . . everything.'

She had on the pale blue dress she had worn to sit for the milkmaid painting. Gervase wore a maroon-and-gold satin waistcoat, and his face was florid. They looked like oil and watercolour hung side by side with philistinic bad taste.

Everyone said what a shame it was that the proper parish vicar could not conduct the service, but the Reverend Baydon had been called away on family business – the court-martial of his brother, so the gossips said, though others said he was simply taking his wife and children up to Bedfordshire to stay with relations. The vicar came over from Hermitage at the particular request of Robin Wootton, and preached a sermon about the seven demons who came in place of the one cast out. Though it seemed, on the face of it, inappropriate, the congregatation responded feelingly. Soldiers were being billeted on households throughout Berkshire – taking over beds, occupying chairs, eating from larders . . . Those householders with daughters said it was very like having the house possessed by demons.

Robin Wootton declined to accept his quota of two soldiers, saying it was against his moral principles. He sent them over the hill to the vicarage instead, which (apart from an unwillingness to perform the marriage) was one reason Reverend Baydon had taken his wife and children up to Bedfordshire. Grace and Suzannah were comely girls. Two soldiers could be worse than seven demons in such circumstances.

Everyone commented on how fondly the bride looked at her guardian as he gave her away, as he waved to the departing wedding carriage. However unusual the arrangement, plainly Wootton had taken his guardianship to heart: the girl was not neglected, her dowry was reputed to be ridiculously large, and patently she carried away from his house as great an affection as any natural daughter might feel for her father.

Of course, the people who said this were busy partaking of a splendid wedding feast at the time, downstairs and up, at the Post Inn in Winding Hatch, paid for entirely out of Wootton's pocket.

Afterwards, Zennor and Robin got back to Hatch House before the servants. The house was preternaturally silent. It seemed to be listening – holding its breath and listening for someone to speak. But perhaps it was just Zennor waiting for Wootton to speak – to draw some conclusive line under the events of the day, to say where it left them in relation to one another. Had his selection been made? Was she now, in fact, mistress-elect of Hatch House? Or had she further tests to pass, levels of satisfactory behaviour to attain before she met his demanding requirements? How long was her education to last, this great apprenticeship for life?

Job's wife, Alice, had embarked on a syllabus all her own, when she heard of Alba's forthcoming wedding. She had taken it upon herself to explain 'the things a motherless girl needs knowing'. And Zennor had sat in on the talk, because all their other lessons had been taken together.

Alice was not a good teacher. She spoke abstractly of 'a man's needs', 'a man's *passions*'. The girls were both familiar with the word. It featured often in Rousseau, and therefore in Robin's conversation. 'Passion: a passionate temperament, lively impetuous feelings.' Zennor had read of it in Rousseau. But Alice did not seem to be talking about the same thing at all. She made it sound like some objectionable disease, suffered by men, like athlete's foot or piles. 'You just have to bear up to it till it pass,' were Alice's words. Rousseau wrote about music and theatre and nature filling him with passion: surely not a man's preserve entirely?

Alice said, 'Just you watch the beasts go to it. 'Tis soon enough over, never fear.'

Zennor had watched the beasts. They brought to mind Oliver Baydon and his threat of sexual violence. Smith at the forge. If *that* was what Alice meant by her abstract ramblings, did it mean that Robin, too, was chock full of sexual hunger? That lust came to him at nights, as it sometimes came to her?

With puzzled, curious eyes, she looked Robin over with this in mind: his body, his way of sitting up to table, the hang of his clothes, the curl of his hair. It was not an objectionable thought – simply implausible. She came to the conclusion that there must be two meanings to the word 'passion' – like the word 'missing', capable of meaning entirely different things without so much as a change of spelling. Missing a target. Missing a person. Missing, as Alba now was, from Hatch House.

Samuel Baydon was missing Sophronia and the children. He tried hard to deny it, since it seemed somehow unmanly, and his parishioners were attending to his every need. They brought him pies or invited him to supper. Curragh's wife agreed to do the laundry, both for him and the troopers billeted in his back bedrooms. She might have liked to refuse, still resentful at losing her job, but she needed the money too much.

The soldiers were intimidated by the parsonage into surprisingly temperate behaviour. They saved their lechery for the barmaids at the inn, tiptoeing in when drunk and swearing only in whispers between themselves. As a Justice of the Peace, Baydon's cases doubled, of course; he presided over cases involving the theft of forks, the death of chickens, drunkenness on Sundays and 'the illicit use of rented premises by Larpier Marchant for the purposes of unseemly and lewd acts'. But he pondered all the while whether he should not send for the children, to have them home again. Grace would hate it, he knew. Grace suffered embarrassment as other children suffered ashthma; but was that reason enough for a man and wife to be kept two counties apart?

Unfortunately, he could not hold Sophronia to blame for deserting him. She had not wanted to go. He had only managed to persuade her by saying that he would get the builders in, while she was away, to investigate the smell and damp once and for all. He had tried to do this, but the army seemed to be keeping all the builders and joiners and civil engineers fully occupied building ships and barracks and ordnance wagons. The French certainly had a lot to answer for.

At night, the big bed which he had once thought to occupy alone felt canted, not level, when he lay down in it – like a ship badly stowed, unsteerable for lack of a balancing load on the port side. It disturbed him that his mind turned so often to Sophronia's side of the bed. He had become acquainted with her body so ... haphazardly, it seemed, on reflection. The woman herself had acquainted him with it by some gradual, educative process, like showing someone around a country rather than giving them a relief map to study. The result was that though he could not quite recollect any one fiercely shocking encounter, he seemed, by some vegetative process, to have turned into a sensualist, an eroticist, a veritable satyr, such that a period of enforced abstinence drove him to the edge of desperation. He had dreams he would have thrashed George for having. Was this any service for a right-thinking woman to have done her husband? He began to plan ahead, for when she returned – opportunities he might make within their restored domestic routine; opportunities for recouping some of what was lost to him by the absence of Sophronia from his bed. He fell asleep thinking this through, and as a result dreamed he was looking for Sophronia all up and down the companionways of a troop-carrier bound for France. He caught glimpses of her, naked, beyond bellying sails, but was impeded in his chase by dozens of whispering soldiers moving always in the opposite direction. He called out to her that there was a war coming, but the wind carried his words away behind him and turned them into seagulls. A purse-seine net of stinking fish was dragging behind the ship, slowing it down, so that Sophronia was easily out-walking the speed of the ship, moving forwards to the bowsprit. He only caught up with her in time to tumble them both into the rigging nets under the sprit. Stretchy as the bill of a pelican, the net engulfed them, he with his arms and legs surrounding her, dimly aware of a vessel closing on them, dropping its gunports, running out its cannon . . .

At three o'clock that morning, with a crash like a ten-gun broadside, the back wall of the vicarage, undermined by ten years of waterlogging, collapsed into the garden. It carried with it the scullery sink, the living-room bureau and spinet along with two paraffin lamps, a section of the load-bearing central wall and the entire small bedroom on the eastern corner of the house. Sam's bedroom. Grace's bed, caught by its feet in the dense rubble of a chimney which fell through the ceiling of her room, was found by daylight hanging vertically down the gaping face of the house. The press in which Sophronia kept her clothes, and which had never been moved from the bedroom she first occupied, fell thirty feet, and smashed on the lawn, spilling petticoats, nightdresses, mourning weeds and a black cane calash in among the winter pansies.

The billeted soldiers, returning home by first light from Larpier Marchant's bawdy house, found the parson, in his trousers and nightshirt, standing out in a gentle fall of rain, contemplating this assortment of clothing spreadeagled across the garden bed in the likeness of a woman. He held an open umbrella in one hand, a calash hood in the other. 'Thought he'd killed somebody,' they said, later in the inn, ''cepting there weren't no body twixt the clothes, and 'alf the 'ouse was down.'

Sophronia Baydon received a strange, garbled letter from her husband telling her that 'God be praised, her house had fallen down, thanks to the macaroni's lake; that the army had rehoused its men and that she was to return home at once with the children, where they belonged. Though he hadn't the means to keep the rain off their heads, he was minded to live alfresco.'

The billeting of troops, and the growing certainty that France would invade, brought world events much closer than usual to the people of Winding Hatch. They read, with spellbound fascination, of the terror in Paris, the death of a king and queen at the hands of ordinary people, and it appalled their English sensiblities. They read of the guillotine, and small children made crude models out of string and knife blades, and cut up catkins, earthworms and mousetails. The sheep-dipping took on a representational shockingness, so did the docking of lambs' tails, the ugly brown potatoes unearthed half rotten in the ground, the carved heads on the beam-ends in church. The most parochial and inward-looking villager was aware of something red and ghastly happening within a three-day coach ride. Blood was soaking through the ground towards them, as the waters of Hatch House lake had seeped under the hill and brought down the vicarage.

And yet at Hatch House itself Robin Wootton did not understand why Zennor suddenly shuddered during the annual crowning of Rousseau.

She had been expecting a sadness – for something to be missing from the annual ceremony in which a laurel wreath was placed on the head of the scowling marble bust. The previous year there had been three of them ministering to the divine philosopher; now there were only two: Robin and Zennor, trying their hardest to embue an invented ritual with the momentousness of pagan worship. The trouble was, it took such a short time, and Rousseau never looked one jot more cheerful afterwards. Somehow tie-wigs and laurel wreaths made anachronisms of one another.

And then, for some reason, Zennor saw the bust for what it was: a head without a body: a head impaled on a pole; and the grotesque knowledge that this was truly happening, day after day, hour after hour, in the country of Rousseau's birth, made her shudder uncontrollably and want to cry.

'Oh Robin, can you imagine?' she said. 'Dying like that? Waiting to die like that? How does anyone keep mastery . . . keep from . . .' The sunlight on the large windows above the terrace made them shine like the blades of a dozen guillotines.

'Ah now, "inner light," Zennor, "inner light." You see why I say that you must confine yourself to the domestic? You attempt too much to try to leap into the arena of world politics.'

'I only . . .'

'The equation, in terms of grief, is too vast for your mathematics. How can you, with your small experience, hope to weigh the brief pain of the few against the protracted misery of the many? The algebra of it is simply impossible for you. Besides, I have raised you to share my own lively feelings, my own passionate temperament. You should not imagine that the victims of the guillotine have quite the same *depth of feelings* that you or I might have in the same circumstance. Consider the cow at the abattoir. And squeamishness certainly clouds history.'

'Oh, it was not squeamishness quite.'

'It may indeed be time for us to progress, my dear Zennor, to questions of morality. If you feel my meagre efforts have equipped you thoroughly. But do please remember: we must always begin with the domestic, and enlarge outwards.'

'I should like to read Hume,' said Zennor, glad enough to change tack, glad too to turn her back on the frowning bust of Rousseau divorced from the passionate feelings of his limbs, his hands, his bowels. But Robin was shaking his head. Apparently Hume was not to be.

'I fear you will have to accept, Zennor, that philosphy – any search for abstract truths, in fact – is simply beyond the grasp of women. It is the woman's place to apply the principles discovered by men. Our friend said that if women were to discover principles and men were to attend to detail, they would live in perpetual strife. And you and I do not wish to live in strife, do we?' He chucked her under the chin as he said it.

She waited, her face upturned, certain that he meant to say more about strife and the lack of it between them. Perhaps he had meant to, but she had deterred him with talk of guillotines and Hume. In any event, he looked at her with that expression which always implied the terrible intellectual isolation of a man trapped on a higher plateau of existence.

At such moments, Zennor felt such a hearty dislike of Robin that she would like to have shut a volume of Hume on his long, aquiline nose. But she knew how to overcome the feeling. She did not subordinate herself to his greater genius; she did not chastise herself for the sin of pride, nor pray for the virtue of meekness. She looked him over, as a stockman looks over a prime beast. She looked him over for what he was: a creature of supreme breeding, secure from the shocks of drought or dearth, possessed of libraries and a rainproof roof, a man who had set his face against snobbery (or thought he had), a man who offered her no violence, no abuse, no brutality. Then, like an accountant at a double ledger, she compared him with her father (what she remembered of him), her uncles, Mr Argent at the Lambeth Asylum, Oliver Baydon, Constable Gervase: all the faceless men who might have taken possession if Robin Wootton had not lighted on her like a magpie on a dropped farthing. Did she care to marry him?

Does the grass care to be watered? Do swine crave to be fed? Nothing in the universe commended itself so highly to her as marriage to Wootton. And even if he did nothing to bring it about, she felt no worse off for that. She was under his protection. And though he told her not to give a thought to the atrocities in France, or the likelihood of war, still she would anyway, because those things also taught her the marvellousness of her own safe and secure state. Of course, he could not feel for Alba or the Parisian aristocrats: he had been born to an inheritance of safety, a wealth of complacency born out of generations of safety.

She wrote to Alba that night, to say that nothing had changed with regard to Robin: he still had not spoken of marriage. She thought that might be of comfort to Alba, if she were still pining. She had no way of knowing whether or not Alba were pining, since they had not seen each other since the wedding. The bride's new home was a good ten miles away, and though Gervase came sometimes, on business, he never brought his wife – not even to dinner. There seemed to be an agreement between the two men that it should be like this. Zennor had written to Alba but Alba had written back only once – a polite, badly spelled note of two lines commending the joys of marriage. Zennor did not know what to make of it.

This time Zennor wrote at length, describing the ceremony of the crowning of J-J, and the grisly thoughts it had roused in her. And she closed by saying that nothing had changed, everything remained the same. Whatever upheavals the world went through, Hatch House remained forever untouched by any but Pan and Apollo and the man in the tie-wig. She thought that might be of comfort to Alba (if she were still pining): to think of Zennor unmarried.

It cost her nothing to write it. For she was blessed if she knew how to make a tragedy out of something so small, so insignificant, as

156

marriage (or the lack of it) to Robin Wootton. And she would read Hume anyway.

Robin Wootton was a man who planted weeds in his garden. No one had ever heard the weeds complain either.

The vicarage was shored up and made weatherproof. Job and Curragh were sent over the hill, with planks and hammers and pockets full of nails, though proper builders were nowhere to be had, thanks to the army. The congregation of Winding Hatch church trembled to think what sermon the collapse would give rise to: of the foolish man who built on water versus the wise one grounded in the Lord? Of the tower called Babel which fell on the good people next door thanks to the pride of its builders? They feared the water-that-is-beneath-the-earth welling up in springs of cleansing wrath; the wronged man rising to excoriate Robin Wootton, at length and in public, from the social high ground of the pulpit – for letting his lake leak. In short, they anticipated war.

But, astonishingly, Baydon showed total restraint. Perhaps in private, within the mould-caked ruins of his once-lovely Tudor vicarage, he was calling Wootton all the place-names under the sun; in the pulpit he talked bewilderingly of foxes and vines, of pomegranates and mandrakes.

'. . . *Many waters cannot quench love, neither can the flood drown it: if a man would give all the substance of his house for love, it would be utterly contemned . . .*'

The Song of Solomon rolled over them like deep waters, and having no clue how to apply it to their daily lives the people of Winding Hatch allowed their mouths to gape, their eyes to shut, and the current to sway them.

Sophronia had returned, and was sitting once more near the front, one arm around the youngest child. Her holiday in Bedfordshire seemed to have brought a good colour to her cheeks, and she watched her husband deliver his address as though he were himself Solomon and his Song perfectly plain in her understanding. After the service, Grace acknowledged the sympathy of the parish with a blush and a duck of the head, but Sophronia was seen to laugh more than once, as she recounted retrieving kitchen utensils from the pond, or imagined the spinet flying through the air like the Harp of Dagda in the House of the Fomorians.

Zennor had found the sermon exciting. Its strangeness disturbed and moved her, and she found herself unwilling to stand about afterwards exchanging the same weekly pleasantries with the same weekly faces. She wanted to get home and find the passage for herself in the Bible, and pick away at its dense weave until she could unravel the threads which held it together.

It was not to be. When she got back to Hatch House, Robin declared over lunch that the time had come for Zennor to become 'active within the social contract'.

The maid serving lunch hurried back with these words to the kitchen. Was it a proposal? 'It hearkened real 'portant!' said the maid.

But Alice pushed out her bottom lip until it resembled the scrolled end of the vegetable tureen. 'Tint love talk, be it?' she said.

It was not love talk. When the maid returned to clear the plates away, Robin was reading to Zennor from *The Social Contract*.

CHAPTER SIXTEEN

New House

When no reply at all came to her letters, Zennor grew anxious about Alba. The child – even the scholar – in her wanted to speak to Alba out of curiosity. How was marriage? What was marriage? Did Alice's ramblings make any better sense viewed in context? In some other part of her, though, unformed misgivings gathered like litter in a backwater. Zennor hoped her gypsy blood was not going to saddle her with the gift of prophecy – or if it did, that it would be a precise gift, not this general, non-specific uneasiness. In the end, she asked Robin when she might go to call on Alba Gervase.

'That particular book is best left closed,' he said, his top lip long and rigid, his hands compressed between his knees. 'Let me never hear, please, that you are in communication with Mrs Gervase. Beyond a word of salutation by way of the constable, I mean. There is a certain level of malignancy contagious as smallpox. And I should hate to see you blemished, child, I truly should.'

'Go to see her? Me?' said George Baydon. 'Why me? Why don't you go?'

'She's miserable, I know she is. She hates me. She blames me, I know she does. I write and write, but she won't answer my letters.' Zennor tossed her head like a horse troubled by flies. The thought of Alba buzzed about her day and night now, giving her no rest.

'But what reason have *I* got to call on her?' said George. 'A married woman?' His hackles stirred. 'Why must you always light on *me*?' His experience of doing favours for Zennor Wootton was not happy.

'How can I ask Mrs Baydon – or your father? They have troubles enough with the house.'

'It is my house too.'

'And you would tell me the truth.'

George was a little placated. 'What truth are you seeking, then?' he asked.

'Whether she's happy, of course,' said Zennor impatiently. 'And whether she hates me.'

A visit to New House involved a walk of ten miles in each direction, and all the way there George racked his brains for a good excuse to call. The house proved to be an ugly, red-brick building with over-tall, braggardly chimneys and pretentious heraldic beasts on the gateposts. As George approached, he saw Gervase at the mounting block, climbing on to an immense bay gelding which staggered under the impact of rider hitting saddle. George had the choice of hurrying forward and delaying the constable, or standing behind a tree until he had gone. A lifetime's experience of Gervase's conversation – concerning foreigners, drunkards, the unemployed, redheads, liberals, young people and Jews – decided George to step off the road. Then it seemed so childish, flattening himself against the bark of a horse chestnut, that he immediately regretted it. Zennor would have wanted him to hide, and that made it worse. In fact the only conversational topic which sprang to mind, now that he was faced with seeing Alba Gervase alone, was Zennor and her confounded tyranny.

Gervase trotted by, the pommel of his saddle completely buried under bulging stomach fat, his chins absorbing the jolts, his face already sweating at the exertion. Within George a dozen different and confused emotions jostled for supremacy. What had Robin Wootton been thinking of, to marry his ward to this gross, pompous buffoon – reward or revenge? And what kind of lamprey was Gervase to take advantage of a domestic scandal to seize on a young wife?

Halfway up the drive of New House, George's feet came to a halt as he called to mind the love affair between Alba and his uncle. Knowing of her harlotry, perhaps he should not even be there. He certainly did not want to be. Alba had overtaken him now in terms of worldly experience, with her secret assignations, her shameless and sordid indiscretions. Gervase, it had to be said, was at least ready to overlook the scandal, to forgo Alba's virginity, to forgive her. Perhaps that made him a better Christian than George, since George (puritanical as only a virgin can be) was not even sure he wanted to spend one hour with such a woman.

The one thing which did not occur to him was that he would be turned away.

'Constable's not at home,' said the housekeeper. She was a ziggurat of a woman, diminishing upwards from her colossal base to a small head and tiny, netted bun.

'Then please present my compliments to *Mrs* Gervase.'

'She's not home neither.'

Ten miles for nothing. George's weariness overcame his earlier misgivings. 'Might I wait?'

'Mrs Gervase d'n receive callers,' said the woman, stepping forward into the doorway as if he might try to push past her.

'Why not? Is she unwell?'

'Who is it?' A small piping voice which he mistook for a child's came from somewhere indoors. Then a huge dormeuse lace cap floated into view.

'Madam is not at home,' repeated the housekeeper.

'Yes! Yes, I am! Who is it? Who?' The shrill whine could hardly be ignored by either of them.

'Madam is not dressed,' said the housekeeper without looking behind her.

'Yes! Yes, I am! Look. Look, I am!' Alba came and peeped over the woman's shoulder. 'Oh, it's George, la!' She was dressed in a sprig-cotton wrapper, which did not seem particularly unsuitable for receiving morning visitors, as far as George could judge these things.

'My father, the Reverend Baydon, asked me to call,' said George to the housekeeper. 'If you were to request her indulgence, I should not detain Mrs Gervase for any great length of time, nor at inordinate inconvenience to yourself.' It wound its way out of him: a sentence of exactly the kind his father would have used if equally embarrassed.

The housekeeper relented and let him in. Yet oddly she did not retire to fetch tea, but took up guard in the corner of the room, her hands clasped in front of her waist.

A duenna, thought George. Gervase is afraid of her entertaining other men! He tried to smile to himself, but found the sight of the wardress staring into middle space oddly chilling. 'Everyone at Winding Hatch sends their warmest greetings,' said George sitting down opposite Alba.

'Do they? Do they?' She seemed neither sceptical nor very interested.

In the good light of the parlour, George could see that the buttons of the sprig-cotton wrapper were fastened wrongly, so that the bodice was pulled out of shape. There were yellowish stains, too, and one of the cuffs was not fastened. Narrow pink ribbons sprang from the ornate lacework of the dormeuse and one brushed against Alba's mouth; every so often her tongue drew it in and she sucked. She did not seem to notice the long silence which fell between them. Her lids drooped and her fingers played incessantly with the wedding ring on her hand, as though it had become stuck there by mistake and she was trying to loosen it. Her reticule lay in her lap, too, clenched tight between her knees.

The presence of the woman in the corner was so oppressive that George, though he rummaged topics of conversation like a burglar through a chest of drawers, could think of nothing, nothing to talk about and lapsed into unhappy silence. The housekeeper peered shortsightedly at the carriage clock on the mantel, and took a step forward, ready to conclude the interview.

'Might you be so kind as to show me your new house?' said George out of sheer pig-headedness, then could not think why he had prolonged his torment.

Immediately Alba stood up to oblige him. She swayed and had to rest a hand against the wall.

'Are you quite well, Miss Alba?' asked George.

'Of course,' she replied, still shrill, half singing. But as she showed him through the house, he noticed that she paused at every doorway and narrowness, as if to estimate the clearance. She kept tight hold of her reticule, too.

A peculiar high-pitched whine accompanied them round the ugly house, like a gnat droning loose somewhere; they had reached the conservatory before he realised it was Alba herself, humming.

Was she drunk? At eleven in the morning? George found himself sniffing the air she exhaled as she drifted slowly, stiltedly through her home. 'I think this is the sewing-room,' she said at one point. There was no smell of drink, only a slight medicinal tang masked by a great deal of perfume.

'It is a charming house,' George said, confronted by one ill-proportioned and cluttered room after another.

'No, it isn't. It's ugly, like him,' said Alba and a laugh trickled out of her like water from a leaky pump.

He had meant her to show him only the public rooms, but she drove a diagonal line up the stairs to the bedrooms above, while the housekeeper hurried along behind, whipping the skirts of her stiff dress to and fro with a noise like sails in a tempest.

Alba threw open the doors of the marital bedroom. The bed was unmade. Pieces of clothing lay about – hair-brushes, a riding boot, a wig stand, a garter. 'This is where,' said Alba. A complete sentence. Her cuff tangled in the door handle. As she tried to pull free, the door banged her repeatedly on the side of the head: she did not even appear to notice. Eventually, the cuff tore, but the ribbon handle of the reticule became tangled instead. George offered to free it.

Through the thin stuff of the bag, he could feel the shape of a bottle – not a flask, he thought – and something else resembling a tea-strainer.

'Miss Zennor was concerned that you did not answer her letters,' he said softly, out of hearing of the housekeeper.

'Letters?' she said, and looked at him with eyes that moved independently of one another without quite focusing. There were patches of red around her eyes, and her lashes were sparse, almost gone. 'Oh Zennor,' she said on a sharp intake of breath. 'Tell Zennor.'

'Tell Zennor what?'

The housekeeper tried to force her way between them to shut the bedroom doors or just to put a stop to quiet conversation. George found his arm holding her off, forcibly pressing hard against the woman's shelving stays. 'Tell Zennor what, Miss Alba?'

'What?' Alba frowned at him, the thread lost, her train of thought broken. She reached up and pulled off her cap. The hair inside it had been ringleted into a *tête mouton* of tight little curls burned shineless with curling tongs. There was a patch of navy bruising to one temple, just below her hairline. Remarkable that she should bruise so soon after the door banging her.

'Go away,' she said suddenly, her voice dropping through two octaves, out of the former, birdlike tweeting. Traces of Lambeth, even after all the years at Hatch House, were plain in the harsh, repeated demand: 'Go away. Go away. Go away.'

George covered three miles of the walk home without even noticing the way. He felt as if he had just witnessed something indecent which he was not supposed to have seen and which he was too young to understand – like a child walking into his parents' bedroom. He wanted to cry without knowing why. What was he to tell Zennor, when he did not know himself what he had seen?

Luckily, when he reached home, he found his father and Sophronia resting from the endless task of moving rubble out of the garden beds. They both looked positively ruddy from spending so much time out of doors. Samuel had fallen asleep sitting on a bench against the wall. So George was able to confine his confidences to his step-mother.

Describing everything he had seen at New House, he laid the responsibility squarely in Sophronia's lap. 'So do you think Miss Alba is ill?'

Sophronia covered his hands where they lay fiddling with the tea-strainer on the kitchen table. 'What do *you* think?' she asked.

'I think she is taking laudanum or some such,' he said, without knowing he had been going to say it. Sophronia inclined her head, to show that the suggestion was not wholly improbable. He was more shocked than she was. 'But what's to do?' he kept asking. 'What am I to tell Zennor Wootton?'

Sophronia was oddly collected and cool. George had become so accustomed to her tolerant, easy-going attitudes that he was surprised to see her eyes close a fraction, her mouth stiffen ever-so slightly. 'I advise you to tell Zennor that you found Mrs Gervase fit and happy and well accommodated to married life.'

'But –'

'In my experience, laudanum is all in all to those who use it. And I see nothing to be gained by disappointing Zennor in her friend.'

George's chief reaction was relief. He had been sanctioned to stop worrying about that strange, febrile, humming woman with the bruised face, up at New House. Alba's use of drugs had placed her beyond reach or deserving (though he was not altogether clear why his step-mother regarded it as such an irredeemable wrong).

He duly reported back to Zennor that he had found Alba happy and well but disinclined to trouble herself writing letters. Zennor was delighted. All her presentiments had proved wrong; she was less gypsy than fool, after all, and she could not have been more pleased. She easily persuaded herself that Constable Gervase had been able to buy Alba's contentment with the dresses and trinkets she had always prized so much.

George was surprised what pleasure it gave him to bring Zennor the good news, to see her face colour, her eyes brighten, her wide mouth enlarge with relief. If conveying good news could be so gratifying, perhaps he ought to think seriously about a career in the Church. For the life of him, he could not think why else he came away from Hatch House whistling.

When Sophronia Baydon prayed longer than usual at the foot of her bed that night, her husband asked her if she were troubled. She looked up at him over her joined hands. 'You are a good man, Samuel,' she said, 'and I thank God for you.'

He smiled, realising that he was being compared with her last husband, the laudanum addict. He just wondered what, at this late date, had raised the comparison in her mind.

CHAPTER SEVENTEEN

Neighbours

'The time is come,' said Robin, 'for Emile's moral parts to awaken – for you, Zennor, to become a citizen of the world which has been revealed to you over the years. At this time, there are only two questions to ask yourself about the plight of the world around you: "How does it concern me?" and "What can I do?"'

'I could write letters for the soldiers,' said Zennor promptly.

She had long since read ahead in her curriculum and foreseen this new landmark. She had already given great thought to the difficulties of her fellow men, and though it seemed to her that they needed almost everything – food, clothing, prayers, education and whipping – she had mastered few skills that were of practical use to them. Only writing. The idea had struck her like a dart – of becoming an amanuensis to some of the illiterate troopers shipping out for the Cape, for Canada and to fight the French in unknown distant theatres of war. They would surely like to set down their feelings, on being parted from their families, perhaps for ever: to leave some tangible expression for a wife or a sweetheart or a swaddling child. Even within an illiterate family she could see the talismanic value of a letter.

Zennor had tested the idea on Sophronia, and Sophronia had called it the 'wonderful notion of a good heart'. Zennor was so pleased that she had clutched the idea to her breast all the way home, like a winning playing-card, longing for the opportunity to lay it down in front of Robin Wootton. Perhaps she played it too fast.

'But war does *not* concern you, my dear Zennor,' exclaimed Wootton in his softest, most apologetic voice. 'War is the prime vice of this unnatural society of ours, *n'est-ce pas*? It goes quite against the true nature of man.'

'That's why no man wants to go,' said Zennor. 'So I thought . . .'

Robin leaned across the table, laying his beautiful hands palm up, as if laying a meal in front of her. 'How can you think to express a tenderness for your fellows by endorsing the very violence which will consume them?'

'Oh, I did not mean to help along the war,' she protested. 'Only to help out the poor men who –'

'Zennor! Child!' groaned Robin, rocking from side to side in barely suppressed disappointment at her small grasp on abstract moral principles. 'Does not a whore justify herself in the very same way?' He breathed out the words, barely audible, so as not to shock too deeply.

Zennor did not labour her plan; she let it go like a handful of sand. Plainly Robin had already thought of a way for her to be of service to the poor, and to persist would only persuade him that she was not yet ready to enter the moral phase of her education. Rousseau had ordained that history be kept back until the Age of Morality. Therefore Zennor sewed up her letter-writing plan, dead as a sailor in canvas. There were whole alcoves of the library in Hatch House given over to history, and she craved access to them.

Perhaps, she mused to herself, perhaps she was not yet capable of selfless moral thought. Perhaps she *was* still so juvenile that she put her own interests above those of other people. Otherwise how could the lure of all those history books make her suppress an idea she knew perfectly well to be sound?

Meekly she submitted to sewing shirts for the children of the poor. That was how Robin pictured her serving the community.

She had not done sewing since Lambeth, and even there she had barely got past tacking. But he assumed the ability would be innate in her, being a girl. Alice showed her some rudiments of needlework, but was irritable – unreasonably outraged, in fact – that Zennor should have grown to such an age without the basic skills of a gentlewoman. Zennor could cut withies, hammer nails, plane wood, prune apple trees, milk a cow and churn butter better than she could sew, but she could do none of them well enough to be of practical use to the community of Winding Hatch; she had no more perfected any of the country crafts than Wootton himself, who had hurried her from subject to subject, a tourist guide on a Grand Tour of agricultural life.

She numbered the day of her visit to the poorhouse among the worst in her life as, measuring-cord and notebook in hand, she walked along the central corridor of the female house, looking for someone on whom to bestow the promise of a shirt. All the fit men had enlisted. All the unfit, and most of the women, were employed on a grand, national scheme of road improvement: that is to say they were out filling ruts and potholes with pebbles gathered off the fields. The only occupants left in the big dark rooms to either side of the corridor were the elderly, the sick and an assortment of listless, hollow-eyed children who drifted sombrely towards her. Like the souls of the dead towards Aeneas, thought Zennor.

Seeing an old lady holding a child on her knee, Zennor said, 'Would your grandchild like a shirt made?'

'A shroud?'

'A shirt,' repeated Zennor. 'I could sew a shirt for your little one. Or a dress.' She was not sure if the crab-apple face belonged to a boy or a girl.

'Sixpence would be a thing,' said the old lady. But Robin had given Zennor no allowance ever since she entered the Age of Morality. He did it as an exercise, a discipline designed to 'undam the channel of social intercourse so oft clogged by a difference in wealth', he said.

Zennor looked around her, breathing shallowly so as to take in as little as possible of the smell: carbolic, urine, disease, damp, the malting-works next door. It was true. Money had choked up the navigable watercourse of these people's lives. Debt had gathered like silt round their feet until they lost all power of movement. Here they were no longer even free to come and go. Poverty controlled every facet of their lives, was miring them under, hour by hour, day by day. With money, she could have sluiced bare this whole building. Like Hercules cleaning the Augean stables just by diverting a silver river, thought Zennor.

'Or a morsel of gin,' said the old lady.

'Please. Let me make a shirt for your little one,' said Zennor, pleading, and the old lady made a gurning motion of her toothless mouth, and set the child down to be measured.

When Zennor got home she could make no sense of the figures she had scribbled down. None of them seemed relevant to the pieces of cloth laid out on the kitchen table. So she went and found the shirts she and Alba had brought with them from Lambeth: they were still rolled up, uncompleted, at the bottom of the press in her bedroom. Alba's was further forwards than hers. It also looked about the size of the child she had seen.

So she sewed it. Its seams were supposed to be run-and-fell, but when she finished the raw edges showed both outside and in. The collar she attached six separate times, to cloth already disintegrating with age, and each time she unpicked it the threads gaped wider. It took weeks. And as she closed the seams, the shirt looked so much smaller than its component parts had done that she doubted it would even fit when it was finished, especially since the child had had quite enough time to grow.

The finished shirt was a source of pride to her, and yet she had seen enough shirts in her life to know it was horrible. It made her marvel at Wootton's shirt across the breakfast table, its seams so smooth, its stitches smaller than grains of sugar. Better cloth, she told herself.

When she took the shirt back, the poorhouse was busier than before, and she had difficulty finding the old woman again. When she did, there was no child with her.

'I brought your child's shirt,' she said, smiling sheepishly. 'I hope the little mite has not grown too big.'

'What child?' said the old woman sourly.

For a terrible moment, Zennor imagined the child had died, while she laboured over pin-tucks and buttonholes.

'Before. You had a child on your lap.'

'Maybe I done, maybe I don't. Tweren't mine.' The intervening time had washed away any acquaintance with Zennor. 'Want to prick me like a cow. Well, you won't!' She drew back from Zennor, petulant, her two thin mottled forearms crossed over her chest, her big rheumatic hands clasped on either bicep. Did she think the shirt was for her?

'I took out all the pins, truly,' said Zennor, but such was the hostility in the woman's pouting lips that the girl backed away, crushing her shirt into a smaller and smaller bundle within one hand.

She wandered through the building looking for the child – any child of a suitable size. She was half inclined to drop the miserable garment on the floor and go. In contrast with the oppressive silence of the place on her last visit, the house was noisy now with sullen, strident voices. There was a restlessness about the groups of women talking around the washing-trough; in the group of men she could glimpse by the door of the other building, across the yard.

To her astonishment, standing in the middle of the yard was someone she knew: George Baydon. He shifted from foot to foot as if cram-full of impatience or irritation, while the warden talking to him kept shrugging and lifting his hands ineffectually. When Zennor went out to them, the warden seized the opportunity of moving off.

'What are you doing here?' asked George sharply. She stopped abruptly a good way away.

'I make shirts for the . . . I made a shirt.' As his eyes drifted down towards the object in question, Zennor pushed it out of sight under her tippet.

Recovering his manners, George went to take off his hat, but was not wearing one. She did not ask, but he felt obliged, by her expression, to explain his presence in the poorhouse.

'My father has . . . offered to pay for inoculation against small pox for the inmates here. Inoculation: it is a new remedy – an excellent . . .'

'I have heard of it. We are against it at our house.'

'Why?' He came back at her with what she thought unreasonable heat.

'Oh, you know,' she said brightly. 'We are against everything medical at our house.' When he saw that she was not talking about her own opinions he mastered his temper without exactly managing to smile. George waved a hand about him angrily. 'None of these are ready to take it! Do they *want* the pox, do you think? Do they *want* to see their children die, sooner than be scratched with a needle?'

'Perhaps they think it is a plot. To poison the poor. To keep down the population.'

'Don't they know, we have the war to do that,' said George, swinging his unworn jacket over first one shoulder then the other, in a fever of frustration. His mind was only half on her; half still wrestling with the intractable poor who refused to be saved from suffering and pestilential death.

'It was a fine, generous notion of your father's,' she said softly, and walked past him to the gate. Beside the gate-house, where a porter barred the way to food and shelter against outsiders, the way to freedom against the inmates, a young woman stood with a naked, long-haired baby in her arms. Zennor pulled out the crumpled, moribund shirt and held it out to the woman apologetically. 'For your little girl,' she said.

The woman set the child down, and Zennor could not quite manage to look away as the child loosed a weak dribble of urine from a sore, red little penis. As the shirt was pulled on over the boy's head, she noticed that he did not even blink his eyes to protect them against the rattle of buttons, did nothing to try to push his hands into the sleeves. His flesh had a brown solidity, though no plump depth to it. He looked, in the coggled garment, like a wood-carved madonna dressed for a church festival, the cloth more living than the statue under it.

'Shoulda give out the cloth,' said the mother. 'I done stitching. Coulda made it up in a day.'

Better, too, thought Zennor. 'You should have the inoculation, you know. Against the smallpox,' she advised. 'That parson wouldn't send a bad thing to you. I know him. He's a good man.' But the mother drew her son against her legs and narrowed her eyes, as if to say the shirt was not bribe enough to make her submit to poisoning. Zennor mustered all her courage. 'If *I* have it, will you?' she asked, laying a hand gently on the child's head.

'No,' said the woman, snatching the child away, and Zennor was relieved. She would have done it, to oblige the Reverend Baydon. She would. But secretly she hated the idea of that cowpox vaccine creeping through her blood, colouring it pied–Guernsey, turning her skin to hide.

When she told her guardian about Baydon's efforts to vaccinate the poor of Wantage, he shook his head, lamenting. '*That* is not what the poor need. They need to be taught a rightness with nature!'

'Vaccination is a natural remedy,' she suggested, without conviction. 'Shall you not be vaccinated, then?'

'No! And neither shall you! Once again science is seeking a simple answer to a problem of its own making. The natural order is disturbed: come sickness and sorrow, and science scurries to its apothecaries for a remedy. Take my advice, Zennor child. Doctors are vexatious to the spirit. Avoid doctors, as I do.'

'You are never ill.' It was out before she knew it, sounding insolent and argumentative, though she had not meant to be. To cover the awful *faux pas*, she plunged (as she always did) into the safe preserve of Rousseau: drew Rousseau in front of her like a sheet of glass, knowing Wootton would not smash it. 'So what can I do? I have to ask myself, don't I? What can I do? Next.'

Robin was not stuck for an answer. He led the way to the round table in the hallway, where the relevant book already lay opened at the relevant page. He read aloud to her, leaning on his fingertips to either side of this, his philospher's stone. '. . . *We must therefore present objects to dilate Emile's heart – to take him out of himself, remove everything which narrows him. We must arouse in him kindness, goodness, pity – not envy, greed and hate . . .*' Robin looked across the table, into the face awaiting his instructions. Although the look on it was a little strange, it was neither envious nor greedy nor hateful. Comforted, heartened that he had not yet erred in her educational nurture, he returned his eyes to the book. '*Emile must go among the poor and suffering!*' he read, closing the book with reverent gentleness.

Zennor's eyes had opened a little wider, but her fingers were still clasped in front of her. 'Yes?' she said, her heart dilating painfully just then at the thought of the little boy in her cobbled, coggling shirt.

He could have sent her, for finishing, on the Grand Tour: the Parthenon, Venice, Florence, Paris. But he had done that himself, and could vouch for there being precious little there to excite a man of feeling: the

170

temples of dead civilisations, the paintings of dead subjects by dead artists; the sepulchres of dead kings. Instead he sent her among the living, those hoping for life: in short, the sick, and in particular the smith's family who were rumoured to be so poorly that the forge was temporarily closed.

'Teach them the virtue of hygiene,' he exhorted her, kissing her on the forehead. 'And remember, tell them to avoid doctors like the plague. The cook will give you some broth for them, and some cleaning items, in case you find the place insanitary.'

'Is it? Insanitary?' she asked, supposing he must have been there to visit the sick himself. But he seemed not to hear.

She very much wanted to say that she was afraid of the smith – that any glancing encounters with him since those first lessons in metalwork at the forge had not made her like him any better or fear him any less. But the man's family was ill, and it seemed uncharitable to be casting aspersions. Smith's lechery would surely have been quenched by worry for his wife, by fatherly anxiety for his little daughters or by whatever unknown illness ailed him.

'Just put they down at the door and take you a walk thereabout,' said Alice, giving her the food, the newly made soap and a scrubbing-brush. 'Let them get on.'

But the prime object of Zennor's trip, she knew, was not quite to feed the Smiths or to clean them up. It was education: to enlarge her soul and charge her unloaded, selfish conscience. She thanked Alice and went out to the carriage.

'I could walk. There's no need for the carriage, truly,' she protested, as her guardian handed her into the landau. Perhaps he did not trust her really to go there? He surely knew her better than that.

'Give Smith my warmest brotherly greetings,' said Robin, patting her gloved hand.

'He always looks so smickerly at me,' she blurted out, as the carriage began to move. But though she did not realise it she had picked up the expression from one of the servants or tradesmen or artisan tutors, and he did not understand.

On the short ride down to the village, she looked down at the soap and brush, and thrust them away under the seat. She could not insult a woman by starting to scrub her floor. It was unthinkable.

'You don't want to be going on in there,' said Job, setting her down outside the smithy. 'That old boy can't hold off petticoats. 'Tis a sickness with him. Say he even lifts his own washing.'

But it was Zennor's turn not to understand. 'It's only right to visit the sick,' she said resolutely. 'I hope they would visit me if I were ailing.'

Job rattling his sinuses unpleasantly at the thought of the blacksmith visiting Zennor's sick-bed, and clicked his tongue at the horse. If he moved off sharply, Zennor would be free to leave her duty presents at the door and run, as Alice had told her. If he hung about, she might feel obliged to knock. Besides, Job had promised himself an hour or two at home, smoking a pipe before taking her home, the Christian show of duty done.

Of course, home was never as peaceful a bolt-hole as he pictured it in the abstract. His wife was there, like the jab of a knitting-kneedle, laying into him as soon as he settled into his chair.

'Never tell me you took her there yonder? What you thinking of, great lummock? *Does* you think on weekdays or what? Never tell me you took her there?'

'Oh, Smith won't try her. Not if he's poorly. Wouldn't dare, neither.'

His wife caught him a blow with a carding comb which left wool clinging to the arm of his jacket. 'Don' you know they got the *scarlet*?' she shrieked. 'Never went in, did you? Never went in y'sel'?'

Job shook his head. But he looked at his hands as he picked the wool off his coat, and wondered if scarlet fever clung just as readily, whether it hung in the air around a house as well as inside it. 'Should I fetch her away?' he asked, struggling to get up out of the low, split chair.

'Don' you dare!' said his wife. 'Let her walk home. You can say you had trouble with carriage. A wheel off. Don' you jus' dare! Ben't I cursed enough having you in aside me, without you fetch the scarlet in, too?' And she hit him with the other carder, leaving a white sausage of exfoliated wool clinging to his hair.

Smith himself opened the latch to Zennor. His nose was wet and pink-tipped, and his eyes rimmed with red, but he was dressed, after a fashion, and looked only as unwell as a man with a heavy cold. Beyond him, in the single room which backed on to the forge, his wife and one daughter lay sleeping in bed, while another three children were bedded down on a palliasse hard up against the chimney-breast. The breast, like a great brick buttress jutting into the room, was the back of the forge furnace, the brickwork discoloured and unmortared by the great heat it absorbed. Since the forge was never allowed to go out, the room behind was immensely hot. The cooking-range was unlit, but Zennor was able to warm the broth just by putting it into the bread oven cut in that monumental chimney. All the while, the children on the floor coughed or whimpered on a level with her hems, like restless dogs. When one of them was sick, Zennor was sorry she had left the soap and brush in the cart. She had to manage as best she could with what the blacksmith found her. All the while she cleared up the vomit, he watched, his lips slightly apart, breathing through a blocked nose, his tongue bulging out his cheek like a gumboil. His bloodshot eyes looked as though he had worn them out with watching.

First and foremost, the place smelt of soot. Their hair smelt of soot, their bedding of soot. The cobwebs which hung in the open roof space of the single-storey building were clotted strings of soot, almost as solid as roosting bats. There was another smell, too, of sickness mingled with sweat.

Each time Smith approached he approached closer than the time before, thanking her for coming, commenting on every detail of her dress, touching as he complimented, chock-full of irony.

'Fine lace.'

'Pretty stuff.'

'Smicker ribbons.'

'Soft leather. You had none when you come to me as a leveret.' But as he bent to lift the hem of her dress and admire her shoes, he was shaken by a bout of uncontrollable coughing. She watched the droplets from his nose and mouth spangle the fabric of her dress. It was as though she were dreaming it, distanced from reality by the feverish heat, the peculiar mix of smells, the shapeless gloom of a room whose closed windows were all but obscured. A dresser had been stood in front of one; a dozen of the iron rods from which he daily cut horseshoes were propped in front of the other. More like a prison than a sickroom, thought Zennor.

The child in the bed stirred and, to keep her from waking the mother beside her, Zennor leaned over the girl, smiling and stroking her hair. 'Soon be well,' she whispered. Such a queer little creature, lacking her front teeth and with spotty skin and hands oddly reddened, as though she were wearing pink lace gloves. 'Could you like a little taste of broth?'

'My bones pain!'

'Your bones?'

'Elbows. Knees. My head.' Even the small amount of daylight seemed too bright for the anxious, frowning eyes.

'Have some broth. It will make you better.'

Their skin was so hot. It was like the chimney-breast: radiating some heat greater than was required by their littleness. There was no sponge or towel. Zennor wetted their faces with a flannel spencer she found hanging on a stool, then thrust it into the top of her dress to cool herself; also to keep Smith's eyes off her sternum. 'Has the doctor called?' she asked him.

'Doctors, tch!' said Smith, which might have referred to their cost or their incompetence. Or perhaps, like Wootton, Smith was philosophically opposed to them.

'A doctor could say what ails them,' she suggested, and his expression suggested that he already knew that. Still, when she asked directly, he shrugged and said, 'A quinsy is all.' Zennor herself had no way of knowing if he were right.

The mother stirred and opened her eyes. She took time to recognise her situation, her predicament. Her heavy hands she could only fling inaccurately in the direction of her object. One hand banged against Zennor, who squatted down beside the low bed. 'Who's this here?' she croaked, thinking perhaps that her husband had taken advantage of her illness to fetch in one of his women.

'It's Zennor Wootton, Mrs Smith. I came to see how you were faring. Can I fetch you something? Some broth?'

Mrs Smith peered at the distant, bulky black shape of her husband, still uncertain. 'Neighbourly, int 'er?' he shouted across the room.

The face on the pillow softened, and she smiled weakly at Zennor, flinging a hand up towards her face, banging Zennor's cheek. Tears rolled unchecked and unnoticed out of the corners of her eyes and into her ears. 'Good of you. Uncommon good of you, miss,' she said. 'Most won't come near the scarlet.'

Zennor's brain swung forwards and banged against the back of her eyes like the clapper of a bell. She did not squeal or drop the woman's hand. She did not jump back from the bed, did not snatch the sheet up over the woman's face to deflect the breath bubbling from her nostrils. She went on smiling, and stroking the hand, pulled the spencer from her corsage and wiped Mrs Smith's sweating throat with it. But inside her head she was screaming the word over and over: *Scarlet! Scarlet! Scarlet!*

She looked at the children lying on the floor and suddenly they were corpses laid out for burial. She looked at the girl with the red lacey hands and spots now easily recognisable as a rash, and thought, She is probably dying. She looked up into the sooty eaves, and death hung there in a black-tasselled canopy of cobwebs, directly over her head.

She did not run directly out of doors. She fed broth until there was no broth left. She wiped little faces and hands until the ewer was empty of water. She did not run out into the road. It would have been both cowardly and offensive to her neighbours. The tolling bell inside her head told her that she was in sore need of a clear conscience. Tomorrow it might be *her* lying in bed with the sum total of her remaining life burning to ashes in the oven of her body. Tomorrow she might die.

'That sounds like Job in the carriage. I must go now.' She heard her voice at large in the room, sounding odd and bright. 'I'll call again, to see you all.'

Smith tried to handle her in the doorway, but her fright made her unusually quick and cunning: if she did not get out of this room it would be the death of her, and no lecherous bully could persuade her of the merit of that. She trod on his foot and ducked under his arm, pulling open the door so that the latch struck him in the back. Then she was out on the road, running for the carriage.

It was not the landau at all, just a flat-cart. Still, she picked up her skirts and she ran, crying out loud, sobbing with fright. Robin had sent her unwarned to catch scarlet fever! She had gone in there and breathed their breath and touched their skin and tomorrow some of them would be dead. Hadn't he known? Hadn't he minded? She had read of epidemics in other parts of the country, cutting a swathe through whole communities, but no one had told her it was loose in Winding Hatch. That it had laid hold of her neighbours. It was as though, while the county kept watch against the smallpox, the scarlet had circled round by country roads, to enter by stealth.

When she reached the path which offered the quickest route home Zennor did not take it. She did not want Robin's help, never thought for one moment of seeking it. She wanted a friend, someone sensible who could tell her how dangerous the scarlet truly was, whether she was in danger of her life, what she could do to be saved. Without a thought of home, she went straight to the vicarage, and climbed in at the kitchen door over a stack of left-over planks, in a clattering lunge.

Only Grace was sitting there, reading a book. 'Where's Sophie? Where is she? Please!' Wordlessly, Grace got up, and went and called up the stairs for her mother. Sophronia came down smiling broadly, as if she had just been told a really excellent joke. She was wearing only a wrapper gown, more proper for the morning, and her hair was remarkably dishevelled, capless.

Zennor threw herself into Sophronia's arms and cried unrestrainedly, pressing her face into the woman's softly plaited hair as she told where she had been and why. 'Will I die? Will I? Will I catch it?'

Sophronia shushed her softly, as if she were a little child, rocking her to and fro, so that the cloth of their dresses whispered together making a similar sound. 'No harm. No harm,' she assured Zennor. 'God will take care of you. God will see to it that you come to no harm. Nothing to fret about. Trust me. Nothing at all.'

Reassurance warmed Zennor like a beam of sunlight. She laughed a damp, shuddering laugh, and kissed Sophronia gratefully on each cheek, calling herself simple and foolish and cowardly. It seemed so utterly silly to have brought her little worries here, to this shored-up, battened, shuttered, ruin of a kitchen. She saw now that there was a pot of camphorated water boiling over the fire. Plainly some of the family were already weathering summer colds.

Samuel Baydon had followed his wife down the stairs and he, too, came into the kitchen. It was as though a thread of Sophronia's dress had caught on his button, for he seemed drawn irresistibly after her, placing a hand on her waist as he stood behind her. He was equally oddly attired for the time of day, in a morning banjan, bareheaded, and wore the same smile as Sophie, of subversive, pent-up delight. For once Zennor's presence in his house did nothing to remove it. 'What's amiss?' he asked, willing to withdraw if it were something unsuitable for a man or a parson to hear.

'Oh, it's nothing,' said Sophronia, stroking Zennor's hair aside with the back of her fingers. 'Zennor has just heard bad news about the Smiths. They have scarlet fever, you know.'

The smile wilted on the parson's face. 'Oh no. I must call on them with communion. Heylipol. The children, too? Hubberholme. Have any died that you've heard?'

Zennor, slow to realise that this question was directed at her, dried her eyes. 'No. No. None. That I've heard.' And Samuel wandered away down the hall and shut himself in his study to pray for the Smiths.

'God will take care of you, chick,' said Sophronia again, cheerily. 'He is very good. 'Way! The scarlet's not much! Best take off all those clothes, even so, and let me wash them through. Grace will fetch you something of hers to put on, won't you, my love?'

CHAPTER EIGHTEEN

Exemplary Woman

When Sophronia Baydon died of scarlet fever, her silence spread farther afield than her noise had ever done. It seeped through the damaged parsonage walls and silenced the tradesmen. It soaked down through the chalkstone into the stream, and left the fish dumbly gaping. It rose into the trees and turned the birds to shrapnel. It holed the black drumskin of the millpond. As far off as Wilton, the windmill stood aghast. The bell in the church did not even ring, castrated of its clapper by unknown hands.

Her constitution weakened by a smallpox vaccination, she succumbed to the scarlet in only three days. Grace, who collapsed a short while later, hysterical with sorrow, hallucinating with fever, was too ill to be told.

At Hatch House, it was Robin Wootton who broke the all-pervading silence over luncheon, with, 'Didn't we always know that medicines were a plague?'

It was as though Zennor's plate had been filled with silence, poisoned with it, so that when she opened her mouth to speak, she could not. Her belly was distended with silence, her brain fogged with it.

'If she'd not let Baydon persuade her to have a cow's pox in her blood, she could have fought off the fever, take my word,' said Wootton, carving ham from a clove-studden shank. 'Dare swear he carried it home to her, too, from visiting the Smiths.'

'None for me, sir, thank you. I have no appetite,' said Zennor. But he loaded the pink slices on to her plate in any case, the cloves embedded like lead shot. She made herself ask, 'Did you know, then, that the Smiths had scarlet fever?'

'No! *Sacré* no!'

His eyes were wide. He was telling the truth. He never troubles to lie, thought Zennor. Never thinks he has any fault to hide.

'It fairly astonishes me that communication can be *so poor* in a small parish like this, that no one told me of it! We must praise God and Our Friend for a sound constitution, eh? You and I are at one with nature. We turn back disease as ducks shed water.'

'Fortunate us,' said Zennor, dull with misery. 'I think I should go and help care for Grace.'

He looked up, startled, dabbing his mouth with a napkin. 'Oh, I think not.'

'I think I must,' she said.

The parsonage door was more substantial than the wall to either side of it, so she knew she could not be kept out. In the event, she was neither welcomed nor barred. The family had turned in on itself. George, Susannah and Sarah, instead of wearing the pallor of grief, were bright-cheeked with colds, the tips of their noses pink. When they buried their faces in their handkerchiefs it was impossible to tell if they were blowing their noses or succumbing to grief: they would not have wanted Zennor to know which. They barely noticed when she annexed a chair in the sickroom and prepared to keep vigil over Grace. There she sat while Grace slept; there she rested a bowl of cold water when Grace was awake and feverish and needed cooling with a linen cloth.

The scarlet took hold in Berkshire that year like rose-bay-willow, both high and low, and the parson, kept busy by it, was rarely home, between the death and the funeral, to receive condolences.

He did not see Zennor for what she was – the perpetrator of their loss. Baydon, too, thought that he had brought the sickness home to his wife on the communion vessel or the sleeve of his coat. Zennor did not disabuse him; no one wants to be hated as much as that.

Altogether, though, he showed little distress, said nothing, displayed only fatigue. When he looked in on his daughter, between a home communion and prayers-for-deliverance, Grace was delirious and mistook him for the devil at the end of her bed; she whimpered and begged him not to look at her with 'those black eyes'. They were indeed very hollow and blackened eyes, as if some sight had had the momentum of fists to strike him.

He himself had no momentum. Zennor had the impression that he only moved, like an unchocked cart, because the ground under him sloped down. At the foot of some gradient as yet unreached, he would come to a trundling halt.

Still, Zennor's chief concern was for Grace, whose sickness she knew she had brought, and must therefore dispatch. Whenever she was lucid enough to be afraid, Grace would search her conscience for the sins which might be reckoned against her if she were called to account. It was like rummaging in a clean linen-drawer for grains of dust: Grace had so little notion of sin that she scarcely knew what she was looking for. More than once she whispered, catching hold of Zennor's wrist, 'I never did anyone harm!' and again and again, 'At least I am a virgin! At least!'

Zennor soothed her as she would a child, this girl her own age, but it rankled with her, all that reliance on an absence; all that trust placed in a negative. She wanted to shake Grace by her bird-like shoulders and shout in her sweating face, 'More cause to get better, then! Stay and see. Stay and find out!'

Once, as Zennor dozed in the chair, she was startled awake by a movement close by. George had come in and was lighting a sulphur candle on the windowsill. 'Against contagion,' he said. The smell was so vile, so choking, that it seemed more of an act of exorcism than a safety measure on Zennor's behalf.

She needed no candle. She no longer doubted her capacity to survive the epidemic. As Robin had said, he and Rousseau had equipped her with a robust constitution. If only they had equipped her with a similar armour against longings and chagrin. Regrets beat like moths against the windows of that bedroom. Rousseau was right: the only truly happy man wants as much as he can achieve, no more. Since she could achieve nothing and was equipped to do nothing, offer nothing, contribute nothing in this evil-smelling room, she only wished she could want, like Grace, nothing out of life but to die a virgin. As for harming no one: that potential was already gone. She already had more to atone for than to glory in.

The day of the funeral was sunny and warm. The coffin had only to be conveyed from the house, across the garden to the graveyard. The journey was so short that the undertaker made the pall-bearers leave by the front door and circle the house by the lane, rather than just stepping out across the lawn. The sexton, as usual, was complaining about the waterlogging of his cemetery by the leaking of Hatch House lake; it had become an obsession with him. (Privately, he had even taken it upon himself to write to the bishop.) The wetness of the earth, he told everyone, had obliged him to sink a grave only five feet deep, and even then there was a gleam of water lying in the bottom.

Grace did not attend. She wanted to, but was dissuaded – she was too ill and, in any case, mourners might be deterred by her presence. As it was, the fear of contagion kept most of the villagers at a cautious distance, outside the churchyard, peering over its wall like the heads of defeated rebels decorating a palisade. Or it may have been Baydon himself that they were avoiding. That infamous temper (his parishioners feared) might have been tried beyond breaking point this time, by the Almighty.

They need not have worried. Baydon behaved himself with admirable restraint, walking bareheaded in front of the coffin, the four children a little way behind, rheumy and coughing with both grief and colds. At the church he adopted the mantle of parish priest, so as to lay his wife to rest according to the Church of England litany.

The parish found it a little shocking, a little chilling that he could muster no valedictory remarks, pay no personal tribute to Sophronia, express no tally of gratitude. Nothing but the words of the funeral service, familiar and pat, dropped glibly off his tongue. The women glanced at one another, creasing their lower lids. The men were just grateful for a short service, given the number they had attended lately.

George Baydon read his step-mother's favourite passage from the Bible – Psalm 30 – and was so plainly moved that those listening needed to remind themselves this was not his natural mother, only one who had helped raise him.

As for Baydon, he was on trial of course, as a parson is always on trial – to see if he can bear out what he has been preaching to others, come year, go year. They watched him carefully for signs of inconsistency, of double standards, rage against the pitiless unkindness of the divine plan. But they saw nothing. A blank.

He seemed smaller – shrunken down, overmastered by the size of his vestments. He leaned, too – perhaps no one but Zennor noticed it, but he leaned forwards, from the feet, like a building undermined by rising water. She had the conviction she ought to right him, get up, then and there, and right him to the vertical. Otherwise some terrible subsidence would follow which shoring boards and pit props could do nothing to limit.

Outdoors, beside the grave, he was a dark cantilever curving out over the trench, block-and-tackle for the lifting and lowering of heavy goods. His feet were planted so close to the edge that granules of earth trickled down – *plop, plop* – into the lying water. The coffin, when it was lowered in, landed with an audible splash, though the rooks in the trees on Hatch Hill did their best to drown it out. The sexton muttered an apology to no one in particular.

Baydon appeared, during the flat recitation of the interment service, to be reading the words off the coffin-sides, for his light brown eyes travelled continuously to and fro, like a reader scanning line after line. Just once he said, by way of a *nunc dimittis* to his departing wife, 'Exemplary woman,' before throwing a handful of earth on to her. He did nothing to quell the crying of his youngest son. Afterwards the woman said that was a disgrace, to leave the little lad uncomforted.

'Perhaps he did not hear,' said Zennor.

When the burial rites were over, those within the churchyard wall and some from outside it formed themselves into an orderly queue, like guests at a wedding, to shake Baydon's hand and offer him their sorrow, as if he might have too little of his own: Wootton, the Knollys, the Martens, the travelling librarian, Curragh's wife, an aunt, an orange-skinned man who was not village . . . 'What can I say?' they asked of a man who said nothing in reply.

But to Zennor, Baydon said, 'Thank you.'

'For what?'

'For trying to save my daughter. For Grace,' though those eyes still flicked to and fro, to and fro, reading his script off her face. She leaned forward and kissed his cheek, without knowing why. At close quarters, she suddenly saw a likeness to the statue in her garden: brows pulled down, the unshaven skin rough as stone. And cold and unyielding.

'Grace will be fine,' Zennor reassured him. 'She is making steady progress.'

He closed his eyes, swaying a little in his self-imposed darkness. Then he shook his head – so imperceptibly that Zennor barely read it as a denial – and looked across at his other four children, as a farmer might look across two fields at his distant cattle. 'Thank you for coming,' he said without a vestige of emotion or engagement. 'Goodbye.'

'She was more than a friend to me,' said Zennor, finding the words in her mouth like pebbles.

His eyes held fleetingly on the air beside her head. 'Exemplary woman,' he said again, irritably.

There were no funeral meats, but that went unquestioned in a time of epidemic. Not unnoticed, but unquestioned.

The effect of the funeral on Robin Wootton was to make him voluble and slightly kittenish on the way home. He picked a big pannicle of cow parsley on a long sappy stalk, and carried it like a parasol. 'Is it not an extraordinary thing, child?' he said, walking sometimes forwards, sometimes backwards ahead of her. 'The mercantile marriage! The bourgeois marriage! There is a man . . .'

'Who?' said Zennor, distracted and disinclined to talk. The sudden thought had come to her that perhaps the vicar mistook his children – the way he had looked at them – their coughs and colds – as showing symptoms of scarlet fever. Perhaps he expected them, like Grace, to succumb one by one to the same fate as Sophronia. She should have said something – the man was barely capable of rational . . .

'Baydon! Friend Baydon! There is a man who has just buried his wife – his twelfth rib! His soul's companion! Admitted, this was not a *grand amour*: not an abandonment to the cries of the flesh . . . but Christ Jesus!' He shook his head in exaggerated bewilderment, though the wrongness seemed to amuse as much as outrage him. 'Do you see what the sacred estate of marriage has been brought to? Secularity! A functional alliance! The engagement of a housekeeper, legitimised by covert wages. A kind of business venture. We collude in it to say, "These people are married." They are not married. They have entered into a convenient living arrangement. Hearts and souls were left at home. Portions and jointures and social station: they are all that's spoken of by the bourgeois bride and groom!'

'Oh, I don't think . . .' Zennor began.

'Oh, believe me! My dear Zennor! Were you watching back yonder? Did you see this man's adieux to the woman who has shared his fireside all these years? Can you imagine Our Friend Jean-Jacques launching into her grave the divine Mademoiselle Galley like a ship – less! like a common barge?'

'I cannot think –'

'*Précisement!*'

She wanted to silence him. She needed to silence his glee. 'Alba . . .' she said, hoping to shame him into silence by touching on his own piece of brokerage. But he only applauded her apt choice of an example.

'Now *there* was a nature born mercenary, you are right. Don't mistake me. I condemn the woman no less than the man, who contracts one of these *material* marriages. They make comfort and plenty their measure of happiness. A roof, a fire and a full belly. Very good! Very well! But where is *Love* in this arithmetical universe of theirs? Eh? Where is *Joy*?' His rhetoric lifted him clear of the ground in great voltas of excitement. 'Where is the cleaving of spirits? The congruent dream! . . . Do you love me, Zennor?'

'Yes.'

She answered as promptly as she could – as soon as the pellet of feather and bone and sinew could be ridded from her owl-throat.

'Yes.'

She said it with force and absolute, incontrovertible candour. Later she would have time to make it true.

'Yes.'

She stopped stock-still to say it – there on the bridge, with its mended rail, its ink-stained water, its ice-cold weed, while at the bridge end he rested one foot on a boulder, in heroic pose.

Then he took it down again. 'I expect you think so, yes,' he said, with resignation. 'I expect you think so. Me, I wait in happy anticipation.'

She ran to catch him up, her black skirts ugly, cumbersome and hot around her legs. 'Wait? For what? What are you waiting for?' she called, as he strode jauntily out through deep hogweed and dock.

'For love, of course!'

'Between us?' she asked, but she was breathless with running.

'For love to leap out and ambush me! For love to lay hands on me! For love to press-gang me into its service! For love!' and with a dramatic about-face, he brought both his upraised hands down on her hunched, hurrying shoulders. She fell up against him, and took her time to recover. Then she held her face up, like a passport, for examination. He was flushed with excitement, twinkling and bright, when everyone else she had seen that day had been sick and sallow with misery. Her throat ran dry. Her sadness at Sophronia's death seemed to sink through her and wedge in her pelvis, painful, like a breech pregnancy that could kill her. God was paying His debts in some way, though whether He was compensating her for a lost friend or punishing her Zennor could not quite make out. 'Between us? Will you? Ever? Could you? Love me?' Her voice came out unnatural, high-pitched, ridiculous.

Birds crawled about in the dark green lushness, loud as visigoths. Small black flies gathered interestedly around their heads to hear his answer. Streamwater belched in and out of a broken zinc pipe.

Wootton's hands slid down to her elbows and held on, as supporting the lugs of a large jar. 'We shall see. All in due time,' he said, energetically brushing pollen off her shoulders as if it were dandruff. 'We shall see.' The tone was avuncular, the smile too.

Zennor crammed herself back into the mould of a dutiful ward, and fell into step with him, treading a few paces behind, reproaching herself with such vanities on the day of Sophronia's funeral.

Next day a letter arrived for Wootton requesting his assistance 'in exploring what can be done to safeguard the fabric and welfare of the church of Saint Gabriel's in Winding Hatch, and thereby the safety of those therein.'

Wootton found it offensive and accusatory 'You see?' he complained to Zennor, taking *The Persian Wars* out of her hand and throwing it aside. 'You see how Baydon occupied himself while his wife lay dying? With complaining to his bishop about *my lake!*' He looked so vexed that she half expected him to stamp. 'Peevish knave! I tell you, it's all small minds and envy hereabout. Dogs-in-the-manger! Because the parsonage is badly maintained, shall the church fall down? Believe me! What you see here are the Pharisees and Sadducees trembling once again in the face of Nature!'

Zennor said nothing, but retrieved her book, marking her place before putting it back on the shelves.

At about this time each day they had taken to walking the grounds, he wearing his rustic round-hat and smock and carrying his shepherd's crook. She realised now that he must have instigated this daily walk hoping that love would leap out, dart in hand, and strike him. Today that idea hadn't even the power to make her smile. She only hoped the level of the lake was high, so that he could demonstrate to her the calumny of those who said it was leaking. She did not much care who was right – the truth is a friable commodity – she just wanted him proved right so that he would stop labouring his argument.

Hatch Lake was full. Something had jammed in the sluice-gate of the overflow. In all but dry weather, the overspill fed a terraced Italian water garden – three descending ponds linked by little ceramic stair-ways. Heavy overnight rain had nicely replenished the lake, but the ceramic steps were almost dry; instead, the water slopped haphazardly over the sluice. A raft of waterlilies had become uprooted from the central shallows and drifted into the sluice-gate, carrying with it twigs, blossom, feathers, weed. Wootton walked out on to the sluice-gate and poked at it with his shepherd's crook. Water splashed over his shoes.

'Shall I fetch the boat?' Zennor offered. It was moored nearby; she had only to untie the painter and pull twice on the thickly varnished oars, and she drifted down on to the sluice-gate. Unshipping an oar and using the side of the boat as a fulcrum, she jabbed the oar-tip under the raft of rubbish, trying to lever it up high enough for Wootton, in his tight-kneed breeeches, to pull it out of the water: a big mat, densely woven, of rotting vegetation.

As he lifted it, a large bright object rolled out and up to the surface, nudging Zennor's oar.

Baydon's hips, heavier than his head, were still under the keel of her boat;

she heard his belt scrape the planks beneath her as he rolled over. His face was slimy from rubbing against the weedy gate, smeared green. But lying on his back among the broken lilies, wearing only shirt and breeches, his hands floating free, the parson of Winding Hatch looked more peaceful than Zennor could ever remember.

Robin turned round cautiously on the slippery sluice-gate, so as to shake his shepherd's crook free of matted, festooning rubbish and be able to hook the body ashore. While his back was turned, Zennor plunged her hands into the water and plucked at the length of rope knotted to Baydon's belt. Her knuckles pressing into Baydon's wool serge belly, she held the knot hidden underwater as she pick, pick, picked at it. The water was bitterly cold; the feeling was almost gone from her fingers before she got it undone. On the other end of the rope was the clapper of the church bell: for a few moments she actually held it, long, harsh, icy, golden, in her numb blue hand. It was so heavy that it almost overbalanced her out of the boat, though it had not been heavy enough to do its job and keep Baydon's body under, hidden. Zennor let the clapper drop and take with it the tell-tale rope, into the secrecy of the lake's mud.

CHAPTER NINETEEN

Consolation

'Disappointed ambition,' said Wootton. 'The man always hankered after cathedral office. Either that or he came looking to meddle with my lake and overreached himself.'

'He leaned out too far,' said Zennor in reply.

'That's your opinion, is it?' said Robin, open to conviction.

'He leaned too far out over the grave.'

Wootton, being unable to make sense of this, decided she had said 'grave' in mistake for 'lake', and nodded in agreement.

He was shaken, no denying it. Nothing so immediately horrible had ever happened to him and he was – not unreasonably – jarred. He did not like changes, alteration, departures from the status quo – not unless he was the instigator, at least. The Winding Hatch living was within his family's gift, and he would probably have to take a hand in the installation of a new vicar. But he delayed writing to the church authorities, presuming the news would reach them in any case. The shockingness might be somehow soaked up by a few cushioning weeks of inaction.

The manner of death was uncertain – dubious enough to rock the village, but inconclusive enough for a coroner to allow burial in sanctified ground given one word from Wootton. George Baydon came over to see him, begging him publicly to discount suicide as an impossibility. But Wootton declined to have an opinion.

As a result, Baydon was buried under the wall of the churchyard – slipped under it like a damp-course – neither inside nor out, neither sheep in the fold nor wolf out of it, in a kind of geographical purgatory. He lay thirty yards, and equidistant, from both his wives.

Robin Wootton did not attend the funeral. Within a few days he had managed to place the sordid deaths in their right and proper context and to recover the personal equilibrium he considered it his duty to feel. He dressed the servants in black pinafores or kerchiefs and put on half-mourning, though he would not allow Zennor to do the same, since he found morbidity unwholesome in the young. Then he consciously and conscientiously put the business behind him.

Not so Zennor. She was still unreconciled to Sophronia's death. Baydon's suicide hit her like a slate from the church roof. She was poleaxed. It seemed to her that the whole world was dying, and all because of her – that life itself was hurtling towards nothing but dissolution. Death, the absentee landlord, had returned to his estates to turn his tenants out of doors.

The nights were worst. During daylight hours she could occupy herself reading – there was no more excuse to go to the vicarage, and how could she anyway? Or else she pretended to study, though her concentration was gone. Thoughts, constructs, theorems, arguments unravelled in her head as fast as she knit them together. But at least during the day the trees beyond the windows flickered and scintillated, animals moved on the hillsides, the post coach raised a distant plume of dust.

Some kind of blame had attached itself to Hatch House. Wootton did not see it, but it was so. Fewer people called at the house; the tradesmen did not stay to talk. The rowing boat was found smashed and sunk one day soon after the funeral. Of course, it might have been the local people punishing Wootton for the injury his lake had done Baydon – a kind of belated solidarity with the dead man. But Zennor could not persuade herself of that. Surely, if that were the case, then Robin would be upset, wounded, sorry, and he was none of those things. She became convinced, instead, that her guilt was known: her hand in Sophronia's death, her failure to comfort Baydon, her concealment of his suicide. Isolated already in the cavernous house, she came to think of their new isolation as deserved, insuperable, everlasting.

And at night the windows were uniformly black, the trees beyond only shifting, shambling shapes full of menace. In the village, no light burned. The dark beat against her like birds; the stillness of the house bore down on her like that cemetery wall.

Zennor felt the weight of that wall. From her heel to her head, she felt the wet weight of shifting earth pressing, pressing on the hollow of her ribcage, on the uncemented keystones of her spine, and the wall above her seemed bound to collapse.

For the first time in her life, death made itself known to Zennor, grabbing hold of her as Smith had done, rubbing itself against her. The grave of Smith's wife and two of his children testified to the brute strength of the beast Death.

Rousseau might fill Emile topful of wisdom, and Emile fill his son, his granddaughter, even unto the seventh generation. It was of no consequence. Previously Zennor had envisaged the world rolling forwards like a cartwheel over ruts, towards somewhere better. Now she could see that it was not a cartwheel at all but a millwheel, fixed and stationary, filling only to empty, filling to empty, filling and emptying without ever moving forward. Ignorance grew to wisdom but begat only ignorance. Emile's child would have to work the same treadmill; no one learned by the labour of any previous lifetime. She was Sisyphus pushing her own personal rock uphill, knowing it was bound to fall back to the very bottom at the end. The only certitude was the repetition of ignorance. The only certain day in which she would be alive was this one. Knowing that made the sky stridently lilac, the sunbeams into rods of gold, the tree roots in the bank a miraculous tapestry. It gave the beasts in the field the wisdom of Solomon, because they knew how to live in the immediate moment, and by instinct, and by their five senses. What Robin had failed to teach her about the natural order Baydon and Sophronia had taught her by dying. It drove Zennor to the brink of hysteria, such was her need to be alive somewhere on the long, arduous, mired journey to being dead.

In that pitch-black, creaking, scratching, rustling, ticking, spidery, draught-haunted, arrogant house, she yearned to be alive, to stop waiting for what the future would deliver and to taste the life that had never quite reached her, for all her years of apprenticeship and waiting. She dreamed her fingers were once again scrabbling with the knots of the rope, except that this time the rope was round her own waist, and she was standing on the bed of the lake, the clapper of the bell shining gold at her feet, the weight holding her under, holding her down.

When she woke, she gulped in air and, with it, twin lungfuls of grief. Instead of water she found herself under fathoms of black grief which made her choke and gag and sob open-mouthed, sitting up in her narrow cot, wanting the solace of Alba or Sophronia – of anyone – and finding no one at any single compass-bearing of the known world.

Slipping out of bed, Zennor ran barefoot along the landing and down to the first floor, where each main state bedroom lay behind double doors glossy under the outstretched fingers. She paused only to wipe the tears and sweat from her face with the sleeve of her nightdress, then opened the door to Robin's room. Never before had she been inside.

He did not stir when she went in. There was a fire, burned low in the grate, but it still gave off enough of a red glow for her to see herself reflected, ghostlike, in the mirror. Her hair was a rook's nest, her eyelids swollen, her nose red. She sat down quite deliberately at his dressing-table, and brushed her hair with his brush, each stroke stilling her sobs, though her heart knocked even louder. She was driving her grief underground, like a river, and half expected her heart to fail, extinguished by that racing subterranean river. It jumped so violently and irregularly. Pressing the cool circle of his fob-watch against each swollen eye in turn, she felt the tick, tick of time passing flicker against her eyeballs.

The room was chill, despite the fire, her hands and feet cold, though the core of her body was hot, volcanic. She got up, meaning to disturb the bedclothes as little as possible as she slid into the bed. But the stool on which she had sat tipped over backwards with a loud thud. In the bed, Robin woke with a start – 'What do you want? Who's there?' Perhaps, just for a moment, he thought she was a ghost.

Then her momentary calm deserted her. Zennor leapt over the end of the bed, tearing the hem of her nightdress a little with the length of her stride. In trying to avoid treading on his legs, and in bumping her head on the low canopy of the bed, she fell ungainlily on top of him, sliding her legs under the coverlet but missing the sheet. He hunched his back against the onslaught, still half asleep.

Her fingers plunged into his hair and tangled, making him yelp. Dragging the sheet from under her, she pressed her body against his curved back and began kissing the base of his jawbone which was all she could reach.

'Hold me, Robin! Comfort me! Keep me alive! I can't bear the darkness! I can't stomach to be all alone and empty!' She flung one leg across his, feeling the coarse hairs of his calf which, even through her desperation, fixed themselves in her mind. His rucked nightshirt made a solid lump against her pelvis; he had turned his hips sharply away.

Sheer surprise let her surmount him. She pulled herself across him till she was straddling his bony hip, her fingers still tangled in his long hair, and her face pressed into the angle of his throat. 'Let marriage alone! Leave marriage! Hang marriage! It's nothing! Choose anyone! But be kind! Tonight, be kind! Do right to me! Be a man to me! Let me be alive, come alive! Please, Robin! Please!' She tried to press his hand against her sternum – to feel that her heart was about to burst. He wrenched it away, knocking her breast. '"All the first impulses," remember? Remember? "All the first impulses of nature are good and right!"'

'Zennor! Enough! Stop this!' He was fuddled with sleep and unprepared.

'"What is, is right!" Yes? "What is, is right!" Our Friend! Jean-Jacques! "All the first impulses." . . .' She might as well have blasphemed, to see the look on his face.

Zennor became incoherent and repetitive, as more and more of her energies went into tearing at his nightshirt, planing him with her hands, as if she were searching for the pocket in which he kept his compassion, his humanity. 'You won't let me be all alone? Not tonight! Please!' Her hips barged against him. Her breasts pressed against his face. Her mouth gnawed at his hair and ears: something remembered from a time before nightshirts, a time before she was born, the night perhaps of her conception, or her great-grandfather's conception. A part of her was asking, 'What does my body remember, that I have never known?'

Previously her sinuses had ached with unshed tears; now the ache had bled down through her body and lodged in her groin.

'*Zennor, enough*! Get away!'

Less than a minute elapsed before Wootton, mustering his wits and strength, plunged his fists into the knot she had made of them and flung her off, bodily. She went backwards over the side of the bed, landing on her shoulders, banging her head on a chair. Her nightdress was up around her waist.

He sat up, hunching a sheet over one shoulder like a Roman senator. The buttons of his nightshirt hung loose – three or four teardrops trembling in mid-air. 'And who taught you *that* manner of play, miss?' He shouted it, malevolent and panting.

'No one. I –'

'And who has kept you sated since you came to heat?'

'What is –'

'Lewd bitch!'

'– is right,' said Pope through the mouth of an eighteen-year-old girl. 'Passion. Very passionate . . . the senses . . .' The embers in the gate shifted, as if embarrassed by the unseemliness of the scene.

'*Do you think, miss, that my home is graced by a hot jezebel with no mind for her virtue?*'

'I needed some gentleness,' said Zennor. Even to her it sounded like a sot in need of a consoling drink. 'I was so . . . . *sad*.' A pitiful, whining excuse.

'I might have whores twenty times a day,' he went on, snorting out the words like feathers from the split pillow beside him. 'Whores come two-a-penny. Why should I breed a whore? Is this the way I taught you to disport?' With every sentence he drew his voice farther and farther up into his sinuses, to where she had kept her tears.

She was very tempted, just for a second to say, 'Yes. Impulse. Nature. Love. Passion.' He had used the words so often over the years that all the shine had come off them. And yes, she had thought those were the substance of his ideal life, his ideal wife. Then the temptation passed, and she drew her feet together and inside her nightdress, sitting in the curl of her legs, looking at the floor. She was humiliated. He would not have settled for anything less.

'We shall talk in the morning, *puella.*'

'Yes, *magister.*'

As she went to stand up, her heel caught in the hem of her nightdress and pulled it down off one shoulder. Quickly, for modesty's sake, she snatched the placket closed at the throat, her head ducked, her face obscured by clouds of bushy hair.

Outside the door, she broke into a run, flying along the landing, her feet hitting the floor with a loud thump, thump thump. She was too desolate to cry, or at least to know if she were crying. The rest of her night was spent sitting in a tight, motionless ball on the pillow of her bed, staring at the blackness wedged in her windowpane, emptying out of her any and every affectionate thought she had ever nursed concerning Robin Wootton.

'Mischief,' said Alice, descending the kitchen steps one at a time with a tray. 'Him's all tragic and hers in 'er 'at.'

Curragh, Job and William sat at the table eating a breakfast of cold eggs and ham.

'Reckon him tried a hand last night, and no joy,' said Job.

They had already debated exhaustively the sounds in the night, the thump of feet along the landing, the opening of one door which, by its opening, made every other door in the house close a little tighter. At times like this, Curragh (who lived out) puffed and grunted his disbelief at their naïvete. In his opinion, Wootton had been 'doin' the child' (as he put it) for years, 'and the blonde one previous'. But the living-in servants knew better. A house gives up its secrets to anyone with half an ear to listen, just as now it would divulge whatever passed beween Zennor and Robin at the breakfast table.

To take advantage of deep, debilitating grief? To put a dear friend's death to lewd and selfish purpose? It was utterly cold-bloodedly vicious. Wootton was mortified. The more he reviewed the events of the night, the more mortified he became. Zennor had sought to launch her assault while his guard was lowered in mourning. She had known how much Samuel and

Mrs Baydon's deaths had afflicted him, and now, within the month, she thought to seduce him, her mind still running along the narrow goat-track of marriage and advancement.

'I have very little to say to you this morning, Zennor,' he said, as Alice left and shut the door behind her. He spoke slowly, like a man crossing a river on stepping-stones placed far apart. 'I simply want you to know that last night you made a wrack of my dreams – of all my dearest wishes.' He held up a hand to preempt any excuse from her, though she had not been going to speak. 'I accept the blame. I was at fault. Plainly I failed to curb your *fantasies*, your imaginings before they grew into vices. Immoderate desires are the seat of all unhappiness. I should have taught you better the virtues of restraint and modesty.'

Zennor sat on the edge of her chair, her walking bonnet already on, her gloves on the table beside her plate. She touched neither food nor drink. Her hands were folded in her lap, her eyes downturned. She had fastened two black ribbons to the leading edge of the bonnet.

'I have considered the possibility, too, that you carry in you the contaminated blood of your natural parents, and that your actions were . . . preordained by that bloodstock. However . . .' His voice was so furred and silken that fleas could have nested in it. 'However, if there is to be any reform in public morals it must begin with domestic morals – we have mentioned this in our lessons – and I simply cannot tolerate the harm your . . . simplicity of nature could do to my life's work. I believe we must consider your future *outside* this household, among people closer to you in humour and temperament. Naturally I will, in accordance with my vouchsafe to you at the start, seek out and secure . . .'

'I hope that first you will consider, sir, my provocation,' Zennor interrupted him, the surge of her voice overwashing his sea-sibillant sound.

'Your –?'

'Have you given thought, sir, to your many qualities? Qualities I might have been powerless to resist?' She raised her dark eyes, but only as high as the butter-dish. 'Are you not framed entirely to enflame the hungry heart?'

He moved uncomfortably in his chair, crossed his legs and turned shoulder and profile towards her.

She went on, itemising virtues: 'A ready wit. A generous soul. An original mind. A quite god-like nobility of spirit.'

He squirmed visibly. 'I am sorry. I really cannot . . .'

'I wonder – I ask myself, Robin,' said Zennor, absently breaking a roll of bread against the table edge as though it were a boiled egg. The crust fell like shell on to her knees. 'I wonder what drew you to the man Rousseau. Was it his passionate nature? His non-conformity? His philosophy of love?'

He waved his napkin exaggeratedly, like a teacher wiping a chalkboard, and shut his eyes tight against her false, fawning flattery. 'I see where you are going. God knows, I am a passionate man . . .' he began, but found himself knee-deep in the swell.

'Passionate?' Both her thumbs penetrated the breadroll. 'As a flounder is passionate. As a fish dead on the slab is passionate.' He sat round again to face her. She said, 'Do you think because you say a thing, that it is true? Shall I be blonde, by saying it?' And she knocked her bonnet backwards off her head. It jutted awkwardly out of the back of her neck, like breeding fettle on a bird, and her glossy, compressed black hair expanded. 'You who borrow your every thought from a single book, like some medieval bigot? You who deign to look down on your fellow man from the great height of supercilious haughtiness? You who let your words of wisdom drop like the antique Sibyl? *Magister?* God in heaven, you're not ten years older than me! You deride your ancestors and despise your betters. You mount up to the high places by treading on the faces of your fellows. And when a thing offends your pretty picture of the world, you paint it out – like Alba. Imagination? Must our imagination be curbed? What ass's dung Our dear Friend Jean-Jacques let fall sometimes! Curb the imagination, is it? Because the imagination feeds desire? Sure, you must have been circumcised of it on the day you were born! What, did the knife slip? Were you gelded of all? No imagination to see into other people's lives. No desires – well, none but desiring always to be God Almighty, one without equal. *One without end!*'

Wootton, who had already thrown both his knife and fork at Zennor in an attempt to silence her, found nothing in his hands but his pocket watch on the end of its chain. He had, in his agitation, snapped its link with his waistcoat, too. He stood up and began to move round the table, swinging the watch on its chain.

Suddenly the door opened, and Alice half entered the room, to no apparent purpose, dithering. Her jawline was swollen with apoplectic unhappiness, her fat hand irresolutely clasped the handle; her black apron was splattered with a constellation of white dough.

Both man and girl looked over at her, seeing her bottom lip try repeatedly to fold itself over her top, so that she should not speak out of turn. 'Can I fetch anything to you?' she asked, with trembling temerity.

The roll in Zennor's hands had exploded into a million fragments; they twinkled to the floor as she stood up and hurried towards the protection of the cook's big body. She was right in her timing. The watch flew out and struck the bonnet with a sharp, hollow rap and then, in error, the cook's plump upper arm with no sound at all, except a thud afterwards as the watch fell to the floor. Alice's lower lip continued to fold over the top one.

'I am going to visit Miss Alba, Alice,' said Zennor, standing up very straight, the bonnet swivelled round on to one shoulder. 'I may be gone a good while.'

Alice's throat distended, like a bullfrog's. She danced a confused dance with Wootton as she tried to stand out of his way. Then he stalked away to change his clothes, and Alice heard Zennor struggling a little with the front door (which often stuck in damp weather).

Still, it was some two minutes before she glimpsed the girl again, cloaked, descend the half-crescent sweep of shallow steps down from the terrace to the front drive. Zennor moved a little awkwardly, almost stooping.

'Loons!' wheezed Alice, pulling a tuft of hair out of the back of Job's head as she swept back into the kitchen. 'You got it all wrong ways about! Gone, she is! All blown up in his face. Weren't *she* disappointed *him!* He weren't man enough for her, reckon. Called him "one without end", as God's my judge!' The men boggled at her. White of egg fell rubbery from Curragh's mouth. 'Heard her! Called him "one without end".'

They stared at one another, silenced for the first time in their lives by the sudden departure of a girl they had never liked. Arms crossed, Alice fingered the biceps of her left arm, unable to account for the pain she felt there. A thought suddenly gave her back the power of speech.

'William! Front drive. Go. Catch up to her. Poor lassie's gone to the constable's house. To call on the yellow one. She don't know. Can't know. Him can't've told her.'

William made a racketing din with his chair legs and ran out of the scullery door. His wife frowned and looked about her without affection at the large clutter of her kitchen, fingering the bruise on her biceps, wondering.

On her way to the front door, Zennor swept up, off the round hall table, one of the morocco-bound works of Rousseau enshrined there: *Emile*. She laid it on the terrace balustrade while she paid one last visit to Jean-Jacques.

Her quarrel was not with him. He had merely furnished the method of her undoing. Somewhere within the suspended motion of her brain she admired and agreed with his thinking. In all probability he had made her what she was – as much as Lambeth or heredity or the travelling library or Sophronia Baydon. It was just that, today, the bust represented Robin

Wootton – that lump of scowling bronze without hands to help her, without feet to accompany her. Still and smug and permanently vexed, the bronze looked steadfastly over her shoulder, the dead flowers of last summer's wreath still circling his brow.

So she put her shoulder to him and overbalanced him. He rocked back, then forwards, only coming adrift of the pedestal on the forward sway, so that she had to jump clear to save her feet being crushed. Rousseau's head opened at a seam – split from crown to ear, allowing the sunlight to shine into the slabby bronze of his brain.

She dropped the book off the footbridge into the stream, staying to watch while the pages broke loose or turned to smeary blankness. She was standing there when William caught her up with the news about Alba. About her 'sister', Alba.

'Can't go there, Alice says, miss! Don't go there. Her's dead these three weeks! Miss Alba's dead.'

She received the news with little show of emotion. 'Was it the scarlet?' she asked after a moment.

'Childbearing,' said William, offering her a boiled egg he had brought along with him from breakfast. 'Childbearing, reckon. Wonder the master dain't tell youm. So you's best go some place different. Alice says.'

It was after an hour or two's careful consideration of her predicament that Zennor knocked at the vicarage door. It seemed an obscenity to be there, but sensible. Eminently practical.

'I am homeless. Without a home,' she told George when he answered the door.

After a few moments, he stepped back from the door to let her in. She only stepped up as far as the threshold. 'I thought: you may have need of a housekeeper. Unpaid. I need only my keep,' she said, 'and somewhere to lie down.'

He did not speak – had not had cause to speak for several days. After the suicide the community had shunned him and his sisters wholly and entirely. His throat had become unaccustomed to speech. There was not a glimmer of light in his face.

'I can work hard,' she said by way of a reference.

His eyes travelled over her face, without curiosity. He had his father's eyes.

'For now,' he said. 'For a time. Why not?'

PART FOUR

The Age of Happiness

CHAPTER TWENTY

'Madly Wise or Wisely Mad'

Revenge. Such a quaintly barbaric concept. Revenge. So very primitive. Often, after finding his book gone and his statue disfigured, Robin Wootton shook his head in incredulous amusement at the interesting phenomenon of petty revenge, smiling ruefully at finding himself the victim of his own charity.

Alice said it was wickedness born through want of slapping, but Robin saw it as evidence of a baser, cruder moral sense at work – a pure egotism which was almost admirable in its animal energy.

Even so, when Robin had found Zennor's black hairs in his hair-brush, he had burned it – thrown the whole brush into the grate. It had curled and burned there, like a hedgehog in a gypsy fire, and rimed the grate with plate-silver.

He sent at once to his bookseller for a replacement copy of the stolen book and despatched the bust to a foundry for renovation and repair.

Barely a month later, he received a letter from the Rousseauian Society in Oxford, whose chairman had heard tell of his 'social experiment' and begged him, in lavish terms, to address the society members at a future meeting.

'Do not suppose, my dear sir, that the unsatisfactory outcome (if so you deem it) in any way lessens our keen interest in hearing the plan expounded by a person of such eminent erudition as yourself.'

Wootton was flattered, though he could not think where the society had gained its information. He did not generally make the arduous journey to Oxford to attend society meetings, finding the undergraduate element rabid in their application of Rousseauian principles. But finding his days suddenly empty of teaching Zennor, he considered that he could spare time to prepare a lecture, and wrote back to the Society accordingly.

'I conclude, therefore, gentlemen – ladies, that my clay, having been exposed long years to the rude winds of desperation and materialism, was already too hardened to be malleable, even in the most tender of hands. Though I have no shadow of doubt that the human spirit is pure gold in essence, I fear that assay proved this particular lode too much alloyed with base metal. Thus my painstaking years went for nought.'

The meeting was held in Holywell Street, in a lecture hall with a ringing echo, and an inn next door. A large element of the audience had spent an hour in the inn beforehand, and were noisily argumentative with each other. Most saw a visiting speaker as proving ground for their wit. They interrupted with questions about the *appearance* of his wards and with suggestive sniggers about their eagerness to please. They lobbed remarks across the hall, dirty as ink pellets, and twice the chairman had to rise to his feet and quell them, pointing out that ladies were present.

There were, indeed, seven or eight ladies, mostly the wives of members, bored or glazed-looking. But in the centre, near the front, a young woman wearing a picture-hat and with a nosegay of flowers in the cross-over of her bodice followed his words intently, leaning forward holding the chairback in front of her with both gloved hands. She seemed not to notice the extraneous noises. At question time, she raised a handkerchief shyly to a level with her ear and asked, 'Might I presume . . . do you . . . are you still . . . in any way . . . is there any friendship left between you and the two girls?'

'Oh yes! Indeed!' said Wootton pouncingly. 'One, as I said, I introduced to a gentleman of standing in the community, and they were married. The other, though she chose to leave, still resides in a house on my land. These things can be amicably done, where there is the will, and where sufficient trust exists between the parties.' There was a loud, communal expression of surprise at his long-sufferingness, in the face of such blatant ingratitude. He decided against mentioning Alba's death, so as not to cast a dampening gloom.

The same young woman approached him afterwards, so quick and darting that she reached him before even the chairman. 'I am so glad you could come. I found your talk so delightful,' she said.

'It was not the most attentive of audiences,' he said, still irritable and hoarse from contending with the drunken hecklers.

'The undergraduates are perhaps a little young to be thinking yet of the next generation,' said the lady.

'They mistake Rousseauism for hedonism,' he snapped, taking a more careful look at her. She was hardly of an age herself to talk of others as 'young': twenty-five, he guessed, with the delicate features of a Dresden figurine, and pewter-blue eyes. After the sun-tanned, large-featured angularity of Zennor's face, this one was a restful experience. A tail of blonde hair emerged from her bonnet to lie in a single tubular coil on the velvet collar of her jacket.

'Do you suppose, Mr Wootton, had your foundling girls been younger, your influence on their natures would have been greater?'

'Oh, certainly – but then, of course, the age difference between us would have been just too great for marriage.'

The chairman hovered at a polite distance, anxious to ask his own carefully accumulated questions out of an open pocket book. Wootton, in gathering up his notes, dropped some, and the young lady immediately ducked down to retrieve them before he could stop her.

'No, no, I understand. You could not have married, then, before the age of – what?' She ran the pewter-blue eyes over his face with a painter's intensity of purpose. 'Forty? But you might still commend the idea to Rousseauian parents, might you not? Raising natural and adopted children together, so that their souls can grow in harmony?'

The chairman sidled round the perimeter of the lady's striped lawn skirts. The words 'luncheon?' 'coffee house?' formed on his lips, though he had not the affrontery to interrupt.

'Do you have children yourself, madam?' Wootton asked.

She laughed, throwing back her head, so that the laugh rose into the eaves and bred with its echo into a whole carillon of laughs. 'No, no! Nor husband nor child! I am not so blessed.'

She introduced herself as Miss Anne Mirafiore, though she spoke with no perceptible accent to accord with the foreignness of her name. 'Pardon me,' she said, 'but sometimes, when I am in Oxford, I like to walk through the Garden of Public Physic – to study the herbs, you know. Might I trespass on your time and beg your company?'

'Oh, but –' the chairman began. He might as well have been behind glass.

Wootton, whose thoughts up until then had been entirely of chops and sherry, found himself instead walking through the Botanical Gardens behind Magdalen College, with a young woman on his arm. It startled him, but it was not disagreeable. She did not dwell on the failure of his experiment but on the substance of his curriculum. She did not want to talk about female preoccupations but about Rousseau and the world his precepts could bring about.

The blending and competing scent of the herbs had a heady, intoxicating effect. The acers were colouring with autumn, blushing and flushing, contending for Wootton's attention.

'It is the wildness of herbs I most admire,' said Anne Mirafiore. 'I find I cannot care greatly for the cultivated garden. Grant me the asphodel and the yellow archangel, and I am happy.'

He considered the possibility that the woman-with-the-foreign-name might be setting her cap at him. She was delightful, she was charming. But if there was one thing he had learned from his great experiment it was to avoid mercenary and predatory females. In the light of his obvious eligibility, he had to be on his guard. He listened with only half an ear to her eulogy on bulrushes, awaiting a convenient pause so as to enquire about her family: it might give an inkling as to her station and ambitions.

Then his ear picked up that she was halfway through bidding him goodbye: '. . . There are fixed mealtimes at my hotel, and I have no doubt you wish to be getting home.' She curtseyed and began to move away.

'Oh!' He was taken unawares and flustered. 'Wait!'

Anne Mirafiore had reached the gate of the park before he caught up with her. 'You do not live in Oxford, then, Miss Mirafiore?'

'Gracious, no. I have a house in London. But I did so wish to hear you talk. The labour of travel was well rewarded, I do assure you, Mr Wootton.' She curtseyed again, smiled uncertainly with that small, lively mouth, and turned to go.

'I shall be in London myself shortly,' he said, trying to toss his voice with the casual abandon of a quoit. 'I have to purchase a new copy of *Emile*. My own was . . . purloined. Perhaps I might call on you while I am . . .'

'Oh, you must let me send you my copy. I believe I know the book by heart, I love it so. . . . No, no, it is the very least I can do in return for the pleasure of your lecture.'

He repeated his request to call, thinking she had overlooked it. 'Have you seen the latest Goldoni? If you are partial to theatre, we could perhaps . . .'

She cut short his sentence with a flutter of pure embarrassment, pulling on her gloves, studying intently a rosemary bush.

'I am sorry, Mr Wootton. You will think me fearsome bourgeois, but my parents are abroad; I live alone – keep my own household, I mean. Presently, I know absolutely nothing of your background. It would be purest disloyalty to my parents to receive a bachelor at my London address. In the circumstances. I do hope you understand.'

It was novel – to have his social standing doubted, not to be recognised as a scion of the Earl of Wootton. It amused Wootton enormously – that *she* should suspect *him* of fortune-hunting. He might have roared his laughter out loud – except that Miss Mirafiore was gone, and he had no means of finding her again, no means of correcting her misapprehension or supplying his credentials.

Every five miles or so, the driver of the coach which carried Wootton between Oxford and Wantage heard an outburst which he mistook for a sneeze, but which was in fact an explosion of frustration, regret and disappointment.

Anne Mirafiore sent the book, however. He had thought (not having given his address) that her offer had been idle courtesy, but there was nothing idle about Anne Mirafiore. She sent it by way of the chairman of the Rousseauian Society, who dutifully forwarded it to Hatch House.

The brief note enclosed simply said, 'I can recommend to you the Goldoni. I attended with my cousin last evening.'

The address on the letter was in Buckingham Gate. It gave him the opportunity to write her a letter of thanks, and may have chanced to mention his uncle the earl and the substantial acreage attaching to Hatch House.

Their friendship, cemented by letter, was largely conducted via the penny post. It grew less formal by the week. Their mutual interests gave them limitless topics to discuss without ever disagreeing; on the contrary, their opinions were always in perfect harmony. He travelled to London four times, and escorted her to plays, but her contempt for 'London society' – 'such opulence and never a thought for the poor at the gate' – meant that they avoided the London circle of balls, soirées, receptions. Her youth, Anne said (and her exquisite clothes attested to it), had been one long procession of ambassadorial functions; the whole circus filled her with ennui.

He could not imagine that. He never once saw her display either boredom or fatigue. She had an energy which belied her fragile, porcelain sweetness, and yet, like someone in a dream, she gave the impression of stepping always away from him – so that he had to increase his stride, concentrate on keeping up.

She at last agreed to visit Winding Hatch, arriving very properly accompanied by two black maids and her cousin, a dark and silent

Italian duenna with long threads of silken facial hair. So attentive was this little entourage that he had no opportunity, for half a day, to speak with Anne alone.

For the first time, he found himself hoping that the beauty of his mansion would impress – but she barely passed comment on it. All her praise was spent on the gardens – the wild flowers, the imported weeds, the unkempt prospects. As she walked, she picked a stem here, a spray there, handing them to him to carry, so that his hands were soon full of teazles, honesty and bracken, as well as peacock feathers picked up from the ground.

Only now did the maids and cousin dissolve away into Muses' Walk and leave Robin and Anne alone beside the Bower of Troth.

The dreamlike quality of the autumnal day, with its wisps of mist and bruise-coloured light, smeared the line between past romantic longings and present realities. This was where he had always envisaged plighting his troth, even though (he realised it now) his imaginings had never before strayed into the realms of genuinely choosing a wife.

Somewhere among the blackberries and burdock, his heart slipped out of him, like afterbirth, in a single, unnoticed contraction and he found himself committed to the idea of having her. No one and nothing less would serve.

His own store of words empty, he naturally borrowed from their mutual stock of second-hand sentiments. '"Feelings come quicker than lightning to fill my soul, but they burn and dazzle me,"' said Jean-Jacques Rousseau on his behalf.

'Are we wisely mad or madly wise?' she asked by way of reply. But it was an entirely rhetorical question.

Only one stipulation did Anne place on their marriage, whispering it with pleading eyes, her fingers plucking anxiously at the kerchiefs crossing her throat – that it should be a village nuptial, closed to the suffocating condescension of grand ladies and gentlemen. She wished it to be open to any and every peasant, milkmaid, tinker or tanner who cared to come and wish them well.

So much did this accord with Wootton's own feelings that he thought he saw his lake seethe with sympathetic emotion, his deer throw up their antlers tossing velvet fragments of happiness into the air. As he nodded his head in agreement, her thumb appeared to catch accidentally in the cross-over tissue of the kerchief, exposing the upper curves of her breasts tightly confined within the small bodice. He stared stupidly, possessed of new lands, possessed of old dreams, possessed of more than he had dared hope.

★

On the wedding day, it snowed. It was only November, and yet the snow came over the Ridgeway like blown-away washing. The benches laid out in the gardens were soon quilted with white, the terrace slushy and treacherous. The villagers splashed up the various lanes and over the potato fields in pattens. With their Sunday best clothes hidden under any coat and shawl and blanket that would keep out the biting easterly, they looked more like refugees than revellers. The painter of inn-signs, employed to record the marriage in pastels, had to wrestle continually with his canvas, as it blew off the easel into his lap. His fingers were blue, his crayons brittle with cold.

The congregation, when it did arrive, sat determinedly towards the back, leaving the front pews for dignitaries. The villagers were unwilling to trust the rumour that they and they alone were the guests. When no dignitaries arrived, they whispered that the earl had surely shunned his nephew for marrying beneath him. But Alice sat majestical in the third pew, and disseminated the news that Miss Anne was 'as rich and uppermost as the almond paste on a Simnel' and 'not a thing to be sniffed at'. She had seen her luggage, and clothes like that, jewels like that, portmanteau pistols and perfumes like that 'were not to be had for florins'. (She did not mention the black maids, judging they might smack more of the fairground than Windsor Great Park. Besides, Anne was forgoing her maids once married, shipping them back to Italy as an unwarranted luxury.)

A wood-burning, cast-iron stove glowed incandescent in one corner of the church, symmetrically balancing the font, as if some children might be blessed with fire rather than water. Whenever the talk lulled, the stove could be heard to ping and sing with a dangerous intensity. Each time the church door opened, the congregation groaned and complained and shouted at the newcomer to shut out the wind. As well as the draught they were exposed to brief glimpses of the artist, sitting in the porch with sacking over his head and shoulder, his face turned longingly towards the relative warmth of the nave, a pleading look in his eyes.

Once more the doors opened:

'Close up and set down!'

'Oh, for Judas' sake!'

Their lowing complaints died at the sight of Robin Wootton, looking perished but magnanimous, in a green coat with so many collars and shoulder-frills that he looked like a pine tree. He had walked from the house so that his houseguests – the bride and the antique Italian gentleman empowered to give her away – might ride down by carriage. (Alice said that *il conte* spoke no English – not a word, beyond 'good-day' and 'goodnight'.)

The skirts of Wootton's coat were sodden to the knees. He threw it across the pew end, then balanced, with one hand on the communion rail, to pull off his sodden boots. The vicar of St Mary's, Wantage was the only one to help him; the rest were unwilling to step so far forward out of their station. Even Job, who was supposed to be standing second to his master, sat tight alongside his wife in the third pew. The empty boots slumped, buckling and damp, as if overcome by fright. Wootton slipped on silk embroidered shoes, but the hem of his full-skirted jacket trembled, either in the draught or because he was shivering so much with the cold.

The fuel inside the stove shifted, and the metal soughed. They waited and waited – a churchful of hibernating creatures, hands pulled up inside their clothing, mouths and noses leaking white vapour. But the bride did not come.

The snow from Wootton's coat melted and dripped on to the floor, filling with water the carved-out lettering of a burial slab: *Hic iacet* . . . But still the carriage did not roll to a halt outside.

Wootton was minded of King Charles, who wore two shirts to his execution, so that shivers of cold might not be mistaken for fear. He rested his hands on his knees, but his knees were jumping. Should he go looking for her? What if he were to return to the house to find her gone: a prohibition from her parents, a cruel joke at his expense?

The inn-sign painter crept into church with the excuse of softening his crayons at the stove. The metal was so hot that the pastels turned instantly to liquid, spat and ran, in small streaks of pungent, coloured chrism. He stood, past caring, warming his hands, opening his jacket to let the heat reach his belly. And still the bride did not come, nor *il conte* with an explanation.

At last, Wootton sprang to his feet, picked up his coat and swung it round him, looking top-heavy in his little salon shoes. Just as he took one step down the aisle, the features of his face all huddled together as if for warmth, the door's hooped handle lifted. Every head turned.

The door rattled at someone's efforts to lift the latch with frozen hands.

Then the bride came in, in the white wool smock of a shepherdess, the bodice tightly ruched, the waistline high up under her breasts. The coach had been unable to negotiate the snowy road, and so she had walked – up Hatch Hill and down, over the crisp, needling cruelty of the frozen grass.

Robin's joy was without measure: the little feet disclosed as the bride lifted her wet hems were whitely bare.

CHAPTER TWENTY-ONE

Bawming the Cherry

Robin Wootton had come to believe all those years wasted on Alba and Zennor a pointless, uncompensated disappointment. Now he realised that they had all been a part of his fate – a delaying tactic on God's part to preserve him from mistaken entanglements until Anne could arrive and lend meaning to his life. He was supremely happy.

His somewhat fastidious nature was mirrored in Anne's extreme modesty. She installed herself, without a word spoken, in the bedroom alongside his, presupposing nothing, taking nothing for granted. When, after three days of marriage, he let himself in and closed the door behind him, there was nervousness in her face – a fear of the unknown, which he found deeply stirring. The shivering rigidity of the shoulders he embraced put him in mind of an unbroken pony, trembling at the touch of the horse-breaker. It conferred on him power and mastery, gave him a sense of ownership which house and land had never done. When she drew up her nightdress, it was as though he were being admitted to a sanctuary, a shrine, a holy-of-holies forbidden to all but the high priest. He worshipped accordingly.

Like creatures in long grass, the occupants of the parsonage kept as still as possible, so as not to attract attention. But inevitably one raw day in February, when Zennor and George were both out and when the tarpaulins over the temporary repairs swelled into the kitchen and bedrooms with every gust of wind, someone else bellied his way indoors.

A young cleric, barely older than George, arrived by barouche to look the property over. His wife was with him – a suety women twice his size, but so quiet-spoken and shy that she paused before every movement, as if in deference to the air she would displace by it. Her husband, a Mr Nehemiah Brough, would set her down in each room like a cabin trunk before commencing an inventory of the room's contents and a lament over the state of its decoration.

'This is really too bad, too bad!' he muttered under his breath, never quite to Grace who was showing him around. Each time she tried to explain – 'The builders are not to be had, you see' – the Reverend Brough would click his tongue or tear off a ribbon of wallpaper or poke a hole in the cankered plaster, ignoring her. 'Our patron Mr Wootton is newly married, you know, or he would have put repairs in hand long since, I'm sure.' Her voice wavered higher and more piping all the while, 'and what with the ground so sodden, what could they do, in any case? Would it not come right down again?' Grace turned the appeal on Mrs Brough, who searched intently in her indispensable for a bonbon.

Ever since the deaths, Grace had walked a twig bridge over chaos and disorder. Her own foundations had been washed away, and the presence of Zennor in the house did nothing to underbrace her. Zennor worked. From early morning, through all the daylight hours, she washed and swept and dusted, sugar soaped the mouldy walls, whitewashed the larder. As the light failed, she moved on to repairing sheets or polishing plate. Through the derelict back wall, a fine tilth of decaying daub blew in on every breath of wind, so that her cleaning came to nothing. Spiders, rats, birds – even a squirrel once – broke into the building, but Zennor pitted herself against them, with her grim, angry face, until she won. And even while she battled against the undefeatable decay there was a stillness about her, a grown-upness, whereas Grace, sitting immobile, with a rug round her skinny, aching shanks, was all turmoil and tantrum inside – too ashamed to show it, too unnerved to grow any stronger.

All the same, faced with the Reverend and Mrs Brough, Grace would have been glad of Zennor just then. The scarlet fever had left her joints inflamed and her hearing slightly impaired, so that it cost her a lot to walk about the rattling house, showing the Broughs its shortcomings. And Mr Brough was tireless in his desire to catalogue every cracked window-pane, every patch of soft plaster, every inconvenience to comfortable living.

'If you don't mind me asking, sir, did the bishop ask you to call on –'

'One spinet. Several notes dumb.'

At last Zennor returned from the mill with a half sack of flour in a hand-barrow, and seeing the barouche brushed the flour husks off her black dress, tucked a strand of hair under her black cap and negotiated the hingeless back door.

'Oh, Zennor!' Grace greeted her in a voice halfway to a sob. 'Here are the Reverend and Mrs Brough come to see around the house, and George is in Wantage selling the horses, and I'm sure I should have offered them refreshment, but they were so very eager to begin, and I don't know but that George has the key to the sherry cabinet and the kettle is empty and I don't believe I can lift the water bucket to fill it, so I—'

Zennor placed herself squarely in front of the Reverend Brough, her hand outstretched. He put his handkerchief to his nose, to demonstrate that his hand was too much occupied for shaking, but she merely waited for him to blow his nose, her hand still outstretched. In the end, he was obliged to shake it.

'And you are?' he said squeamishly.

'Zennor Wootton. I lodge here. As housekeeper. Miss Baydon has been unwell. Might I ask your interest in the house?'

They were in the middle hallway. Grace sat down on the second stair, resting a hand on the newel post which rocked to and fro a little, like a tooth loose in its socket. She had not succeeded in asking, but she knew the reason for the visit as well as Zennor did, without forcing a reason out of the tight-lipped and grudging Mr Brough.

'I hardly see how my wife and I shall support it,' he said now from behind his handkerchief. 'We had no idea of the extent of dilapidation. But my bishop has requested that I occupy the living vacated by the previous incumbent. So I must require that the property be vacated by the week's end.'

Mrs Brough, after making two or three attempts to extricate herself from the sofa, stood up and smiled benignly at everyone, tightened the string of her indispensable and turned sideways to negotiate the door. She assured them all that she would be very happy in their house 'once it was set to rights'.

'Shall I ask that Constable Gervase accompany me on Saturday next?' asked her husband belligerently. 'He may be able to help you with your belongings.'

'That will not be necessary,' said Zennor. 'Nor even desirable.'

They could not claim to be surprised. For weeks they had been anticipating it, and only the long silence of the Church Commissioners had helped them ignore the facts. Winding Hatch must have a vicar, and the new vicar must have a house. Their house.

'Oh, I wish George would come!' said Grace, slipping her hands under the rug Zennor laid over her lap. 'He would know what's to be done!'

'That's simple. You must shift ground,' said Zennor. 'Rent somewhere.'

Grace was not listening. 'George means to enter the Church. I know it. He has never said so, but it is just the profession for him. An educated man. So many of our friends are . . .' Her brother, in concert with God, represented continuity, a barbican against sudden catastrophic change. If George were to enter the Church Grace, like the world, could continue lying safe in the palm of God.

'So he may, but not by Friday,' said Zennor sharply, jarring God's elbow. 'You must rent rooms – in Wantage for choice. There is book-work there.'

When George did come back from selling the horses, his humiliation clinking in a stiff leather purse, he found Sam, Sarah, Suzannah, Grace and Zennor sitting with the parlour lamps unlit. Grace stood up and flung her arms round his neck, and Zennor said, 'The new parson came.'

Then they all sat down together, a family without adults, so that George and Zennor, by their size, might have been mistaken in the semi-darkness for the mother and father, had they not sat down at opposite ends of the room.

Zennor repeated that they must look for rooms to rent in Wantage or Oxford, where there was book-work to be had for George. They looked at her blankly, this outsider from over the hill, wanting something kinder. But she sealed up her face against them, tightening her full lips, tucking away her troublesome hair, making practical plans. Samuel Baydon's suicide had ruined them – made pariahs of them. With the post of parish highway surveyor vacated by the parson's death, George had applied for it, knowing that the honorarium might make the difference between survival and penury. His offer had been declined in the tersest words. He was tarred with the brush that had blackened his father's memory. 'Two bedrooms will suffice,' said Zennor. 'One for Sam and George. One for Sarah, Suzannah and Grace. Best would be a single floor, without stairs for Grace to climb.'

'But where will you sleep?' asked Sam, picturing her curled up like a cat in front of a carved, Adam fireplace.

'I shall find live-in work. I am not in the equation.'

George lurched awkwardly out of his chair, pulling at the neck of his shirt, angry. He went outside and up the stairs, taking three steps at a time. He called from the landing, still angry, by the sound of him, 'A word, Miss Zennor.'

She took a lamp, since the stairwell had become a single shaft of darkness at the centre of the unlit house. He was waiting at the head of the stairs for her. The lamp in her hand lit first his knees, then his cuff, his father's watch, a cheek in need of shaving. Exhaustion had settled on him like a pall. Zennor stopped three stairs down.

'There is no need,' he said. 'To go.'

'Why? If the bishop needs his property . . .'

'What? No. I didn't mean – I meant . . . I realise your position here is . . . tenuous. Unorthodox. But you were never . . . You never paid great mind to . . .'

'Orthodoxy?' She would have liked to help him, but she had no idea what he was trying to say. That the sale of horses left him able to pay her a wage? 'I don't give a fig for orthodoxy, but you won't need me. When you're in rooms. Not a place, nor a space. Not a space nor a place,' she repeated with a crooked smile. 'It was a purely temporary . . .'

A knock at the front door sent a frisson of alarm through them both, like a fox's scratching on a henhouse. Down below, Grace pushed her hands deeper under her rug, abdicating any duty to answer the door. Sam wanted to go, but Zennor got there before him, hurrying down the stairs with the lamp, driving him back into the parlour with a single fierce glance.

It was Anne Wootton.

Zennor looked beyond her, glanced past her for a sign of Robin, but the bride was alone. She was in riding habit, and the horse stood tethered to the field fence opposite, a lumpen shadow in the encroaching dusk.

'Forgive me calling on you without an invitation, but I was riding past. I shall forget a thing, if I don't say it now.' She stepped inside, a breaking wave of sandy silk trailing in little hissing ripples over the threshhold.

'I regret, Mr Baydon is not—' Zennor began, wanting to spare George the humiliation of being told twice to vacate his home.

'No. Naturally. He is dead,' said the woman in front of her. Realising her mistake, she went on, unabashed, 'Oh, you mean the son? No matter. It is an easy message to deliver. Perhaps you would be kind enough to mention my request when he returns?'

'Request?' First the new vicar wanting his house, next the bride wanting what?

Anne Wootton took up a position in the room in which the yards of her voluminous skirt flooded between the furniture, marooning little Sam on the window-seat. She put her hand on the child's shoulder, and bent to look past him. 'What a lovely garden. Of course, a garden is very agreeable to a house. I would be asking much of you to forfeit such a fine established plot.'

'Reverend Brough has already called on us,' said Suzannah bitterly.

'Reverend Brough?' Ann's face, as she turned it towards them, admitted no knowledge of Reverend Brough. 'It is simply that the gate-house – the gate-house, you know. At the foot of the drive. It has stood empty for more than a year now. And buildings fall into such disrepair – well, how could you fail to know it?' Her gloved left hand, while appearing simply to steady her against the window bay, fingered the bleak mould cankering the plaster. 'You would be doing me the greatest favour if you would consider moving there. I do so hate to look out and see windows unlit; like blind eyes in a face, I always think. And a chimney without smoke? Horrid. Of course, it has only two bedrooms. I have to admit; it would be asking a great sacrifice of you. I don't know how I could possibly recompense you – except that the estate could keep you furnished in fuel, I think. And game birds are yours for the taking. Do you think that you might manage – all the six of you? – to oblige me?'

'Oh yes!' Grace's rug slid to the floor. In her imagination she had already made the move. 'You, Zennor, Sarah, Suzannah and I can sleep in one bedroom; George and Sam in the other.'

'No, I –'

The Baydons looked towards Zennor. Without realising it, they had come to look her way whenever a problem arose. In the silence that followed, a tell-tale – a sliver of glass wedged into a fissure in the wall to mark its subsidence – tinkled to the floor and broke into granules of rainbow.

'This is Mr Wootton's wish?' Zennor queried. Over Anne Wootton's shoulder she could see Suzannah frowning with irritation at her apparent ingratitude.

'We are as one in all our thinking,' said the bride sentimentally, though her eyes did not drop and her cheeks did not colour; she went on looking at Zennor quite levelly. So did the others. That flustered Zennor.

'Well, I'm sure it is hardly for me to say,' she said, wiping her hands uneasily on her white apron. 'Mr Baydon shall decide when he comes home. Myself, I shall soon be gone.'

Grace dropped her rug again. Sam jumped up, crushing the glass tell-tale underfoot. Suzannah and Sarah added their astonishment. Only Anne Wootton seemed unsurprised.

'Please don't,' she said, letting her eyes rest heavy on Zennor, like someone leaning a ladder against a wall. 'Consider remaining in the village. I feel sure the gate-house would benefit from a conscientious housekeeper. And I am perfectly certain Miss Grace has need of you.'

Zennor blinked and stepped back from the intensity of those pewter eyes. 'I don't think Mr Wootton would –'

But she had to give way. For Anne Wootton insisted that she and her husband were of one mind; there was nothing she could give which he would prefer to withhold.

Robin, when he finally came to hear of it, on the day of the removal, was embarrassed and mildly nettled by the thought of Zennor living at the end of his drive. But he found he could not quite frame his objection in words. So he was obliged to let the arrangement persist.

Before long, however, he did forbid Anne to go riding her big bay mare around and over Hatch Hill any more. For she was expecting a child, and an heir to Hatch House was far too precious a burden to jeopardise.

So relieved was the viscount that his nephew had refrained from marrying one of his wards, that he was ready to look favourably on any superior match, despite having no acquaintance with Anne's far-flung family. He found Robin's political theory as wrong-headed as French republicanism: indeed, he assumed they were directly related, and took to calling Robin the Ragged Pantaloon of the family. But at least the young fool only waxed wordy about his beliefs and (to quote the viscount precisely), 'at least the bloody woman was fecund'. He did half-heartedly instigate investigations as to the woman's breeding stock, although personally he saw no reason to doubt talk of a diplomatic background.

Not six months into her pregnancy, Anne Wootton knew how she wished to celebrate the birth of her child. 'The old customs fall away so, Robin,' she said one evening, as she permitted him to rub almond oil into her pale belly and purpling breasts. 'Nature wants for her proper dues.'

He could not quite recall how he had come to be accorded this immodest privilege, although he remembered her reassuring him: 'the worship of beauty is as natural as self-love'. He understood worship – libation – the artistic ritualisation of everyday life, so that when she phrased it like this his hygienic nature felt licensed to comply – even to comply when she worshipped him in a similar way.

'I should like to pay nature her due when our child is born, Robin. Deck her out, in some way. Deck her out, do you see?' If fact her vision was not so imprecise as this suggested. It was wholly thought through, with ribbons to be supplied by Wenhams of Kintbury, and wreath-making twine bought in bulk from a funeral-florist, and teams of men employed with billhooks to cull fifty thousand dog-roses from the hedgerows of the Lambourn Valley.

Soon the whole of Winding Hatch anticipated the birth more keenly than

Christmas. Anne had been so assiduous in getting to know her neighbours, and so often she had spoken to them of bawming the cherry; they began to think they must have known of the custom long before her arrival, and simply let it slip their minds.

The cherry trees in the big orchard at Hatch House, anticipating wonders, swelled too, in expectation, thrilled into blossom, loosed pink tears of joy at the honour in store for them, festooned themselves with blood-red fruit. The first cherries appeared on the very day (or so these things are remembered) that Anne Wootton gave birth to a son.

From as far afield as Fawley and Ashbury they came, to the sound of drums and bird scarers. By cart, on horseback and on foot they streamed in, collecting their wreaths and drinking their allocation of free ale at the Post Inn. Spontaneously they came, with never a word from Wootton. Just one nod from the weary mother to Alice and the midwife, and the county round about galvanised itself to celebrate in the time-honoured fashion the bawming of the cherry.

In truth, time had never honoured a Berkshire ritual of bawming. And yet, when they were reminded of each little touch, each small particular, it seemed like a practice newly fallen into disuse. And they drank ale from tankards with a single cherry bobbing against their lips; they each wore a cherry-red ribbon round a sleeve or in their hair; they raised toasts to the cherry and to maidenheads broken in the name of love; and they converged on Hatch House to spit the bright white cherry-stones on to the sun-dark lake.

Standing at the bedroom window, his baby son in his arms, Robin watched with delight. First the deer stampeded in a dappled rush, from one end to the other of the prospect. Then the pheasants and partridges flew up from their covers. The music arrived even before the procession came in sight, fading and swelling with each contour of its route up from the village.

At last the first strings of villagers, dressed in holiday clothes, ribbons fluttering, picked their way tentatively through the long grass of the orchard to hang their rose-wreaths on the branches, plucking down a cherry each in exchange. He saw Curragh and wife glancing uneasily back at the house, unsure of themselves. How right, how very right it all seemed: that happiness, if not wealth, could be held in common at a time like this, shared equally by men and women of all degrees. Robin held his son up to show him how blessed he was in his fellow men.

But Job and Curragh and Smith, the osier woman and the tradesmen were followed by more flocking hordes, trampling in across the garden and round the house with their horses and carts and dogs and large batches of children. They stripped the cherry trees like starlings, then turned back towards the lake, milling and wheeling to avoid new crowds pressing in behind. They trampled the long orchard grass flat, and made new routes to the waterside wherever a path grew too choked. Soon the dry-stone orchard wall was pushed down in a dozen places, baring its toothless gums at the house

Wootton's delight turned first to dismay then to panic as a seemingly never-ending barrage of noise and celebration invaded his grounds. When the cherries were all gone and every bough festooned with wreaths and ribbons, the celebrants moved on to the apple orchard. Their boots, as they took the long way round, broke all the green plant-tops off the growing potato crops. A fight broke out in the stable yard. Children drank from the Italian water-garden, their boots scuffing the pink Italian rock out of the watercourse and into the lower pond.

Up in his Palladian ark, Robin Wootton watched his estate submerged under a deluge of humanity. His eyes stung with dust from the trampled barley. A field of young wheat – the first for several summers – parted like the Red Sea in front of the children of Israel. His knuckles rapped on one of the big sash windows, but could not attract the attention of the three drunkards billhooking more blooms from his rose-garden. Then he saw that, quite fatally, the baker's wagon (commissioned by his wife to distribute pies and glazed bread to the bawmers) had driven up on to Muses' Walk, drawing the crowds right through the heart of the garden in order to reach their lunch. Ducking down, Wootton tried to shout through the open base of the narrowly opened window, but the drums and bird scarers, the handbells and the singing drowned him out. His own noise only served to alarm the baby in his arms and set it squawling. It flung out a pair of bare pink arms as though to save itself from a vertiginous drop to the terrace below.

Wootton recoiled into the bedroom and looked around at his wife. She sat half-reclined among the pillows, smiling serenely at him. Given material proof of so much life and love, it seemed monumentally petty to complain about the damage to his floribunda.

CHAPTER TWENTY-TWO

Furniture

The bills which came in for the bawming of the cherry were larger than Wootton had believed possible. He had never given more than a passing thought to money, but then he had never received accounts before – three in one week – amounting to two hundred guineas. The orchards were so damaged that there could be no apple harvest whatsoever, and the potato fields had to be replanted for fear of yet another bread famine in the autumn.

The revellers had dispersed, like flies from a corpse, and set the country-side ablaze with outrage, all of which was heaped on Wootton and the Wootton estates for encouraging mayhem. The viscount wrote expressing his hopes that nothing like it would ever occur again.

'We shall have to find some other way to celebrate our joy,' he told his wife.

'What, not bawm the cherry? After I gave my word to do it every year?' She widened her pewter-blue eyes at him in pained astonishment, as though he had banned the Eucharist to save on wafers.

'Well, yes – you and I – the village, perhaps, but –'

She offered to pay the cost out of her own means. (It was quaint, he thought, but only right philosophically, that she should speak of having means still hers to dispose of.) He refused to let her, of course, but was left feeling not only two hundred guineas poorer but frugal and mean as well. After all, she asked nothing for herself, nothing whatsover – not for dresses or banquets or balls. She fed the child herself, in the public rooms, which, quite frankly, appalled him; and she took to raffia-weaving, making him a deplorable hat which affection obliged him to wear.

But at night she gave of herself in such ways as made him praise God for giving him a passionate nature, for sending Rousseau to liberate his instincts for happiness.

Naturally, he was anxious to show her off to his regular dining companions – the Dunches, the Knollys. And she did not disappoint him. When he expounded on the war, or the penal system, or the inevitable demise of monarchy, she was all sweet concurrence, laying her opinions down alongside his like a draper suggesting lining harmonious with a fabric.

The gentlemen did not take offence, though the ladies fluttered their fans hard, as if to deflect the snowy words from falling on their husbands' brows. But whatever she said to them in the withdrawing-room, after dinner, won the ladies over to her as well. He had no way of knowing *what* she said, only that it fired the ladies' cheeks redder than the porter. Unfortunately, though they became quite reconciled to Anne herself, instead they snubbed him at his own front door, urging their husbands away, from a distance, as if from playing with a particularly large and rabid dog. As he bid them goodnight the women actually sniffed at him, as at a pile of ordure dropped unexpectedly in the hallway, and were already hissing secretively into their husband's ears as they climbed into their carriages.

He asked her about it. 'I fear they do not care for our politics,' said Anne, shrugging her beautiful, bare shoulders. Then she added thoughtfully, 'It's true. Privately they do not seem to care for you. Perhaps they had hopes you would marry one of their daughters.'

'They have no daughters,' said Robin, still watching after the coaches, even as they passed the lights of the gate-house. 'Not a daughter between them.'

'Then perhaps they had ambitions to be your lover,' she laughed, already unlacing, there, on the terrace. Robin turned back into the house, the familiar feeling hard once again under his ribs of having been cruelly wronged.

Zennor lay in bed, waiting for the birds to sing. Sarah ground her teeth in her sleep. Suzannah turned over, winding herself in her bedding tighter and tighter, without waking. Grace's sleeping face was as white as a death mask. But only Zennor lay awake, waiting for the birds to sing.

As soon as the sky lightened, they would come to the bramble bushes in the angle of the wall, picking the berries she could not reach, deep inside the barbed, sprung coils. Spring had wound the bushes, summer encased them, and autumn had triggered their escapement. Now the birds and the Baydons ate blackberries every day, as autumn wore away.

But for Zennor time had stopped. She felt as if her spring had been

217

wound, but no one had freed the cogs; or else they had seized, for want of oil. As with most gate-houses, the windows of the room were very high, affording no view but the sky, which was overcast and starless. There was still too much furniture for the size of the bedroom, but how could that be helped, with four girls sharing? A press, an ottoman, a blue-and-white vase. Some shelves of books. Out in the living-room, the Reverend Baydon's desk still occupied pride of place. His and Sophronia's umbrellas hung behind the door. But most of the surplus furniture had gone – sold to a gentleman-farmer whose mother-in-law's house had burned down. Everyone's disaster profits somebody, thought Zennor.

On the day they had left Winding Hatch parsonage, the gate-house had strained to swallow all the furniture which had belonged to Samuel Baydon. George had wanted to leave it behind, but Zennor had insisted on Job and Curragh (sent by Anne Wootton, to assist in the move) loading the clock, the press, the dresser, everything, and walking beside it as far as the gate-house. She oversaw its careful stowing in the single-storey building. 'Sell it by all means, but do not give Brough more than he already has,' she said.

'What does this dross signify?' said George, full of disgust, pitching a metal ladle against the firedogs. A gigantic spider, black as the ash, scuttled out into the open hearth then ran for a gap between the bricks. 'Joinery. Pots. Goods and chattels.'

'They signified to the man who made them,' said Zennor, patiently lining a drawer with straw and packing it with china. 'They signified to your father when he bought them. They'll signify to the pawn shop, if nowhere else. Only the rich say things don't signify.' She picked up the ladle and straightened its buckled handle.

'I say it,' said George belligerently. 'I want none of it.'

Grace, however, sat at the spinet, arms spread, holding either end of the keyboard, as if to shield it from impending disaster. Suzannah sat on the stairs holding her step-father's Bible, and Sarah sat underneath her mother's shawl, like a canary in a cage, while Sam tore up and down the garden playing a desperate game of cricket against himself. George could see he had no great support for sloughing off the family's wordly goods.

Before the day was out, they filled the gate-house like a furniture depot, leaving no living space between – a forest of cupboards, rolled carpets, inverted tables, an underbush of umbrellas, pan racks and footstools. Sam and Sarah's beds stood vertically against the wall, and their bedding had to be spread on the bedroom floor, under the dining-table, where they slept with the firedogs at their feet like sepulchral carvings. Suzannah and Grace also wormed their way into a bed in the second bedroom, each with a piece of cheese and slice of bread, while Zennor and George were left standing marooned among the dove-jointing, each with a china cup of milk for supper. Lamps stood balanced precariously, one on the flourbin, one on a pile of books, one on the seat of Sophronia's dining-chair.

'And you still think all this was needed?' he said, his shadow huge, crook-backed where it reached the ceiling and bent over. Her lesser shadow was thrown by a different lamp – smaller and bending the other way, so that they overlapped at the shoulder.

'Once, when I was at Lambeth,' said Zennor, 'a girl came there with a table on her head. She had walked all the way from Whipps Cross with a table on her head. It was the only thing she owned. There was no parting her from it. It made her who she was. A person with a table, you see? Thinking back, I can see that now. Not a person without. A person with a table.' Then, assuming he would understand better: 'Rather you sell it, than Brough.' She was holding the jug of milk, and offered him more, but it was an awkward operation to pour it, hampered by a drying rack and a firescreen.

'Is that ours? From before?' He nodded at a large oil-painting properly hung on the wall beyond the piled clutter, so that it had a look of belonging. Zennor turned round, and peered between a cabin trunk and a fasces of curtain poles. The painting was of Horatio holding the bridge.

'It is from the house. Mrs Wootton must have moved it here. For us. How kind.'

'In case we wanted for furnishings, you mean?' he said, and the absurdity bubbled up through his lugubrious gloom, in a kind of hiccough which spilled his milk.

A curtain, rolled up and crammed between the low ceiling and the top of the dresser, suddenly broke free and bounded down on them, loosing a cloud of dust and a tinkling of spoons. Zennor put up her hands and, fending it off a lit lamp, heaved it onwards like a bale of hay. It slid across the spinet and flumped down at George's feet. The dust made Zennor cough, and the cough turned to laughter, until she had to lean against the mattress beside her and bury her face in the ticking, for fear he thought her unfeeling, callous, light. Appalling, to laugh at such a time, among the jetsam of wrecked lives, the flotsam of sunken hopes. But she could not stop herself. Glancing up, meaning to apologise, she saw that his face had coloured deeply. As he reached round the rolled turkey rug and the bathtub, she thought he was trying to smack her arm, to chastise her, but he could not reach. The bathtub, propped off the the horizontal, began to slide, and they both had to reach out to restrain it. He was more successful, with the result that the contents tipped over her – brown earth and something buried in it: long, tuberous, green fingers.

For a moment, George thought he was seeing grave plunder – the decomposing fingers of one or other of his parents scrabbling over her breast. 'What? What is it? What are they? God's breath!'

Zennor plucked the green fingers out of her décolletage. 'Asparagus. Your father's asparagus crowns. You know how he prized his asparagus crowns? They don't transplant, people say, but we can try. I thought I would try.' She did not know what the look on his face meant, or why he was picking his laborious way around and over and under limbs of furniture to her side of the bath. She talked faster, to fend off his anger. 'When I picture him . . . when we sing the hymn . . . casting down their crowns around the glassy sea . . . that's how I picture him. Your father. Presenting his asparagus to God. To the Master Gardener.'

Worse and worse, she thought, scooping the straggling root fibres and clots of soil back into their bath, unable to back away, because of the settle and carver penning her in. I am making things worse and worse. The handkerchiefs of her morning gown were full of loose soil; she could feel it filtering through and down between her breasts, trickling down her stomach. She pulled out the loose streamers of cloth and shook them into the bathtub.

For a moment, seeing the shadows jump, she thought that some other piece of furniture was on the move, turned sharply, and put out her hands. And her fingers closed around his head. More grains of soil trickled down inside her dress. At least the skin of her stomach prickled, as if topsoil were falling on it, and she could feel the filigree roots straining after the dark and moisture of her body. She did not let go of his head; the hair was softly cold and springy. Horatio on the bridge felt faint for want of blood.

'People call it the consolation of the poor,' he said.

Incredible that she still did not know whether he was hostile or friendly. 'How can we be poor? With all these?' She rocked her head towards the plethora of worldly goods, still joking, still pretending to joke. The carver jabbed her in the back. The firescreen reflected back the heat of her body's grate. Her mourning black had become Nile mud, rich and seasonal. Their intertwined shadows were already overlaying one another. It was not the consolation of the poor. It was the consolation of the empty, and the lonely and the bereaved. It was any and every consolation. She had sensed that long since, but never achieved the proof. She pulled his face down against her throat.

At least she tried. His head resisted her; his shoulders pulled away. Her thumbs were still by his eyesockets and part of her wanted to gouge out his eyes for being shut, for refusing to look at her, as Robin had refused. He had fought her off, too: repulsed her; been repulsed. A trench of horror opened up, and she was alone again. Her hands sprang away, as if from blackberry thorns, and she clutched the two strips of gauzy tissue across her chest.

And that was why she lay awake listening for the birds to begin singing, and the ticking of the clock which stood in the living-room. Her own mainspring had been overwound; if she were to put a hand to her breast she doubted she would even feel the kick of a heart. They ate blackberries every day, the Baydons and the birds. But Zennor simply waited for the season to end, for the dark juicy fruits all to be gone, even from the deepest heart of the bush, so that the birds would stop coming, stop singing, and so that she stood some chance of sleeping again.

Sarah and Suzannah came home the same way each day, from the dame school in the village – over the footbridge and between the tall hogweed. Today, suddenly, a shaft of light struck them, like an Epiphany, whitening their faces and shrinking their pupils: light beaming off glass. When their eyes recovered, they could make out the oblong gilt frame around the big mirror which, in moving, had caught the sun.

They were accustomed to the big curve of Hatch Hill rising like a green sea swell out of calm oceans; but they had never seen tables and chairs floating on it before, pedestals and beds and couches. It seemed, from a distance, that a green flood was sweeping the contents of Hatch House out of doors and away, twirling and turning like pieces of wreckage – a surreal cavalcade of furnishing moving all in one direction: over the hill, past the ruin, and out of sight.

The girls ran the rest of the way to the gate-house, to tell George, but he was still up at Wantage. He had got work as a clerk with the Old Bath Machine Company ('on the despatch and delivery of unaccompanied parcels travelling by stage'). Neither was Sam home from school. But Grace was always home, and Zennor was there too, cooking potato cakes on a griddle. 'Zennor! Zennor! The furniture is all up and off!' gasped Sarah, flapping a hand.

Just then an armoire and a little boot-locker came by the gate-house. Smith the blacksmith was dragging them along on a pallet sledge, stopping every few yards to kick the doors of the armoire shut. Zennor unconsciously put an arm round each of the girls and drew them back into the doorway.

When Smith saw them, he said, 'You want to get yous up there. S'comin out, every bit.' There was a cast-iron fireback on his sledge, too: a man and woman standing beneath a tree, and a snake around the trunk. Zennor remembered it from the fireplace in her bedroom.

'Why? Are they leaving?'

Smith only shrugged and grimaced and spat a large pat of phlegm on the ground.

'Well, what did Wootton *say?*' Zennor insisted.

'Ben't there,' said Smith, and easing the loop of rope circling his shoulder he leaned into the task of dragging his booty home.

'Are they robbing the house, Zennor?' whispered Sarah.

'Is it the revolution come?' said Grace behind them. She had taken to wearing her blanket over her head if she stepped outside, to keep the sunlight from troubling her eyes. All three looked to Zennor for an answer. Why was Hatch House furniture streaming out of doors?

'I'd best go and find out,' said Zennor, and set off at a run.

Like ants decamping from one nest to another, chains of energetic souls were carrying away the contents of bedrooms and kitchen, icehouse and scullery, linen-rooms and withdrawingrooms – a shocking, mindless rout – and not by strangers, but by people she knew! Mrs Beeny and little Norbert, Harry Furzelow and the Cullompton twins. Job and Curragh, William and the groom.

She recognised each item – had memories associated with each bowl and pan and china plate. It was horrible to see the house haemorrhaging out its beautiful fixtures, as the holiday plunder of hooligans and vandals.

'What are you doing?' she asked William, running alongside him. 'What's happening?'

'Oh, 'tis all right, miss,' said Alice, answering for him. 'We have her word for't.' She was carrying a copper salmon kettle and a glass-funnelled lamp.

Then, out of the terrace door, came little Sam Baydon, struggling with a sewing basket and a framed lithograph of a parakeet. Zennor grabbed him by his queue of hair and shook him the way she had not been able to shake William. 'What do you think you are about, young man? Have you taken to thieving now? Is that what they teach you at school? To loot and thieve?' And she smacked at the top of his head with an open palm, over and over. Sam pulled his neck into his collar and bent at the knees, still clutching the basket. 'It's all right! The master said! We were let go to do it!'

'Robin said? Wootton *said* you could take all this?' She crouched down in front of him, sitting on her heels. The baker, carrying an astral globe like a huge belly in front of him, barged her off balance as he stepped out of the terrace door, and apologised, though he did not stop to help her up.

'Not *Wootton*. The *school*master!' said Sam, agitated by the sight of the globe, by the thought that he had chosen too soon, had missed better choices. '*She* came to the school. Mrs Wootton. Said people were all to take what they lacked. Something they lacked.'

Zennor gave him a look which suggested she knew a liar when she saw one. But she let him go, for she had just caught sight of Anne Wootton – caught a glimpse of blue-and-white glazed cotton, a yellow straw bergère, on the swing in the cherry orchard. Zennor picked up her skirts and ran. It seemed a very long way. 'Mrs Wootton! Mrs Wootton!'

The woman on the swing held out her legs stiffly crossed at the ankles, toes pointed, *le dernier cri d'élégance*, for an Arcadian. Her dress was of the short, *pet en l'air* style, leaving her calves and ankles bare. With great deliberation she hung back from the ropes of the swing, her arms at full stretch. 'Ah, Miss Zennor,' she said, in her rich, smiling voice.

Zennor pointed back at the house. 'The village,' she said, labouring after words large enough to describe the pillage. 'The village . . . They are carrying off . . .' Even as she spoke, little boudoir chairs promenaded through the apple orchard next door, along with a couch upholstered in tabaret: alternate stripes of watered blue silk and grey satin.

'They have my permission,' said Anne Wootton, her tabaret eyes unnerving in their calm. 'Robin and I do not believe in owning more than we need. Material simplicity but emotional plentitude. Those are our watchwords. You must have heard him say it yourself, a dozen times.'

'A hundred,' said Zennor. 'I heard him quote it a hundred times. I'm not certain I ever heard him think it.'

'With health and daily bread, we are rich enough,' said Anne. (It was astonishing that in such a short time she had contracted from Robin the same self-certain cadences of speech, the same gospel-sprinkling of Jean-Jacquobite sayings.)

'Is he not at home?' Zennor asked, on a sudden impulse.

'Robin? Oh, no. He has gone to London,' Anne said, abruptly starting to swing higher. 'Home presently, I think.'

'Emotional plenitude,' said Zennor to herself, retracing her steps rapidly towards the house. 'Emotional fiddle-faddle!' But she was breathless with astonishment, more than with running. And occupying more and more of her thoughts was the library at Hatch House – her childhood preserve, her private realm. She had a vision of its shelves stripped bare, its roof prised off like the skin from a drum and its dark interior flayed of its leather and gold-blocked hide, the bones of its shelves laid skeleton bare.

But though the house, empty of its carpets, rang with footsteps, the library had been barely touched. The writing desk had gone, and the lamp. The fire grate had gone too, and the rug. But so little bearing did books have on daily life in Winding Hatch that hardly one was missing from the shelves.

Zennor went straight to Samuel Butler and Daniel Defoe, to Webster and Cobbett and Donne. The more titles she saw, the more she was reminded of, darting to and fro, cursing with exasperation the thief who had taken the movable steps and cut her off from the delectable upper shelves. More, Lovelace and the Apocrypha. Little by little, the same material frenzy infected her that had brought the whole village pelting to grab up every pretty, useful or valuable object. A retreating army would not have made such rack of the lovely house, of its monochrome staterooms, its opulent salons. Bacon, Jonson, Fanny Burney . . . Her arms too full of books to open the door, Zennor paused, no hand free to turn the handle of the libary door. It was then that Robin Wootton chose to return from London.

She heard the shouting outside first, and setting the books down in a pile at her feet slipped her hand out through as narrow an opening as possible. Then, easing the key from the lock between first and second finger, she locked the door from the inside. Then, she dropped back into one of the dark alcoves, between the shelves, wanting to be invisible. Even without making out particular words, she could tell it would not do to meet Robin Wootton in his present mood.

Much as Sarah and Suzannah had first seen it, Robin Wootton saw the contents of his house spill out over the Berkshire countryside. A dozen of his ancestors, piteous as the victims of a lynch mob, looked down from the hill at him, as the portraits off his staircase were carried aloft.

Robin too thought, Revolution, as his carriage rolled past a woman with his bedlinen piled high on her head. He jumped down and grabbed her – grabbed the linen – then caught sight of Jethro Hogg carrying a music-stand and a trout-rod. *What do you think you're doing?* he yelled in their faces, but they looked back at him offended, resentful. 'We wuz told,' they said.

'We wuz told.' Every face said it to him, whether it was the child carrying his artist's reticule or the simpleton clashing his silver tureen lids together for cymbals. Robin lashed out with the fishing-rod, grabbed hold of coat tails and hair-queues, but they shook him off with unapologetic reproach. Had his voice lost all authority, that his billiard table contrived to sail away like a weed-green man-o'-war, and he could do nothing to stop it?

He took things out of their hands and told them to get off his land. But while he threatened one with the magistrate, another came up behind and picked up what he had retrieved, so that he had to recover it all over again.

'*For Christ Jesu's sake!*' he was screaming, as he leapt up the steps of the house. '*If you've harmed my wife and child, I'll see you all hanged and damned in hell!*'

But Anne was there to greet him in the octagonal morning room, grass stains fresh on her white silk-stockinged feet and calves, her expression as calm and luminous as in the Oxford Garden of Public Physic.

'*What in God's name? What in God's name?*' Robin panted, flailing the fishing-rod so hard that the reel unlocked and let fall a silver saliva of fishline in a spooling pool on the bare, marble floor. '*What in God's name . . . ?*'

His wife crossed to him and circled his face with her palm and the soft inside of her wrist. 'I simply carried out your wishes, my love,' she said, caressing him. 'What have you always told me? What have we always agreed? What is wealth for, if not to be communicated?'

Across the silent hall, Zennor crept on bare feet, her shoes carried in the skirt-front of her dress, along with a small library of books. She could hear muffled voices from the morning room, the high wail of Robin's agitation, the soothing murmur of his ideal wife propounding their mutual idealism.

As Zennor slipped surreptitiously out of the garden door, she noticed something propped against the curtain. No one had chosen, then, to make off with Robin's shepherd's crook.

PART FIVE

The Age of Wisdom

CHAPTER TWENTY-THREE

Motives

From door to door Robin went, demanding the return of his property, for all the world as if he had been robbed rather than misunderstood. He was successful at first, surprising households before they had even put away their acquisitions. But after Winding Hatch got wind of the change in philosophical climate they put out of sight all they could, and claimed, to a man, to have taken no part in the one-day redistribution of wealth. When the final tally was made, so many of the contents of Hatch House were missing that Wootton could not hope to keep the matter secret. To pre-empt disinheritance or possibly even notice to quit, Robin travelled to Wiltshire to explain matters to his uncle the viscount; to win the old man round, or at least win forgiveness.

Gradually the villagers came out, like woodland creatures after rain, to count the cost of the storm. There were rumours of reprisals and retributions against the wife who had taken upon herself so much too much. But the rumours were quickly dispelled, for Mrs Wootton rode out on her big roan mare and was seen everywhere, absolutely everywhere, as cheerful as May, whereas Wootton was out of the county. The elderly smiled indulgently to think of the crimes true love is ready to forgive.

In truth, Wootton's esteem would have soared locally – except that he was not there to receive the plaudits, and Anne Wootton was – a figure promising legendary times of bounty and excitement in the village's uneventful history. Nothing like this had happened before her arrival, and so the praise was given to her – even though the furniture had been Wootton's.

By contrast, a numbing mundanity had set in at the gate-house. The sheer to-ing and fro-ing of the girls to dame school, of George to Wantage, of Zennor piloting Sam through the shoals of a home education, left no energy for discontent, forward planning or even regret. Distilling from her books and her own dilettante education the things she deemed of any practical or pleasurable use, Zennor put together an education she considered suited to Sam's expectations. It frightened her that someone so lamentably under-educated as she should be entrusted with the education of a pastor's son. But there was nothing for it. His pre-paid school fees were now all used up. To pay more was out of the question. And George – though she every day expected him to forbid her meddling – said nothing.

Nothing. Nothing. Sometimes she thought even his disapproval would be better than the silence which held between them. Like the beams which span a street, bracing apart the houses on either side, it did not exactly interfere with day-to-day traffic, but she did not know what disaster it was meant to be averting, that silence, that solid wedge of silence.

As George Baydon arrived at his place of work he passed, in the doorway, an oddly familiar stranger. Beneath the clay-thick paint of foppish cosmetics, the features had the bloated dissolution of any city rake. The wig was huge – like a docked sheep's rump with a face embedded in it. The black ribbons fastening the queue hovered, as flies do, behind the sheep. George saw a gilded gunpowder spot, an earring, an eye irritated by face powder, and a soft straw basket carried underarm, which squeaked and writhed – a lapdog presumably. The stranger was tall, his swollen neck accentuated by layer upon layer of collars to his coat, and there was an unsavoury smell lurking beneath the nutmeg sweetness of his toiletries.

Only after standing aside for the passenger, and seeing him climb into the morning stage, did it occur to George whom this absurd buffoon reminded him of.

Waiting for him beside his desk and ledger, George's manager stood fretting and rattling the soft membranes of his nasal passages. 'Am I to do your duties for you, Baydon, and pay you also? Thanks to your tardiness, I have had to fill three forms of lading already.'

George was slow to apologise, his thoughts still taken up with the fop. 'Who was that last?' he asked, glancing at the documents. He could barely read his manager's elaborate hand, but no name on the papers resembled any he knew.

'Why? Would you claim acquaintance, sir?' said his manager with a sneer which encompassed both George and the effeminate fop.

The name on the form – O. Cromwell, Esq – the details of the luggage sent ahead – '*2 seachests, ½-barel lid, oakrib, padlock and strap (wove): Nul insure*' – told him nothing. But George's unease was not dispelled. Like a morsel of food caught in a tooth he could not let it alone. He was half inclined to ride an hour home to Winding Hatch – to call at the vicarage and satisfy himself he was mistaken. But he knew that he would not have a job tomorrow if he left today, and he could not afford the luxury of curiosity.

At the end of the day, as dusk fell, he was only just mounting up when Wootton's empty chaise rolled into the market place, come to collect Robin Wootton off the last stage of the day.

There is no hurrying out of Wantage. A rider has to dismount to climb the hill up to the Ridgeway before descending the long, twisting, shallow gradient past Challow and Childrey and Sparsholt. Two covered coaches were negotiating it at the same time as George; both belonged to gentlemen he knew, though he felt no desire to knock with his whip on their roofs: the society of disagreeable gentlemen was something he no longer had to endure. Suddenly it came to him out of nowhere: the identity of that fop boarding the stage with a live creature in a basket. It had been his uncle, Oliver Baydon. But his puzzlement over the false name, the altered appearance, was set aside when Hatch House came into sight and both the carriages in front of him turned into the driveway. Zennor and Grace stood on the gate-house step, to watch them pass.

'That's the seventh today,' Zennor said, before George had even dismounted. 'And never a one with the blinds up.'

'Like witches to a coven,' said Grace, Cassandra-like under a lace-edged, Irish linen tablecloth.

'A soirée,' said George. 'Cards.'

'They leave again within the hour,' said Zennor. 'It is more like a papal audience.'

'House by house?'

'Man by man. Coach by carriage. . . . Or a valediction.'

'But Wootton's not home. He's on the road behind me. Ten minutes back.'

Zennor nodded, as if to say she knew full well, at any moment of the day, the whereabouts of Robin Wootton. George had often supposed that her soul must trail after the man, over hill and highway. 'Last time,' she said. 'Last time, she gave away the furniture.'

A full moon came out like a clash of cymbals, which made Grace whimper and creep indoors. She did not like the daylight, and she did not like the dark, only the soft, lamplit hinterlight of the house. A high wind was moving cloudy wisps across the moon so fast that it appeared to fly, cannon-fired, across Hatch Hill. And yet down on the ground there was hardly a breath of wind. The house and its grounds seemed to be holding their breath to see where the chain-shot moon would burst, what it would demolish.

As his coach rolled by, Robin Wootton saw the two figures at the door of the gate-house. But since he made it his practice not to acknowledge Zennor – to ignore her presence within his garden walls, he pulled the blind sharply down.

So it was not until he alighted from the chaise that he found the carriageway in front of his terrace crowded with other vehicles. Four stood hugger-mugger, the horses mouthing softly to one another, the coachmen sitting on the steps. His own driver barked territorially, and the drivers shifted ground, crunching away over the pea gravel, into the dark recess of the curved steps. The upper storey of the house blared with light. There must be three hundred candles burning to death on the first floor.

Robin's heart gave an inexplicable lurch of alarm, as he fancied he saw at a window a demon face – a black face – underlit by a candlestick, suddenly turning away at the sight of him. He pulled his cloak round him, even though the night was warm, and ran up the steps. The front door stood ajar.

No soirée this, for the hall was unlit. Light leaked like melted butter under the doors of the morning room, and where the staircase wound round and over his head, he could hear an insistent rhythm, like the drumming of a death-watch beetle. Starting to climb, he found his legs barely prepared to carry him.

'A half-hour yet,' said the man on the upper flight. 'Some gorbelly is only just gone in.' The rhythmic rap came from the toe of his boot which he was sliding slowly and repeatedly along the wrought iron of the banister. 'I come after.'

'Who *are* you?' asked Robin. His voice echoed on the stairwell, now that the portraits were missing.

The stranger, a fashionable Londoner with pox-pitted cheeks and a Cadogan wig powdered blue, had taken off a sky-blue coat and hung it on the hook vacated by the second viscount's portrait.

Robin withdrew, fell back, for want of understanding, to the entry hall. 'Anne?' he called. '*Anne!*'

The stranger leaned over the stair rail. 'I told you, sirrah! There's others afore you. Can you not keep your wick lit so long?'

Anne was not in the morning room, either. Six men were sat there playing ombre or piquet. They looked up with only mild interest as he came in, like sleepy pensioners in a coffee house. Robin recognised his feed merchant, his auctioneer. His lawyer stood up sharply and moved back towards the wall, as though some centrifugal force were spinning the room. Indeed, Robin could feel it spin under his own feet.

'Where is my wife, Mr Finch?' he said, and the lawyer, his hand still full of ombre cards, fanned his face like a duenna with a lace fan, answering in a panicky voice. 'Where she wishes and intends, sir. Of her own volition. With friends of her own choosing.'

The men stared at Robin with a mixture of shock and impudence, of fear and hostility. Outnumbered, he could not return such an intensity of stare and was forced backwards into the doorway. A hand touching his shoulder from behind made him swing round with a cry. It was one of Anne's black maids – one of the two she had employed while single: the demon at the window.

'Madam will see you now,' said the maid.

'See me?' He followed her up the stairs, past the sky-blue jacket, past the blue-wigged Londoner strumming the balustrade with his boot. 'Queue-leaper!' the fellow protested.

Before the maid reached the landing, Robin made a bid to take back control of the evening. He pushed past her, tripping on the top step, but regaining his balance and running on to his wife's bedroom door. He rattled the handle, expecting it to be locked, but it was not. The double doors swung away from him so hard that they banged against the wall on either side, and tried to swing closed on him again. 'Anne?'

The flesh he could see did not belong to his wife. The fat, lardy undulations of Constable Gervase's rump and back quivered and clenched, as his ambitions collapsed on the very brink of fruition. Keeping his face averted, he crawled flailingly away over Anne's legs and over the far edge of the bed, slithering down head-first on to the floor. The bedding followed after him, leaving Anne naked, her chest and stomach livid red from the chafing of chest and belly hair.

'At last,' she said. 'I had to keep the poor constable two hours unsatisfied, waiting for you to come in sight.' Her voice was thick and rasping, as if scorched by alcohol from the many bottles littering the room. But she did not slur her words. 'Others came, but my heart was set on having Gervase here now, just now.'

Out of sight, Gervase whimpered. His clothing, piled on a chair in the corner, was beyond hope of recovery, but a small, plump hand crawled over the bedside and snatched his wig. Then he heaved himself to his feet and lunged towards the door, white, gross, like a beached seacow.

'I'll kill you, sir,' said Robin; it was the only expression he found in his mouth.

But Anne was too fast for him. Sliding a hand under the heap of pillows, which raised her up as if for childbirth, she drew out a pistol – one of her own duelling pistols – and fired. The ball struck Gervase in the back of his left thigh, and his momentum carried him crashing on into Wootton, screaming, porcine.

It was as if the foundations of the house stirred, as those downstairs heard the shot. Running feet rang in the hall. Somewhere a door banged: a babble of swearing; outside, shouted orders to the coachmen, and a disturbance to the gravel like a wave-shifted beach. Someone shouted, '*He's killed her!*'

What did it mean, this scene of biblical carnality, of priapic hell? For what unsuspected crime was his conscience punishing him with nightmares of such grotesque sin? Cramps. Night cramps, surely, that he should dream a naked man was pinning his legs against a bedroom door, bruising his shins, warming his feet with blood. Robin cast his mind back over the day, struggling to remember at what moment waking had given way to sleep, exposing him to these foul, sweating dreams.

'Are you not going to help him?' enquired the woman in the bed. 'He is your kin, when all's said.'

'Kin?'

'By marriage, at least. You married my sister to him, after all.'

'Your sister?'

At the end of a long, inverted telescope, a bed stood like a distant island separated from him by miles of sea. The image was sharp; he could even hear the syllables of the naked siren on its rocks, though they barely made sense to him. He must remember to recount his dream when he woke. And yet to whom could he repeat such vileness?

'Your protégée. Alba Padock? You must remember! The yellow one. The one you took from the side of me like a foal from its mare. At that horsefair. At Lambeth.' The woman pushed her arms into the sleeves of her wrapper, leaving her breasts uncovered. 'For a time I was envious. But I thrived, you know, I thrived. In my own way. There are other ways of making good in this world, than to catch the eye of a philanthropic Rousseauite.' She lifted her long limp hair out from inside the wrapper, leaving her clasped hands on top of her head tangled in the sweat-darkened curls. The posture made her breasts tilt upwards and her ribcage show through her flesh. 'Ours is an excellent age for whores. The gentlemen downstairs will tell you that.

'Then one day I chanced on a customer – a man from hereabouts, who knew of the "great experiment". You might recall him – Oliver Baydon? The parson's brother. He was quite well able to tell me what had become of my little sister. Of little Alba Padock. What a deal he knew of Berkshire's great enlightener. Of his detractors. Of his two wards. He could tell me all the circumstances of my sister's marriage – how you contracted her a marriage, mindful of her welfare. Not a marriage to her taste, to be sure, but a marriage. Not to a creature worth the shit of a distempered cat – but a match, when all's said. And with a settlement, too! My friend told me what consideration was put into it; how deeply you contemplated its merits. More! I found how this man Gervase cherished his bride . . . with fists and a riding crop and laudanum to keep her quiet and docile. And for what? For being "Wootton's cast-off", "Wootton's stale", he called her. "Nor true Berkshire, neither. An incomer. A foreigner."'

The woman slid off the bed, fastening the wrap, taking up the hair-brush from the dressing-table and starting to brush her yellow hair with her left hand. In her right was the second pistol of the pair.

'Have you any notion how very much the constable loathed the both of you? "Wootton's used wiping rag," he called her, as he knocked out her teeth. Oh, naturally, he would not decline the honour – would you, Gervase? Refuse a favour to his feudal master? Never. His career would have surely stumbled. And an alliance with the Woottons: that was greatly to his taste, oh yes. And there was the settlement! Far too handsome to neglect. So he swallowed his pride and saved his vengeance for his wife. In a way, it suited the malice in him, to be bound to a soiled wife. It gave him cause and motive to practise his bestial abuses with a clear conscience.' For the first time the woman's voice exhibited some emotion – broke out of its sardonic, sing-song, nasal chant into a little crescendo of grief. Then she broke off, and when she spoke again, she had regained the impersonal, hypnotic rhythm which, along with her snake-like weaving to and fro, kept Wootton mesmerised.

'When she was with child, Gervase threw her against a mounting block, and her womb was split. She died before ever I met Oliver. So I never chanced to meet her again. After that day at Lambeth.

'So, you see, I had no chance to ask her: 'How shall I make him pay? What recompense am I to ask? For a sister.' No. I was obliged to chart my own course. A little reading. A small investment in letters. A drawing-in of favours from my many, *many* esteemed . . . acquaintances. And lo, I made of myself an ideal wife for the Rousseauian gentleman of Berkshire – shaped myself to his *fantaisies*. No more than I have been doing for gentlemen these fifteen years, when all's said.

'Not a life's work. But I was thorough, wasn't I? By the time I brought you to Oxford, I could match you phrase for phrase, hypocrisy for hypocrisy. I was thorough. You must grant that.

'And you such a very *giving* man! Once we were married, how could I help but learn by your example? To give. Goods and cattle. Cattle and goods. We are man and wife, when all's said. What can I give away that isn't a mark of your *giving* nature? Today I gave more to your neighbours than your neighbours can ever repay!' and she pressed her hands, pistol and all, into the small of her back and groaned lightly.

Wootton, like a man drowning, who dares not open his mouth, made one desperate bid to break surface, to breathe again. He wrenched his feet from under Gervase who, for long minutes, had lain still as a stone, hoping to be overlooked or mistaken for dead. But as Robin rolled him over he could not help but blurt in agony, and put out both hands to his shattered leg. The result was that Wootton tripped and fell forwards, his fingers reaching only the hems of Anne's gown.

She had ample time to stretch out the second pistol and fire once again, this time full into Gervase's face.

Then Wootton tumbled her on to the bed, aware even as he felt the curves of her body, of a fear of touching this Lamia, this succuba, this Lilith. Pinning her down with his body, he reached for her throat, to wring it.

It was no more than she had expected. 'Where's your son, Wootton?' she asked, her voice distorted by the thumbs on her vocal cords. 'Where's John Jack?'

He let her go at once, looked to the door, looked back into her face.

'Where is he, Robin? What have I done with him? I've given so much away tonight. What have I done with John Jack? Kill me, and you'll never know.'

He scrambled to his feet. The cord of her wrapper caught round his wrist. He shook it off like an asp. 'Where? What? What have you done?'

She was breathing heavily, face flushed, eyes big. The veins in her neck were swollen, as they were in the act of love. Act of love. Act of dedicated hatred. 'Perhaps I have killed him. No. Not so unnatural, surely? Go and see. Go on. Why don't you? Go and see. Perhaps I've drawn the circle closed: Jean-Jacques to John Jack.'

He hit her — as hard as he was able to with arteries full of water and a heart clogged like a sluicegate. Then he ran for the door, calling his son's name. He had to heave Gervase's body clear of the door before he could get out of it, and the corpse turned on him its featureless face. He sobbed with the exertion of it, and kept his eyes shut until he struck his head on the door handle.

The house below was silent now. The sky-blue jacket still hung on the portrait hook, but its owner was gone, along with the rest of the audience invited to witness and partake in Wootton's cuckolding: his wife's ultimate redistribution of private belongings.

They took with them the news that Wootton had found Gervase covering his wife, and had shot him, or her, or both. What else would explain the gunfire?

And how was he to contradict such scandalous errors? The only witness to the killing was Anne Wootton, and by the time Robin had run to the nursery, forced the locked door, searched the empty room, the bedrooms to either side, scoured the house for signs of his son, either living or dead, she too had melted away, evaporated, disappeared like the waters of a lake drying to nothing under a summer sun.

He returned to a bedroom empty of anything but blood and horror. Of Anne Wootton, her black maid, or any other accomplice there was not a sign. But for the few golden hairs in the bristles of his hair-brush, Robin could almost have imagined the woman a figment of the madness invading him through every seam of his blood-splashed clothes.

CHAPTER TWENTY-FOUR

Solutions

One of Zennor's first tasks, as housekeeper of Hatch House, was to clean the bloodstains from the carpet and wall of the master bedroom. Curragh and William had lugged the body out: she never saw that, but she undertook to clean the bedroom herself, did not delegate the work to a maid. Legends are made of such things; legends and stories of curses and jinxes and ghosts. And Zennor cared about the house too much to have it suffer calumny at the hands of gossip-mongers.

It was widely supposed that Robin Wootton had shot both his wife and her lover, but then that was as Anne Wotton intended and she was a thorough woman. Like a meticulous suicide she had left notes of all kinds with Mr Finch the lawyer. There was one for the third viscount. Finch had helped her compose it, in return for an invitation to the 'Day of Carriages':

> Since that the girls taken in by your nephew were both adopted and given to wear the name of Wootton, it is arguable in law that they have some title and lien on the property. Mindful of the disquiet this might bring to your honour's peace of mind, and given the small ambition of the surviving girl, may I commend to you the following . . .

Zennor's silent compliance could be secured (she went on to suggest) by establishing her as housekeeper in Hatch House, and her protector, George Baydon, as estate manager.

To Zennor she wrote:

> Resort not to the law, my dear; you have not the means to buy it. Depend, rather, on the doggedness of your presence, the which gives stronger title than justice. By my example you have seen this. Do not question your deserving,

for Gervase possessed my sister Alba and by what intrinsic merit? The viscount and small gentry are possessed of half England and by whose gift?

Wootton's interest is forfeit by his hypocrisy, and myself I have no mind to stay any longer parted from my true nature. Do not hinder me in this, for the sake of thy sister Alba, whose soul flies restless up and down.

It was a strange style, echoing the tuck-pleated rhetoric of Lambeth sabbaths. The paper trembled in Zennor's hand as she read it, as though a draught were blowing all the way from Lambeth Asylum or the whorehouses just outside its walls. It was soon followed by a terse letter from the third viscount to George, inviting him, without reason or embellishment, to take over management of the estate of Winding Hatch.

Their altered state settled over them like a change in the weather – something distant, whose cause it was not in their power to alter or understand. It brought barely more excitement to the neighbourhood than a red sky in the morning. Perhaps the shocking unspoken-of events of the 'Day of Carriages' robbed them of all capacity to be astonished.

The viscount had quite thought to send his nephew overseas – to the West Indies or the Americas. But there proved no need to expel him either from respectable society or from the villa. Wootton's undoing had already been achieved by Anne Wootton. She simply wrote to him:

'*Your son will be raised as Rousseau's own.*'

Those words alone were all it took to secure Wootton's damnation. He disappeared from Winding Hatch as completely as his bride and child.

Naturally, it was assumed that he had fled abroad to escape hanging. But whereas his family could easily have bought him immunity from the law, nothing could suspend the sentence Alba's sister had passed on him.

A figure of staging posts and hackney ranks, he began to travel the length and breadth of London's boroughs, then farther and farther afield, like a comet whose eliptical course lengthens with each skirting of the sun. To the asylums of Lambeth and Dulwich, to the orphanages of Windsor and Leicester, to the poorhouses of Portsmouth and York he travelled, rattling by turns over ruts of ice and cracking drought, his soul dislocated a little way from his body, his heart jolted insensible, bloodshot eyes no longer distinguishing between town smoke and harvest dust.

His obsession was so complete that he was quite incoherent to all the matrons and wardens, his questions elided into a garbled, unintelligible foreshortening. He could not conceive that others required details, dates, descriptions, names; his mind was so full of them that he assumed the whole world must know of his predicament. 'A boy,' he would say, drawing the lashless lids back off his eyes, basilisk-like. 'A tiny boy! Left by a whore!'

Perhaps she had lied. Perhaps, somewhere, Anne Padock and Oliver Baydon were secretly raising John Jack as their own – along traditional lines, with stick and kisses. But Robin did not believe it. He believed absolutely in his wife's malice. He knew for certain that Anne had done as Jean-Jacques Rousseau had done: she had abandoned her baby at the poorhouse door, to be brought up by charity and state.

Despite all his ideals, all his compassion for the human race, all his finer feelings, that had been Rousseau's solution to the practical problem of his own children existing, unwanted. He had left them at the poorhouse door. What hope, then, for Robin's son? And the thought of his own flesh and blood, his beloved John Jack wailing consolable weeks away in the stony cell of some poorhouse, was gall and wormwood to Robin. The child, after all, had Wootton's immortality clenched in his small, pink fist.

'A boy. My tiny boy,' he said, while wardens and matrons and beadles ran dubious eyes over the travel-stained stripes of his empire-brocade waistcoat, the eggshell and ale on his redingote, the shallowing heels of his shineless boots.

Meanwhile, his house floated adrift on the green Berkshire countryside, like a skeleton ship waiting the opening of its sea-cocks before sinking out of sight. A handful of souls continued to light its lamps, prune its trees, wash its flagstone, flick up its dust, but it lay effectively becalmed, run aground. It waited for Wootton to return, though he did not. It waited for the third viscount to instal some other scion of his family, but the old man had other plans, other ways of chastising his miscreant nephew.

He wrote to the investment consortium of the Wiltshire and Berkshire Canal Scheme, inviting them to drive their waterway through the estates at Winding Hatch. He had developed an appetite to demolish all things romantic.

Within weeks, the land was fractured by excavation, and a fissure had been opened up across Wootton's paradisal garden. The Bower of Troth was demolished for the sake of its timber. The Muses' Walk was made a turning circle for carts delivering construction materials.

But the ship that was Hatch House was refloated and gathered way. Navvies and overseers from as far afield as Ireland and the Kentish mines doubled and trebled the population of Winding Hatch. The Reverend Brough (who had thought to tend a pleasant little country sinecure) found not only his patron gone, disappeared, but his church crammed to bursting each Sunday with an army of craftsmen, labourers and itinerant strangers of variable character.

Rooms in Hatch House which had been sealed up against the ravages of daylight and the want of fuel were opened up again to house surveyors, engineers, visiting investors, labourers, dependents and casualties. In place of the silence which had hung like a tarpaulin over the mansion, a raucous, racketing din surrounded and filled it every hour of the day.

While still awaiting the pleasure of seeing his nephew's dismay, the third viscount died, whereupon not a single member of his surviving family laid claim to the Berkshire house subsumed in a sea of sand and rubble and overrun with workmen, its trampled vistas cut through like cheese with a wire of water.

Standing at the kitchen table, at not much past six in the morning, Zennor carved slices of beef which Sarah spread with mustard and Sam augmented with a large slab of bread. The range behind them blazed like the mouth of hell, guarded by Alice with a fork and tongs. Suzannah was supposed to take the two pennies in exchange for each breakfast sold, but she was in love with an engineer, and had become otherworldly and unpredictable, taking long, solitary walks to contemplate her happiness.

Grace, who generally managed to hold herself aloof from the horrid squalor of communal breakfast, found herself enlisted in Suzannah's place. Each time she reached out for the money with her right hand, the woollen shawl dropped back off her hair, and she pulled it up again with her left. Her cheeks flinched at the noise of the pennies clattering into the cash box on the table. She told George she was not well, but he simply drew her up a chair to sit in while she took the tuppences. The smell from the mustard pot made her queasy, and the heat from the range made her faint.

A wiry-haired Cornishman six feet tall and as thick-set as a ship's bollard, offered her his money from the inside of his cap, presumably because his hands were so often dirty. 'Hair so fine shoulden be hid,' he said.

Grace ducked her head. 'Saint Paul says that women should keep their heads covered,' she said, on a single, sighing outward breath.

'Then he were prolly thatch'oled,' said the man, ruefully showing the baldness at the crown of his own crisp hair. 'Most men are wicked jealous of a woman's thatch once they's lost they own.' And he laughed: an easy, popping laugh, like cider fermenting in a barrel. Grace did not answer, neither did she pull up her shawl the next time it slipped off her hair. 'Thy's a fair little republic here,' said the man, to no one in particular. 'Rare little republic.'

'The owner would be pleased to hear it,' Zennor replied, vigorously carving a brisket.

'Wuz here once. In yonder room with the long sashes. Begging of work.'

Both Zennor and George looked with more attention at his face, but had no way of recognising him. The orange rind which had once disguised his natural colouring had peeled away over the years to reveal a man of around forty, no more, and good wages had fleshed him out. Stiff Abney took something from his pocket and, putting it in his hat, held it out towards George. George looked into the hat. It was a shilling. 'Youz father lended me some such when I wuz needful.'

'My father's dead.'

'I know, God rest him. Then you'd best tek it back, if you will. Stiff Abney's the name. I'm a pump-maker now. Hide work, and I know hides. There's none meks a pump better, if you'll pardon my pride. There's a living to be made from pumps.'

Grace looked up at the pump-maker, idly smoothing her dishevelled hair.

'My best regards to your wife, Mr Abney,' said George.

'Oh, still a widower, Mr Baydon,' said Stiff, though he said it to the parson's daughter rather than the parson's son. 'Three children living – some nigh old as him.' He nodded towards Sam. 'But still a widower. Perchance I could show you my present pump at work draining the workings. It's a very excellent pump.'

And Grace, though she had not been aware till then of a strong interest in extraction pumps, said that she would be very glad to see it. So once again there was no one to take the tuppences for breakfast.

George expressed unease at his sister befriending a widower twice her age with children, but Alice, raking the ashes out of the bottom of the stove, only shouted above her own noise: 'Ask me, the children tipped the scales his way. Where a family's going to come hard, why go without? There's plenty widowers take a second wife and make them both happy by it.'

Zennor suddenly noticed that there were tears running down the blade of her carving knife, diluting the blood of the beef, salting the slices. Tears. And they were hers.

As soon as she was able, she slipped away from the noise of tin plates and rattling buckets of night-stale, the sharpening of shovel edges and the shouting of team-masters, and climbed to the top of Hatch Hill. A young man with a theodolite was taking note of triangulations, elevations and bearings within the landscape. At the sight of her, he quickly offered to go. 'Do you wish to be alone, ma'am?'

The smile she turned on him made him close the theodolite tripod on his fingers. 'No,' she said and gave a little shrug. 'But there is nothing to be done, it seems.'

Gauche and shy, and wanting to swear because of the pain in his fingers, the surveyor moved off to the other side of the hill and when he heard someone else trailing up the steep incline made himself scarce.

It was George. As he climbed the last few yards, Zennor was put in mind of Pilgrim in *Pilgrim's Progress* toiling up the Hill called Difficulty, with his unremovable pack.

This morning George had come with things in mind to say. 'You won't always be troubled by such a din and a clamour,' he said. 'One day it will be a stream outside the door merely.' He had brought her cape: the wind was always brisk up on Hatch Hill. He did not look her in the face, so as not to embarrass her if she were still crying. He did not refer to her tears, either.

'The din does not trouble me,' said Zennor, examining the same view as he. 'The house is alive now; it has a life now. Before, when I lived here, it was too . . . It was like a reflection in a pond. Waiting splashing.'

Once or twice he started to say something, but did not succeed. Poor Pilgrim, she thought. When at last he succeeded in framing a sentence it took her completely by surpirse.

'He may yet come back,' George said. 'And see your republic.'

'Pardon me? Who?' She was startled. 'Wootton, do you mean? Pray God, not till the pickmen are gone from the billiard room, or then the cat would be among the bir −' She did not finish, since he was looking at her so strangely, in a way she did not understand. 'Is there news, then? Is he coming?'

'No. No news.'

'Do you fear him coming home?'

'Yes.'

'Because we would be put out of the house?'

He looked at her even more oddly. She drew in her chin and looked intently at the view.

'God grants none of us safe tenure,' said George ecclesiastically. 'For me, he could have the house and welcome.'

She waited, until she thought she must wait in vain for him to say any more. 'What, then? The return of despotism? An end to the "republic of Winding Hatch"? It's true; all the Rousseau will be gone out of him.'

She was beginning to recover; the wind over the hill could usually be relied on to carry away her black moods, her regrets, like so many pieces of furniture. She was unprepared for him to come back at her with such bitter sarcasm.

'Not his *passion*, though, say? He will be the "passionate man" still, as he ever was.'

She peered at him warily, seeing that she was on trial for someone else's crimes. 'Wootton? Passion? He hadn't one speck! Not a spark in the whole grate. Don't judge Rousseau by Wootton. I like a deal of Rousseau. I suppose even Socrates had fools in his following. And even Wootton started out with good intentions. He just lacks the *nature*. Some people are born without eyes. Robin was born without a great fund of . . . human feeling. Oh dear. Am I disloyal to the man that made me? I'm sorry. I'm too tired to be proper and gracious in my speaking.'

'I am not −'

But she was deep in thought. 'Your *father* was the only passionate man I ever knew. He was like a man who dressed in a hurry and forgot his skin − a layer or two, you know? Mrs Baydon once said to me that love crept up on him like a beast: he never saw it, because he was too scared to look over his −'

'*Don't speak of the man*,' snapped George. There was a closing down within his face, a dark menace which at any other time would have stopped Zennor's flow like a sandbank. But something inside her had breached. If she had to leak away into the ground, she might as well spill herself in words. Quite enough nonsense had been talked on this hill already.

'Your father believed you were all going to die. God should have spoken up louder, if He did not want to be mistaken. Well. I dare say the mistake is put to rights now. Why do you look at me like that? I'm still angry with God. Aren't you? You've got no place to be angry with anyone else. He should *speak up* . . . and I don't see what purpose was served by Him driving your father to his death. Love takes so long to grow. Why root it up when it's just coming good?'

A glacial silence fell between them. She kept her head cocked back, as if to say she held to her words and he could go hang if he expected her to swallow them.

'Your position here is . . . invidious,' he suddenly said, changing the subject.

'Oh! Why?' She trembled again, despite her defiance, despite the cape.

'People frequently . . . tradesmen − at breakfast time − incomers . . . they often assume we are man and wife.'

'Yes. I know. I'm sorry.'

His hands broke free from his sides and made an inchoate gesture.

'Oh. No. No, no. It's nothing to me ... what people think. You know that.'

'Even so. You would prefer not. I see that. Of course. But you must see my predicament. Where else could I be a housekeeper? Or turn such a profit? Among my own kind.'

He snorted: a noise halfway between a hiccup and a cough. '*Your own kind*,' he said. 'Where is there another like you?'

He was right, she knew. She was neither fish nor fowl: did not belong anywhere in society's farmyard. It was not quite friendly of him to remind her, but at least it showed an understanding of her plight. Zennor straightened her back. 'What remedy do you suggest?'

She was almost sorry she had asked, for it would clearly have been kinder to feed hot pickle to one of the deer. Both hands went up to his head, and he turned first towards Oxfordshire, then Hampshire, then Wiltshire, before walking off altogether to the far side of the knoll, where he could look down at the parsonage where he had been born. When he did not come back, Zennor went and stood beside him; it did not seem right to leave a creature in such obvious distress. It was from just here that she had thrown Oliver Baydon's musket into the nettles, and felt the bullet pass through her petticoats.

'I could offer you marriage,' said George.

'Not for the sake of my reputation, thank you,' said Zennor sharply. 'Out of practical good sense, if you will, but not for propriety. That's a nonsense. To couple for the sake of chastity.'

The deer took another mouthful of pickle. Its eyes watered. 'No,' he said. 'No.'

'Yes, for the sake of my soul, but not for my reputation.'

'Your soul?'

'My soul, yes, George,' she said briskly. 'Lust is a sin, you recall? Perhaps I could give more of my mind to God if it were not so taken up with speculation: How would the skin of his belly feel against mine? How does his sweat taste? What would be the weight of his body on mine? How does the bush burn without being consumed? Do the bowels ache more in emptiness or in fulness? ... I was raised to *curiosity*, George. These things trouble me. Where can I apply for an honest answer?'

There was a loud crash. The young surveyor had mistakenly returned, at the worst possible moment, thinking they had passed on over the hill and down. They both turned and watched him struggling away again with the three separate legs of his dropped theodolite.

'But you love Wootton,' said George.

'I most surely do not!' she retorted indignantly. 'He taught me too much good taste to love such a . . . such a *Vicar of Bray!* Whatever made you think it? How offensive! There were times when I might have taken comfort from him – if comfort could have been wrung from the man. But love? That's something entirely different. *That*, sir, is asparagus. If you value my opinion. Well? Do you?'

'Oh, I . . .'

'If you value my opinion, you and I would do very well married. In a while. Finally. Better than some. What does it signify *why* people marry? Cheeriness afterwards is down to practice, isn't it? Like playing the spinet. The secret, it seems to me, is not to ask too much. If you put the butt close enough, your arrows will hit it oftener, won't they? Industry and small expectations and a morsel of charity. And patience, of course. To wait for the asparagus to come. And God holding off His malice, of course.' She ended with her head on one side, still thinking. 'But I'm base stock. Weeds are always looking to thrive in the wrong beds. You mustn't pay any attention to me.'

George found himself imprisoned in the peculiar Eden of her imagery: the whistle and thud of archery, the tinkling of the spinet, the smell of good crumbling black mulch. It confused his senses. Inside his head seemed noisier than the kitchen had been.

Zennor threw back her head and sniffed the air – full of sileage and excavated clay, lake silt, nettles and the smoke of bonfires. She felt much better for speaking her mind, even if it brought the sky's roofbeams down on her head, even if the world fell off its hinges for being set swinging. Picking up her black skirts in both hands, and giving an unconscious flick of the hips, she crossed back over the hill and started down it in long, sideways strides, towards Hatch House. She was halfway down before it occurred to her that she still did not know whether he wanted her to leave.

George did not go after her. There would be plenty of time later for conversation.

He could easily tell Zennor later. He could tell her he had been in love with her for as long as he could remember: had thought of her as a foretaste of brimstone, she burned so in his blood.

Later, George would be able to tell her his plans for the house – its potential, after the canal was built, as a mercantile headquarters. Warehousing, boatbuilding, leets and slipways, houses, schools – a crossroads development at the heart of the country's waterways.

There would be time to discuss the best way of raising a child –